D[illegible]
in the
CITY
of
BRIDGES

J.C. CERON

GOLD COAST BOOKS LLC

NEW YORK • DELAWARE

This book is a work of fiction. Names, characters, businesses, places, events, locales, and incidents are either the products of the author's imagination or used fictitiously. Any resemblance to actual persons, living or dead, or actual events is purely coincidental.

Published by Gold Coast Books LLC goldcoastbooks-llc.com

Book cover design by ebooklaunch.com
Map design by dmc.creativedesign.com
Edited by Julie MacKenzie, Free Range Editorial

ISBN: 979-8-9862554-0-8 (e-book)
ISBN: 979-8-9862554-1-5 (softcover)
ISBN: 979-8-9862554-2-2 (audiobook)

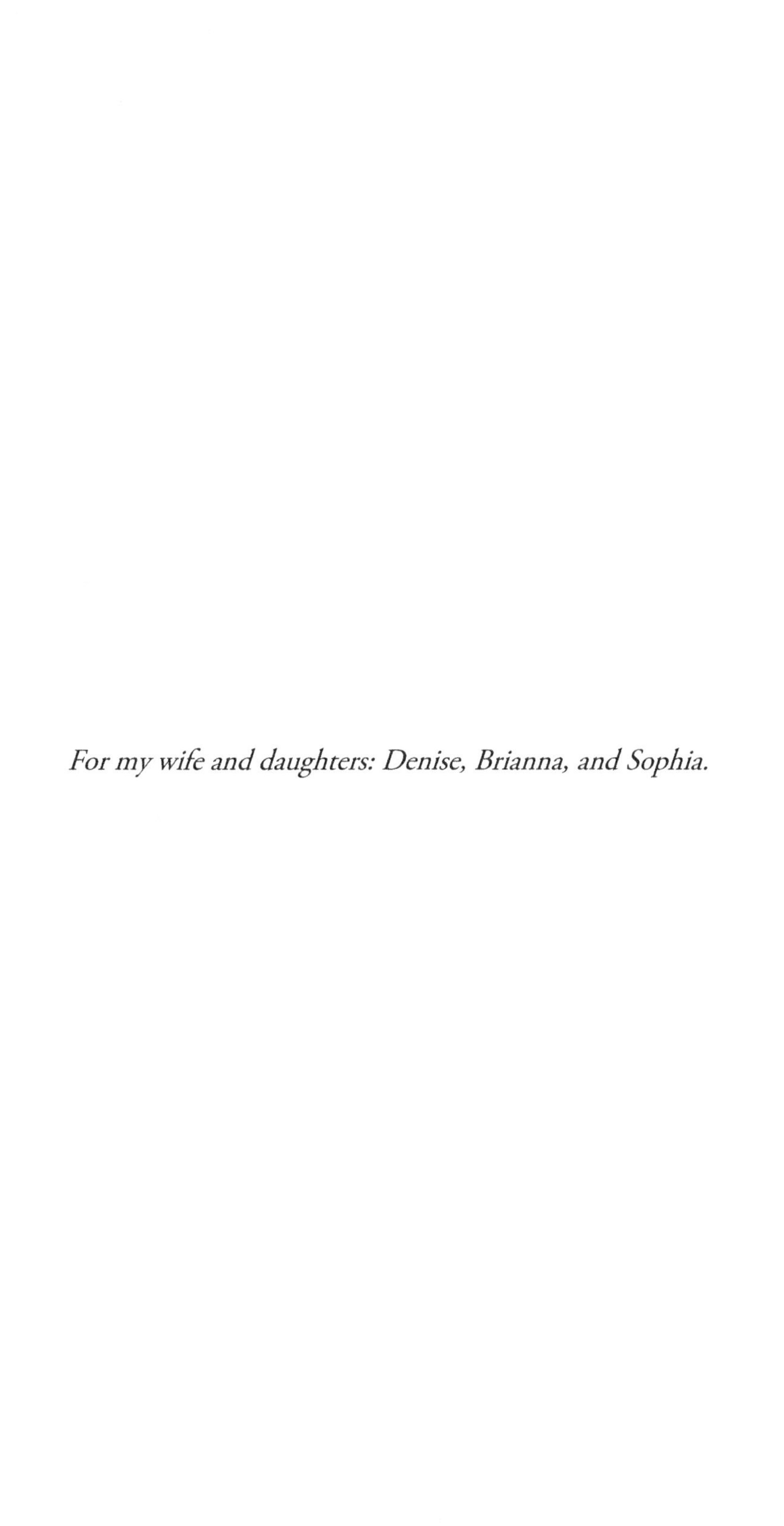

For my wife and daughters: Denise, Brianna, and Sophia.

Contents

St. Mark's Square

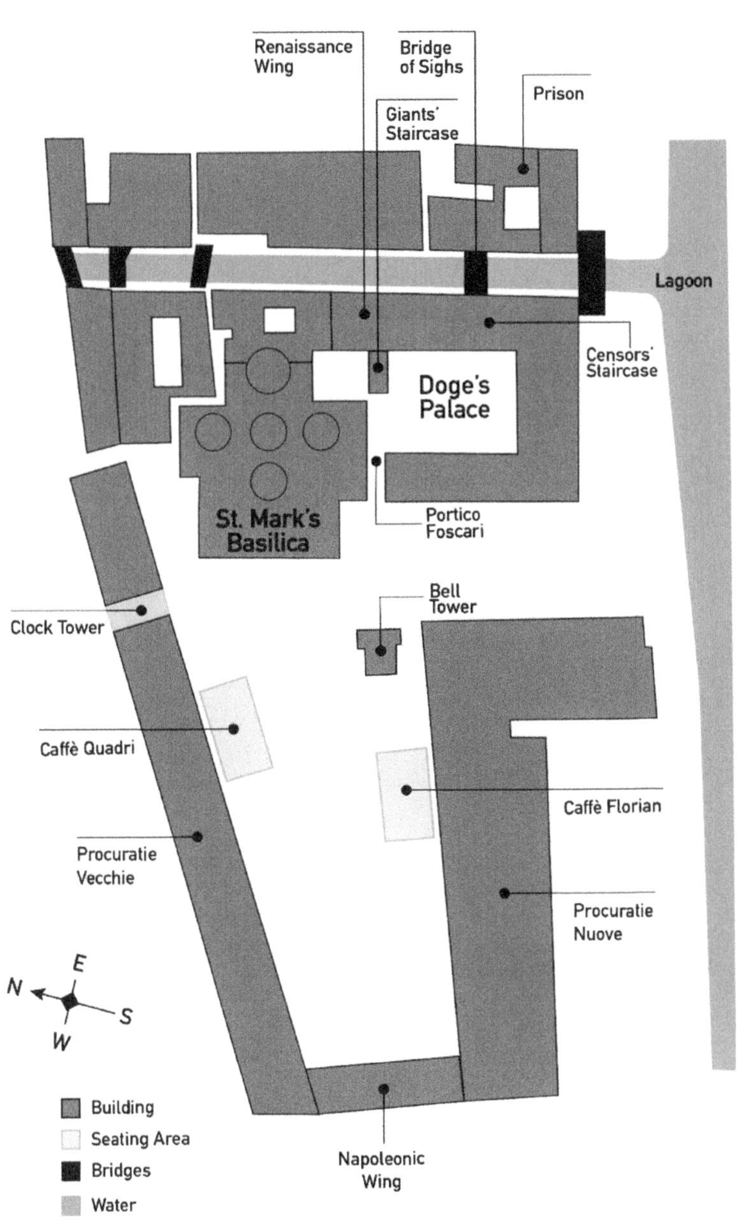

Chapter One

The Snitch

Day 1

Monday, 0945 hours

The view was spectacular. From my table in front of the world-famous Caffè Florian, St. Mark's Square in Venice was like a Renaissance painting on exhibit. The bell tower soared in the foreground, and a brushwork of clouds lit by the warm Mediterranean sun hovered over St. Mark's Basilica. There in the white heaps, I imagined half-hidden cherubs and angels spying on the tactical operation unfolding in the square below.

Undercover and underfed (a proper breakfast wasn't an option at the start of my hectic morning), I posed as a tourist. For my disguise, I wore cargo shorts, a Brooklyn Nets cap, and a bright red polo shirt. Concealed under my shirt, an encrypted radio and a holstered SIG Sauer P226 were clipped around my ample waist. Not part of my disguise was a wallet in my pocket with a versatile set of identification: Miles Jordan, Detective First Grade New York Police Department, FBI Joint Terrorism Task Force Officer, and Jamal's Big & Tall Gold Star Customer.

"More gelato, *signore*?"

I turned to the waiter and hesitated. What harm could come from another bowl of that creamy rich confection that played the palate like Coltrane played the sax? The answer was always more than I thought.

"Just coffee, please."

Flipping through a US newspaper, an article about the growing rift between the White House and the Israeli prime minister caught my eye. As I finished reading a long, gossipy paragraph listing the snubs and dwindling decorum between the two governments, my radio earpiece came alive.

"Eagle Eye, from Echo Two. The subject's still in the Imperial Rooms. No contact with the target yet."

Eagle Eye was our unit, the surveillance team. Echo Two was my partner, Detective Vincent Santoro, NYPD, also a member of the Joint Terrorism Task Force or JTTF, a counterterrorism force made up of various law enforcement agencies and police departments. JTTF normally dealt with domestic terrorism, but for this high-value target, our unit fell under the FBI's Legal Attaché Program, which gave us jurisdiction to operate in Venice with the full blessing of the Italian government.

The subject was Aarzam El-Hashem, a sleeper agent turned snitch. He was bait, there to rendezvous with his boss, the world's most wanted terrorist. A bad guy known to us only as The Scorpion. A large force of Carabinieri (the Italian military police) and JTTF agents was standing by, ready to take down The Scorpion when the order was given.

"Echo One, from Echo Two," Vincent said.

I squeezed the push-to-talk radio mic clipped to the inside of my shirt collar. "Go, Echo Two."

"I hope you're laying off the gelato. That stuff's like my grandmother's homemade manicotti—highly addictive and detrimental to the pursuit of fitness."

"Now you tell me."

"Really? *Marone*, Miles, your belly sticks out like—"

"Echo Two, from Top," Killian O'Neil, the Supervisory Special Agent, barked over the radio.

"Go, Top," Vincent said.

"What kind of goddamn operation do you think I'm running here? Knock it off!"

"Copy that, Top." Vincent's radio screeched.

I sat taller, adjusted my cap, and shot a glance to my left. Spread between the Procuratie Vecchie, the building across the square, and the Procuratie Nuove, the one behind me, was the Napoleonic Wing, the third in a trio of connecting buildings surrounding the square in a U-shape. On the second floor of that wing, inside a museum, was the subject.

"Eagle Eye, from Top," O'Neil said. "How do you read this unit?"

One by one, our six-member team sounded off. I went first, followed by Vincent, who was tracking the subject from inside the museum. FBI Special Agent Antonio Ruiz covered the stairs to the museum, while his partner, Max Colt, occupied a table in front of Caffè Quadri in the building across the square. Port Authority Detective Tony Tufu was stationed near the Doge's Palace, next to the basilica. Last to call in was Kamaria Uba, who came to us from the Carabinieri's Special Operations Group for organized crime and counterterrorism. She was posted by the clock tower near the basilica.

Several more radio checks with other units followed, including the Carabinieri assault team commander.

"All units, from Top," O'Neil said. "Stay sharp and stick to the tac plan."

The tac plan, or tactical plan, originally called for drones and sharpshooters on the rooftops to track the subject. But with a three-hundred-foot bell tower looming over the square and lines of tourists waiting to visit the top, that option was out. Given the stakes, we couldn't afford a blown cover. In fact, we hadn't even wired the subject. What if he was met by other operatives and searched before meeting the real deal?

We'd opted for a six-member team to cover the subject and blend in with the tourists. Three main public access points led in and out of the square: one south of the basilica and the other two north. The Carabinieri assault team in hiding was ready to seal all routes and flood the square.

A tight trap.

In the cool September breeze, I could smell the brine and decay of a thousand years coming off the Grand Canal. The tourists were plentiful. Many chose to waste their hard-earned euros on bags of maize for the ballsy pigeons that littered the square. Most viewed the spectacular sights before them through the lens of a phone camera instead of with the naked eye. In their eagerness to reduce everything around them to data they could quickly upload to social media for all their real and imagined friends to see, they never truly appreciated the treasures before them. Then there was the insult of the selfie, made easy with those absurd telescopic phone holders. It encouraged people to turn their backs on buildings and monuments that have awed and inspired for centuries.

As if to make up for their lack of respect, I admired the Procuratie Vecchie across the square, noting every window, arch, column, and carved detail of the three-story structure. I wanted to remember it exactly as it had been since the sixteenth century when the Venetians rebuilt it to house their movers and shakers. It was a thing of uniform beauty, as natural and balanced as a honeycomb.

"Eagle Eye, from Echo Two," Vincent said. "The subject is checking his phone. Stand by."

This was the moment we'd been waiting for. My heart beat faster. My hearing got sharper. I shifted in my seat, feeling the reassuring nudge of my hip holster and the poke of the SIG's magazine.

Vincent said, "The subject is mobile. Repeat, subject is mobile."

Less than a minute later, Ruiz said, "Echo Two, from Three."

Ruiz was standing in the arcade of the Napoleonic Wing, his uninjured arm disguised in a bright red sling.

Red was the color of the day for undercover officers.

"Go, Echo Three," Vincent said.

"I have visual. Subject is coming down the stairs, brisk pace. You're clear to move out."

The subject soon strutted out of the arcade. He was thick-bearded, dark-skinned, of average height and build. In khaki shorts and a white safari shirt, he looked like a casual tourist. But his eyes gave him away: black and lifeless, the eyes of a killer. Even from afar, I saw those eyes flicker, quick as a snake, from under a shock of unruly black hair.

Ruiz followed a few yards behind, red sling and all, carrying a foldout map.

"Eagle Eye, from Echo One," I said. "Subject is moving east across the square, passing my location. I'll lose him in the crowd in sixty seconds."

"Copy that, Echo One. We got eyes," Vincent said.

I spotted Vincent's huge muscular frame, barely contained in a casual blue suit, moving parallel to the subject. He had a red carnation pinned to his lapel.

"Echo Four, y'all. I see the hairs on his chinny-chin-chin," Agent Colt drawled over the encrypted airway. He abandoned his table to feed the pigeons like a dozen other tourists were doing. The white cowboy hat he wore overshadowed his red string tie.

The subject halted and reached for his phone. I lost Vincent and his red carnation in the arcade of the Procuratie Vecchie. Ruiz paused to consult his map with a convincing frown. The subject worked his phone, presumably reading incoming text messages and tapping off quick responses.

"Eagle Eye, from Three," Ruiz said. "Subject is moving."

The subject headed toward the two vending carts in the middle of the square. He passed the first cart loaded with knickknacks and loud shirts and caps no native Venetian would wear and made a beeline for the second.

"Eagle Eye, from Echo One," I said. "The subject is on line for the maize cart."

"Maize? What are they gonna make him do? Feed the pigeons?" Vincent asked.

Fifteen minutes later, the subject moved on with a bag of maize in hand.

"Eagle Eye, from Three," Ruiz said. "The subject's proceeding east toward the basilica."

I dropped a pile of euros on the table and moved out to the middle of the square. As I kept a visual on the subject while catching glimpses of Ruiz and Vincent, one of the double-hung windows in the Procuratie Vecchie caught my eye. It was now open, the white venetian blinds behind it swaying in the breeze.

"Echo Five, from Echo Two," Vincent said.

"Go, Echo Two," Detective Tufu said.

"We're halfway to the church. You got visual?"

"Negative, but I will soon."

"Copy that."

At the end of the square, Vincent, Ruiz, and Tufu were converging on the basilica, covering the subject on three sides.

"Echo Six here," Kamaria said. "I am seeing the subject now and changing my position."

I couldn't stop glancing back at the window.

"Eagle Eye, from Echo Two," Vincent said. "The subject's scanning ahead. He must expect contact with the target soon."

The venetian blinds rose slowly.

"Eagle Eye, from Echo One," I said. "I'm cutting across the square."

"Echo One, from Top!" O'Neil snapped.

"Go, Top."

"You better have a goddamn good reason for falling off the tac plan."

"It's probably nothing, Top. Quick walk-by. Still moving east."

"Eagle Eye, from Three," Ruiz said. "The subject is turning around. Repeat, the subject is backtracking. Checking his phone again."

I weaved through the occupied tables of Caffè Quadri, where Colt had sat just minutes before.

"Eagle Eye, from Echo Two," Vincent said. "The subject stopped in front of the maize cart. Why'd he go back there?"

At twenty-five yards from the window, I froze. The short barrel of a rifle protruded from the open blind, pointing in the direction of the basilica.

Before I could yell "Gun!" the muzzle flashed.

Chapter Two

Pandemonium

Few things short of an earthquake or a hundred-foot monster tearing up downtown Tokyo cause as much pandemonium as the crack of gunfire. In the crowded square, the sound reverberated. The pigeons were the first to flee, taking flight as one ominous dark cloud. Then frantic tourists ran in all directions, battering and trampling one another. Tables that a moment before lined the square in orderly rows were overturned or shoved aside. Plates and glasses flew and shattered. Waiters too slow or too stunned to retreat into their restaurants were stampeded.

Pushed from behind, I fell hard on one knee but managed to keep my eyes on the window.

The rifle was gone.

A shadow watched.

"Shots fired! Shots fired!" Vincent said over the radio. "The subject is down. Need a bus!"

Heart jackhammering, I added, "The shooter's on the second floor of the Procuratie Vecchie!"

O'Neil's voice boomed, "All units, from Top, initiate lockdown! I say again, initiate lockdown!"

I glanced at the small square to the left of the basilica. An advancing wall of blue military uniforms clashed with the tide of fleeing tourists. In the mayhem, Colt's white cowboy hat was kicked and trampled along with caps, T-shirts, and kernels of maize from the overturned vendor carts. I turned back to the window.

The shadow was gone.

"All units, from Echo One," I said. "The shooter is on the move. I'm going in!"

From under my shirt, I pulled out the gold badge hanging around my neck. I drew my SIG Sauer and rushed down the arcade, yelling, "*Polizia!*" I pushed against the crowd until I found the corridor that led to the other side of the building. A Carabinieri soldier standing there pointed his weapon at me.

"*Alto!*" he shouted.

"Polizia! Pol—"

He fired a short burst from his submachine gun.

The sound was deafening and froze me to the core. The spray of bullets went high. Chunks of plaster rained down. People rushing through the corridor dove for cover.

The trigger-happy Carabinieri, a kid in uniform, had failed to acknowledge my verbal identification or note that I was wearing red, the color of the day for undercover officers. He'd also missed the badge hanging like a billboard on my chest. He must've been too distracted by what he saw first: a huge black man carrying a full-sized 9mm handgun. Who could blame him for shooting first and asking questions later?

I raised my weapon sky-high and shook the badge. "*Polizia! Polizia!*"

The kid—Lorenzo, according to his nameplate—gaped at me. The gravity of his fuckup quickly sinking in.

"More shots fired!" Vincent shouted in my earpiece.

I glared at Lorenzo. He lowered his weapon and stood rooted, eyes on his boots.

"Eagle Eye, from Echo One," I said. "Disregard, accidental discharge."

"Accidental discharge? What the fuck, Miles?" The alarm in Vincent's voice was palpable. "What's your location?"

Three more Carabinieri soldiers burst into the corridor. Outfitted like Lorenzo with combat boots, fatigues, ammo vests, and submachine guns, they looked ready to take on an army. After a brief exchange, one of the soldiers led the way to a small private entrance used by the building tenants. The door was wide open. People committed to the latter part of the fight-or-flight response were stumbling through it. They were safer inside, but hysteria often incites reckless action. The soldiers with me were swarmed by the people rushing out of the building with demands for protection and information. More Carabinieri approached the side of the building to form a human shield. I weaved through the people traffic and rushed inside.

I hustled up a flight of stairs and stopped at the landing, gasping for air. My heart was in overdrive. Just two years shy of forty, the last thing I needed was another heart attack.

I emerged from the stairway into a long hallway that ran to my right and left, the width of the building. The offices facing me looked out over the square. On the walls hung mirrors, tapestries, and smoke detectors, their red power lights blinking at steady intervals. Chandeliers cast warm light throughout, lending a soft glow to the white marble floor. A stationary security camera in the ornate ceiling eyed the stairwell.

Ruiz blared in my earpiece, "All units, from Three, the subject's in shock. We're losing him! Where are the paramedics?"

A door slammed.

I glanced at both ends of the hallway. It was empty. Did the shooter slam that door? No animal was more dangerous than a cornered one. I turned off my radio. The only sounds were footsteps and voices from the floor below. I took a deep breath and turned left. Counting as I moved, I estimated which offices had windows above the café. I reached a trio of candidates—all behind the eye of the camera—and tried the doorknobs.

One was unlocked.

Chapter Three

The Bell Tower

The man had a bird's-eye view of Venice that stretched as far as the Italian Alps on one side and beyond the Venetian Lagoon on the other. But the whole of his attention was on St. Mark's Square.

The five domes of the basilica looked the same from his vantage point as they did from the square. The sloping clay tile rooftops of the Procuratie, however, were a letdown, considering the craftsmanship of the façades. It was a view hidden from patrons seated at café tables or pedestrians. He had been both a patron and a pedestrian many times, always in grudging admiration. Now he felt duped. He dwelled on his disappointment for only a moment. His business lay in the unfolding chaos.

Minutes before, heavily armed Carabinieri units had stormed the square from multiple points. He'd expected the use of that strategy to seal the square. The ensuing gridlock resulted in a tangle of bodies thrashing like ants at war. As fascinating as it was to watch, the thought of being among them made him shudder. He hated crowds. He hated their intuitive need to follow. Men stopped thinking and simply acted. An act without thought was as dangerous as a sword with a dull blade.

A thrashing of bodies had also ensued on the observation platform of the bell tower, where he stood alone in one corner peering through the tall open-air arches that supported the belfry. A small group of tourists had turned into a senseless herd, jostling for spots near the elevator. It was the only exit available to them, and it would take at least two trips to get them all down to the ground floor. Conditions were ripe for panic.

It was not a prospect that concerned him. The stairwell—closed to the public for decades—was open to him, thanks to his talent for getting in and out of places few could access.

The Carabinieri below shouted instructions through bullhorns. Despite the howl of the wind, he heard their pleading words and soft demands. It seemed absurd. A panicked herd does not heed words. Why hadn't they come mounted on horses? Wasn't that the best way to control cattle?

He reached into the inside pocket of his lightweight dress coat for a square of rice paper and tapped a neat line of tobacco across it. The tobacco came from a pouch he kept beneath his shoulder board. Still watching the square, he rolled and shaped a cigarette with his nimble fingers. As he pinched the cigarette between his lips and fished in his pockets for a match, a woman who had broken from the group suddenly stood behind him and demanded that he do his job. He ignored her, even as she tugged on his arm. When he found the wooden match, he turned and struck it across her forehead. When that failed to set its supposedly strike-anywhere tip ablaze, he struck it against the wall. He lit his cigarette as the woman wailed and scurried away.

The fat man.

What to do about the fat man? Described as the perceptive one, he was as stubborn and persistent in his mission as he was at gorging himself. The proof traveled loud and clear through the encrypted radio airways. In a venue full of activity, where thousands of details were vying for attention, the fat man had sensed that something was amiss. What had he seen?

"Eagle Eye, from Echo One. I'm cutting across the square."

When he heard those words in the radio earpiece, he quickly scanned the square. To his dismay, the fat man was heading in the direction of the assassin instead of the mark he was there to protect. The entire plan was on the verge of unraveling until the crack of gunfire put that safely out of reach. But his relief was short-lived. On that same radio frequency, he heard the fat man was in pursuit of the assassin.

You miss nothing, do you?

He took several drags of his cigarette, always exhaling through his nose. A scheme for maiming the fat man was taking shape.

The struggle below waned as more police arrived. Those with bullhorns, to his surprise, managed to steer the cattle to the arcades of the Procuratie. A sense of order was being restored. That was not the case by the elevator. As the clang of the ascending car grew louder, the commotion by the elevator intensified. By the time the doors opened, the ever-predictable herd was in full panic.

He flicked what was left of his cigarette through the open arches and walked over to the stairwell door. He had already picked the deadbolt lock. All he had to do was open the door. It resisted his shoulder at first but caved on the second try. Assaulted with a musty odor and air so stale it seemed impossible to breathe, he took a moment to adjust. Then he plunged into the blackness. By the time he reached the bottom, he had settled on the details of his scheme for the fat man. He gave no thought to the police activity he'd find at the foot of the bell tower. His Carabinieri officer's uniform would let him slip through the lockdown.

Chapter Four

Procuratie Vecchie

The unlocked door was solid wood, probably capable of withstanding a tactical battering ram. I put my ear to it. No sound. Standing back by the hinges, I leveled my weapon and pushed the door with my foot, like stepping hard on a gas pedal. The door swung open. I stepped into an office crowded with dark wood furniture and smelling of lemon furniture polish. With both hands on my weapon—close to my face and tilted forty-five degrees sideways—I swept the tight space for bad guys. It was clear.

Behind the desk, a rifle leaned against the windowsill. Short, with a walnut stock, a folding bipod, and a scope, it had a low-capacity magazine inserted behind the pistol grip. I recognized it immediately as the Walther WA 2000, a rare and distinctive weapon once featured in a James Bond film with the Dalton guy nobody seems to remember.

It was an odd choice. Why use a rare weapon? Why leave it behind?

I found no shell casings, which meant the perp knew they were evidence and took them. Though unlikely, it was possible to pull latent prints from fired shell casings. A few feet from the rifle lay an empty canvas duffel bag. It was navy blue with "Venezia" embroidered in gold letters along the sides. A common tourist bag that seemed long enough to carry the rifle. I wasn't betting it had usable prints, but I could hope for hair, oil, or skin-flake DNA.

Beyond the open blinds lay a perfect view of the square. Paramedics hunched over a body. Carabinieri units swarmed around them. Tufu methodically scanned the area, his Glock drawn and ready. Ruiz talked into his mic. I turned on my radio.

"Got here too late, Top," Ruiz said. "The subject is dead."

Aarzam El-Hashem. The subject. The snitch. The killer I swore to lock up in a Rikers Island jail cell was dead. So was my reason for joining the Feds, joining the task force.

Almost a year earlier, Vincent and I had caught a triple homicide in the swanky brownstone community of Park Slope in Brooklyn. The crime scene was as heartbreaking as it was gruesome. El-Hashem had beheaded a crooked banker with a butcher knife from the victim's own kitchen and shot the wife and nine-year-old daughter execution style. Now dead, El-Hashem would never face a courtroom to answer for those crimes. The victims and the people of Brooklyn had been cheated, thanks to a cowardly shooter.

I rushed out of the office and nearly collided with a large hooded figure. He veered deftly out of the way and sped forward. It took a moment to realize it was a monk in a chocolate-colored habit. A monk in Italy was not unusual, one that big and agile was.

Heavy combat boots?

I leveled my weapon.

"*Alto, Polizia!*"

He stopped.

"*Mani! Mani!*" I waited to see his hands.

He raised his arms and turned around. The sleeves of his habit slid down, exposing meaty, calloused hands and ropy forearms. His head was down, and the hood shrouded his face. I ordered the monk to drop the hood. He hesitated but complied when I repeated the order. He had a blond crew cut and a nasty jagged scar along his jawline.

"On the floor, now! *Pavimento!*" I said.

His face gave away nothing.

I squeezed my push-to-talk mic. "All units, from Echo One. I have a suspect on the second floor of the building." He circled slowly, forcing me to do the same. "White male, six foot four, heavy build, wearing a—*pavimento, pavimento!*— Request back—"

The monk ducked. Cut sideways. Charged.

He slammed me sideways against the wall, knocking my gun loose, then landed two rapid-fire punches on my kidney. A forearm swing from downtown followed. My head snapped back. I dropped to one knee—same knee I bruised back at the square. His legs made good targets. His groin did too. But he'd crippled me. I lacked the power or stamina to launch a counterstrike. He broke off the attack and turned to flee. I lunged and caught his waist. We crashed prone on the hard marble floor. I had the wind knocked out of me and lost my grip. He shook me off, sprang to his feet, and headed straight for a room near the stairs.

"Echo One, here. Where's my backup?"

O'Neil shouted at the Carabinieri assault team commander over the radio. "Why isn't anyone on the goddamn second floor?"

"Echo One, from Echo Six," Kamaria said. "I am inside, coming to your location."

"Echo Four, y'all," Colt said. "Just a few yards shy of the building. Hang on, Echo One!"

Carabinieri soldiers finally came out of the stairwell. I was both relieved and unnerved. Would the idiots start shooting up the hallway?

"He's dressed as a monk," I said into my mic. "*Monaco! Monaco!*"

The soldiers moved to intercept the fleeing monk. The suspect sprinted, reaching the room first and throwing the door open.

"You are hurt?"

Still stunned from the fight and lying facedown, I turned to look up. Kamaria Uba was standing over me. Her weapon—a sleek, sexy Beretta—was in her hands, pointed low and away.

"Umm, just catching my breath," I replied.

She helped me up. A pained grimace marred her flawless ebony skin. "Your face is broken."

I touched the left side of my face and winced. It was hot and swollen. I tasted blood. Even my teeth hurt.

"Where is the bad man?" she asked.

Shit!

With Kamaria fast on my six, I staggered toward the room and through the doorway into a large unfurnished space smelling of fresh paint. I ignored the confused soldiers standing in the middle and looked for other doors. There were none. I rushed to the windows. All were locked.

"Where did he go?" Kamaria spun in a circle. "Only escape is the door."

"There has to be another way out. He didn't just disappear." I scanned the room again. "The fireplace!"

I hustled over to the mantel and knelt in the hearth. I looked up. "He must've climbed the chimney. Seems wide enough."

"He is on the roof!" Kamaria issued orders in Italian to the Carabinieri soldiers, and they rushed out of the room.

How could he climb so fast? It was a long way up, and there were no handholds inside the chimney. He could have climbed by pressing his limbs against the walls, but that required a lot of time and effort. Maybe he had an accomplice, someone on the roof with a rope.

I leaned a hand against the back wall of the fireplace. I noticed horizontal and vertical cracks in the mortar that held the stones together. The cracks joined to form a jagged rectangle. I put my palms on the rectangle and pushed. It shifted.

"Wait!" I called to Kamaria, who was almost out of the room.

I pushed harder, and the rectangle slid back to expose a short tunnel. I squeezed through the opening and into a small room illuminated only by the meager light coming from the tunnel. A wooden trapdoor was in the middle of the stone floor. I gripped the iron ring bolted near the edge and pulled. A rough-hewn circular shaft fell away like a deep well. A row of iron rungs anchored in the stone descended into the murk below.

"Here!" I yelled.

"I know you are here."

Her voice startled me. I didn't expect her to be right behind me.

"Ask if anyone's familiar with this shaft or hidden passageway. We need to know where this leads."

As she radioed in, I inspected the shaft with the small, superbright tactical flashlight we all carried. The rungs were rusted but looked thick and sturdy.

The answer to Kamaria's question came back negative. Command had building blueprints that didn't show the hidden room or where the shaft led. The assault team on the roof reported no sign of the suspect.

Kamaria pointed at the shaft. "He must escape here."

After testing a couple of rungs with my foot, I started down; Kamaria followed.

At the bottom, I shined my flashlight on the walls. A brick corridor broke the monotony of the stonework. Empty candle sconces lined the sides like an honor guard. Leading with my weapon, flashlight pressed against the gun's stock, I moved forward. The arched ceiling was low, forcing me to stoop. Kamaria fell in behind, sweeping her flashlight over the walls and floor.

The corridor meandered at odd angles. The deeper we went, the stronger the smells of rotting wood and stale water. Heavy mildew covered the brick. At one point, the corridor made a sharp turn. A huge rat greeted us there. I shrieked.

"The big man is afraid of a little mouse?" Kamaria asked, doing a bad job of suppressing a snicker.

"No, it's just—*that's* not a mouse. That's a rat! I've seen big ass rats in Brooklyn, but not like that."

She went around me and chased the rat away. I followed her, feeling like a fool but glad the giant rodent was gone. Behind me, the sound of voices and hurried footsteps grew louder. Other uniforms from the assault team must've followed us and were catching up.

We approached a medieval wooden door made of heavy planks bound together with rusted iron bands.

I reached for an iron ring just as Kamaria spoke into her mic. "All units, from Echo Six. The suspect has abandoned his disguise." She squatted next to the monk's habit, shining her flashlight on the empty folds.

I yanked the door open. A vacant canal stared back, the wake of a fleeing boat confirming the shooter's escape.

Chapter Five

Headquarters

After the excitement of the morning wound down, Vincent and I headed to headquarters for a three o'clock emergency meeting. It was a short walk east of St. Mark's Square. We traversed crowded streets and crossed short bridges over narrow canals. Along the way we passed several trattorias where the pasta was handmade and savory sauces were simmered with ingredients that had never seen the inside of a can. But with no time to stop for a proper meal, lunch was a mix of tiny sandwiches and pastries I picked up along the way.

We stopped when we reached a small square bordered by eighteenth-century town houses with storefronts, a white Gothic church, and the Carabinieri's headquarters in Venice. We were early, so we sat on a stone bench.

Vincent drank a bottle of water and chewed on a protein bar that looked like tree bark. "He actually shot at you? With a submachine gun?"

I nodded. "And missed the barn by a yard."

"*Holy Shit!* Frigging guinea."

"It was a kid." I ate my last pastry. "Couldn't have been more than twenty."

Vincent took off his suit jacket and folded it over his leg. He ran a hand through his slicked-back blond hair. The sleeve of his dress shirt seemed on the verge of tearing under the strain of sheathing his massive bicep.

"Fuck him," Vincent said. "He coulda put you in the morgue."

Now that Vincent mentioned it, I looked myself over to make sure a stray round hadn't chipped the paint or punched a hole in the barn doors.

Vincent put his heavy hand on my shoulder and squeezed. "You okay?"

We'd been through a lot, Vincent and me. We were brothers, sharing a bond that extended well beyond our professional relationship. A bond that would last until death came for us. It was that simple. It was black-and-white.

"I lost the shooter." I looked away. "So, what do you think?"

"Your mea culpa will give me the frigging runs, is what I think. You were two steps ahead of everybody. You saw the shooter, for fuck's sake!"

"I lost him."

"Cut the shit, Miles." He chewed the last bit of tree bark and said with his mouth full, "We had a million people there, and nobody knew about that escape route. We *all* lost him."

For a few minutes, we watched tourists and Venetians haggle over prices in the town house shops.

I said, "I held back information, back at the square."

Vincent shot surreptitious glances at people browsing the storefronts. "I'm all ears."

"I said I saw the blinds open and then the muzzle flash, but there was more."

"You ID'd the shooter?"

I shook my head. "Never really *saw* the shooter. Just a shadow. But I saw the rifle protruding from the window."

Vincent tapped his fingers along the edge of the bench. "And that's important because…?"

"Because I don't think the shooter is a pro."

"He took the shell casings, didn't he?"

"Yeah, but would you expose yourself like that? Flaunt a rifle out a window? In a square full of photo-happy tourists?"

Vincent rubbed his chin. "How else do you make that shot?"

"Dunno."

"Then call an expert, call M&M. It's about 0900 stateside."

I took out the cheesy smartphone the FBI insists on forcing its patriotic agents to use, one engineered by Koreans instead of Americans. In my ever-expanding contact list, I searched for Manny Martinez, a sharpshooter for the NYPD Emergency Services Unit—a euphemism for SWAT.

Manny answered on the second ring. "Martinez, ESU."

"M&M, Miles Jordan."

"Miles! *Que pasa,* bro? Long time. Heard you left for the Feds."

"JTTF."

"Nice. I hear that's a good gig. Vinny went with you?"

"Of course. He'd be lost without me." I glanced at Vincent, who was flipping me the Italian version of the bird.

Manny laughed. "Tell Vinny he still owes me a drink at Scores."

"Will do. Listen, Manny, we've got a situation. You got a few?"

"Yeah, shoot."

I gave him a quick rundown of the day's events, cramming in as much detail as I could. There was a long silence when I was done.

"Well? What do you think?" I asked.

Manny made a sound like a cicada. "Your shooter is an amateur. No trained sniper sets his weapon out of a window. A pro sets up inside. You would never see the rifle. In this case, I would've raised the blinds a few inches or cut a square in the slats. Then set up a couple of feet behind and put my shot through that opening. Also, shooting from an angle is tricky. I would've located elsewhere, like opposite that church, from what you describe. And then there's the sun to consider. Where was the sun at that time of the day?"

"It was mostly shining on that side of the square."

"Another tactical mistake. The glint from the scope."

"Okay, what about leaving the rifle behind?"

"Very unusual. You must've spooked him and ruined his extraction plan. Snipers don't intentionally leave their weapons behind."

"And the weapon? Why that rifle? Something special about it?"

Radio chatter filled Manny's side of the line, and he waited for it to subside. Then he said, "That rifle is short, which might make concealment easier. If your perp strapped it to his leg, for example, it might disappear under a monk's habit. But other than that, I can't think of any good reason to use it. At that range, any rifle would do. Using a rifle that rare is a liability. Easier to trace."

Though it seemed far-fetched, I saw it working. Strap the rifle to his leg and walk with a limp. Then use the habit to conceal it. However, that didn't explain the duffel bag.

"Gotta go, Miles. We just caught a ten-thirty. Possible hostage situation. Call me when you're back. We'll hit the bar."

"Thanks, man."

A ten-thirty was a robbery in progress. The thought of playing cops and robbers on the streets of Brooklyn instead of terrorist hide-and-seek brought a wave of nostalgia.

I missed home.

I missed Brooklyn.

"Miles, one more thing," Manny said. "Your shooter knew exactly where his target would be and when. That's the one thing he got right."

I looked Vincent in the eye and said to Manny, "We know."

When I ended the call, Vincent asked, "What do we know?"

"That we've got a mole."

Chapter Six

Finger-Pointing

A squad of soldiers marched into the square. Leading them was Colonel Giuseppe Marino, the commander of the Venice Carabinieri. He was a short man who cut a lean, fit profile in his sharp blue uniform. His polished knee-high boots glinted in the sunlight. A saber rattled at his side. He made eye contact and shook his head.

"Check out this little pisser, looking for a goat." Vincent jutted out his thick, boxy jaw as if daring Marino to take a swipe at it, but the colonel ignored him and kept marching. "Twenty bucks says he'll check that activity tracker twice before he reaches the building."

I knew better than to take the bet; Marino was obsessed with step counting. And sure enough, before I could finish the thought, he glanced at the activity tracker on his wrist and then again seconds later.

With wrought iron window balconies, clay tile roofing, and a terra-cotta stucco exterior, the headquarters of the Venice Carabinieri looked like a Tuscan villa. If not for the Italian flag fluttering overhead or the words carved to the right of the stone entryway—Carabinieri Comando Proviciale Stazione—you might mistake it for some fat cat's house or walk in looking for a vacant hotel room.

We followed the procession through the entryway, across a garden with a working fountain, and past a set of double doors.

What the exterior of the building lacked in institutional touches was more than made up for inside. The plaster walls were painted apple green and finished off with rubber base molding. Dark asbestos tile covered the floor. The only reprieve was an incongruous pink marble staircase. I suspected the interior of the building had been "modernized" and the staircase saved by budget cuts.

We climbed the stairs to the second floor. A pair of overstuffed couches in the hallway faced each other. Displayed above them were photographs of Carabinieri commanders. Some were sepia, dating back to when the camera was a recent invention. All were taken against the backdrop of the iconic St. Mark's Basilica. Out of twenty portraits, give or take, Marino's was encased in the largest and gaudiest frame of all.

The noise of heated words grew louder as we approached the task force squad room.

"Finger-pointing time." Vincent wrinkled his nose and slowly opened the door.

The squad room was large and rectangular and smelled of stale cigarettes and espresso. Italian and American flags stood side by side in a corner. Windows covered one wall. Framed photographs of agents killed in the line of duty, award plaques, and safety and procedural posters filled another two. The corkboard on the wall at the front of the room usually caught the eye first. Two years of task force work covered every inch of it. An organizational chart represented the command structure, as we knew it, of the terrorist organization we were investigating. For known members, mug shots or surveillance photos were used. Glaring white index cards stood out as stark reminders of all the scum we still had to identify. Each photo or card was neatly labeled with names, aliases, or code names. The most conspicuous feature of the pyramid—and the most frustrating—was the sole blue index card pinned at the top. It was inked in red Sharpie: The Scorpion. Next to the chart were maps of the US, Europe, and the Middle East.

Today, however, the corkboard took a back seat to the team gathered in the middle of the room. With the exception of Kamaria, who sat on a nearby desk, everyone had a role in a three-ring circus.

Scruffy-bearded Tony Tufu and clean-cut Antonio Ruiz were in each other's faces, spittle flying and fingers jabbing. Opposite them stood Max Colt with his corduroy sports jacket pulled open and his right hand resting on his service weapon. He looked ready to quick draw if the pair of lanky Carabinieri officers he was wrangling with didn't change their tune.

But the main attraction, in the center ring, was O'Neil and Marino. At six foot five, O'Neil towered over Marino. He was forced to stoop, close to the tipping point, to get his face within inches of his Italian counterpart. Marino glared back, stretching out his neck as far as it would go and underscoring every other word he uttered with violent hand gestures.

"Let's go for a beer before they see us," Vincent said.

From her neutral corner, Kamaria waited quietly with her arms crossed. Her neat, shoulder-length cornrow-braided hair was in a ponytail, held in place by a gold ring she'd brought from the Horn of Africa. She was a jungle cat, lithe and sleek.

"There he is!" Marino pointed a finger at me. "Your man, Mr. O'Neil, let the assassin escape. *Incompetente!*"

I was now in the center ring.

"For crying out loud." O'Neil straightened up. "We've been through this four goddamn times! Nobody let the shooter escape. He got away. It happens. Miles was the only one who spotted the guy and gave chase. Yet, out of two hundred law enforcement personnel we had sealing that square, not one got to the second floor in time to back him up!"

This was a new experience. When the brass had to choose between pissing off a politically connected somebody or throwing a detective nobody under the bus, you could bet the farm on the latter. Watching O'Neil back me up was the bright spot in an otherwise shitty day.

"What we should be asking," O'Neil continued, "is why your blueprints said nothing about that hidden room or the passageway below the square."

Marino waved his hand dismissively. "No, no, no. Not *my* blueprints. I get them from the Consiglio Comunale."

"Where?" O'Neil asked.

"*Come si chiama?*" Marino snapped his fingers. "City Hall? They give me blueprints, but no one knew these secrets. But your man, he knew. And he put my Carabinieri on the roof to chase birds! Then, like magic, he find the secret room." Marino turned that pointing finger at O'Neil and shook it. "Why, Mr. O'Neil, does your man do this? Strange, no? And more strange, why he don't answer his radio?"

I turned it off in the hallway, asshole, so I could hear—

"Maybe he wants to be hero, eh? Catch the assassin alone."

Hero?

"Or maybe"—Marino crossed his arms and jutted his chin—"the rifle he find is *his* rifle."

I charged. Desks in the way flew aside as if a tsunami had hit them. But before I could get a hand on the little shit—not that I knew what I intended to do—I hit a wall called Vincent Santoro. Marino, to his credit, didn't flinch. His lieutenants did, both jumping back.

"Now he attacks a *comandante* of the Carabinieri. *Incredible!*"

Marino marched toward the door, brushing past Vincent and me. His lieutenants hesitated then walked around us and jogged to catch up.

As he opened the door, Marino said over his shoulder, "I will see this man of yours, Mr. O'Neil, removed from this team!"

CHAPTER SEVEN

REGROUPING

The blind rage that gripped me left the room with that asshole Marino. I glanced at Vincent and then at the team. All eyes were on me.

"I'm cool," I said. "Let's get to work."

"We *will* discuss this later," O'Neil said with a scowl.

The team quickly restored the scattered office furniture.

O'Neil wheeled his office chair to the front of the squad room. "Gather around, people," he said.

We followed suit and sat around him in a semicircle. Behind O'Neil, crisscrossing lines of yarn pinned by thumbtacks spanned across the maps on the corkboard. Each distinctly colored line represented the movement of a suspected or known terrorist or sleeper agent. Black was for the subject, the snitch, El-Hashem. His line stretched from various parts of the Middle East to Europe and across the Atlantic.

I glared at the thumbtack pinned on Brooklyn.

El-Hashem had come to my city and shat in my backyard. He'd killed a guy who probably deserved it and a wife who visibly enjoyed the fruits of her husband's shady labor in the clothes she wore and the cars she drove. That I could keep professional. But then El-Hashem committed the ultimate crime. He killed an innocent kid. On my watch! That made it personal.

Bloodred lines of yarn on the maps tracked the suspected movements of The Scorpion. They were short, erratic, and unconnected—a sobering picture of how little we had on him.

O'Neil crossed his legs and put on a pair of black half-frame glasses that set off his silver crew cut.

"This day started out mild and sunny and ended up a shit storm," he said. "And a lot of that shit is rolling downhill with great momentum. A simple grab-and-bag turned to shit. But that's water under the bridge, people. The Scorpion is still out there, and the Israeli prime minister's visit is five days away. That's our focus now."

Without the red sling, Ruiz's arm dangled at his side, a huge diving watch acting as a pendulum. "How do we catch The Scorpion now? Some of us—you included, Top—have been chasing the son of a bitch for two years, and the closest we ever got was El-Hashem. The same El-Hashem now decomposing in a morgue."

A silence as thick as a bowl of seafood risotto hung in the room. Ruiz was right. We were chasing a ghost. All we had left to go on was a shaky police sketch gleaned from El-Hashem's recollection of the last time he met The Scorpion—fourteen years ago.

"Who wanted El-Hashem dead?" I asked. "Who would benefit?"

"Isn't that obvious?" Ruiz said.

"Is it? Who?"

"The Scorpion. Who else?"

"The Scorpion activated El-Hashem for a terrorist attack on European soil. Why activate a reliable sleeper agent he had well hidden in New York only to have him killed?"

Three months earlier, El-Hashem had received a coded phone call that activated him to carry out a terrorist attack. The call was forwarded by a CIA listening post in Guantanamo, where El-Hashem was enjoying Uncle Sam's hospitality. Instead of a specific date, target, and location, he got a confusing itinerary that started in Morocco and ended in Istanbul. He was put in play, and once he reached Istanbul—accompanied by undercover agents—he met with a contact who pointed him to Venice. There, he was to receive his final instructions from The Scorpion himself.

Given Venice as a location and the approximate arrival date by boat and car, we put two and two together, and the target became clear. The Israeli prime minister was set to visit Venice on Friday morning—the day we were calling D-Day. His visit would start with a speech at the Doge's Palace, followed by a tour of the historic Jewish Ghetto. A series of meetings with his Italian counterpart and a delegation from the Vatican to discuss humanitarian efforts in the Middle East rounded out his three-day visit.

Ruiz said to me, "Reliable sleeper agent? You guys found him in six hours. We flipped him in eight weeks."

We didn't know for sure if El-Hashem had acted alone or was ordered to murder the terrorist organization's crooked banker and his family, but the Feds believed—operating on blind hope really—they could hide him in Guantanamo and flip him to work for us while keeping his handlers completely in the dark. It was a calculated gamble that up until today seemed to be paying off.

I said, "We're operating under the assumption that The Scorpion doesn't know we flipped him."

"Then we're being obtuse," Ruiz said, "and need to rethink this."

"What do you mean?" O'Neil asked.

Ruiz replied, "Somehow, The Scorpion found out El-Hashem was our asset and activated him for a fake gig here in Venice to set him up."

That set off a round of speculation and disagreement with everyone talking at once and no one listening. O'Neil let it ride out for about ten seconds then restored order. We went around the room and everyone had their say. Last to go was Kamaria.

"I believe truly that Venice is safe," she said in that sweet voice, one with tones of soul and soprano.

"Safe?" O'Neil peered at Kamaria over his half-frame glasses. "How so?"

"Sleeper agents, like El-Hashem," Kamaria said, "become targets when they are suspected traitors. This is true. Still, consider this. The Scorpion believes El-Hashem is loyal and plans to meet with him. At the square, he sees El-Hashem struck down by bullets. He sees many, many Carabinieri close the exits. And, he is thinking"—Kamaria tapped her temple—"the police followed El-Hashem and then killed him when he was of no more use. That must mean they are very close. They have set a trap. The Scorpion hides in the crowd and escapes. Knowing how close the police had come, he would not risk attacking Italy now."

"I suppose that's plausible," O'Neil said. "It's also a great decoy. We think it's too hot for him here, we lower our guard, and he attacks here anyway."

My throat went dry and scratchy. "There's another sleeper agent. Here in Venice."

Someone groaned. Someone else said, "You had to say it?"

Kamaria leveled those beautiful hazel eyes on me. "Can we believe a sleeper agent is here after all that occurred this morning? What if we are wrong? Focusing here, we leave Europe exposed, do we not?"

O'Neil removed his glasses and tapped a temple tip on his lower lip. "Europe has been exposed for years. That hasn't changed, Kamaria."

"This is true, still consider this. If The Scorpion had plans for Venice, then he acquired or was provided the resources to execute them. If he cannot use those resources here—and use them, he must—where else might he use them? Where many, many people gather. Look to European football matches and the climate change meeting in Brussels. Both in occurrence this week."

Kamaria was my kind of investigator. Always thinking outside the case file.

"She's got a point." Ruiz gestured at the corkboard. "We have red yarn in England and Germany and some in neighboring Brussels. We could team up with Interpol, work all last known whereabouts—"

The team erupted again, slinging opposing opinions around the room like mud.

When things settled, Ruiz added, "Look, it's logical. El-Hashem was directed here and killed by The Scorpion or one of his henchmen. That gets rid of a snitch and throws us for a loop, while the real attack happens far from Venice."

Feeling a familiar old ache in my lower back, I stood and paced the room. The arguments and theories continued. At the first sign of a lull, I stopped and turned to the team.

"If The Scorpion was behind the hit on El-Hashem, then finding the shooter is our only hope of getting a line on him or the intel we need to thwart an attack." I held up my hands. "Before we get into another round of whether an attack is imminent and what the venue might be, let's weigh the possible targets. Kamaria has offered a couple of juicy possibilities. And so have Ruiz, Tufu, and Colt. But is there really a juicier target than the Israeli prime minister?"

I made eye contact with everyone.

"And is there a better venue than right here in Venice, where he'll be in five days?"

Chapter Eight

Objectives

After a ten-minute break, we settled in our chairs to continue the team meeting.

"I agree with Miles," O'Neil said. "First, we need to continue to operate on the assumption that The Scorpion is planning an attack here in Venice, and his target is the Israeli prime minister. Second, we need to locate and apprehend the shooter."

Colt tilted his cowboy hat back, drawing his eyes out from under the shadow of the brim. "Y'all reckon that yellowbelly is still in Venice? Seems a long shot."

"Got that right." Tufu scratched his scruffy beard as if something had taken up residence there and was on the move. "Why would the shooter hang around? He's probably halfway to some desert shithole by now."

I said to Tufu, "Or he's enjoying a hearty meal down the street."

"All right, enough of this," O'Neil said. "Let's see what we've got. Tufu?"

"El-Hashem was shot twice," Tufu said. "The first round nicked the upper arm. No big deal. The second was the Grim Reaper. Hard to say exactly what damage it did until we see the medical examiner's report. Too many factors. I can tell you the round went into the upper back and punched a fist-sized hole in the chest. Blew out a lung, maybe a part of the heart too. He was a goner before the medics got to him."

"Both rounds exited the body, then?" O'Neil crossed his legs. "Did we recover them?"

Tufu grinned. "We got lucky. The techs were able to pull them from the wood panels of the maize cart. They sent them off to firearm analysis."

"Good. When do we get the report?"

Tufu scratched his beard again. "Wednesday."

O'Neil stretched out his arm palm up. "Wednesday? Didn't you put a rush on it? We should have it tomorrow."

Tufu shrugged. "This is Europe, Top. Working overtime is practically a capital crime."

O'Neil took a deep breath. "What else?"

"Tried getting additional intel out of him before he checked out," Tufu replied, "but he faded fast."

Ruiz shot Tufu a look.

"Got something to add, Ruiz?" O'Neil asked.

Ruiz turned the bezel on his huge diving watch as he spoke. "I tried keeping El-Hashem alive and needed help, but all Tufu was interested in was interrogation."

"Questioning," Tufu spat.

"We'd already turned him," Ruiz said. "What more was there to extract? Our job was to keep him alive!"

"He was dead anyway, and dying men sometimes spill secrets."

"It was stupid and incompetent."

Tufu sprung out of his chair. "Fuck you, Ruiz!"

"Hey, can it!" O'Neil removed his glasses and pointed a temple tip at Ruiz and then Tufu. "We don't have time for this crap. Now settle down, or I promise you both dog shit transfers. Are we clear?"

It was a potent threat. As FBI, Ruiz could be shipped to the Dakotas or some other Fed-forsaken outpost where agents go to fade away. The Port Authority brass could drop Tufu in a detective slot for the bus terminal—a command nobody wanted—or put him back in uniform to babysit motorists in the Holland Tunnel or on the George Washington Bridge.

Ruiz nodded curtly, but Tufu wasn't getting it. He remained standing, a death stare on his face.

"Do I have to repeat myself?" O'Neil asked Tufu.

Vincent leaned over and said to Tufu, "Sit the fuck down, Tony. You wanna finish up your twenty writing tickets on the GWB?"

Tufu glanced at Vincent then at me and suddenly seemed to understand. He sat down with a crash.

O'Neil turned to Colt. "Where are you and Ruiz?"

"We got video." Colt smiled. "That interior hallway camera Miles here pointed out was set for streaming video to a local server. We bagged the hard drive and a thumb drive that was plugged into one of the ports."

O'Neil sat up. "And?"

"Video's pretty as a peach! Has a real nice facial of the sumbitch along with footage of Miles playin' linebacker like he was skunk drunk."

My face flushed hot.

"We also got footage from four external cameras and some phone video submitted by witnesses at the square," Colt said. "But there ain't nothing there to fuss over. Next step is to run stills of the perp through facial recognition software and all that."

"Good." O'Neil pointed at Colt. "Keep me posted." He then turned to Kamaria. "You're up, K."

Kamaria said, "I have volunteered to replace Officer Tufu in following firearm analysis, as he will be busy with other matters. Agent Ruiz will supervise my findings."

O'Neil nodded.

Kamaria continued, "I have given our technicians the short killing rifle. They say it is most uncommon. I will investigate its history."

O'Neil said, "Maybe we hit pay dirt. Find the current owner or a former owner. Never know where that could lead. Vinny?"

Vincent said, “Me and Miles pulled three dozen of Marino’s people to do an exhaustive canvass of all the apartments, offices, and businesses in and around the square. Nobody we talked to saw the shooting. Many heard the shots. Coupla witnesses claim they saw a monk fitting the suspect’s description entering the building about a half hour before the shooting. They also claim he was with two other monks. Marino’s people are running background checks on those witnesses.”

“Is that common, monks in that building?” O’Neil asked.

“You wouldn’t think so, but yeah,” Vincent said. “There are administrative offices and apartments there under lease by the church.”

“What’s next then, more canvassing?”

“We’ll keep canvassing today. And tomorrow, we’re following up with the church bigwig.”

O'Neil looked surprised. “The cardinal?”

Vincent nodded. “We have an appointment with His Eminence.”

Colt asked, “Why talk to the church if we reckon the perp ain’t a monk?”

Vincent replied, “Assuming our witnesses are credible, he was seen with other monks. There could be a church connection.”

Colt tipped his hat.

“There are numerous church officials you could have brought this to,” O’Neil said. “Why the cardinal?”

I said, “To expedite this part of the investigation and avoid red tape, we should talk to the top guy.”

O'Neil thought that over a moment. “Okay, fair enough. But how’d you get access without me having to song-and-dance through channels?”

“Easy,” Vincent said. “I asked his secretary if she’d heard about the guy who was shot in the square. After a litany of ‘yeses’ and ‘oh my Gods,’ I told her it was the work of a killer monk. You shoulda heard that woman scream.”

O'Neil cracked a rare smile. "What about that underground labyrinth? Was it thoroughly searched?"

"Far as we know, Marino's people are still down there scouring the place," Vincent said.

"Keep me posted," O'Neil said. "Miles, walk us through this thing. In excruciating detail."

I described the day's events in excruciating detail as requested, leaving out the parts about getting shot at by the Carabinieri, the rifle sticking out of the window, and my conversation with M&M.

"All right," O'Neil said. "Any questions?"

When the Q&A was over, O'Neil stood. "To recap, Colt and Ruiz will run stills of the perp through facial. Kamaria will take over firearm analysis."

O'Neil turned to Tufu. "As we discussed before the meeting, I want you to pick up the old leads we have on The Scorpion, see if anything new shakes out after this incident."

Tufu flashed a thumbs-up.

O'Neil cleared his throat. "Miles and Vincent will continue canvassing the square until their interview tomorrow with the cardinal. In between all of that, people, we'll continue to follow up on the public tips that keep pouring in." He paused. "Keep in mind that our primary objective now is to thwart an attack and ensure the Israeli prime minister's visit is uneventful. Nailing The Scorpion is secondary."

The sound of moving chairs and bodies filled the room. Forming a single file, I fell in behind Colt. The way he walked was amusing, a slight swinging out of each leg as it moved forward as though his cowboy boots were fitted with spurs and he was leery of getting tangled up.

O'Neil pulled me aside. "Charging at Marino was goddamn stupid. What the hell were you thinking? He'll take this straight to the SAC—a hardline good ol' boy. You know what that means?"

I knew exactly what it meant. The SAC, the Special Agent in Charge, the man running the task force, was the type who'd wear white robes and burn crosses if that were still a thing in the Deep South.

"Marino will spin it. The SAC will eat it up. And you'll be off the case. All I can do is stall them. But I need something."

It was hard to look O'Neil in the eye. "I'll find something."

"Find it fast."

Chapter Nine

The Courier

Nabeel dropped his cellphone and fell to his knees. He barely heard the crash of glass and metal or felt the sharp sting of the tile floor. He just knew the weight of the desert had fallen on his bony shoulders.

Your son's cancer has spread.

That's what the doctor had told him. How could that be? Had Allah abandoned him? Was he not a good Muslim? Did he not follow the teachings of the prophet—peace and blessings be upon him?

Amir, his only son, was five years old. So small and tender. So slight of strength. With a smile that never faded from his thinning face, no matter the pain the cruel disease inflicted upon him. No child deserved such a fate. Least of all, his Amir.

He must go now to a good hospital, the doctor had decided. He needs far better care, the doctor had insisted. We cannot do much more for him, the doctor had lamented. All of that required money, money he didn't have. Money that would take him months to earn as a humble courier. Months his son didn't have.

And what of Dalia, his sweet wife? How was he going to break the news to her?

"Dalia, Amir needs better care, but we cannot afford it. He will die, love of my heart, and there's nothing we can do but try to comfort his final days."

The words tortured his mind and shredded his heart when he said them aloud. And he wept. When the tears subsided, he prayed. When his knees bled from kneeling, he paced the confines of his tiny rented room. When the pacing exhausted him, he rested in the only chair he owned.

Murmurs and laughter drifting in through the small open window seemed cruel and accusing, as if the strangers outside were speaking about him and laughing at his plight. He knew that was absurd. He was no one.

The tip of his tongue picked and probed the hole where a front tooth he'd lost to decay—an incisor—once completed his smile. He became vaguely aware of a persistent ringing. Confused, he glanced around until he saw his cellphone lying on the tile floor where he'd dropped it. *Who could that be?* The ringtone was generic, not the one he'd assigned to Dalia or anyone he knew. He pulled himself out of the chair. By the time he bent over to reach for it, the ringing had stopped. He picked up the phone anyway and turned it over. The glass was shattered. A web of lines spread from a corner. In the black of the screen, he stared at his reflection, broken and disconnected, the shards of his former self. He swept his thumb over the surface, expecting to be cut but feeling only the lines of the cracks.

The phone rang again and simultaneously vibrated in his hand. He bobbled it but managed to hold on. The screen was still serviceable, displaying an unknown caller through the cracks. Perhaps it was a mistaken connection or a phone trickster. He tapped the screen to take the call.

"Nabeel Haddad?"

The man on the phone had a deep, commanding voice. It instantly made Nabeel anxious. *Is this another doctor? Will I listen to more bad news?*

"Is this Nabeel Haddad, I kindly ask again?"

"Yes." Nabeel swallowed. "Yes, I'm speaking."

"Peace be unto you."

"May the peace and mercy of Allah be with you as well."

"I see you are a good Muslim, Nabeel Haddad. Just as I've been told."

Nabeel frowned. "You know my name, but I have not the gift of knowing yours."

"My name is of no importance, but what I have to say is. I know of your plight."

"My plight?"

"Your son is dying."

There it was again. In simple Arabic. The grim reality hitting him like a bucket of ice water. "How do you know this? Who are you?"

"I can help you, Nabeel Haddad."

"Help me?"

"Better doctors are expensive. Good hospitals, even more so. I can help you attain both."

Nabeel shot out one long arm and groped the air until his fingers curled around the back of the chair. He pulled it close. The bone-rattling sound of the hollow metal legs scraping the tile floor was not enough to encourage him to move, to close the gap. He settled in the chair as if his knees were tight rusted hinges.

He held the phone tight and pressed it hard against his ear. "I am listening."

"I have a package, a very important package. One that must be delivered at night, well after the Tahajjud. Both the contents of this package and the identity of the man to whom you are to deliver it are of no concern to you. Do you understand?"

The Tahajjud, the voluntarily night prayer, was not new to Nabeel. Since Amir's illness was discovered, he had performed the mandatory five prayers required of every good Muslim as well as the Tahajjud. Delivering a package after that prayer meant well after midnight. He never cared about the contents of a package and barely acknowledged its recipient. But this odd hour of delivery was something new. Something uncomfortable.

"Do you understand? I kindly ask again."

"I understand." Nabeel felt instantly ashamed of the lie. "Please, resume."

"I am prepared to pay handsomely for this service. How handsomely? Listen closely."

When the man told him the figure, Nabeel felt like weeping. He would make eight months' worth of wages in a single night. Eight months!

Nabeel mumbled, "What must I do?"

The man did not respond. Instead, he exhaled sharply as if smoking a cigarette.

"Are you still there, sir?"

"I am here, Nabeel Haddad, I am here. Tonight, I will call this number. I will give you an address. I will give you a name. You will not write anything down. You will commit the information to memory. Do you understand?"

"Yes," Nabeel said, nodding.

"You will go to that address and ask for that name. A man will give you the package and instructions. All you are required to do is deliver this package and forget that you ever saw it or that this conversation ever took place. Do you think you can do this?"

Nabeel suddenly felt his thobe get tighter, clinging to his skin like a sheen of sweat. "I must ask one question, sir." Nabeel's tongue picked and probed. "Why must delivery take place after the Tahajjud? Transportation is tricky—"

"That is not your concern. The instructions are simple and not open to discussion." The man paused. "You are one among many discreet couriers from whom I can choose. Have I made a mistake?"

"No! I can do this."

"Good, then we are agreed."

"Wait." Nabeel was on his feet. "I am ashamed of my rudeness and I apologize, but how … how do I know you will pay me? How do I know you are not just a phone trickster?"

The sudden silence on the other end of the phone gnawed at his heart. He wanted the offer to be real. He needed it to be real.

"Hello? Sir, are you still there?"

"Go to the kitchen cupboard and look inside the coffee mug."

Nabeel looked up at the small cupboard hanging above the compact sink. "I will find something there?"

"You will."

"Have you … have you been inside my room, sir? I have nothing of value."

"There is no lock I cannot defeat. But do not worry, Nabeel Haddad, I am not here to rob you. Go to the cupboard and see."

The phone line went dead.

Nabeel rushed to the cupboard and opened it. Finding the mug was easy. It stood like a palm tree in a desert. He put his phone down on the scrap of countertop next to the sink and reached for the mug. Inside was a white envelope. There was weight and thickness to it, which made his heart beat like the wings of a hummingbird. He carefully opened it and peered inside.

Allah had not abandoned him.

Chapter Ten

The Smokestack

Il Ciminiera, or The Smokestack, was the local cop bar. It was inconveniently located a long walking distance from Carabinieri headquarters. On the outside, it boasted the impressive Venetian Gothic façade of the many palaces in Venice. If not for the bright neon sign glowing above its heavy oak doors, the place could be confused for just another historic building facing the Grand Canal. Inside, however, it was a rebellious departure from the old-world style that dominated much of the city. Once you crossed a small foyer, it surprised you with the industrial look of steel trestle columns and stamped concrete floors. Sodium light fixtures hung from chains bolted into the high rafters. Panels of welded metal forming factories with smokestacks decorated the brick walls.

I sat at one end of the bar counter with Vincent, while the FBI guys sat on the other. Between us gathered a rowdy crowd of Carabinieri officers wearing their fancy uniforms with loose ties and open shirt collars. Tufu and a couple of task force officers I didn't know occupied a table in the dining area.

We were all wearing the same clothes we'd had on during the operation at the square, although the suits, business casual outfits, and even the shorts, polo shirt, and cap I wore were no longer crisp and fresh, as though the stress of the day had worn and prematurely aged the fabrics.

Glancing at Ruiz, who was in a huddle with Colt, I asked Vincent, "What's the beef between Ruiz and Tufu?"

Vincent squeezed the lime in his vodka. "Ruiz couldn't put pressure on El-Hashem's wound to stem the bleeding because Tony was too busy shoving his foot in it and asking questions."

"Ah." I grabbed the beer in front of me.

"Tony said there was no surviving that wound anyway, but you know Ruiz. That pompous ass thinks his Harvard law degree makes him all-knowing. Never mind that Tony did three tours in Iraq as a medic."

"Tufu was a medic?"

"Yeah, and a good one. Got the medals to prove it."

I sipped the Chimay Première, a beautifully crafted Belgian beer, aerating in a tulip glass.

"El-Hashem died ugly," Vincent said. "Take satisfaction in that."

Maybe it was the knot in my neck I kept kneading or the cheese platter between us I kept picking at instead of polishing off that gave me away. I was lit up inside. A simmering rage rippling under the cool-cat Miles Jordan exterior.

"It's not justice for the kid." I took another sip of beer. "She was there, in that living room. Just five … five feet from her father's severed head."

"She didn't see that. She was shot first."

That's how we read the crime scene. El-Hashem was there to punish his organization's double-dealing banker. He was there to make an example. Logically, that meant shooting the kid first, letting her parents watch. What could be worse for a parent? Then shooting the grieving wife. The banker was last, his hideous murder drawn out. What had been worst? The butcher knife gradually slicing his throat or knowing he'd gotten his family killed?

I said, "Maybe she didn't see her parents die, but she knew something bad was going to happen. And she was terrified, man."

Vincent shuddered. "That crime scene was gruesome. Banker's blood everywhere. Even on the girl. I thought working homicide meant you got used to gruesome. You don't, do you?"

"A lot of things you do." I could say that with authority; I had ten years in homicide, five more than Vincent. "But not the kids."

Vincent glanced at his watch. "Almost twelve hours since the shooting, and we got nothing."

"We'll get something."

"Yeah, well, I'm not feeling optimistic. Colt and Ruiz can't find a facial match for our suspected shooter. Kamaria tracks down the rifle owner only to be told he reported it stolen seven years ago." Vincent downed his vodka and signaled the bartender for another round. "Canvassing the square for witnesses hasn't given us shit, and don't get me started on public tips. Those always draw out the crazies."

"I know the score. We'll be fine."

"*Marone,* can't I wallow in self-pity and defeat for five minutes? Just five minutes?"

I smiled.

Vincent started on his new drink, which the bartender had set down along with another beer for me.

"Any guesses?" he asked.

I threw surreptitious glances around the bar. "You mean the mole? No, not yet. You?"

"Has to be a Fed. You can't trust them on a good day."

I rolled my eyes. "You got anything more substantial than that?"

"What do you mean?"

"You know what I mean. Interagency distrust and rivalry will rule the day until we uncover the leak. I get it, but it'll hurt the investigation."

Vincent looked away and shrugged. "Fine. It could be the Italians too. But I'm pinning my hopes on a Fed. They're always treating us like the hired help, too stupid or unqualified to be called agents. That's why we're task force officers. TFOs—Team Fuck Offs."

"Howdy, boys!" Colt called out as he navigated through tipsy bodies and a haze of cigarette smoke. "Why y'all sitting over here like you ain't part of the team?"

"We never got the invite," Vincent said. "We're the TFOs, remember?"

"Y'all don't need an invitation. Just flash them toy Yankee badges y'all got and you're in."

Colt laughed.

Vincent smirked.

I said to Colt, "I thought you lost that hat back at the square."

"Lost a hat, that's right. Got stampeded on would be more like it. This here's a backup."

"That's another hat?" Vincent frowned. "You travel around with identical hats?"

"Think cowboy hats are all the same?" Colt took off his hat and pointed. "The band 'round this one's rattlesnake. Brown cowhide with a silver buckle was on the other."

Vincent nodded as if he'd been the beneficiary of great wisdom. "How come you always wear a white hat?"

Colt slipped his hat back on, and a toothy grin formed under his horseshoe mustache. "'Cause the good guys always wear white."

"Right," Vincent said. "Dumb question."

"Well, catch you boys later," Colt said. "I've got to see a man about a horse."

After Colt drifted off to the bathroom, we sat in silence.

"You know, Miles, I almost let you get at Marino."

"Good thing you didn't."

"What were you gonna do?"

"Frankly, no idea. I just wanted to shut him up. The fucking gall. Implying I had something to do with this."

"Can he really get you booted off the task force? Because if he can, and does, I'll kick your ass. *You* talked me into riding shotgun on this thing."

A sobering reminder.

Soon after Vincent and I had El-Hashem in custody, the Feds descended in force on our busy Brooklyn South precinct and scooped him up. They hosed us down with national security bullshit, and there wasn't a damn thing we could do about it. Given that El-Hashem was a high-level sleeper agent with access to The Scorpion, the Feds needed his cooperation. They made it clear that the only prayer I had of pinning the triple homicide on that scumbag was to join the task force. Once The Scorpion was in custody, El-Hashem was mine. It sounded like a win-win before it all turned to shit.

"Oh, bullshit," I said. "You came along for the European tail."

Vincent threw his head back and laughed. "That's just a fringe benefit. I'll go wherever you go. We're partners."

We tapped our drinks.

"What did O'Neil say to you?" Vincent asked a couple of minutes later.

I nibbled on a crumb of blue cheese. "'Get a lead quick.'"

"How quick?"

"Tomorrow. We need one by tomorrow."

"All we got is an interview with a priest."

"Not just any priest. The church's version of divisional brass."

"Oh right, with all that clout comes miracles."

"You never know."

Vincent got off his stool. "Gotta take a piss."

Taking my beer glass, I turned the barstool to watch the crowd. Tufu was enjoying a bowl of shrimp and linguine fra diavolo, the delicious house specialty and the only dish served in a bright red ceramic bowl. At the other end of the bar, the Feds dined on tasty fried appetizers and dark brews.

Kamaria was hanging out with a group of other Carabinieri officers. Suddenly, Colt pushed through the crowd and grabbed her arm. He said something in her ear and led her aside. Under his white good-guy hat, Colt scowled and his mouth moved fast. Kamaria stood with her arms crossed. When she tried to walk away, Colt grabbed her arm again. This time, she yanked it free and gave him a look that would wilt stone. Then she stomped off.

What was that all about?

Chapter Eleven

Magic Words

Day 2

Tuesday, 0015 hours

Vincent called it a night. As he got up to leave, he issued a stern reminder of our morning gym session and then a skeptical look when I promised to be there. The FBI guys and most of the uniformed Carabinieri had already vacated the premises. Tufu and his buddies were in the process of doing the same. I sat on my barstool and drank another beer. The Europop music had either mellowed, or my ear had numbed.

"The big man is all alone?"

Only one person called me "the big man." I would've preferred "the handsome cat," but we don't always get what we prefer. Still, it was cool. Whenever she said it, the words rolled off as a term of endearment, not a jab at my weight.

With a glass of white wine in hand, Kamaria stood breathtakingly close. Her hair was loose, cornrows falling neatly around her shoulders.

"I'm not alone anymore."

She slid onto the barstool next to mine and pointed at my glass. "Beer is it? I thought Americans only drink Jack Daniels on the stones."

I chuckled. "On the rocks, Jack Daniels on the rocks."

"Now you make fun of me." Her smile was a breeze on a hot summer night.

"Whiskey's for forgetting. Beer's for savoring the moment."

"Then you are savoring the moment?"

I could smell her: lilac and freesia. "What do you think?" I playfully wiggled my eyebrows.

"I think you drink too much beer."

"Guilty as charged, Officer Uba." I offered my wrists. "Are you bringing me in?"

"You are not drunk enough."

"No? Just give me another hour, then."

We laughed.

"My commander was wrong to judge you so harshly," she said.

"You think so?"

"I saw the video, your struggle with the bad man. You fought bravely."

It hadn't been much of a fight. I played punching bag. What bravery did that require? Still, it was nice of her to say that.

She pointed at my battered face. "Does it hurt?"

"Only when I stop drinking."

Her smile turned conspiratorial. "Then we must beckon the bartender."

We ordered a round and then another. We laughed, got serious, and laughed again. Life was chocolate and all things sweet.

When the mood felt easy enough, I asked, "Everything okay between you and Colt?"

"You saw us argue." She made eye contact. "We had a relationship. It grew serious for him but not for me."

"And you broke it off?"

"I have tried. He is not taking it well."

"Have you talked to anyone about it?"

She shook her head. "You are the first."

Despite a silly feeling of pride that she'd confided in me, I felt uncomfortable, burdened with a sudden responsibility. "I could talk to him. Sometimes a man-to-man talk—"

"No, Miles. The work rules. The rumors. There would be trouble for him and trouble for me."

I nodded.

"Speaking of work"—Kamaria moved closer—"tell me, why do you do this work?"

I put down my beer glass. "Catch bad guys, you mean?"

"Yes, why do you catch the bad guys?"

"I need a job."

She raised an eyebrow, a warning of a deeper examination. "You were a lawyer in America. You became a policeman for a very good reason. Come, tell me."

I gazed at her hazel eyes. "I needed the action."

"Why?"

I paused. "Not something I talk about."

She put her glass down on the counter and leaned even closer. "Tell me."

I traveled back thirty-two years to an icy February afternoon in 1983. *My mother, brother, and I stood on the corner of Saratoga and Atlantic Avenues in the East New York section of Brooklyn. Two-story residential town houses were as grimy and rundown as the businesses overlooking the avenues. The only source of color came from patchwork graffiti on the streetlights and brick walls. Traffic was loud and heavy. Car fumes laced with the sweet aroma of fried dough from a nearby Dunkin' Donuts were nauseating. My brother made demands. My mother told him to hush. I made breath clouds in the cold air, pretending I was Puff the Magic Dragon.*

"My brother was killed by a stray bullet."

She put a hand over her mouth.

"He was nine years old, my brother. I was five at the time. Never really got to know him, but I've missed him my entire life."

We looked at our reflections in the smoky mirror behind the bar.

"Did the police catch who did this?" she asked.

"No, the case is still open." I drank more beer. "I grew up believing the police never worked the case. Why would they? The homicide of a black kid was just a statistic."

She wrapped her arm around my waist and put her head gently on my shoulder. Her tender touch took me by surprise. I stiffened, afraid that the slightest move might chase her away.

"After that, all I wanted to be was a crime fighter. Captain America. Use my shield to stop stray bullets, my big muscles to catch bad guys." I shrugged. "I was just a stupid kid. Looking at the world through crayon-colored glasses."

She lifted her head off my shoulder and glanced at me. "Why then did you become a lawyer?"

"My parents were both teachers. Education was king in our household. My father told me I could be anything I wanted to be but only after I got a thorough education. That meant an advanced degree. So after college, I went to law school. Then took a job at the prosecutor's office. I worked my ass off for three years and put away a lot of bad guys. But it wasn't enough. I envied the cops who caught them. I still wanted to be a crime fighter."

We quietly nursed our drinks and caught glimpses of each other in the mirror.

Kamaria asked, "Did you investigate your brother's killing?"

I took a moment to reply. "A year after making detective, I pulled the case file. Turned out my brother's murder was investigated twice. Once by the original detectives and years later by a cold case unit. Both investigations were professional and thorough. Both failed to produce a suspect."

The bartender wiped down the counter, navigating a towel around our drinks.

"That's enough about me," I said. "What's your story? Why are you a cop? And in Special Operations, no less?"

She reached for her wine. "I need a job. And do not ask why. I do not speak of it."

"Now you're making fun of me."

Her smile faded. She emptied her wineglass and set it aside.

"I was your brother's age when war came to Somalia. People say no war is worse than civil war. This is true. Your friends become enemies. Your neighbors betray you. Your family dies around you." Hard lines formed around her mouth. "One day, I heard a knock on the door and ran to the window to see who it might be. Close to the glass, just a fist away from the blinds stood a boy I knew. A boy from primary school. He was all teeth, big ivory teeth, smiling as he always did. But his eyes were strange. Open, yet not seeing. Moving, yet still. That was a sign. I did not know it then. I asked what he wanted. He begged for medicine, medicine for his ill parents.'"

I pictured the banker's little girl running to the door.

"He insisted that death was upon them."

Believing monsters existed only in movies and books.

"I opened the door."

Until she saw one crossing the doorsill.

"The boy rushed in, holding a gun as big as he."

And her world turned black.

"My mother, my father … all became fire and blood."

I reached for her shoulder and hesitated.

"He did not shoot me. He did not see me, though it was I who opened the door. He walked out of our house as a guest would do. No trouble on his mind. No anguish in his heart."

The bartender walked over and said the bar was closing in a half hour. He asked if we wanted a last round. We declined.

"I should have known," she said.

"How could you? You were just a kid. He was a kid."

"No, he was a man. The khat made him a man. A man behind a blind is like a lion in the grass." She wiped away a tear.

The use of the mild narcotic khat, whose leaves are chewed to achieve a high, was rampant in Somalia. Now I understood what Kamaria had seen in the boy's eyes.

"I came to Italy a refugee," she said. "I lived in an orphanage of Catholic nuns. It was close to a Carabinieri *comando*. The policemen visited us on Christmas and brought gifts. I liked their uniforms. I liked what they made me feel—hope. There was never hope in Somalia. So I wanted to be one of them. After university, I joined the Carabinieri. I speak and write Arabic and was assigned to Special Operations and antiterrorism. And now, I'm here having a good time with you."

Silence sat between us.

What could I say? Sorry your parents died so horrifically. At least you survived. You were very fortunate. Few people are ever as lucky as you. Shower her with survivor's guilt. *Yeah, real smooth, like a bed of nails.*

Then the music changed to something jazzy, and I knew what to say. I took Kamaria by the hand. "Did I ever tell you that I'm a great dancer?"

"You are a dancer?" She smiled. "Oh, I want to see."

We walked to the middle of the empty dining area. I held her close and took the lead, gliding over the dance floor like Ali had in the ring.

"It is true! You are a very good dancer."

"You should see me dance salsa."

We danced until our hearts were racing. We forgot about the world and all those nasty scorpions in it. When the music stopped, we still held each other.

The bar staff was busy turning off lights, emptying ashtrays, and flipping chairs on tabletops to make room for mops. Kamaria wrapped her arms around my neck, stood on her tippy-toes, and pulled me close. Her breath was a warm tingle on my ear, her bare shoulder a tantalizing inch from my lips.

She whispered magic words. "Take me to your hotel room."

Chapter Twelve

Phantom Helicopters

Sitting on the edge of a creaky bed that reeked of sweat and sex, he pressed a freshly rolled cigarette between his lips. He rummaged through his pockets until he found a wooden match. Holding it in his fist, he struck the tip with his thumbnail. The brief sizzle and the phosphorus scent always calmed him. He tilted his head sideways and lit the cigarette. After taking a deep drag, the man tapped the ash on a square of rice paper that lay flat on the neighboring nightstand. Smoking was not allowed in the cramped room, so an ashtray was nowhere to be found. Still, people had smoked there before. Burn marks on the nightstand and the mattress said so.

Lifting his bare feet off the floor, he swung his legs onto the bed. He lay down with one arm folded between the lumpy pillow and his head, the other free to hold the cigarette. The man took another drag and blew the smoke from his nostrils. He tried hard to ignore the ceiling fan that pulled the drifting smoke. The fan would put his mind in a bad place. Still, he couldn't help himself. The rotation of the blades, the humming of the small motor that powered it, were like a snake charmer's flute. Soon, the shadow cast by the blades, illuminated from below by the lamp on the nightstand, brought back the dark memories of the phantom helicopters.

When they wanted their presence known, the helicopters roared through the sky like winged lions. When their missions required stealth, death came as a bolt of lightning without thunder. He had seen the fire of the helicopters up close, those raking lines of hot lead spewing from rotating machine guns. He had seen the missiles too, piercing tanks with the ease a spear pierces a man.

His worst experience had come on a black, moonless night, shortly after the invasion had begun. His soldiers were gathered around their tanks, eating and drinking in glum silence. The desert air was cold enough to cloud a man's breath. In the chill, he picked at his food and grew restless. As his men turned to sleep, he decided to take a walk. First, he carefully packed away what remained of his meal. With his supply lines in tatters, nothing was wasted. He buttoned his shirt collar and set out in a random direction. In the vast openness of the desert, every direction led to more of the same. It was like walking in circles without turning. What he didn't know at the time was the direction he had chosen, which had him cresting a sand dune and rolling a cigarette on the other side of it, would save his life.

The phantom helicopters—choosing to remain unheard and unseen from positions several kilometers away—launched a vicious assault. He had been thrown forward by the shock wave of multiple simultaneous explosions. Darkness came as earsplitting sound and searing heat.

Hours later, he woke to a sickening smell. It wasn't roasted pork. It was burning flesh. And before he had set eyes on the charred remains of his soldiers in the light of dawn, a hate arose in his heart.

All throughout the short war, he saw the phantom helicopters and heard the terrible pop of their long blades and the buzz of their tails. Lying on that bed decades later, he still saw them. Still heard them. The searing heat still on his back.

A tap on the door drew his attention. Three more meant he could open the door.

He placed his unfinished cigarette on the burn-scarred nightstand and carefully climbed off the bed. He reached under the edge of the mattress for his loaded 9mm Beretta. He moved quietly to the door and peered through the peephole, keeping the gun at his side. The visitor he saw fit the description he had been given.

The courier was a scrawny man in a white thobe with arms too long for the sleeves of the garment and a beard too full for his boyish face. Still, a hundred men in Venice could fit that description. It was the missing incisor in the courier's yellow smile that set him apart. He scanned the man's forehead and dark eyes. The skin was dry. The eyes focused. A suitcase wrapped in airport cling film hung steady from his hand.

He listened for sounds in the hallway. No one stirred. He opened the door and hid behind it. The courier put the suitcase on its wheels, extended the retractable handle, rolled it through the opening without entering the room, and waited for the door to close, just as instructed.

Through the peephole, he watched the courier bow slightly and turn around. There was a lightness to his walk, a silent song in each step that announced the coming and going of a man without burdens. He knew that was a lie. Things were often not what they seemed.

He watched the hallway long after the courier had left and listened intently until he was sure the only sounds were of snoring in one room and the hum of a fan in another. Then he turned to the suitcase.

It was a carry-on with a hard polycarbonate shell. He retracted the handle and picked it up. It wasn't heavy. Its contents didn't rattle as he turned it on all sides to inspect the cling film. Satisfied that it hadn't been tampered with, he walked over to the bed and lay the suitcase on the mattress. He pulled a box cutter from his pants pocket and cut the cling film. The suitcase was locked. Around his neck dangled the only key. He unlocked the luggage, pulled back the dual zippers, and flipped the lid open. The contents were tightly packed and organized, so the critical components were easy to identify. He folded his arms and smiled. Except for the vest, which would come later, everything was there, disguised as an innocuous collection of items that would pass for a repair kit to an unsuspecting eye.

Once those items were assembled and fitted on a vest, a committed soldier wearing that vest would become a tool of war. One as unheard and unseen as the phantom helicopters.

Chapter Thirteen

Morning After

The knocking on my hotel room door woke me.

My jaw felt stiff; a dull ache discouraged me from moving it. My mouth was sour. I stank of secondhand smoke and probably too much beer. I reached across the bed, knowing she had left for an early meeting but hoping for a surprise.

Kamaria and I had shared a night of fireworks. It was hard to believe. Perhaps it was the alcohol or the stories of mutual loss that had made us weak. Or the frequent loneliness that comes with the job. Whatever the reason, the result was magical.

I rolled on my side and reached for the other pillow. It smelled of lilac and freesia.

More knocking.

"Open up! This is the gym police! We have a warrant for your arrest."

Oh shit, Vincent.

"I'm coming, man!" The discomfort in my jaw spiked a little. "Chill."

As I lumbered out of bed, I glanced at the loveseat we'd tossed our clothes on. Mine were still there, apparently strewn in the order of removal, which was an embarrassing revelation. My Brooklyn Nets cap was last in line.

"On the count of three, I'm coming in," Vincent said.

"Cut the racket!"

"One..."

"You'll wake the neighborhood."

"Two..."

"Forget it! Now I'm not opening the door."

"Come on, hurry up. I gotta take a piss!"

I snatched my boxers off the loveseat, pulled them on, and staggered down the hallway. I turned the deadbolt and yanked the door open. Vincent stood there in a muscle tank top and shorts, pumped and sweaty, hopping on his toes.

"Where's the commode?"

I pointed over my shoulder.

As Vincent urinated with great enthusiasm, I grabbed his gym bag off the hallway floor and closed the door. It was hefty. I let my imagination run with the delicious idea that a half dozen Boston cream donuts—imported from an awesome little bakery in Upstate New York—were secretly stashed inside.

"That's the problem with proper hydration." Vincent flushed the toilet and turned on the faucet. "When you gotta go, you gotta go."

He came out, wiping his hands on a towel. "Your face looks like you dropped it at Grand Central Station and five commuters stepped on it."

"Just five?" I shooed him aside and stood in front of the bathroom mirror. One side of my jaw was swollen. Faint purple bruising was beginning to show. I moved my jaw side to side, working through the pain. "Ouch."

"Got your pecker caught on something?"

I poked at different points to gauge the extent of the swelling. Oddly, the uninjured side of my jaw hurt more.

The floorboards creaked.

"Smell a woman in here," Vincent said.

I reached for my toothbrush.

"Who was the lucky lady? Come clean. You don't wanna leave it up to my imagination."

Working the brush gently, with mechanical precision, I tried to think of an answer that would wipe off the devious grin I knew was plastered on his face.

"Don't tell me it's that hot concierge, the one with the boob job." Vincent paused. "Nah, she's definitely into me, so that's not it."

I reached for the mouthwash.

"The chick at the juice bar? Oh wait, you don't go to the juice bar. You don't even go to the frigging gym."

I gargled.

"Got it! The French hostess at that trattoria we like ... whatchamacallit?" Fingers snapped. "Mamma Lola. That it?"

I rinsed. "I don't kiss and tell."

"That isn't healthy. Men are naturally wired to confide in their buds all manner of mischief and sexual exploits. Otherwise, there's a buildup of astrological and psychological tension that can lead to impotence."

I snickered. "You're so full of shit."

"Well, at least"—a cellphone rang—"hold on ... gotta take this. It's the Lufthansa stewardess we met on the flight over. She's in Venice on a layover."

While Vincent played Staten Island Casanova, I carefully shaved and combed my half-inch-long hair, which was due for an appointment with the barber. When I finished, I walked out of the bathroom, rubbing a glob of aftershave on my broken face.

"Shit."

Vincent looked up from his cellphone. "What?"

"Forgot to floss."

"You know, if you gave your body half the love you give those perfect choppers, it would run almost as good as mine."

"I need clean underwear."

"Sorry, can't help you there."

I rummaged my dresser drawer.

"It's the cashier at the bakery, the one who's always smiling and throwing you free mini cannolis."

I turned around. "At three a.m.?"

"The first clue!" He tapped away on his phone. "Says here Il Ciminiera shuts its doors at two a.m. on a school night. So, I'm betting you closed the bar with someone. Oh, oh. Now I'm thinking you hooked up with a cop! And the only logical candidate is—"

Don't.

"—Kamaria!"

I looked away, caught myself looking away, looked back at Vincent, and knew I'd been caught in a tell. I turned back to the dresser.

Vincent whistled. "Now that's a helluva score. I did try getting in there, but she was immune to my charm. Thought she was a lesbian."

I rolled my eyes. "Right. Any woman who doesn't fall under your spell has got to be a lesbian."

He laughed.

I dug out a pair of clean boxers. "Why didn't I shower? I'm all out of whack, man. You're distracting me."

"Go ahead and shower. I have to shower too." Vincent started for the door.

My cheesy, Federal-issued cellphone rang. I took it off the nightstand and checked the caller ID. "Hey, Top."

"Colt and Ruiz got a hit on the video. You won't believe who this guy works for."

As O'Neil gave me the rundown, I felt the onset of nausea.

"We're on our way." I hung up.

"What'd he say? You have that 'oh, shit' look on your face."

I looked Vincent in the eye. "The team has a positive ID on the shooter."

"That's good, isn't it?"

"Not when he's CIA."

Chapter Fourteen

French Mirror

Colonel Giuseppe Marino stood in front of a full-length French neoclassical mirror. Propped against an oak-paneled wall in his office, it was a hulking, seven-foot tribute to French craftsmanship. It was also his favorite possession. He loved how it wreathed his reflection in ionic columns, a handsome base, and a broken pediment. The effect made him a third of a meter taller and more regal than the pope himself.

The visor of his peaked cap was polished to a high gloss. Above it, in gold thread, shone the exploding grenade with the rising flame insignia of the Carabinieri. A symbol of power and tradition. The real power, however, came from the colonel rank insignia on his shoulder boards, one tantalizing step below brigadier general.

Making general was his lifelong ambition. He was born to command men and bred to steer through the murky waters of Italian politics just as his ancestors had been bred for the open seas. Late at night, he'd often pose in front of his mirror while donning the shoulder boards of a brigadier general. If there was a knock on the door, he would exercise the God-given power of his rank to tell the offender to fuck off.

He eyed the four rows of ribbons on his dress coat. Individually, each ribbon represented a medal earned for a specific achievement. Collectively, they inspired awe and demanded respect. Respect any sane citizen, tourist, or uniformed subordinate exhibited. Even the criminals and refugees who contaminated the slums had enough sense to demonstrate that respect.

The Americans were the exception.

The arrogant Americans treated him like the leader of a third-world peasant army who must be patronized. And they meddled. Before the American politicians had bullied or bribed their spineless Italian counterparts into allowing the FBI to stick its nose in Venice, he alone had been entrusted with the city's security. Now, he had to share that responsibility and the glory that went with it.

Outrageous!

Turning away from the mirror, he marched a few paces and stopped in front of his second-favorite possession: his glass display case housing a crowded collection of medals and cups for first-place finishes in pistol-shooting competitions. Even there, the Americans stuck their noses in where they didn't belong. Before O'Neil's arrival—over two years ago—no one could compete with Marino. Now, he had O'Neil matching him almost shot for shot at the annual police competition. *God, when will I be rid of the American rabble?*

At his desk, he glanced at the activity tracker strapped to his wrist. Twelve thousand steps; eight thousand to go. He removed his cap, placed it gingerly on the desk, and settled into the large executive chair. To Marino, the chair was just right, but the oversized desk was neither long nor wide enough. He reclined and drummed his fingers on the armrests.

The day had been a clusterfuck.

Waves of follow-up calls since the shooting had turned into a tsunami. First, the press corps. An unidentified man shot in Piazza San Marco by an unknown assailant who was still at large wasn't good enough for that horde of leeches. They kept demanding to know why the police response had been so swift and overwhelming. Had the victim been under police surveillance? Had a Carabinieri operation gone bad? He wanted to scream "Yes!" and offer the Americans up for sacrifice. Instead, he parroted what was expected. "Can't comment on an ongoing investigation." "Yes, we're pursuing leads." "No, we don't have a suspect." "We're still working to identify the victim." "There's no evidence this is connected to the Israeli prime minister's upcoming visit."

My God, where did they get such imaginations?

As irritating as those calls were, they were easier to stomach than the bosses and politicians. Trying to gauge how they might stand to gain or lose from the shooting, the hacks demanded answers. Their minions lined up conference calls, private calls, large meetings, small meetings, and one-on-one meetings for those with enough clout.

Feeling a shiver, Marino sat up, hopped off the chair, and marched to the fireplace. The fire was dying. He raked the embers until the hearth glowed red then laid two fresh logs on the grate from a nearby rack of firewood. Soon flames were licking the logs.

He watched the fire.

The most damaging question from the hacks was the one he had the poorest answer for. Entrusted with the safety of the city, why had he allowed a known terrorist to walk freely about one of the most touristed piazzas on earth? Bad things were bound to happen! His defense hinged on the available intelligence, which, he argued, had required that the operation proceed exactly as it did. That invited ridicule. Had the shooting also been part of the plan? Insinuations of conspiracy, incompetence, and misuse of resources threatened to smother him. He had to act fast. He had to refocus attention elsewhere.

Where better than the Americans?

Marino did an about-face, stomped his boots—one, two—and marched back to his desk and sat.

He would start by distancing himself from the intelligence that had driven the operation. It had come from the Americans anyway.

Granted, he had taken credit for producing most of it, but that was a minor complication. He would just change the narrative: the Americans chose to ignore his reliable intelligence and proceeded instead with their own faulty conclusions. The internationally renowned FBI refused to listen to the silly Carabinieri. What did the Italians know about the war on terrorism? Yes, that was a good start, one with a jab to national pride.

What if the shooting had been sanctioned?

The thought was sudden and jarring. For a fleeting moment, he stopped breathing. If the shooting had been sanctioned, they would've told him. They had to tell him. Didn't they?

His eyes drifted to four neat stacks of folders, binders, and paperwork resting on his desk. To the casual observer, these were simply the tools of bureaucracy. However, hidden in plain sight was a folder that didn't officially exist. It contained random invoices. On one of those invoices were three phone numbers. Each was a fake, but when truncated and merged correctly, they produced a real number.

He pulled out the folder, located the invoice, and snatched up his desk phone. Was it smart to call from his office? He stared at the receiver and tossed it back in the cradle. He folded the invoice and put it in the breast pocket of his dress coat then got up, retrieved his cap, and marched toward the door.

CHAPTER FIFTEEN

BETWEEN THE LINES

The island of Murano was a thirty-minute boat ride from St. Mark's Square. Known for its glass art, it was home to a hundred glass factories, many passed down from one generation to the next. In one of those factories, I had a meeting with CIA Field Supervisor Franklin Shears and his agent Aaron Kaufmann—the man the team had identified as the suspected shooter.

I got off the water bus and walked down a crowded street split by a canal. Small bridges connected the two sides, which were flanked by brightly painted town houses and glass storefronts glistening in the twilight.

My phone rang. O'Neil. "Hey, Top, just got off the bus."

"You're early. The meet is at the Mondolino Glassworks—2030 hours sharp. Walk to the back of the shop. Ask for the factory and sit in the first row. I just sent you the address."

My phone chimed with an incoming text message. "Got it."

"Ever deal with spooks, Miles? Spooks in the field?"

"Negative."

"They're a slippery lot. Say a whole lot but don't tell you a goddamn thing. You have to take everything they say and read between the lines."

O'Neil had been a spook for ten years before switching to the Feds. He still had contacts there and had spent most of the afternoon calling in favors to arrange this meeting.

"Why would they only meet with me?"

"Goddamned if I know. Call me the moment you're done."

Putting away my phone, I thought I saw a fast-moving figure wearing black sunglasses. Odd. The sun had set. I turned to look. Nothing. A minute later, I glimpsed the same sunglasses in the crowd. I stopped to look again. Waited. Walked. Stopped abruptly. Scanned. Still nothing. I shook my head. This cloak-and-dagger shit was getting to me.

With forty minutes to kill, I browsed storefronts for glassworks and new flavors of gelato. Eventually, I spotted the Mondolino Glassworks Shop and Factory, nestled in a commercial strip. I approached the shop window and peered inside. The usual collection of vibrant glass figurines, vases, sculptures, and chandeliers was on display, including a three-foot black stallion rearing on its hind legs. The stallion was magnificent. The detail in the work and the dramatic illusion of movement in the pose had me ogling like a kid at a toy store Christmas window.

The shop door squeaked open. A balding old man in a rumpled linen suit emerged. He stood next to me (a little too close) with his hands clasped in front of his paunch.

"American?" he asked.

"Yes."

He didn't smile. He didn't invite me inside.

"You like?" He pointed at the stallion with an arthritic pinky. "Many euros this." He dropped a number.

I whistled. "That's a lot of zeros."

"That way"—he pointed over his hunched shoulder—"you find cheap."

In ten seconds, he had sized me up as someone unable or unwilling to afford a fine work of art. I wanted to believe it was the baseball cap and shorts I was wearing. Would a suit have made a difference? I didn't think so.

Then the man almost tripped over himself to open the door for a white couple, ushering them inside like they were old friends.

As he let go of the door, I gripped the handle and gave him a look that encouraged him to get out of the way. Inside, I was immediately intercepted by a middle-aged woman with the dour expression of having a mouthful of lemon wedges. She asked what I wanted, not if I needed help. When I asked for the factory, she escorted me to the back of the shop. There, she opened a door that led to an atrium. Once the black man was safely out of the shop, she closed the door behind me and locked it.

I wanted to bang on the door, stomp into the shop, slam my Amex down on the counter, then point to the stallion. That would show them I did, in fact, have the means and the will. Then sit back and watch them kiss my enormous ass for the entire thirty minutes it would take to process the hefty sale. But those people didn't deserve a nickel of my business, and I doubt they would have learned anything from the experience.

At the other end of the atrium stood a double doorway. The sign above it read *fabbrica*, which I took to mean "factory." I stepped through into a warehouse. Open skylights in a two-story ceiling were obscured by chain-hung fluorescent light fixtures that lit up a work area with two brick ovens. The room was warm despite its size and the efforts to ventilate it. The work area was cordoned off with rope threaded through wooden posts. Three long rows of empty benches facing the work area were lined up one behind the other. I walked to the front bench and sat. My phone clock said I was eight minutes away from my clandestine meeting with the CIA—the guys who did the government's dirty work on foreign soil. Now I was rolling with spies.

How was the CIA involved? The team believed Agent Kaufmann was the shooter. I had too until they ID'd him as CIA.

Your shooter is an amateur.

The CIA wouldn't send an amateur to do their dirty work. Were there two shooters? The amateur I saw and a well-hidden professional? It was possible. But why was the CIA there in the first place?

As a man in overalls entered the work area and poked a blowpipe into the glowing mouth of one of the ovens, I formed a theory. It was so improbable, the more I thought about it, the finer I strained it, the more plausible it became.

A man in a green-brown tweed jacket over a rust-colored vest sat behind me. He had a pointy nose, darting gray eyes, and a thin mustache.

"Good evening, Officer Jordan," he said. "I'm Field Supervisor Franklin Shears."

He didn't offer his hand and neither did I. "Detective Jordan."

"Yes, we know." He tugged on his cuff links. "Decorated NYPD detective first grade. Fifteen years on the force, mostly in Brooklyn South. Exceptional arrest record. Law degree. Former prosecutor. Twice divorced but no kiddos."

His accent was strong Bostonian, and I suspected an arrogant Ivy League pedigree.

"You have my file," I said, "but I couldn't get a line on yours."

His eyes stopped darting. "That might have something to do with pay grade, Detective."

I scoffed. "Bet it does."

"It's not an insult, just a hard fact security clearances work on." He leaned forward. "Who we are is really not important, is it? What is important is that we're here."

"Meaning what?"

"Meaning we're here to share intel."

A man sat behind Shears in the last row of benches. The jagged scar on the right side of his face was unmistakable.

Shears glanced over his shoulder. "You've already met Agent Kaufmann, though not in the best of circumstances. Pity. We're all on the same team."

I scowled at Shears. "Are we?"

"Sure we are. One big happy family since nine eleven. CIA, FBI, NSA, ATF, you name it. A chummy alphabet soup. Don't you think so?"

"Well, let's see. You guys assassinate our snitch—the only line we had on a most wanted terrorist. And in the process blow a two-year operation." I paused. "The only reason we're even having this conversation is because we made your agent. So, do I think we're on the same team? No, I don't fucking think we are."

"There's no need to raise your voice, Detective." Shears' eyes darted again. "But I'm glad you mentioned it. It's precisely the misinformation we're here to clear up."

"Misinformation?"

He spread out his arms. "Simply put, we're not responsible for Mr. El-Hashem's unfortunate fate."

"Assassination."

Shears feigned indignation. "Such an unsavory description, but use it if you like. It still doesn't change the fact that we had absolutely nothing to do with it."

Kaufmann shook his head.

"The demonstration is about to begin." Shears sat taller. "Have you seen glass blown and shaped? It's something to behold, especially at the hands of these Venetian masters. They've been making glass the same way for seven hundred years. Turn around and watch. You'll enjoy it."

The man in overalls, the master glassblower, extracted the blowpipe from the oven with a red-orange blob at the end of it. He walked over to a worktable and rolled the blob back and forth along a flat steel plate, occasionally blowing in the other end of the pipe. The blob's color darkened as it cooled and took on a roughly cylindrical shape.

"If Agent Kaufmann wasn't the shooter," I said over my shoulder, "then you have a good explanation as to why he was there, right?"

"I do."

Wielding the blowpipe, the man put the blob back in the oven for a few more turns in the fire, then he pulled it out and walked over to two parallel steel workhorses. He sat on the stool between them, resting the blowpipe across the workhorses.

I said, "I'm listening."

"He was on a special assignment."

"What kind of assignment?"

"That's classified."

"Oh, here we go. The classified card."

"Glad you understand."

I did understand. The classified card was the government's "fuck off" when they wanted you to mind your own business. And Shears was free to use it liberally.

"Why didn't your agent identify himself? Why didn't he stand down?"

"It's complicated."

"Complicated how?"

"That's classified."

The man rolled the blowpipe back and forth over the workhorses. With a pair of foot-long tweezers, he shaped the rim, gliding the tool along the edges and widening the opening while still rolling the blowpipe back and forth.

I said, "We could do this all night. I ask a question you don't want to answer, you give me the fuck-off. But that'll get old pretty fast, so I'll offer you a theory."

"A theory? I'm intrigued."

"It's no secret the current White House administration and the Israeli prime minister have no love for each other. You agree?"

Shears was silent as the glassblower cut a strip of molten glass with a pair of shears and attached it to the pitcher he was making then worked quickly with the foot-long tweezers to shape it into a handle.

"Agent Shears, do I have your attention?"

"Complete and undivided."

"Then you agree?"

"Go on."

"Let's suppose someone with enough juice in the administration decided that in the best interest of our government's executive branch, the Israeli prime minister had to go, so a friendlier version could replace him."

I shot a glance at Shears. He was no longer watching the man at work. He was staring at me, poker-faced.

I continued, "But there's a problem. You can't just take out a prime minister. Certainly not the head of state of a key ally. So what do you do?"

Kaufmann clapped as the glassblower removed the newly fabricated pitcher from the end of the blowpipe and propped it on the table with the steel plate. A hollow sound coming from an audience of three.

"You realize you're making a dangerous accusation," Shears said.

"I haven't made any accusations. This is all hypothetical. Should I continue?"

"Please do."

"At some point, this very powerful someone catches wind of a possible terrorist plot on the Israeli prime minister and the task force's effort to stop it. Here's a golden opportunity. Take out the only link to the mastermind behind that plot and give the attack a chance to succeed."

Shears snickered. "You have a vivid imagination. I'll give you that."

"Maybe, but it fits. Explains why your agent was there and why he fled the scene. How could his presence there be explained? You could argue the CIA was just doing its job, taking out a wanted terrorist. But why go there if you don't have to?"

The glassblower worked quickly on another blob of molten glass, pinching and pulling it with the business end of those huge tweezers.

Shears asked, "Did you witness Agent Kaufmann fire a weapon at Mr. El-Hashem? Did you find a rifle in his possession?"

A cat. The master glassblower had made a figurine of a cat.

I turned around. "No, I didn't see him fire a weapon or see him in possession of one when he took a cheap shot at me. But the fact remains that your agent was there, under suspicious circumstances, and fled the scene when I identified myself as a police officer. That makes him a prime suspect."

Shears crossed his arms. "Let me offer an alternate theory, one more plausible than yours."

"I'm listening."

Shears took a folder from Kaufmann and handed it to me. It was army green, about a quarter-inch thick, and had CLASSIFIED stamped across it in bold black letters.

"Classified? I thought this stuff was above my pay grade."

"Consider your security clearance upgraded."

Bullshit. I bet all the folders in the CIA had CLASSIFIED stamped across them, even those with the takeout menus. I opened it.

"Not here," he said. "Later, in your office. Let me give you the aerial view." Shears played with his cuff links. "What do you know about Cardinal Luca Perricone?"

Cardinal Luca Perricone was the leader of the archdiocese, the chief of the Roman Catholic Church in Venice.

"Not much," I said. "My partner and I had a meeting scheduled with him today, but we canceled when we found out you guys had shit on our parade."

If the jab rankled Shears, he didn't show it.

"Perricone is known for his fiery speeches. He's a gifted orator, a TV evangelist on steroids if you will. He's also strongly anti-Islam, often calling for stringent limits on the number of Muslim refugees and immigrants entering the European Union. Naturally, any terrorist incident involving Islamic extremists is fuel for his speeches. Some say his goal is to stem a decline of

Catholicism by rallying Christians together. What better way to do so than by pointing out a common adversary? Others say he's just an opportunist with sights on the papal office. Either way, he gains by the successful execution of a terrorist attack—particularly one on home turf."

"So the cardinal did it? Is that it?"

"Someone acting in his interests."

"Who?"

"A fanatical Catholic organization. La Mano Santa, or The Holy Hand. They've taken a keen interest in Cardinal Perricone, rallying stoutly behind him."

"Never heard of them."

"You're fairly new to the counterterrorism game, so I wouldn't expect you to. Moreover, The Holy Hand is an obscure organization suspected of carrying out attacks on Muslim institutions, clerics, and mosques. They operate in the shadows."

Like the shadow behind the blind?

"Okay, let's assume The Holy Hand gets dirty for their favorite cardinal. How did they know where El-Hashem would be and when? And about his connection to The Scorpion or a possible terrorist attack?"

"The Holy Hand has a source inside the Carabinieri or the task force."

The mole.

I glanced at the folder Shears had given me. "That name isn't in this file, is it?"

"Correct. It's not in the file because we don't know who it is. But we give you the name of the man who does."

Kaufmann tapped Shears three times on the shoulder. Morse code among spies? Shears nodded.

"Before we get into that, Agent Kaufmann would like to extend a sincere apology for the little run-in he had with you. It wasn't personal. It was the job."

I glanced at Kaufmann. "Why doesn't he tell me himself?"

Kaufmann stretched his neck and pointed at the scar. It ran longer than I'd thought, the tail end looping down from his jawline, pink and angry, and running across his throat.

"He can't," Shears said. "Our agents often pay a high price for serving their country."

Someone had done a number on Kaufmann, slicing him up like a butt of roast beef. Any desire I had for payback quickly dissipated. I said to him, "Water under the bridge, Agent. You owe me a beer."

Kaufmann cracked a grin, stood, and left the factory.

I said, "Who's this guy who supposedly knows the inside source?"

"Ignazio Bonaventura, the leader of The Holy Hand. A difficult man to locate." Shears pointed at the folder in my hand. "But we're steering you in the right direction."

I thought about that while keeping eye contact with Shears. Then I held up the folder. "If this goes nowhere, your man remains our prime suspect."

"We gave you a name and a lead. As promised, cooperation. One big happy alphabet soup." Shears stood and walked out into the aisle. "Our job here in Venice is done. Luck to you, Detective."

As he walked away, I knew Shears was taking dark secrets with him. Yet, contrary to what O'Neil had said, the CIA had told me plenty. They confirmed their agent was there on special assignment, and his apprehension would have been problematic. They also revealed their contingency plan. If Agent Kaufmann's mission blew up, the file I held in my hands (now conveniently declassified for the lowly detective class) would focus attention on Cardinal Perricone and The Holy Hand. Why else disguise Kaufmann as a monk?

Whatever we thought we had on the CIA was strictly circumstantial. I knew it. Shears knew it. Shears also knew that our only play was to take the bait he offered.

Chapter Sixteen

In the Black

Outside the Mondolino Glassworks factory, the night wore a clear dark sky and winking stars. Tourists crowded the street, strolling toward the water bus piers. I suspected most of them were headed back to their hotels to put on dinner attire and hit the restaurants of mainland Venice.

That sounded like a plan; I was starving.

Holding the CIA folder tight, I fell in with the crowd. Walking among lively families and couples, tour groups, and lone travelers put a spring in my step. People came in all shapes and sizes, colors, and ages, wearing everything from shorts and flip-flops to sundresses and three-piece suits.

My phone vibrated. O'Neil. "Top, I was—"

"Told you to call the minute you were done. Why do I have to chase after every goddamn one of you? What did Shears tell you?"

"Denied everything."

"Goddamn right he did. And?"

"Gave me a lead."

"A lead?"

"He called it a lead. A fanatical Catholic organization he says is good for the shooting. He claims they have a mole inside the task force or the Carabinieri."

"Which organization?"

"The Holy Hand."

O'Neil fell silent.

"Top, you there?"

"I've heard of them. A lot of suspicion of terrorism, but nothing solid ever seems to stick. Did Shears give you anything, a file perhaps?"

"A dossier."

"A dossier … now that's something. Spooks don't cooperate or even give the illusion of cooperation unless they absolutely have to. Some higher-up decided they absolutely had to." O'Neil paused. "Didn't tell you why his agent was there, did he?"

"He said that information was above my pay grade."

On a shirt collar, I caught a fleeting glimpse of black sunglasses.

"'Course he said that," O'Neil said. "Tell me about the dos—"

Hanging up on O'Neil and turning off the phone was a risky move. Nothing rankled the man like being cut off. It didn't matter if the drop in communication was unintentional, coerced, or subject to reasonable laws of physics. But better to piss off O'Neil than ignore a tail.

Ahead, the street forked. I took the right prong into the mouth of an alley. Faint footsteps followed. A hundred feet then another right, another alley. This one was deserted but well lit by gas lanterns bolted to the walls of the town houses that lined it. I walked casually. About a quarter of the way in, I stopped at the top of a staircase to my right and pretended to consult my phone. The clack of steps behind me didn't stop or change pace. I drew two conclusions: either I was being paranoid and behind me was just a citizen of Murano ambling home after a long day of kissing ass or browbeating tourists, or I was being followed by someone with some training.

There was only one way to find out.

The staircase led to a residential area that was poorly lit. I put my phone away and descended the stairs. The alley got darker the farther I went. There was barely enough light to see the bottom step. I missed it, landing hard on my foot. A violent jolt settled in my knee, and I gritted my teeth to suppress a howl. Some part of that complex mechanical joint had shifted, clearly in a way it wasn't designed to. Every hobbled step after came with a jab of pain. *Fuck.* I needed a bum knee like I needed another twenty-five pounds.

I limped deeper into the alley, searching in the feeble light for a recessed doorway big enough to conceal me. When I found one, I pressed against the doorjamb. Given the poor visibility, I decided not to draw my weapon.

At the top of the steps stood a tall figure with a slim, masculine build. His arms were at his sides, bent like his hands were buried in the pockets of a jacket. He descended the stairs furtively, quietly.

This was no citizen of Murano. This was a tail.

A surge of adrenaline primed my body. As I braced for the confrontation, he stopped short, just a few feet shy of my position, and stood there, apparently listening for movement or waiting to sense it.

Straining to see in the gloom, I tried in vain to add detail to his description. He was just a shadow. A shadow with a little more bulk and height than I'd seen at the top of the steps. That didn't worry me. His concealed hands did.

He resumed his forward motion, close to the doorway. His breathing was shallow. The brush of his clothes crisp. When he was past me, I bent over and put the folder on the ground. The lesson learned from my encounter with Agent Kaufmann was that spooks struck first and apologized later. If this was a spook sent to keep tabs on me, he would understand. If not, then at least I had the upper hand.

I crept up behind him and buried a low uppercut in his kidney. As he arched back from the impact, I yanked his shoulder and spun him around. I could make out enough of his facial outline to land a jab on his left eye socket.

He went down in the darker reaches of the alley. Groping for him in the black, my foot caught on something and the knee gave way. This time, I howled in pain. Frustrated and unable to pursue, I watched him stumble and flee down the alley where the light was better but still not good enough.

Who was that guy? Why was he following me?

CHAPTER SEVENTEEN

DANTE'S DOOR

Day 3

Wednesday, 0720 hours

The sky over St. Mark's Square was overcast. A chilly wind coming off the Venetian Lagoon stirred a misty rain. Water puddled across the worn flagstone, creating makeshift birdbaths for marauding gangs of pigeons. Sidestepping the puddles and their foul visitors, I crossed the square with Vincent.

He asked, "You told O'Neil about your little misadventure last night?"

"Told him I'd been followed."

Vincent ran a hand through his damp hair. "What'd he say?"

"That it could've been anybody."

"Even CIA?"

"He said that wasn't a CIA play. They handed over information. They were washing their hands and moving on."

Vincent stopped. "You know, going alone to that meeting was stupid. I told you, screw the CIA. Take backup. We had leverage. We caught them holding their dicks, for fuck's sake."

"Nothing happened."

"'Cause you got lucky. What if the play was to ice you?" Vincent was talking with his hands, squeezing his fingertips together and shaking them in front of his face. "Never again,

Miles, you hear me. I'll cuff you to my frigging belt if I have to. Let 'em call us rejoined twins for all I care."

"Conjoined."

"Conjoined what?"

"You mean conjoined twins."

"Whatever!"

"Love you too, Vincent."

"This is serious, Miles. You coulda got your fat ass shot off, or worse."

I was tempted to ask what could be worse than having my ass shot off. The visual alone was enough to make me nauseous. What would hold up my pants? But I decided not to. Vincent had used my first name twice in less than a minute. That meant he was close to pissed off. Unless a perp was on the receiving end of that, it was best to defuse him.

"All right, man." I held up my arms in surrender. "You're right; it was stupid. Won't happen again. Screw the brass and bureaucracy. We stick together, salt and pepper."

We continued walking.

A handful of tourists was milling around in cheap yellow ponchos. Native Venetians under small umbrellas hurried along in tall rubber boots, the same boots they wore whenever the square flooded. Too cool or too American for rubber boots and umbrellas, Vincent and I relied on our polished shoes and dark summer-weight suits to keep us dry. That plan was shaky at best.

"It was a guy following you, right?"

"Of course it was a guy."

"You sure?" Vincent looked dubious. "You never saw his face."

I sighed. "Six one, six two, slim build, dark clothing. The lighting in the alley was bad, but I'm sure he was white."

"Bet it was a spook, maybe looking to retrieve that file." Vincent pointed at the black plastic file carrier I had pinned under my arm. "Once he got it, your ass was dead meat."

"I just told you it wasn't a CIA play. Think about it. Their entire agenda was to draw suspicion away from the CIA. Not attract more if I'd suddenly gone missing."

"Maybe they got a rogue agent. You ever thought about that?"

I gave him a blank look. "You watch too much TV, man."

"Fine. You don't like that theory? Try this one. It was the frigging mole. And his job was either to keep an eye on you and report back to his handlers or steal that file and make you disappear."

"That's better. I didn't consider that."

We fell silent as we climbed the short steps of the basilica. We'd been in Venice for almost a month and had only seen it from afar.

The entire façade was decked out in patterned marble cladding. Tight clusters of multicolored columns with distinct capitals formed the piers on which five round-arch portals rested. Each portal had a mosaic ceiling bordered with bands of carved foliage and figurines. Above the main portal, at the top of the tallest of five ogee arches that adorned the second level, stood a winged golden lion against a field of blue—the symbol of Venice.

"And I thought St. Patty's was nice. Wow, this is beautiful!" Vincent tapped his chest. "Take note, Miles, nobody builds 'em like the Italians."

Vincent had a point. St. Patrick's Cathedral in Midtown Manhattan, with its Gothic architecture and towering twin spires, was a worthy home for the Roman Catholic Archdiocese of New York. But frankly, it couldn't hold a saint's candle to the Venetian basilica.

First through the bronze doors was Vincent. He dipped his fingers in the holy water font, crossed himself, and dropped to one knee in the large vestibule. I followed close behind.

The ceiling rose high enough to compel visitors to lift their heads. Gold glass tesserae covered the ceiling and the upper walls.

Mosaics of saints and biblical scenes stood bright against the shimmering gold. The five domes that topped the building rose higher still, forming a cross, with the largest of the five at the center.

"*Scusami*, are you police?"

I turned to the soft voice. It had come from a gangly man dressed in a fine black cassock with fuchsia trim. A matching fuchsia skullcap covered most of his short silver hair.

Vincent cleared his throat. "Yes, Father, we're with the Carabinieri and the FBI. We have an appointment with His Eminence."

"I am Bishop Tommaso Cusa, here to escort you. Please, follow."

Bishop Cusa walked as he had stood, his hands clasped in front of his waist just an inch below a large gold crucifix that dangled from his neck on a thick rolo chain. He led us through the vestibule, around the nave, and down a side aisle. There, we stopped at a formidable wooden door. From somewhere under his cassock, he pulled out a large antique key, the kind that opens dungeons in the movies.

I pictured a room full of medieval torture devices and a gang of hooded men lying in wait for the intruding Americans. When Bishop Cusa opened the heavy door, the only thing waiting for us was a stone staircase.

"The cardinal's private stairs, to his private chambers," explained the bishop. "Please, close the door behind you. It must lock."

Vincent and the bishop climbed the uneven stairs with ease. I lagged behind on a bum knee and an unhappy stomach. The Italians built roads, monuments, and buildings that have stood for centuries, but they couldn't provide a man his most important meal of the day. Instead of eggs, bacon, bagels, grits, and pancakes, all they could muster were lightly buttered breads, fruit-filled pastries, and paper-thin slices of cheese or salami.

At the top landing, the bishop unlocked another door with the same key. It opened on a marble hallway more in tune with the basilica's opulence, decorated with a pristine Persian rug runner, elaborate plasterwork, and ceiling frescos. At the end of the corridor, bolted eye level to the wall, was a polished bronze plaque that read Cardinale Luca Perricone. It was obviously meant to draw the eye, but the black lacquered door next to it stole the show.

Heavily carved, it had nine circular panels arranged in rows of three. Each panel depicted a gruesome scene of suffering humanity being roasted over spits, hung by the neck or ankles and weighed down by serpents, skewered with pitchforks and spears. All at the hands of grinning beasts and long-horned demons. The Latin inscriptions on the scrolls along the bottom of each circle eluded me.

Perhaps it was the grimace on my face or Vincent in the act of crossing himself for the third time that induced Bishop Cusa to give an explanation.

"The nine circles of hell. Dante's *Inferno*."

Vincent nodded like he completely understood, though I suspected the only Dante Vincent knew was a hot pickup bar on the Upper East Side.

My take on the door was simple: abandon all hope, ye who enter here.

Chapter Eighteen

The Cardinal

When Bishop Cusa opened Dante's door, the fires of hell did not await.

We entered a large, dim, sparsely furnished, anticlimactic room. All of the usual grandeur of the basilica was reserved for the high ceiling. Even the bare marble walls seemed dull and unassuming. The air was musty, as though the tall, draped windows hadn't been opened in centuries.

Bishop Cusa closed the door behind us. Our footsteps clacked across the marble floor. A gaunt old man, dressed in the traditional red cassock and skullcap of a cardinal, sat small and emaciated behind a plain wooden desk with a phone, a water pitcher, and a glass. There were no picture frames on the desktop. No computer. No standing crucifix. In fact, the only cross in the room hung from a thick chain around his scrawny neck. Unlike the desk and the chairs that faced it, the crucifix was flashy: gold, embedded with semiprecious stones.

As we approached, the cardinal stood and said in a booming baritone (incongruous for such a small man), "Ah, *bene*! Punctuality is one of God's virtues. I'm Cardinal Perricone." He offered his hand to Vincent.

Vincent was a practicing Catholic in that he went to church every Sunday the job allowed, gave up alcohol and brunettes for Lent, and did not eat meat on Good Friday. All else, however, was off the table. He once told me that Catholicism was one of mankind's great rackets. You could sin like a hooker from dusk on Monday until dawn on Sunday. Then have your sin slate wiped clean at Sunday mass if you sat through all the bullshit and dropped a check in the collection box. So it was surprising to see the deference he gave the cardinal.

"Your Holiness, I mean, Your Eminence, it's a pleasure to meet you." Vincent bowed and kissed the gaudy episcopal ring on the old man's bony hand. "I'm Detective Vincent Santoro with the New York Police Department, assigned to the FBI's Joint Terrorism Task Force. And this is my partner, Detective Miles Jordan."

"You are not FBI?"

"We work closely with the FBI."

"Santoro, you are *Italiano*." The cardinal, blessed with either perfect white teeth or the best dentures money could buy, smiled like a showman. "Your parents are from where?"

"Staten Island, New York, Your Eminence. My grandparents emigrated from Bologna."

"Ah, northerners. Olive oil from the north is *eccellente*. Any *famiglia* left in Bologna? You do speak *Italiano, corretta*?"

Vincent shook his head. "No family that I know of, and my Italian is lousy. A word at the beginning, a word at the end, and a lot of *spazzatura* in between."

The cardinal chuckled. "You pronounce, well, like a northerner. Practice is what you need."

Vincent shrugged. "Been practicing since coming to Venice."

"*Bene, bene*. Are you a good Catholic?"

"Yes, Your Eminence, I try to make mass every Sunday when I'm not working."

The cardinal flashed his showman's smile and nodded his approval like a good-humored grandfather. He then aimed that smile at me and extended his hand to shake. It felt cold and clammy, but his grip was firm.

"Jordan ... the name is familiar," he said. "American football?"

"Basketball."

"Ah, basketball. I remember. Please, sit."

The two matching chairs that faced the desk were rigid and uncomfortable as though deliberately designed for short stays. While securing the file carrier on my lap, I glanced around the room, expecting to see more.

Reading my mind, the cardinal gestured at the walls. "This room is much too large without the bookcases. They covered every wall to the ceiling. Then the marvel of technology reduced my library to this." He held up an iPad.

I chewed on that. "Powerful visual. The impact of technology."

"There was a time when a device like this would be seen as the work of the devil." He glanced at the iPad and put it gently on the desk. "How can I be of service?"

Vincent took out a notepad from the inside pocket of his suit jacket. "We're investigating the shooting, Your Eminence, that occurred on—"

"I have contacts in the Carabinieri. I know why you are here."

"Oh." Vincent glanced at me. "We didn't know that information was made—"

"You believe the man responsible for this terrible crime is a member of the clergy."

"That was our—"

"A man wearing a habit isn't necessarily legitimate, is he? Anyone can obtain the cloth through the Internet. Is it not true that a great many things can be acquired through this tool that were not readily available before its invention and commercialization?"

"Yes, sir, we've—"

"The devil—the ever-cunning opportunist—has made great use of this tool. If the instructions for bomb making and the necessary materials are available to anyone with a twisted motive, why not a simple monk's habit?"

"Agreed, on all points, but we—"

"I assure you that no member of this church would condemn his soul for all eternity by carrying out such evil. You are wasting your time, Officers."

"Actually, that's not why we're here, Your Eminence, sir," Vincent said quickly and paused as if bracing for another interruption. "We have new information that has changed the focus of our investigation. We're looking for a man you know, a member of The Holy Hand."

Some men of power recline in their big office chairs and chew unlit cigars. Others sit rigid, with hands folded. Cardinal Perricone was a steeple man, propping his elbows on the armrests and forming a steeple with his fingers. I suspect he did it to flaunt the gaudy ring.

The cardinal asked, "The Holy Hand, you say?"

"La Mano Santa," offered Vincent.

"I know who they are!"

The good-humored grandfather veneer had vanished. In its place was the grim, deeply furrowed mask of a man not used to being caught off guard.

To keep him off-balance, I said, "Then you'll be able to tell us the whereabouts of Ignazio Bonaventura."

The cardinal reached for the pitcher of water. "You believe I know this man?"

"You've had dealings with him," I said.

"Dealings?" With a hand that was surprisingly steady for such an old man, he filled his glass. "How do you mean?"

Vincent said, "We hope you'll tell us, Your Eminence."

"And why do you believe I know this man and have had … dealings with him?"

"In the course of our investigation," Vincent explained, "we obtained information from a reliable source."

"A reliable source? Who?"

I said, "We can't say."

The cardinal grinned, apparently expecting that answer, his face splitting along new and deeper fissures. He turned his head from Vincent to me. "In matters concerning God, I go on faith alone. In matters concerning man, I need more than words."

I opened the file carrier, thumbed through the CIA file, and pulled out six eight-by-ten surveillance photos. I handed them to the cardinal.

He lined them up on his desk and studied each one. "I was not aware I was under investigation."

Vincent said, "You're not, Your Eminence. Mr. Bonaventura is. Anyone he comes in contact with … well, goes in the file." Vincent pointed at the folder carrier on my lap.

The cardinal eyed Vincent sharply. "What you have here"—he waved a dismissive hand over the photos—"is a church official sharing a few meals with a member of his parish. Saving the souls of one's flock requires more than mass and confession. It requires social interaction. It requires building relationships. This is hardly unusual. Are these the dealings you were referring to?"

"Well, Your Eminence, not exactly. There's the delicate matter of financial transactions."

The cardinal squinted. "Financial transactions?"

From the CIA folder, I pulled copies of bank statements and handed them to the cardinal. "Yes, financial transactions—payments, to be exact. All originating from bank accounts linked to The Holy Hand. Payments to fund various projects that come under your name, Cardinal."

The cardinal flipped through the statements, giving each a cursory glance.

I continued, "And when you look closely, a pattern emerges. An act of radical Islamic terrorism is followed by one of your incendiary speeches against Islam. Days later, a mosque is burned or a cleric is found dead in his home, and a money trail leads to your coffers."

The cardinal slammed the bank statements on his desk. "You're not suggesting that I-I—how dare you!"

"I don't have to suggest anything." I held up the file. "The media and the public can draw their own conclusions."

"You would release this to the press?"

I sat deadpan. "Leaks happen."

The cardinal's face flushed, turning an unhealthy pink, and his mouth trembled. For a fleeting moment, I thought his head would burst. Then, in a show of incredible self-control, his expression morphed. The pink faded. His smile was back.

"Ignazio Bonaventura." He said the name with a flourish. "Yes, I have had dealings with him but not in the way you imply. Foremost, I will confirm that Mr. Bonaventura is the leader of The Holy Hand. The crimes you mention have never been proven by the Carabinieri to be the work of his organization. The Holy Hand are known for their devotion to the faith and charity, which explains those transactions you speak of." He turned his ring. "However, the Holy Father in Rome is concerned about their unfavorable publicity and has asked me to look into the matter. I have reached out to Mr. Bonaventura numerous times so I may encourage him and his followers to pursue peaceful means of protest."

I said, "You're admitting Bonaventura and his organization resort to violence?"

The cardinal paused. "Admit that Bonaventura and The Holy Hand are violent? No, I have made no such admission."

"You said you hoped to encourage him and his followers to pursue peaceful protest. That implies they're doing the exact opposite."

"I said, 'encourage'? Ah, I misspoke. I meant 'ensure.'"

A slip?

"Okay. What do you and Mr. Bonaventura talk about?" I asked.

"Racing, mostly. We are both tremendous fans of Formula One racing."

"What about The Holy Hand?"

"He considers the topic a spiritual matter and will only discuss it under the sanctity of the confessional. I cannot help you there, officers."

How convenient.

"We wouldn't expect you to, Your Eminence." Vincent smiled. "We just need help locating him."

The cardinal turned his office chair around and faced the tall, draped windows. "And what will you do to this man, officers, if you find him?"

"Just ask him a few questions," Vincent said.

"What questions?"

"We can't discuss the details of an ongoing investigation," I said.

The cardinal spun around and scowled at me. "How will you ask these questions? I cannot be the cause of harm coming to this man."

Vincent leaned forward, propping his forearm on the desk. "We're not gonna torture him or anything like that, Your Eminence. It's just a conversation."

The cardinal swung his penetrating eyes back and forth between the two of us. His expression softened, and he sighed. "He is a difficult man to find."

Vincent leaned back. "He doesn't live in Venice?"

"He has no permanent address."

At the risk of another scowl, I said, "A man running a charitable organization, as you describe it, has no permanent address? That's suspicious. Don't you think, Cardinal?"

"Why is that suspicious?"

"It makes him mobile. He can pick up and leave at any moment. Why would he need that kind of mobility?"

The cardinal reached for his water glass. "You'll have to ask Mr. Bonaventura."

Chapter Nineteen

Verbal Judo

As the cardinal reached for the phone, Vincent and I exchanged nods. The play had worked. A minute later, Bishop Cusa opened Dante's door.

"Yes, Your Eminence?" he said.

"Go to archives and bring me Papal File Sixty-One."

"Sixty-One? The file on—"

"La Mano Santa. Bring it, please."

Bishop Cusa shot us a death look before he bowed his head and said, "Yes, of course."

Vincent jumped out of his chair. "Mind if I come along, Father? I have a spiritual problem I'd like to discuss."

Cusa hesitated then held Dante's door ajar. "Of course. The walk to archives is long. We will have some time."

The moment they were gone, the cardinal gestured at the door. "This is what we do. This is how we tend to our flock."

"Very noble." I smiled at the cardinal for the first time. "Your English is good, by the way. Did you work abroad?"

"I completed my doctorate in Dublin and served the archdiocese there for twenty years. Later, I spent a decade in Canada."

"Any time in the States?"

"You mean America?"

I nodded.

"To visit." He studied me over his steepled fingers. "Are you Catholic, Officer Jordan?"

"Southern Baptist."

"Christian still." He paused. "Are you a religious man?"

"No, I can't say that I am."

"You've lost your faith, is that it?"

I took a moment to reply. "I witness the dark side of humanity often enough to know it has no boundaries. People do horrific things to one another. For money, for greed, for jealousy. Or just plain evil."

"And that has shaken your Christian faith?"

"I don't see how a just God would—"

"Evil comes in many forms, but it ultimately manifests itself in the actions of men. You must not lose your faith. God does not allow evil to prevail. He has many soldiers at work against it. You and Officer Santoro are among them. As am I." The cardinal pointed behind me. "That door, you did see that door when you entered this room?"

"It's impossible to miss."

"And that is precisely the point. The door is meant to remind all who enter this room that we are mortal, made of weak flesh and brittle bone. Someday, we will face God's judgment. The decisions we make in our short stay on earth have consequences. If we do evil or allow it to prevail, our souls will burn for eternity in some region of hell. Dante understood this well enough to describe nine levels of hell in his famous poem. Those are the carvings on the door."

"The inscriptions describe each level?"

"*Corretta.* Limbo, lust, and greed"—the cardinal counted off on his fingers—"wrath, heresy, violence. There is fraud and treachery. That's … eight. What am I forgetting?" He eyed me sharply. "Ah, gluttony!"

Perhaps to lessen the insult, he added, "Gluttony comes in many forms, not just as a physical manifestation."

Until he got to gluttony, the cardinal was on a roll. He'd aroused my interest and managed to make a few stray hairs on the back of my neck take notice. But the insinuation that my love of beer, sweets, and junk food, which hurt no one but me, would someday land me in the same hell reserved for the murderers and rapists I've devoted my life to locking up had, frankly, pissed me off.

"Now that we've covered my sin, let's talk about yours, Cardinal."

He arched his eyebrows.

"Anti-Islamic speeches that incite violence, violence often aimed at innocent people. It's all here." I tapped the file carrier. "In more detail than you might find comfortable. Where does that fit in Dante's *Inferno*? What level of hell would that be? Violence?"

He sat deadpan. "It's not my intention to incite violence. The mere suggestion insults me."

Touché.

The cardinal made a hasty stack of the photos and documents we had given him. "These mystery agents you and Santoro will not speak of have constructed a false narrative."

He pushed the stack toward me. I caught it before it flew off the edge of the desk.

"My goal," he said, "is to unify the Christian faith to stand against a common evil. If violence results in the pursuit of that noble cause, I find comfort in the belief that it's the mysterious way our heavenly Father has chosen to work."

"So the violence doesn't bother you?"

With a blank expression, the cardinal brought his hands together and caressed his heavy gold ring. "All violence pains me."

"But not enough to deter you."

He turned the ring. "I'm simply God's servant."

"A lot of people see you as an instigator. From what I've read here," I said, returning the stack of photos and bank statements to the file carrier, "I do too."

"We are on the same side."

"Same side of what?"

"Of Christ."

"As opposed to … Islam?"

"Of course!" He slammed an open hand on the desk, the unhealthy pink returning in patches to his face. "Is there a more vile example of hate and violence toward the West? Toward Christianity? Islam is your enemy as much as it is mine."

"Islam is not my enemy."

He shook his skeletal fist. "Everything you fight is done in the name of Islam. Islam *is* your enemy."

"Terrorism is my enemy, not Islam. If I'd lived five hundred years ago, Cardinal, the government system of the Catholic Church would have been my enemy, not Catholicism."

The cardinal pulled back as if I'd thrown a snake on his desk. "The church, your enemy?"

"The Inquisition."

"You dare compare Islamic terrorism to—"

"A twisted interpretation of Catholicism that led to the death and torture of thousands. It was, in effect, state-sponsored terrorism. Men with control agendas claiming God's law."

The cardinal regarded me with a faint smile. "A student of history, are you?"

"I read more than dessert menus."

"Well, Officer Jordan, I'll admit your argument is clever." He took a deep breath. "I will not defend the dark history of the church. Times were different then, and often those agendas—as you call them—served a greater good."

I said with a sneer, "I don't see how murdering and torturing people for their beliefs serves—"

"Let's not waste each other's time on a lengthy debate. I have neither the time nor the energy. What is important to remember is that Christianity has moved forward, and we have achieved a higher level of civilization. Those I speak against still cling to barbaric notions. They fight to destroy a thousand years of progress."

"Then speak against them and not the religion as a whole. Just as Catholicism was used for evil, any religion can be corrupted for nefarious purposes."

I was so engrossed in the verbal judo with the cardinal that I didn't hear Dante's door open.

Bishop Cusa said, "I have the file, Your Eminence."

The cardinal looked up. "Officer Santoro can bring it here."

The bishop hesitated.

"That'll be all, Bishop," the cardinal added.

The bishop gave the folder to Vincent and left.

Vincent settled in his chair and handed the file to the cardinal. The cardinal riffled through it until he found the page he was looking for. He dropped the open folder next to the phone and lifted the receiver.

"You're going to call him?" I asked.

The cardinal held the phone halfway to his ear. "Isn't that the entire point of your visit?"

Vincent cleared his throat. "It would be better, Your Eminence, if he didn't know we were paying him a visit. That could lead him into temptation. To disappear, I mean."

"He has done nothing wrong. Why should he flee? Besides, I do not lie to my flock." The cardinal cradled the handset between his shoulder and ear as he punched buttons on the phone.

I stood, reached over, and gently took the phone from the cardinal. "Just give us the address, Cardinal, so you don't have to lie to your flock." I put the phone back on the cradle.

Maybe it was my height and bulk looming over him or the hard expression on my face that took the edge off his sharp scowl. After a brief stalemate, he sighed.

"Very well." The cardinal pulled out a pen and notepad from his desk drawer and wrote in large cursive. "As I mentioned, he has no permanent address. However, The Holy Hand owns apartments." He tore the page off and held it out.

I took it. "Four?"

"I can't tell you precisely where he is since I can't call and ask him." The cardinal enjoyed getting in a last jab by flashing a gotcha smile.

"Anything else we should know?" I folded the page and slipped it into my suit jacket. "Company he keeps or places he frequents?"

"He lives alone." The cardinal reached for his water. "As for other places, try communal terraces. All the apartments have access to one."

We thanked the cardinal for his cooperation and headed out. I opened Dante's door, surprised by how smoothly it swung for such a large, thick slab of wood. Bishop Cusa was waiting in the hallway, beckoning us with a forced smile. I held the door open for Vincent, who rushed through the doorway as if demons bent on pulling him into Dante's hell were reaching out for him. I chuckled, which earned me the Italian bird flip.

As I crossed the threshold, the cardinal said, "Find your faith, Officer Jordan. In your line of work, it's the only thing that will keep you sane."

Chapter Twenty

Remorse

The moment Nabeel Haddad entered the Western Union shop in the Santa Croce section of Venice, he felt uneasy. The envelope he carried in his small messenger bag containing eight months of wages had come too easy. He knew that from the start, but he was too overwhelmed with worry over Amir's disease to care. Getting the money required to improve his son's medical care was foremost in his mind. He never gave a thought to the motives of his benefactor or the source of his money.

The shop was small, a mere slice of storefront on a tight commercial street, easy to miss if not for the large black-and-yellow blade sign projecting halfway into the narrow street. Inside, business was slow. The only customer was a Muslim woman hunched over a nearby table filling out paperwork. Her eyes were too friendly, and her lips too red for her humble blue hijab.

Behind a bulletproof glass enclosure sat the clerk, a young man with hair as spiky as the spines of a cactus. His head moved to the noise blaring from the large wireless headphones he wore, and his eyes were glued to a video playing on his smartphone. He looked up only when Nabeel knocked vigorously on the glass. Apparently not happy with the interruption, the clerk frowned and pointed to the table where the woman stood. With his middle finger, he made a rude and exaggerated hand gesture for writing. Nabeel bowed slightly and walked to the table. Picking a spot far from the woman, he took a form and a cheap blue pen from a tray. By the time he finished filling out the form, the woman had left.

Nabeel opened his messenger bag and hesitated. Why was he chosen? He was no one. His initial unease gave way to a sudden sense of dread as if doubting his good fortune would make the money for his son disappear.

It had been good fortune, had it not?

It had been Allah's will.

Who was he to question it?

With the tip of his tongue jabbing at the hole of his missing front tooth, he grabbed the envelope and walked over to the window. If the clerk was suspicious of where or how Nabeel had acquired such a sum, he showed no sign of it. The transaction was quick, perhaps too quick. Nabeel suspected it was either because large cash transactions were common, or a young man as carefree about his hair and the manner in which he conducted himself would be the same about his job.

The clouds were still unhappy when Nabeel left the shop, but the drizzle and cold wind didn't faze him. He was beyond physical discomforts, too preoccupied with his growing sense of dread. Soon, it took on the manifestation of a shadow he kept expecting to find over his shoulder. Even the knowledge that the money was on its way to his wife did little to calm him.

Dalia, his wife, would calm him. He pulled out his cellphone.

"How is little Amir?"

"Our son is happy in the company of his cousins."

"His pain … is it great?"

"He deals with the pain well. He is young, stronger than we think."

A tear escaped him and a second threatened to break him, but he couldn't cry with his wife on the phone. He stopped to compose himself, not caring if he disrupted the flow of people in the narrow street.

"God willing, soon he will not deal with so much pain," he said. "I have sent you money, all of the money the doctor requires."

His wife did not respond.

"Dalia? Did you not hear the good news?"

"All of the money, Nabeel? For the new hospital as well?"

"Yes," he said, nodding, unable to repress a prideful smile.

She was silent again. This was not what he'd expected. He waited for joy and sweet words and blessings to Allah. Instead, he got silence, which only heightened his unease.

"Dalia?"

She asked meekly, "Have you arranged a loan?"

"A loan?" He leaned against a wall. "Why would I arrange a loan?"

"The required sum means many months of labor. How—"

"I earned it."

"So quickly? You are a humble courier with humble wages."

"A man called. He knew of Amir's illness and said he could help us. I took it as a gift from Allah. All the man required was delivery of one package and that I ask no questions."

"How did he know of Amir?"

It was a fair question, one he should have considered.

"The mosque, I suppose. Many assemble, and the imam calls prayers for Amir."

"This man, he paid that sum for one package?" Her voice was rising. "Oh, Nabeel, what have you done?"

She had always been smarter, the brighter flame in the room. While he would fall for it every time, Dalia could always spot a menu swap at a restaurant (a lower priced menu presented before ordering a meal and a higher priced menu at the time of payment). She could shame a phone trickster, while he hung on every lying word. She would scam the scamming taxi driver with low-value foreign coins she'd collected from her small carpet shop and laugh about it later. Dalia kept him out of trouble.

After promising his wife that he would be careful, that he would not accept easy money again, he ended the call.

No one pays such a sum, sweet husband, to courier a box of shoes.

Her words burned in the pit of his stomach like spoiled dates.

He hadn't told her how he'd received the payment. If he'd revealed that an envelope was left in the cupboard of his room, she would point out that someone untrustworthy had broken in. He also hadn't told her about the man who gave him the package to deliver. The Armenian with the shrill voice and the wandering eye. Talking to that man was like talking to a chameleon: one eye fixed and focused, the other drifting alarmingly to the edge of its socket. Nabeel had had trouble deciding which eye to look at while the man instructed that the package never be left unattended or in the care of anyone else. What frightened Nabeel was the man's grim warning: if the package was opened or tampered with in any way, the consequences would be dire.

Nabeel had assumed that meant the full return of payment. Now with a shudder, he wasn't so sure.

What had that package contained to warrant such a large payment and earn him that warning? Why had the man in the room hidden behind the door? As invisible as a ghost. As mute as a rock. The time of delivery had bothered him from the start, but it had just seemed like a strange inconvenience. Now it took on a new meaning—it was meant to avoid curious eyes. What could be so troubling that it had to travel to a seedy part of Venice in a wrapped suitcase, at a strange time of night, and delivered to a man without a face?

Yes, what have I done? Who have I helped? And to what end? Oh, merciful Allah, guide me. In your infinite wisdom, tell me what I must do. You have put me on this path for a reason.

As the words settled in his mind, he felt the reassuring presence of Allah, and things became clear, as clear as Dalia would see them. There was evil here he was meant to resist.

He unlocked his cellphone. When the operator for the Carabinieri's public tips hotline answered his call and asked for his name, Nabeel stood tall, ignored the question, and told the police his story without hesitation.

Chapter Twenty-One

Water Taxi

Bishop Cusa dropped us at the door of the basilica. He gave a curt farewell and hurried back inside.

"Couldn't wait to get rid of us," Vincent said.

I buttoned my suit jacket and pinned the file carrier under my arm. "Was he as testy on your walk to archives?"

"Now that you mention it…"

"You see him hesitate when the cardinal asked for the file on The Holy Hand?"

"Yeah, like he thought it was a bad idea."

The rain had stopped, but the chilly wind persisted. Thick, gray clouds threatened a sudden downpour. Still, the square was crowded.

"What do you think?" Vincent asked.

"About Cusa?"

"About the meeting."

"We got what we came for."

"You think the cardinal's dirty?"

"I'm still chewing on that. One thing is clear, he knows more about The Holy Hand than he told us."

"Oh, without a doubt. Which is why I'm leaning toward dirty. He dropped the good-guy act the moment we mentioned The Holy Hand. Then played dumb when we brought up Bonaventura."

I shrugged. "He did the political calculus."

"What do you mean?"

I had a sudden and inexplicable urge for a breath mint. Maybe it was the bad taste the cardinal had left in my mouth. While I fished around in my suit pockets, hoping to find a stray Tic Tac or a forgotten Life Saver, I said, "A firebrand cardinal with ties to Bonaventura—the leader of an alleged Christian terrorist organization—is not good PR for a scandal-ridden church. It's another black eye. When the cardinal said the church brass asked him to look into The Holy Hand, you can bet they were really telling him to rethink his relationship with Bonaventura. So he wasn't admitting anything unless he had to."

We fell silent for a moment.

Vincent said, "That CIA file was golden, the key to unlocking the cardinal. Surveillance, financials. Who knows how long it woulda taken us to connect those dots."

"And we wouldn't have a reason to, at least not at this point in the investigation."

"Come to think of it, the spooks really put a lot of effort into it."

"They had to. They needed a distraction if things went south." The search for a breath mint came to a disappointing conclusion when all I found was a ball of lint and a spare button. "And it worked. We're now looking in a completely different direction."

We stopped for a large tour group clad in yellow ponchos and absurd fisherman rain hats as though a surging Nor'easter was expected to hit the square at any moment.

Vincent said, "The money trail's shady, no matter how hard the cardinal tries to dress it up as charity. It smells like a payoff."

"For what?"

"A papal hook."

"I'm not following."

"The bishop told me the cardinal is on the short list for pope."

Agent Shears had described the cardinal as an opportunist with papal ambitions. Cusa's comment had confirmed those ambitions and given new meaning to the money trail.

"That's a good point. The Holy Hand would be even better connected. When were you going to tell me this?"

He glanced at his watch. "Exactly nine seconds ago. Perfect timing."

I shook my head, and we started walking again.

"You know, El-Hashem's homicide only seems to benefit the cardinal," Vincent said. "Think about it. Keeps The Scorpion out of an eight by six, free to chase his terrorist's wet dreams. If The Holy Hand has a mole in the task force or the Carabinieri, they look good to me for the shooting."

I said nothing.

"You don't agree?"

"If it plays out like that, we're screwed. No line on The Scorpion or his sleeper agent."

"Hmm. Let's see what we get out of this Bonaventura. Speaking of which, the cardinal didn't like the idea of us talking to his boy. Wonder why."

"Maybe he has secrets to tell."

"So you do think the cardinal's dirty."

We stopped at the base of the eastern granite column that served as a pedestal for an ancient bronze sculpture of the winged lion.

"How do we play Bonaventura?" I asked.

"Mamma mia, not even a G-string under there." Vincent was eyeing a curvy brunette in white fitness gear who stood incongruous against the backdrop of ponchos, boots, and umbrellas. "Roman goddesses running loose here, imagine that. You think she needs directions to Mount Olympus?"

I blocked his view. "Focus, man."

He looked over my shoulder. "Oh, I am focused, believe me."

"Vincent!"

"All right, all right, don't lose your panties." He let his eyes linger a moment longer. "Where were we?"

"Bonaventura."

"Right, how to play him." He threw his head back and finger-combed his damp hair. "Like we know for a fact The Holy Hand did the hit."

"Works for me. Let's find a ride."

Gondolas were pulling in and out of the jetties along the canal. We had four addresses to visit; a slow-moving gondola wouldn't do. I spotted a motorized water taxi moored about thirty yards away.

"There!" I pointed. "Let's move before we lose it."

We rushed to the water taxi. My knee was acting up again, a dull ache that made me slower than usual. Luckily, my partner caught the captain as he got off the boat. When I reached them, I shoved the list of addresses the cardinal had given us into the captain's weather-beaten face. Vincent, speaking fast Italian, ordered the squat middle-aged man back into the cockpit. Once we were seated and tucked away under the small canopy, the captain backed his boat and steered into the canal.

Over the roar of the motor, I said, "What's this spiritual problem you laid so thick on the bishop?"

Vincent grinned. "I just wanted to get in a confession. I figure forgiveness from a bishop is a virtual license to sin."

I looked away and smiled.

Chapter Twenty-Two

The Carpenter

Bishop Cusa was back in the room where he had watched His Eminence write a note and hand it to police. Officially, the small space served as a storage area. In practice, it was Cusa's personal refuge and listening post. Located next to the cardinal's office and fitted with hidden peepholes and a pair of shotgun microphones connected to a recording device, it made for the perfect spy den. Though he didn't like thinking of it that way. Its existence was strictly precautionary, a means of protecting the cardinal.

The bishop clenched the chain of the large crucifix hanging around his neck. He rubbed his thumb along the links, counting them like rosary beads.

The current situation was quite perilous indeed.

Why had the cardinal cooperated so thoroughly? Papal File Sixty-One was a secret church document, one that did not officially exist.

Had he been coerced?

Had he been threatened?

He would listen to the recording later. In the meantime, how to proceed?

Action?

Inaction?

Both had consequences. Which was less perilous?

Lord, how should I choose?

He paced the small room with his head down and his hands clinging to the crucifix. After a few minutes, he stopped. He had made a choice, the kind that weighs heavily on men of faith. He found solace, however, in the fact that he was not alone. God was guiding him. Today and always. Working his divine will in the most unexpected ways.

From under his cassock, the bishop extracted a cellphone that was not registered to him or to anyone who actually existed. He entered a phrase in Latin to unlock it and accessed the short contact list. He selected the number for Il Falegname—The Carpenter. He let it ring four times and disconnected. He continued pacing until the phone rang minutes later.

Bishop Cusa put the phone to his ear and said, "Please check the roof. I think it's about to leak."

Chapter Twenty-Three

Mr. Bonaventura

The first three addresses on the cardinal's list were a bust. The trip to the last location involved a tangle of major and minor canals that led deep into the residential district of Cannaregio.

After navigating beneath a trio of low-clearance bridges, the captain called out, "*Cinque minuti!*"

"Five minutes." Vincent opened the CIA dossier and was quickly transfixed by the photos of a man with thick, shoulder-length brown hair and a neatly trimmed French fork beard. "*Marone*, he looks like Jesus Christ—well, the picture of Jesus Christ I grew up with."

"I suspect that's not a coincidence. He is the leader of a fanatical Christian organization."

"How can I bad-cop Jesus Christ? Nonna Geppina would kill me."

Nonna Geppina was Vincent's grandmother, a formidable octogenarian who could lavish you with a bounty of homemade pastas and pastries at the drop of a phone call or beat you with a wooden spoon if you so much as tasted a lick of food before saying grace, took the Lord's name in vain, or spoke unflatteringly of former President Ronald Reagan, whom she referred to as "Mr. Ronny."

"Nonna Geppina will never find out," I said. "But if she does, we'll deny everything and say anything to save our seats at her table. Besides, he's not Jesus Christ."

"I *know* he's not Jesus Christ, but I *see* Jesus Christ." Vincent dropped the photos back in the dossier. "Are we gonna squeeze him? This is an Italian citizen, you know. Our jurisdiction here is flimsy. What if he files a complaint? What if the media catches wind of it? Marino will rake us over hot coals. Probably speak in tongues too."

Back in Brooklyn, we rolled with the law. Only once we deviated from it when a life was at stake and we'd run out of options. As a lawyer, I could never justify playing fast and loose with the law, but as a cop, I knew getting the job done meant sometimes bending the rules, even to the breaking point.

"The Israelis will be here in less than forty-eight hours. This guy's our only lead. He has to give up the shooter or convince us The Holy Hand had nothing to do with it." I paused. "If he's not cooperative..."

Vincent slowly closed the dossier.

The captain drove the boat past rundown buildings. Most of the stucco exteriors were worn away, exposing raw brick and mortar. The stench of the water was stronger, as if that side of town had the worst of everything. Still, Venice did not fail to amaze. Instead of cars, the garages of the homes on the canal housed motorboats, rowboats, and gondolas. Real estate listings in the area probably went something like this: lovely, three-floor Venetian Gothic town house, circa 1500, with century-young terra-cotta tile roofing and original plate glass windows; amenities include electricity, indoor plumbing, and a boat garage with room to spare for that old family clunker.

The only watercraft I didn't see were Jet Skis. Maybe they were illegal. Considering the popularity of the irritating Vespa scooters in other Italian cities, I was relieved that Jet Skis didn't enjoy a similar following in Venice. The noise alone would mar the serene ambiance of the great city's residential areas.

The captain slowed and maneuvered the taxi into an empty boat garage.

"Another bust?" Vincent turned to me. "You think maybe the cardinal tipped off this guy?"

Ropes and tools hung haphazardly on the brick walls of the garage. A worktable stacked high with rusted junk was shoved in a corner. The place smelled of gas. A fifty-five-gallon tank perched on the jetty was the likely source.

"Wouldn't make sense," I said. "The cardinal's a politician. He wants us to go away and knows that won't happen until we talk to this guy."

"Right, but an empty garage says nobody's home, just like the other three did."

"We still have to check."

Vincent handed me the dossier.

The captain cut the motor and secured the mooring line. He agreed to wait somewhere close by, so long as he could keep the meter running. Vincent got the captain's cellphone number and stepped off the boat. He then gave me a hand. My poor sense of balance on floating surfaces, coupled with my bum knee, made it a precarious operation. I held my breath until we managed to get all of me safely onto the jetty.

Vincent opened a nearby doorway as the taxi's motor turned over. "Stairs. The apartment is three alpha."

And so began another three-flight climb up creaky wooden stairs—the fourth of the day—and it wasn't even noon. Everywhere I went, there were stairs. Whether it was the task force office, my hotel room, a bar, a restaurant, a church, or visits to The Holy Hand's numerous apartments, there were stairs. Always stairs. What did the Venetians have against good old elevators?

I reached the top landing. Vincent waited in a narrow hallway, facing a door marked 3-A. I joined him and leaned against the doorframe to catch my breath.

Vincent folded his arms. "One day you're not gonna make it. You're not gonna keep up in a situation where it's critical to keep up or show up."

Heat spread across my face. "Today … today is not that day, is it? And when it nears … I'll give you ample notice … put in for a new partner."

"Oh, come on, don't get dramatic. I'm just trying to motivate you, for fuck's sake."

I reached for the door knocker. It was probably older than the Brooklyn Bridge, covered in green and white rust, and shaped like a lion's head biting down on a heavy ring. I listened for stirring on the other side. Nothing. I rapped it again with the same result.

Vincent directed my attention to another flight of stairs at the end of the hallway. "Terrace."

I gestured for him to lead the way.

At the top, a wide entryway opened to the terrace. The floor was tiled. Stubby stone columns topped with planters served as posts for the wrought iron guardrails running along the edges.

Vincent stood just inside the entryway under a manual roll-down gate, the kind used to secure storefronts. He chin-pointed at a quadrant of the terrace that was out of view. I limped over to see. The Jesus look-alike from the CIA dossier stood by a table under a wooden pergola. He wore faded jeans and a windbreaker, hardly dressing the part of Christ. He was busy knotting the end of a rope to the rock-climbing harness he had strapped around his waist and wiry thighs.

"What's he doing?"

Vincent shrugged. "Maybe making his great escape."

"He'll have to tie the other end of that rope to the guardrail first."

We approached.

"Ignazio Bonaventura?" I asked.

In good English, which I'd expected since the dossier indicated he'd been schooled in Montreal, Bonaventura said, "The last couple of turns are key." He was looping the multicolored rope around a confusing pair of knots. Nothing in his body language or expression suggested surprise.

He was expecting us.

"There." He pointed at the knots. "Figure eight follow-through, backup fisherman's."

"You are Ignazio Bonaventura?"

Probably annoyed I wasn't impressed or interested in his fancy knots, a frown creased his soft Jesus Christ features. "I am."

"I'm Detective Miles Jordan, and this is my partner, Detective Vincent Santoro. We're with the FBI, working closely with the Carabinieri."

Ignoring my offered handshake, he dragged the coil of rope he was tethered to with his foot and pulled out one of the four chairs set around a square table. Not bothering to remove the harness, he sat and crossed his arms over his chest. He did not invite us to sit.

The remaining chairs were wet. The tabletop had been wiped. A pitcher of water, identical to the one on the cardinal's desk, rested on a wooden platter along with an empty glass. We took off our suit jackets and lay them on the wet seats. I dropped the dossier on the table and sat.

"You climb?" I asked.

Bonaventura glanced down at the harness. "I fancy the sport. Master the knots, they say." He paused. "You came to talk about climbing?"

I smiled. "No."

"What is it this time?"

I leaned forward, putting my elbows on the table. "You've been questioned by police?"

Bonaventura scoffed. "You know I have."

"I mean recently, as in the last two days."

"No, not that recent. Ask your questions."

"Mr. Bonaventura, we're—"

"Iggy."

"Excuse me?"

"Call me Iggy. No English speaker—you included—can pronounce Ignazio or Bonaventura in proper *Italiano.* And that irks me."

Iggy? Why not Jerk?

I smiled my good cop smile. "We're investigating the shooting that occurred on Monday in St. Mark's Square."

I studied his face. No reaction. His vibrant blue eyes never blinked.

"To be specific," I continued, "we're looking for the shooter and anyone involved."

Bonaventura drummed his fingers on his folded arms. He glowered with such intensity I expected to see the sudden manifestation of the wrathful God of Abraham all good Baptists are taught to fear.

Instead of spewing fire and brimstone, he said, "I know nothing. I wasn't there. I was here, working."

"Working? What kind of work do you do?" I asked.

His eyes darted back and forth between us. "You know what I do."

"You're the leader of a militant Christian organization."

"Militant?"

"Some call it a terrorist group."

His eyes narrowed. "That's absurd."

"Not according to this file we have on The Holy Hand." I patted the dossier. "Sheds a lot of suspicion—"

"Suspicion! Suspicion is not proof! The Holy Hand has powerful enemies in the press who labor to spread fantastic lies in an attempt to silence us. We are a charitable organization, one with a voice. We speak for Christian unity. We speak against Islam and its anti-Christian agenda. We speak against the hordes of non-Christians invading Europe. And it makes the press crazy."

"Racism has a way of rousing the media."

He smiled. A slightly chipped front tooth was the only imperfection on the man's face.

"That's always the angle." He pursed his thin lips. "Disagree with radicals, and they label you a racist. Well, allow me to enlighten you. Christians come from all backgrounds, economic and social, and are of all races. Their devotion to the Christian faith makes them one people in the eyes of God."

"As opposed to, say, a Jew or a Buddhist?"

"We are not warring with Judaism or idolaters. We are warring with Islam. We have been for a thousand years."

Vincent cleared his throat loudly as a way of telling me the interview was going off the rails.

"Mr. Bonaventura—"

"Iggy."

"Just how does your organization carry out its anti-Islamic message?"

He shook his head. "I don't understand the question."

"You said it's a charitable organization with a voice. How is that voice heard?"

"Peaceful protest."

"Protest how?"

"We march, we demonstrate ... we have a website. A strong social media presence as well."

"How do you decide it's time to protest or demonstrate?"

"We ... well, it depends on the kind of statement we feel compelled to make. If the EU announces that more refugees will enter Europe, we march. On social media, our message goes out daily."

"Or when Cardinal Perricone gives one of his incendiary speeches. Isn't that right?"

"Incendiary?" He tilted his head. "You mean controversial."

"I mean incendiary since they often lead to violence."

"Violence? I don't understand."

"After a speech, you order a protest, and soon—"

"I told you, we—"

"—a cleric is killed, a mosque is firebombed."

"Enough!" Bonaventura jumped to his feet. "I have answered your questions."

"Sit down, Iggy," Vincent said. "We're just getting started."

Chapter Twenty-Four

Upended

Instead of taking Bonaventura into a dark room, tying his hands behind a wooden chair, and shining a light in his face, Vincent opted to make use of the tools at hand. Leveraging the climbing harness Bonaventura never took off, the coil of rope he was tethered to, and a few knots of his own, Vincent hung the man upside down from the pergola like a butcher shop sausage.

Vincent inspected his handiwork. "I'm no climber, but these knots should hold."

"You can't do this!" Bonaventura squirmed. "You gave Cardinal Perricone assurances!"

Vincent squatted in front of Bonaventura. "How do you know we talked to the cardinal?"

"He … he said that you wouldn't do this."

"Do what?"

"Treat me like an animal!"

"So the cardinal tipped you off. Well, he neglected to mention that Detective Jordan gave assurances. I didn't."

Spittle lathered Bonaventura's lips. "Detective Jordan!"

I grasped a heavy cast iron chair and dragged it. The grating sound the hollow legs made on the tile floor set the tone. When I was close enough, I sat.

"Vincent, give us a minute."

"No problem. Gotta make some phone calls anyway." Vincent stood and left the terrace.

Bonaventura hung with his arms crossed. The climbing harness was pulled tight around his waist and thighs. His legs were bound by shorter ropes to the main line to keep them vertical. Veins swelled across his forehead, and his long hair swept the floor. Only his French fork beard stood defiant, resisting the pull of gravity.

"He's a former marine, my partner. Two tours in Iraq. Medals for valor. But he came back missing something up here." I tapped my temple. "There were rumors … bad things he did over there. To prisoners."

Bonaventura crossed himself.

I added, "No one could control him then. No one can control him now."

Vincent's honorable service record said nothing about abusing prisoners, but a little spoon-fed lie at the right moment of an interrogation can be pretty effective. For the first time, fear flashed in Bonaventura's eyes.

"We promised the cardinal no harm would come to you, but I need your help. Can't do it alone."

"I don't understand."

"The sooner you answer my questions, the sooner I can get my forgetful partner out of here."

Bonaventura said nothing. His forehead was spotted with sweat.

I continued, "We have to trust each other. You and me, working together, we can get you out of this in one piece. With your face intact and your fingers and arms still working. Are you with me?"

Again, he said nothing.

"Hear that?" I turned my head sideways to listen. "That's my partner coming back. Are you with me?"

He nodded.

"Good. Now, follow my lead."

In a loud voice, I said, "Will you cooperate with us, Mr. Bonaventura?"

"Yes, I will cooperate. I want to cooperate."

"You heard that, Vincent? Mr. Bonaventura has agreed to cooperate."

"You sure?" Vincent approached. "I can start with his fingers."

"No, please." Bonaventura shook his head. "I will cooperate, yes."

I pulled my suit pants at the knees a couple of inches for comfort and brushed away imaginary lint from the fabric. "Did The Holy Hand have anything to do with the shooting?"

"No."

"What was the motive?"

"We had nothing to do with that shooting."

"Oh? Not *that* shooting?" I rubbed my goatee. "Which shooting then?"

"Which shooting?"

"That's what I'm asking you."

"We don't shoot people." He watched Vincent circle. "We help the poor."

"What the hell does that mean?" Vincent bumped Bonaventura with his hip, setting the man swinging like a pendulum.

"Don't do that! I suffer sickness of motion." Bonaventura shut his eyes.

Vincent chuckled. "Motion sickness?"

"Yes!"

"Come on, Iggy, you expect me to believe that bullshit? You live in Venice—boats everywhere."

"I walk. Venice has four hundred bridges. Why do you think they call it the city of bridges? Unless you must go to Murano or Lido, you can walk anywhere."

That explains why there was no boat in the garage.

Vincent said, "Well, what about this climbing business then? Ever occur to you that climbers sometimes end up hanging upside down and swinging much worse than that?"

"I get proper training; I will not make mistakes," Bonaventura claimed. "But here, I have no control. This is torture."

"Answer the question," Vincent said. "What do you mean by 'help the poor'?"

Bonaventura grimaced as if switching between threads of conversation required physical effort. "We raise money for Christian causes. Education, food, medicine."

"Sounds expensive." I shifted around in the chair. "How do you raise the money?"

"I'm getting sick."

I gestured to Vincent. He grabbed one of Bonaventura's legs to stop his swing.

Resting my elbows on my knees, I leaned forward. "How do you raise money?"

Bonaventura opened his eyes.

"We have—" he swallowed "—carnivals, fairs, dinners. Sometimes raffles."

"Why did The Holy Hand carry out the shooting?" I asked.

"What? Why did we do the shooting?" He paused. "I don't know."

I leaned back. "You don't know? But you admit The Holy Hand was responsible."

"No, I don't. We didn't do it."

"Mr. Bonaventura, if you don't cooperate, I won't be able to help you." I crossed my arms. "You haven't denied the shooting. Instead, you told us that you didn't know why The Holy Hand carried out the shooting. That sounds like an admission to me."

"Not what I mean."

I pointed at him. "Did you give the order?"

He clenched his fist and shook it at me. "No! No! No!"

Vincent said, "We have somebody who says you guys did it."

"Who? I demand to know who is saying this fantastic lie. We have many enemies who say fantastic lies about us."

"Maybe you're the fantastic liar, Iggy." Vincent pushed Bonaventura's thigh.

Bonaventura groaned. "My God, you have to stop this." With the strength in his arms apparently exhausted, he dropped them and immediately realized that he could touch the floor and stop his swing.

"Who are your big donors?" I asked.

"What? Who are the big donors?"

"Yeah, who?" Vincent asked.

"Businesses, private businesses."

Vincent pressed. "Like who?"

"Who?"

"Who? Who? Who?" Vincent raised his voice. "What are you, a frigging owl?"

Bonaventura clasped his hands together in a pleading gesture. "But I don't understand."

"He's asking what specific businesses donate to your cause," I explained. "Restaurants? Shops?"

"Yes, restaurants, shops too … and the glass factories."

"How many were involved?" Vincent asked.

"Involved? In donations?"

"Don't be a balloon head, Iggy. The shooting. How many were involved?"

"I don't know. I had nothing to do with it."

"But someone in your organization did. Who?" I asked.

"No one!"

I threw my head back in exaggerated frustration and said to the sky, "So you had nothing to do with it?"

"Yes … I mean no."

I dropped my head to look at him. "Which one is it?"

"I had nothing to do with it."

"But you knew about it," Vincent said.

"No, I don't know anything."

I said, "So it happened, but you weren't a part of it. Is that what you mean?"

"No! You're confusing me."

"Confusing you?" Vincent pulled out his Spyderco police knife. "You're confusing us." He flicked his wrist to spring open the serrated blade and approached Bonaventura.

The Holy Hand's leader screamed. He squirmed like a fish on a line.

"Relax, Iggy, I'm not gonna cut you. I just need another piece of rope."

Vincent walked behind Bonaventura and cut a yard's worth of rope from the coil. He seized Bonaventura's wrists and tied them behind his back. Vincent could've used handcuffs and saved himself the trouble, but I knew he wanted Bonaventura to see the knife's wicked blade.

With his hands tied, Bonaventura could no longer stop or slow the swinging Vincent subjected him to.

"Who are your donors?" I asked. "Give us names."

Bonaventura didn't reply.

My cellphone rang. It was O'Neil. I directed the call to voicemail and turned off the ringtone.

"Mr. Bonaventura, you're not helping me here," I said. "So, how can I help you?"

Eyes still shut, Bonaventura said, "You're killing me. My head will explode. I will die."

"Relax. Your head won't explode from hanging upside down. You could, however, go blind or have a heart attack. Brain hemorrhaging is another possibility. But, believe it or not, the most common cause of death for people in your situation is asphyxiation. See, heavier organs, like your liver and intestines, will slowly crush your lungs. The lungs are designed to sit on top of those organs, not below. We forget, or don't realize, that the parts inside our bodies move and can even dislodge. But don't worry. You'd have to hang like that for twenty-four hours or more, and that's not going to happen if you answer my questions."

"Blind? I can be blind?"

"Who paid you to do the shooting?"

"No one paid."

"So you did it for free?" Vincent waited. "Bullshit. What was the motive?"

"We didn't do it!"

I held up my hands. "Okay, Mr. Bonaventura, let's take a break from this line of questioning. Let's talk about your spy in JTTF."

"Stop this swinging … I will vomit."

"Who is The Holy Hand's spy inside JTTF?" I continued.

"Who is the spy?"

On the upswing, Vincent smacked Bonaventura on the forehead. "Stop repeating every question, Iggy."

Bonaventura winced. "I don't know! What is JTTF?"

When I told him it stood for Joint Terrorism Task Force, he gave me a vacant look, so I asked, "Who do you know in the FBI?"

"Who do I—stop hitting me!"

Vincent grinned. "Then stop repeating the questions, Iggy."

Getting smacked was reducing the arc of his swing. His eyes, now bloodshot, flickered wildly. "I'm so confused."

I exaggerated a sigh. "You don't understand … you're confused. We're running out of time, Mr. Bonaventura. And I believe Detective Santoro here is running out of patience."

"You better frigging believe it."

Bonaventura swallowed. "I don't know the FBI.'"

I gave Bonaventura a hard look. "Who wanted Aarzam El-Hashem dead?"

"Who wanted—" Another smack. "I don't know this man!"

"Well, somebody wanted him dead. Was it the cardinal?" I loosened my tie and unbuttoned my collar. "Did the cardinal want him dead?"

Bonaventura glared at me. "I told you, I don't know this man."

"Stop lying, Iggy." Vincent squatted and grabbed Bonaventura by his hair. "You knew who he was and where he was gonna be. The exact time and place." He yanked Bonaventura's hair to underscore the point. "Somebody inside the FBI gave you that information, and we need to know who the fuck that was!"

"I don't know." Bonaventura whimpered. "This man you refer to … a terrorist—was a terrorist."

I leaned in. "So you do know who Aarzam El-Hashem was."

Vincent let go of Bonaventura's hair.

"Only what I see in the news today. That's what they said. That's what they called him."

"You lied," I said.

"No, I'm confused."

"What about the Carabinieri? Does The Holy Hand have a spy there?"

After another ten minutes of back-and-forth, our only lead swayed gently in the cool breeze, reduced to a sobbing Bible-quoting mess. He made a convincing victim—Jesus Christ suffering for our sins. He was either a great actor, or he really didn't know anything about the shooting.

We stood at the dreaded fork in the interrogation. Do we believe him, or do we keep up the pressure until he breaks and either gives us what we need or lies just to make us stop? I was leaning toward believing him. Vincent's unclenched fists and sagging shoulders said he did too. Believing Bonaventura, however, meant our only lead was a dead end.

Why would Agent Shears steer us to a dead end and put his agent back on the hook? That didn't make sense. There had to be something here. Maybe we were asking the wrong questions.

While Vincent paced, I waited for Bonaventura's blubbering and rambling to subside. "Mr. Bonaventura, are there members of The Holy Hand who work for the police?"

He didn't reply.

I tried again. "Does anyone in The Holy Hand work for the police? The Carabinieri? The FBI?"

He nodded. "Yes, one. There is one."

Vincent stopped pacing.

"Who is it, Mr. Bonaventura?" I stood. "Who in The Holy Hand works for the police?"

He licked his cracked lips and said in a faint voice, "Let me down ... I will tell you when I can sit."

I turned to Vincent. "Cut him down."

The moment he was back on terra firma, Bonaventura threw up his breakfast. We helped him to his feet and put him in a chair. He wiped his mouth and beard along the sleeve of his windbreaker. Bloodshot eyes, disheveled hair, and faint welt marks on his wrists offered the only physical evidence of his ordeal. The rope Vincent had used to hang the man upside down was still knotted to his harness and lay in a heap on the floor.

Bonaventura complained of double vision and a migraine, with a moment of panic when he thought he was going blind. His elbows were propped on the table, his head propped on his hands.

I pulled up a chair next to him. He reeked of shampoo, sweat, and vomit. "Now, tell us who in The Holy Hand works for the police."

He lifted his head and kept his eyes down. "A key member ... name is—"

The back of Bonaventura's head exploded. The outward force propelled his skull forward, crashing his face into the tabletop.

My immediate and absurd thought was the blood rush to Bonaventura's brain from being suspended upside down had spectacularly done the impossible, just as he had feared. However, the pop and the gaping wound—consistent with the damage wrought by a bullet entering the front of the skull and exiting the back—made the situation clear.

As I hit the floor, Vincent returned fire. I landed hard on my right side and got jabbed by my own holster. To reach my gun, I needed to roll. But I was wedged between the heavy cast iron chair and the base of the table.

The sudden screech and clang of moving metal drew my attention to the entryway. The roll-down gate was fast descending.

I pushed off the base of the table and knocked the chair backward. By the time I managed to roll, draw, and get into some semblance of a tactical shooting stance, Vincent was at the gate. It had dropped too quickly, hitting the floor with a crash. He never got a hand under it, so he was left struggling to wedge the heel of one hand between the subtle edges of the corrugated panels while holding his gun with the other. Embarrassed and angry over my clumsy response, I hobbled over. Together we tried to lift the gate, but we couldn't get any purchase on the sleek metal.

Then we heard a click.

"Shit! We're locked out." Vincent let go of the gate. "Is there another way outta here?"

We backed up and looked for another exit.

A minute later, the roar of a motorboat coming to life cut the air. We hustled to the edge of the terrace and looked over. The boat was small, white, generic, the kind found everywhere in Venice. The driver was clad in dark clothing with some kind of cap. He was further obscured by the distance and the darkening sky.

Vincent aimed his firearm at the boat. "Too far."

"And moving too fast," I added.

We watched the boat race down the canal and turn out of sight in the distance, knowing we just let another shooter get away.

Chapter Twenty-Five

Crime Scene

The Carabinieri's crime scene unit was photographing the gore that less than an hour before had been Mr. Ignacio Bonaventura. Uniforms near the roll-down gate were completing a canvass of the stairwell and boat garage on the off chance the shooter had left a weapon or other evidence behind. A pair of Carabinieri detectives conferred in a huddle.

I stood next to Vincent at the perimeter of the crime scene, which spanned the pergola and most of the entryway. We'd already given our statements to the detectives.

While waiting for the cavalry, Vincent and I had done our own walk-through of the crime scene. What remained of Bonaventure's head was on the table. One arm was folded awkwardly under the carnage. The other dangled off the table, motionless. His body was still in a sitting position, propped up by the table and heavy chair. We found two shell casings about twelve feet from the victim, which we attributed to Vincent discharging his weapon in response to the muzzle flash he'd glimpsed at the entryway. We left them where they lay for the crime scene techs to photograph and collect. We did not find any for the shooter.

When the tech with the camera signaled that he was done with the long, medium, and close-up photographs of the victim, Detective Alonza Giordana approached the body. She put on a pair of latex surgical gloves, giving each an extra tug that made it snap. She lifted Bonaventura's head to expose his face. From a very neat and very precise hole in the middle of the forehead oozed a thin, jagged line of blood down the left eye socket. The vibrant blue was still in the eyes as though part of Mr. Bonaventura clung to life there. The tech with the camera moved in for close-up shots of the face.

I said to Vincent, "Dead-center head shot at twenty-five yards. Our perp is an expert shooter."

"You can make that shot."

"I'm an expert shooter."

"Whatever." Vincent finger-combed his hair back. "Cop? Military?"

"Could be one, could be both. It could also be a professional hit. One shot, no shell casing. Had a predetermined escape route. No panic, no rush. Well planned."

Vincent sighed. "Well, whoever it was, he was sent here by the cardinal. Nobody else knew we were coming."

"Bonaventura knew we were coming. Why tip him off and then have him killed? The only logical reason for the cardinal to call Bonaventura was to get him to cooperate, to make us go away."

"You don't see it?"

"See what?"

"Iggy was shot only after we cut him down, when he was ready to talk."

The memory of Bonaventura seated at the table, hair tousled, eyes bloodshot, alive one moment and dead the next, played in my mind. We hadn't used pliers or electricity. We hadn't subjected him to waterboarding or used his face as a punching bag. Still, we'd crossed a line. We'd broken a rule. One that led to his death and gave us nothing to offset the guilt in return.

I hung my head. "That means … the shooter was here all along. Listening. Waiting."

"And the moment it became clear Iggy was gonna spill the beans—*bam!*"

I nodded.

"So we're back to square one," Vincent had to add. "Now what? We gotta find this shooter too?"

"Maybe it's the same shooter."

"Same one who hit El-Hashem? Nah, different MO. One operated like an amateur and the other a pro."

"Different set of circumstances. So we can't rule that out, at least not at this point."

Vincent shook his head. "That would take an enormous pair of balls. Shoot our snitch then shoot Iggy—both times right under our noses."

"Either way, one or two shooters, this is all connected."

"What's next? Sweat the cardinal? Maybe hang him upside down in the basilica." Vincent chuckled. "Imagine the wrath of Nonna Geppina over that one. You'd never get a whiff of her food, and I'd never walk straight again."

I watched the techs process the crime scene. They looked like busy termites in their hooded, baggy white overalls, the words "Polizia Scientifice" stamped in large letters across their backs.

Vincent chin-pointed at Detective Giordana. "She keeps watching us. She knows we're full of shit."

"How? You did all the talking and you're a master bullshitter."

"Very funny." Vincent threw another glance Giordana's way. "She's great at detecting bullshit. It's more than the cop in her. I can tell."

Before the homicide detectives arrived, Vincent and I had agreed on a filtered version of events for our individual statements, a version that excluded our meeting with the cardinal and our enhanced interrogation method. It was also vague as to why we'd paid Bonaventura a visit. Knowing The Holy Hand had an asset inside the police, releasing the unfiltered version was not an option. Only O'Neil—whom we'd succinctly updated earlier to the tune of a half dozen goddamns—would get the whole story.

"And she's a good detective, I hear," Vincent added. "Don't know anything about the balloon head she's paired with. It's Longo, right? But I know he's senior to her, probably making twice as much with half her IQ. So she's out to prove something."

Detective Giordana crouched. She seemed interested in Bonaventura's wrists. Abruptly, she called over one of the techs. A moment later, he handed her a paper bag. Earlier, I'd watched the same tech bag the rope Vincent had used to bind those very wrists.

I said to Vincent, "If they decide to run that rope for DNA..."

"Not gonna worry. We didn't shoot the son of a bitch."

With the paper bag in hand, Giordana approached us. Over a dark suit, she wore a lightweight raincoat that fluttered easily in the wind. Her glasses were square-framed and oversized, extending well beyond the boundary of her eyebrows as if chosen to ensure her eyes got full prescription coverage no matter where she turned them. She was stocky but light and agile on her feet. I bet she could do a double back vault and nail the landing in high heels. Unlike her partner, Giordana didn't speak a word of English; we learned that when we gave our statements. So it was no surprise when she held up the paper bag and fired off a stream of Italian.

I leaned into Vincent's ear. "What did she say? I only caught bits and pieces."

"You want the skinny or the full monty?"

"Monty."

"She says Iggy has ligature marks on his wrists, marks she thinks are consistent with the rope that's in the bag she's holding. She plans to run it for DNA and then demand samples from us for comparison. Do we want to change our bullshit statements?"

Like a pair of lying kids busted for breaking a window during a game of stickball, we shook our heads in unison.

Her brown eyes, enlarged by the farsighted prescription of her glasses, methodically scanned every square inch of our faces.

She released a long sigh that seemed to ask, "What do I do with you two?" She pinned the bag under her arm and pulled out her notebook. She thumbed through a quarter inch of well-worn pages, stopped abruptly, and read out loud.

When she was done, Vincent said, "She read the part where I pin that rope on Iggy and his obsession with knots. *Marone*, the bullshit sounds worse in Italian than it did when I made it up in English."

"Did she read mine?"

"Nah. She just said that it's very convenient that you only saw whatever supports my statement."

"Damn."

"Told you she's a great detector of bullshit."

I glanced at her partner, a lanky, rumpled caricature of a Mickey Spillane private eye character, complete with trench coat, cigarettes, and a fedora. He was off in a corner, texting and smoking as if standing at a bus stop instead of investigating a fresh homicide.

Issuing another round of rapid-fire Italian, she shut the notebook and jabbed it at Vincent to underscore each point. When she finished, she crossed her arms and waited, the paper bag and notebook held firmly in each hand.

Vincent said, "She's also not buying our explanation of the climbing harness strapped to Iggy. She thinks we came here to torture him for information, and we'll be brought up on charges if she can prove it. She's giving us a last chance to change our statements."

We shook our heads again.

She threw her hands up in the air and pointed at each of us.

Vincent said, "She's ordered us not to leave town until—"

"She completes her investigation. I know, I got most of that." I tilted my head. "Wonder what her partner thinks."

"She's mad enough. I'm not gonna ask."

One of a cop's most conflicting situations is getting caught up investigating another cop. No one wants to go there. The guy you investigate today is the same guy you might have to trust with your life tomorrow. Do you want to piss him off? Give him an appetite for retribution? What's even worse is the long shadow you cast with other cops. The fraternity you can always count on to watch your six can turn on a dime and abandon you. Still, if you are a good cop, you'll go where the evidence takes you, despite the risks and the blowback. That's where Detective Giordana now found herself, a place synonymous with a minefield.

I said, "Tell her we need to see Bonaventura's apartment. It pertains to our investigation."

Vincent relayed the message.

Giordana called over the tech. When he was close enough, she shot out her arm to hand him the evidence bag and told him she was escorting us to Bonaventura's apartment. Then she called out to her partner.

Trench Coat flicked his cigarette over the terrace guardrail. To remind everyone he was still in charge, he blurted several useless instructions to the techs and uniforms—useless because everyone was already following those same instructions issued previously by his partner. Giordana rolled her eyes as we waited for Trench Coat to finish his little show and join us. When he finally did, she gave him a quick summary of where we stood. He barked something about Bonaventura's apartment being off-limits to anyone not involved with the investigation.

I nudged Vincent. "Tell them we know how to work a crime scene and any extension of it. We won't touch anything, and we'll share what we find."

Trench Coat barely let Vincent finish, replying—with an index finger held up like a bird flip—that only one of us could go.

"You go ahead," Vincent said.

A moment later, I followed Trench Coat and Detective Giordana down the stairs toward what I hoped would be a new lead.

Chapter Twenty-Six

Laser Straight

Trench Coat was the first one through the door of Bonaventura's apartment. He had waved off Giordana—more like pushed her aside—so he could lead the way. I read it as another peevish reminder to her, and to me, that this was his investigation. It earned him a dirty look from a red-faced Giordana. I gestured for her to go ahead of me. She hesitated, shooting a glance at Trench Coat, but quickly shrugged it off and stood taller. Expressionless, she gave me a barely perceptible nod and went into the apartment. I followed close behind.

Bonaventure's apartment was a small, no-frills square space. The walls and ceiling were painted dull gray, too thin in parts to cover up patches of plaster. There was a bath but no kitchen. On our left stood a small wooden dresser. On the right, a twin bed pressed against the wall. There was no night table. No place for an alarm clock or a lamp. The only room decor (if you could call it that) was a cheap oval mirror hung too high above the dresser and a wooden crucifix keeping watch over the bed. If it weren't for a carry-on and a camo knapsack stacked in the corner, we would've had no reason to believe the apartment had been occupied.

Directly in front of us was the only luxury the room afforded: a pair of French doors leading to a narrow balcony. The doors were shut, making the room feel stuffy and even smaller than it was. Trench Coat glanced around and barked orders at

Giordana. He strode to the glass doors, pulled them open, and went out on the balcony to light a cigarette.

In slow, well-enunciated Italian that I could follow, Giordana reminded me it was their extension to the crime scene. I was to touch nothing. I could, however, take as many notes and photos as I deemed necessary for my investigation.

Still wearing surgical rubber gloves, she started with the dresser. The top drawer contained three unassuming stacks of pressed clothing and underwear, which she removed and placed on top of the dresser. She examined each article and frisked for hidden objects. When that yielded nothing, she opened the second drawer. It housed a Bible and a book on rock climbing. She flipped through the pages of each, finding only a five-euro bill subbing as a bookmark. The bottom drawer was empty, so she turned her attention to the knapsack. As she arranged the contents on the wooden floor, I counted four packets of trail mix, a map, a worn wallet with credit cards and other identification, an Italian passport, a cellphone, and a few toiletries. Giordana dropped the cellphone in a plastic bag she pulled from her raincoat pocket. The phone would go to the techs, who would try to hack it and review its contents. The carry-on was less interesting, holding only a pair of well-traveled hiking boots and some socks.

All told, Bonaventura's belongings amounted to a simple collection of light travel items. They said nothing about the man and even less about any connection to, or knowledge of, a police contact.

With my cellphone, I took photos of the items Giordana had lined up neatly on the floor. Then I took pictures of the bed, the dresser, and the open drawers. I asked Giordana if she could move the dresser, which she did after slamming the drawers shut. Behind it was nothing but dust and chipping wall paint.

I spun around the room, looking for something that we'd missed, like a closet or a crawl space. I pointed to the bed, or rather under it. Giordana, who was far more nimble, dropped to a push-up position. She looked under the bed, sweeping her glasses from side to side like a search beam, and shook her head.

Although the techs would do another sweep for prints and DNA that didn't belong to Bonaventura (in case he'd been visited by his killer), the room felt like it was hiding nothing. I was about to check the terrace when the condition of the bed caught my eye. It was made with deliberate precision. The sheet and blanket fold ran laser straight and was set perfectly square to the edge of the bed. The sides were tucked in with no visible creases. And so taut was the blanket that a drill sergeant's quarter could easily bounce a half a foot off any part of it.

Had Bonaventura been in the military?

Chapter Twenty-Seven

Debriefing

The captain of our water taxi didn't let the long delay of a homicide investigation get in the way of his payday. He had waited patiently for our phone call. With his meter running at double the standard rate, I suspect he would have waited for hell to freeze over.

As we boarded, Vincent told the captain to take us back to St. Mark's Square. From there, we would walk to the task force office.

It was time to give O'Neil another update, so I reached into my damp suit jacket for my phone. The voicemail banner on the screen reminded me that he'd called during Bonaventura's interrogation. I tapped the screen to access voicemail.

"O'Neil left me three curt messages to call him back," I said. "Did he mention it when you called him about the homicide?"

Vincent shook his head. "All he did was blow a fuse."

I called O'Neil. He picked up on the first ring.

"Where are you?" he barked.

"Still in Cannaregio but on our way to the office. We just finished going over Bonaventura's apartment with the Italians."

"And?"

"Nothing solid, but the techs still need to pick it apart."

"So we've got nothing."

I paused. "Just a hunch."

"I need more than a goddamn hunch, Miles. We're exactly nowhere on this case, and the prime minister is due to arrive in less than two days!"

The line went silent. I thought O'Neil had disconnected until I heard the deep breathing of the man's slow simmer.

He suddenly said, "Twenty minutes, off-site meeting and debriefing. I'm texting over the address."

"Is that enough time for everyone? We're still trying to get to the Grand Canal."

"Then you better step on it."

The call disconnected.

"What's the story?" Vincent asked.

"Something's going down."

"What did O'Neil say?"

"We have twenty minutes to get to an off-site meeting. This is the address." I showed him my phone.

Vincent glanced at the screen. "That's not the usual off-site location. And it's out longer than twenty minutes from headquarters, so he must be there already."

"Give the captain the new address, and tell him to step on the throttle or whatever makes this thing go faster."

* * *

Under a darkening sky, we made it to the Grand Canal. Less than ten minutes after that, we arrived at our destination. The captain pulled alongside a weathered jetty, a few yards behind a Carabinieri boat. He cut the engine and set out to secure the mooring line. On the quay stretched a one-story brick building with a pitched terra-cotta roof.

"What's this place?" Vincent asked.

I shrugged. "A factory? Warehouse, maybe?"

"With windows like that?"

A long row of lattice windows was fitted into narrow openings crowned with lancet arches. It wasn't the type of frontage you'd expect to find on a commercial building.

"I guess we'll find out," I said.

Vincent paid the captain.

As we climbed out of the boat, the sky opened up. Rain fell hard and fast. Vincent jogged the length of the jetty. I hobbled. By the time I reached the doors of the building, I was soaking wet and practically hopping on one foot.

"You better wrap that knee," Vincent said, closing the door behind me.

As we shook off the rain in the lobby, the smell of coffee wafted from the spacious interior. I conjured up tasty images of chocolate chip lattes, triple s'mores, vanilla bean mochas, and caramel cappuccinos topped with four inches of whipped cream, nuts, and Reese's Pieces. It made me realize how hungry I was, but with things shaking as they were, the need to feed had to wait.

We walked inside. Coffee beans crunched underfoot—a strangely soothing sensation. Passing a row of steel columns that ran down the middle of the structure, we spotted O'Neil at the far end. He was seated cross-legged behind a wooden snack table. Stacked nearby were two plastic lawn chairs.

"Where is everybody?" Vincent whispered.

"Looks like it's just us."

O'Neil waved us over. "Sit down, boys."

Vincent reached the lawn chairs first. He pulled them apart and dropped them around the snack table. We sat.

O'Neil peered over the top of his half-frame glasses, which were signature-perched at the end of his long nose. "The rest of the team will not be joining us."

Perhaps to delay something unpleasant I sensed was coming, or to lighten the mood, or simply out of a sudden misplaced curiosity, I said to O'Neil, "I didn't know you drove boats, Top."

"What?"

"The Carabinieri boat outside. You're the only one here, so I assume you drove it."

"Pilot. You drive a car, you pilot a boat. I grew up on my old man's hundred-foot crabber, so you bet your ass I can pilot a boat. But I didn't ask you here to discuss boats or my old man. Now, tell me what the hell happened."

We spent the next half hour briefing O'Neil on our meetings with Cardinal Perricone and the late Ignazio Bonaventura. We stuck to the facts as they'd occurred, omitting hazardous details like suspending Bonaventura upside down and coercing cooperation from a Roman Catholic cardinal with the threat of a media leak.

O'Neil sat perfectly still, with downcast eyes, no doubt running both the political and investigative calculations his role required. Judging by the growing frown on his face, he wasn't liking the results.

His first question went to Vincent. "What prompted you to discharge your weapon?"

"I caught a peripheral of a muzzle flash. When I turned to it, I saw the perp standing in the entryway, pointing a weapon at us. It was dark in there, so I couldn't make out specific details."

"Bonaventura was shot only after he agreed to cooperate?"

"That's right, Top," I said.

"And what do we make of that?"

Vincent replied, "The shooter had us under surveillance, so somebody put him there. And the only somebody who knew we were gonna talk to Bonaventura was the cardinal."

O'Neil scowled. "A Roman Catholic cardinal is behind the hit on the leader of a Christian organization suspected of terrorism? Is that what we're saying here?"

Hearing it out loud, the notion sounded ridiculous.

Vincent cleared his throat.

I tugged at my wet suit in places it was sticking to me.

"That's Vincent's working theory at the moment," I said.

"Not yours?"

"I think the cardinal wanted him to cooperate so we'd go away quietly. I don't see any other reason to call him."

O'Neil took off his glasses. "Maybe he called to threaten him. Keep your mouth shut or else. Or maybe the cardinal told someone else and that someone else is behind this."

Vincent and I turned to each other. "Cusa!"

"Who the hell is Cusa?"

I replied, "Bishop Cusa, the cardinal's assistant. He was the only other party there. Shit, we totally forgot about him."

"There where? In your interview with the cardinal?"

"He wasn't present during the interview, but he was there before and after."

"What do we know about this Bishop Cusa?"

Vincent said, "Not much. We didn't know he existed until this morning."

O'Neil put his glasses back on. "Whether it's this bishop or the cardinal or both, this points to The Holy Hand. Which means those two are either members or in cahoots with that organization. Is that how we're approaching this?"

We nodded.

O'Neil said, "You two realize this is exactly how the CIA was hoping we'd play it?"

After an awkward silence, I said, "That's where the case is taking us, Top. Bonaventura confirms The Holy Hand has a police asset. And when he's about to give it up, he gets blown away. Who else can we suspect if not The Holy Hand? There's motive and opportunity."

O'Neil sat deadpan.

I added, "And with a police asset, they also had the intel the first shooter needed to hit El-Hashem, such as time and location."

"Do we think it's the same shooter in both cases?"

Vincent shrugged.

I said, "We don't know."

"Hope it is. Two shooters would make this case acutely more complex." O'Neil stretched out his long legs and leaned back. "Over the phone, you mentioned a hunch. Let's hear it."

I pulled out my phone and searched for the photos of Bonaventura's bed. I handed it to O'Neil.

"That's the bed in Bonaventura's apartment. Notice how precisely it's made. You can put a ruler to the fold and find it's perfectly straight. No slack or wrinkles anywhere on the top blanket."

"So?"

"Only a soldier makes a bed like that."

O'Neil raised his eyebrows. "You think this guy was military just because he makes a neat bed?"

"Not just a neat bed. An *exceptionally* neat bed. It's easy enough to check when we run his prints."

"Miles is right, Top. That's a soldier's bed. I should know."

O'Neil glanced at Vincent then turned back to me. "And if it turns out he was?"

"Then we'll cross-check anyone he served with against active police personnel databases."

As if a fog were lifting, O'Neil nodded. "Okay, that's a lead. This Bishop Cusa is another. And speaking of police, who are the homicide detectives?"

Vincent replied, "Alonza Giordana and Something Longo."

"Fredo Longo?"

Vincent snapped his fingers. "Yeah, that's it."

"Giordana is a sharp knife. Longo is a politician. He's also Marino's lapdog."

Interesting.

O'Neil continued, "How did we handle them?"

"We told them as little as possible," Vincent said. "So little, they think we're full of shit."

"Good. Since we don't know who to trust, the less people know, the better. Now, tell me about the Bonaventura interview."

Vincent glanced and me and then looked back at O'Neil. "What do you mean? We just went over that a few minutes ago."

O'Neil crossed his arms. "Tell me the parts you left out. Like why Bonaventura was willing to give up his police asset. It was obviously worth killing for."

Getting ambushed with a question that had only two responses—a blatant lie or the ugly truth—was embarrassing, given that we were two experienced interrogators who often used the same tactic. We should have anticipated and planned for it. Our only option now was to tell the ugly truth.

I put an open hand on my chest, the classic mea culpa gesture. "It was my call, Top. The clock is ticking, and we have no traction on this case. We had reason to believe Bonaventura could give us that traction, but he wasn't cooperating. So I opted to squeeze him."

O'Neil gaped. "Squeeze him how?"

"No waterboarding or nothing like that. Just PG-rated stuff, honest." Vincent smiled.

O'Neil pointed at Vincent. "You think this is goddamn funny?"

"No, Top. I'm just—"

"Are we going to have a problem over this?"

Since the cat was already out of the bag, there was no point in keeping it from the litter box.

"We might," I said.

"We might? We might how?"

"You sure you wanna know, Top?" Vincent asked. "You still have plausible deniability, I think."

O'Neil's glare could peel paint.

Vincent told O'Neil what we'd done to Bonaventura and what Giordana was planning to do with us.

"You hung the man upside down in a climbing harness?" O'Neil was wide-eyed.

There was a moment of silence, the calm before the O'Neil storm. It gave us a chance to brace ourselves.

"Goddammit!" O'Neil stood. "We're guests in a foreign country with barely enough jurisdiction to wipe our own noses, and you two pull a stunt like that?"

There was nothing to say. We gambled and lost.

"Of all the goddamn ammunition you could give Marino, you hand him a cruise missile? He's been itching to pin something on us. Anything that'll make us look like chumps and send us packing. You can bet your asses he'll be all over this. What the hell were you two thinking?"

I'd already explained what we were thinking at the time. No point repeating it. Besides, O'Neil wasn't looking for an answer. He was venting, and rightfully so. He now had to deal with the blowback, which would be raw and concentrated, given that we had nothing to offset it. All we had to show for the entire ugly episode was another victim.

O'Neil dropped in his chair. His shoulders sagged, and lines formed around his mouth.

"Miles, I need your gun and shield."

Chapter Twenty-Eight

Free Agent

Vincent jumped out of his seat, knocking the lawn chair backward. "Oh, for fuck's sake, Top, we just scared him a little!"

O'Neil's tone softened. "Sit down, Vinny. This is not about Bonaventura."

Vincent hesitated.

"Go on, sit."

Vincent picked up his chair and sat.

O'Neil said, "Miles, you're on modified duty until further notice. I'm to put you on a six p.m. flight to New York. This is coming straight from the SAC."

Of course it came from the Special Agent in Charge, the good ol' boy O'Neil had warned me about. This wasn't the first time the brass had asked for my gun and shield. Five years earlier, I'd shot a knife-wielding child murderer and rapist in self-defense. The bullet severed his spinal cord, sentencing him to life in a wheelchair. The scumbag lawyered up with the slimiest ambulance chaser in Manhattan, and together they set out to sue the city of New York for a fortune. The lawyer claimed since I'd been hell-bent on catching his client that I'd shot him out of vigilantism, not self-defense.

It was a dark time. My career, my reputation, and possibly my freedom hinged on a split-second decision. Sleep eluded me. Relationships suffered. My health declined. I'd turned to food as never before, trying in vain to fill a harrowing void that robbed me of purpose, of the job I needed to do.

"Miles? Miles!"

I flinched. O'Neil was snapping his fingers in my face.

"Are you paying attention? Did you aim your service weapon at Carabinieri personnel on the day of the shooting or not?"

"What?" I sat up. "They aimed at me. Shit, they *shot* at me."

O'Neil took off his glasses and tossed them on the snack table. "They shot at you? And you don't say a goddamn word about it?"

"Told you," Vincent said.

O'Neil gave me a stern look, which somehow seemed more severe without his glasses. "You covered up for a reckless cop?"

I looked back, not saying a word.

O'Neil propped his elbows on the armrests of the lawn chair. "Well, Mr. Blue Wall of Silence, that was all Marino needed. He found out about it and reshaped it to great effect. As far as the SAC is concerned, you panicked. You recklessly aimed your weapon at Carabinieri officers trying to assist or deliberately tried to keep those officers from reaching the perp as part of a yet-to-be-determined conspiracy. One aimed at taking out El-Hashem and embarrassing the Carabinieri. Either way, you're damaged goods. Now I have to take your gun and shield."

I didn't move. Getting asked for your gun and shield was like being told to hand over a kidney.

O'Neil stretched out his hand. "Miles, don't make me ask again."

I stood, reached for my hip holster, and drew my weapon. After removing the magazine and ejecting the chambered round, I set the pieces on the snack table along with my shield.

"Oh, this is fucking ridiculous." Vincent was up again, pacing behind me.

"My hands are tied, Vinny," O'Neil said.

"Yeah, well, mine too." Vincent stomped over to the snack table and threw down his shield. "Get another ticket to New York."

"Jesus, Vincent." I picked up his shield.

O'Neil pointed at Vincent. "Sit your ass down. I have no intention of putting Miles or anyone else on that plane."

Vincent ran his fingers through his hair and dropped into his seat. He took his shield back when I handed it to him. O'Neil gestured at me to sit as well.

"If we uncover the mole, and it turns out to be Carabinieri personnel, then we'll have leverage," O'Neil said. "Just imagine that kind of heat. Marino's bullshit'll stink, and the SAC will have to reinstate you, Miles."

"Maybe Marino's the mole," Vincent said. "How sweet would that be?"

O'Neil considered that for a moment. "Doubt it. He's too career driven and political. But we should suspect everyone until we don't have to."

Lightning flashed through the narrow windows, casting tall, restless shadows. We listened to the rain pelt the tile roof.

Vincent asked, "Top, did you have to pick such a spooky spot to meet?"

O'Neil glanced at our surroundings apparently noticing the warehouse interior for the first time. "Next time, I'll make sure it's warm and cozy. Just for you, Vinny."

Vincent shrugged. "Just saying."

Thunder boomed overhead. The report inside the building was explosive.

I winced.

Vincent adjusted his tie.

O'Neil didn't flinch.

"We can't risk Marino finding out that we're hunting a mole," O'Neil said. "Kamaria is Marino's link to the team, so we have to keep her on the outside."

"On the outside?" I frowned. "She's one of us, Top. She has no love for Marino."

O'Neil said, "Ultimately, she works for him. Her career rises or falls on his watch. If he starts asking questions, making threats or promises, she'll cave. We can't afford that. Besides, we're only talking about a day or two. After that, it probably won't matter."

"She's walking the gun and running firearm analysis," I reminded O'Neil.

"We'll only exclude her from the internal investigation. Her work is still relevant to the El-Hashem shooting."

"Where is she on that? On the rifle?" Vincent asked.

O'Neil replied, "She's running down where it landed after being stolen from the original owner. Only Marino keeps sidetracking her with administrative tasks he says are urgent. Now that I think about it … it might be part of a ploy to derail the investigation."

"Derail how?" I asked.

"Marino went out of his way to get you thrown off the team—not that it took a whole lot to convince the SAC." O'Neil gave me an I-told-you-so look. "It's disruptive to the investigation and demoralizing to the team. Then there's the firearm analysis. We still don't have a report matching that rifle to the round that killed El-Hashem. Kamaria keeps saying there's a delay with the lab. Meanwhile, Marino has the power to speed that up or slow it down."

Though I was sure we had the weapon used to kill our snitch, the fact that the rifle was left behind cast doubt. It could be a decoy, planted so we'd waste time and resources chasing it. We needed official confirmation.

Vincent asked, "Why? Why would he do that?"

"Like I said, Marino is a politician. He's looking to make general in the worst way, and anything that embarrasses the Carabinieri under his command threatens that ambition. So maybe he knows—or fears—there's something there and wants to keep it buried."

Vincent stretched his neck muscles. "What's the plan, Top?"

"The plan hasn't changed. Ensuring the Israeli prime minister's safety is primary. Anything we get after that is gravy. Though some of the details do change. The first we just mentioned, keeping Kamaria on the outside of the internal investigation, focused on firearm analysis, and walking the gun. Ruiz is mentoring her, so I'll tell him to step in and get that moving. Tufu and Colt can take a hard look at Bishop Cusa, see if and how he's connected to The Holy Hand."

O'Neil picked up his glasses from the table. "Vinny, I want you to follow up on the hunch. See if Bonaventura has a military record and who he served with if he does."

"What about me?" I asked.

"You'll sit on the bench until we have something I can take to the SAC."

"Won't the SAC expect me to be on that flight?"

"Your replacement was booked for a ten a.m. flight out of JFK—the only flight today with a vacancy. He never made it. His car broke down on the Belt Parkway. I had a good man driving that car. Now, you have a heart condition, don't you?"

The brutal memory of searing pain cutting across my chest while staring down the business end of a .40 caliber Glock came rushing back. Reflexively, I put my hand on my chest. "It's not an issue."

"I'll tell the SAC that your heart condition flared up when I asked for your gun and shield, and the doctor insisted on rest. That'll buy us at least twenty-four hours." O'Neil held up his index finger. "Now, listen to me very carefully. Do not run a side investigation. No phone calls. No database searches. Not a word to anyone remotely connected to this case. Stay away from command or any pertinent location. Got it? Are we absolutely clear?"

I pressed my lips together and nodded.

After a brief silence, Vincent asked, "When are we telling the team?"

"As soon as we're done here," O'Neil said. "You and I will head back to command. I'll brief people individually. Miles, you'll head back to your hotel room and stay there until I send for you."

O'Neil must've seen dejection on my face because he added, "It's not all bad. You get to rest up that knee. You're limping like a three-legged dog."

As Vincent led the way out, thoughts of being sidelined in a stuffy hotel room turned my stomach. When I considered Kamaria's unfair treatment, I understood it was a necessary and temporary policy of exclusion but not one I was bound by orders to follow. In fact, I didn't have to follow any orders. I was off the team and technically no longer under O'Neil's command.

That made me a free agent.

Chapter Twenty-Nine

A Personal Favor

Colonel Giuseppe Marino marched at a brisk pace down Riva degli Schiavoni, the famed promenade running along the Grand Canal. Struggling to keep up was Carabinieri Detective Fredo Longo.

Marino said over his shoulder, "How can a man as thin as you, with legs as long as a gondolier's oar, move so slow?"

Longo picked up the pace, his open trench coat fluttering in the chilly wind. "Your pace is difficult to match, sir."

Marino grinned. It was true. He was in superb physical condition. His daily step count averaged twenty thousand, an impressive feat for a man managing a large military police force while catering to the whims of insufferable politicians. He accomplished this by opting to walk everywhere, often receiving updates and issuing orders on the go. However, this form of mobile communication was limited to his immediate staff of handpicked lieutenants, all of whom could keep up. Not like Longo, who smoked too much and had the stamina of a fig.

Marino glanced up at him. The man was wrapped in a tacky trench coat topped off with a ridiculous fedora. Longo was an embarrassment to the Carabinieri. Still, he was tolerated.

Longo was loyal.

Longo followed orders.

Longo never asked questions.

"Where are you on the Bonaventura case?" Marino asked.

Longo gave an update long on procedure and short on substance.

"You have no leads?"

"Not at this time, sir. I believe the killer is a professional. No detectable mistakes. Had a well-executed plan that outfoxed the Americans."

Marino grinned again. *Outfoxed the Americans.*

"Did the Americans say why they were there?"

Longo had fallen back a few steps and had to jog to catch up. "They were deliberately coy, sir, and disrespectful. They would only say it pertained to their investigation and could not discuss it. I don't believe—"

"What about your partner, the woman?"

"My partner, sir?"

"What was her impression of the crime scene?"

"Amateurish"—a blast of wind forced Longo to grab hold of his ridiculous hat—"and nonsensical, sir."

Giordana was a lot smarter than Longo could ever hope to be. The mere fact that Longo couldn't see it was proof enough. She was ambitious and stubborn and bent on single-handedly changing the male-dominated culture of the Carabinieri. She was a rising star who could be contained for only so long—God knew Marino was trying his best. After all, it wasn't luck or random chance that had landed her a half-wit like Longo for a partner.

"Nonsensical?"

Longo told him about the ropes they'd found at the crime scene and Giordana's theory. "I told her not to waste time on that absurd notion." He snickered. "Bonaventura was shot, not strangled."

Marino couldn't help but smile. What an opportunity! He stopped, causing Longo to overshoot and then double back.

Marino asked, "Hasn't it occurred to you that perhaps the Americans committed this murder after torturing the poor fellow?"

Longo's face turned pink. "Well, sir, it's still very early in the—"

"Take the lead on this. Abandon the search for the boat. Tie Giordana to a desk and get the Americans to submit DNA. Have the laboratory run tests on those ropes as a priority. If so much as a single American cell is found, I want to know about it immediately. Understood?"

Going from pink to red, with trace evidence of a frown, Longo replied, "Yes, sir."

"Good, carry on."

Marino navigated the crowds gathered outside the Doge's Palace, never stopping or slowing his pace. His activity tracker read sixteen thousand steps. Good. He'd hit twenty on the walk back to his office.

Passing the two granite columns at the square's ingress (impossible to miss when entering the square from the Grand Canal side or walking along the Riva degli Schiavoni), he glanced at the statue of Saint Theodore, perched high above the column of San Todaro, holding a shield and a spear while standing firmly on a crocodile. Given what he knew of the inner workings of the city, it was most likely that Theodore had been no saint at all. Just another insufferable politician, prancing around in big shoes and wiping them clean on the backs of more-capable men. Perhaps that's what the crocodile was meant to symbolize. It was a frustrating dynamic, similar to the one he had to endure with Cardinal Perricone, whom he was to meet at the Royal Gardens up ahead.

What does the cardinal want? An update on the murder perpetrated in front of his church? Details of Marino's security plan for the upcoming arrival of the Israeli prime minister? Or was it about Bonaventura? The old man had sounded tense over the phone.

The Royal Gardens were located behind the Procuratie Nuove. Despite the impressive name, it was just an ordinary arrangement of grass, trees, and benches. The cardinal always insisted on meeting there, and it suited Marino's step count since the old man liked to walk and talk along the gravel walkways, even when the weather was unfavorable.

At the gate, he spotted Bishop Tommaso Cusa, looking grim.

"The cardinal is upset," Cusa said as Marino approached. "Speak delicately."

Marino gave the bishop a slight bow and entered the Royal Gardens. Directly in front of him was a raised circular concrete flower bed. The cardinal sat on one of the empty benches surrounding it, waving his arm as if to identify himself among a throng of Roman Catholic cardinals milling about in black cassocks and stark red skullcaps.

Marino marched over. "Your Eminence, I came as soon as I received your message."

The cardinal looked more shrunken and weather-beaten than Marino remembered.

"You mean you came as soon as it was convenient." With unexpected agility, the cardinal stood. "Walk with me."

They followed the flower bed halfway around then turned down a narrow walkway. Loitering pigeons pecked at gravel.

"When were you going to inform me of Ignazio's murder?"

Porco dio! Was nothing safe from leaks? He wanted to seize the cardinal's throat and squeeze from it the names of those loose-lipped traitors.

"You are aware that I have a vested interest in his organization. I should have been informed immediately."

"Your Eminence, you'll have to forgive me. It's never appropriate for a professional police organization to disseminate information prematurely. That could lead to … complications. I appreciate that you must remain well-informed, but in this case, it was most inappropriate of your sources to go behind my—"

The cardinal waved a liver-spotted hand, the substantial

episcopal gold ring on his index finger impossible to miss. “Save the lecture, Colonel. Tell me of this terrible crime that has been committed against a faithful member of my flock.”

“The Americans are involved. Santoro and the fat one.” Marino sidestepped a trail of pigeon droppings. “I urged our spineless mayor not to allow them to operate on Venetian soil, no matter what the politicians in Rome demanded. My command was fully capable of safeguarding the city from any terrorist attack and pursuing leads the Americans might have had. Now I have two bodies in three days as a result and more questions than answers.”

The cardinal was about to say something but seemed to reconsider. He turned randomly onto another walkway. At length, he said, “What do you mean ‘the Americans are involved’?”

“They were there when it happened.”

“Involved how?”

“We believe they tortured Mr. Bonaventura.”

“Tortured? Are you certain?”

“We are searching for DNA evidence on ropes found at the crime scene, ropes we believe were used to tie up the victim.”

The cardinal stopped walking. His face contorted and grew paler, which was jarring, given that he was already ghost white. “Merciful Father,” he said, making the sign of the cross.

“Why they were there with Mr. Bonaventura is a mystery,” Marino added. “They refused to give my detectives an explanation.”

The cardinal pursed his thin lips. “They’ve made Ignazio and The Holy Hand a focal point in their investigation of the murder in the piazza.”

Marino frowned at the cardinal. “I know nothing of this.”

The old man resumed his stroll. Marino followed.

“Ignazio and I were under surveillance. You know nothing of that either?”

Now it was Marino’s turn to stop abruptly.

The cardinal gestured at an empty bench. "Let's sit awhile."

Marino hesitated, struggling with an overwhelming urge to march straight into the task force's office, corner O'Neil, and demand answers. He would not give in to it, of course, any more than he would choke the old man.

Misfortune favors the impulsive.

He took a deep breath and joined the cardinal. Though they sat quietly, the noise inside Marino's head was deafening. He was so engrossed he let a pigeon peck at his impeccably polished boots before kicking it away.

"Your silence is telling, Colonel. It appears both investigations have gotten away from you." The cardinal glanced at Marino. "Do you see why it's important that I stay informed?"

Marino gritted his teeth.

The cardinal continued, "The Americans came to see me about the murder in the piazza, prepared with a file. A file containing surveillance photos of Ignazio and me at lunch on several occasions. This file also included financial documents, including a thorough listing of charitable donations The Holy Hand has made to my various projects."

Marino felt his chest tighten. "Did they say where they got this file?"

"They would only say it came from a reliable source."

Marino muttered, "A predictable deflection."

"It would help for you to find out who."

"I'm well aware of my duty!" Marino snapped.

The cardinal gave him a sharp look but said nothing.

After a short, awkward silence, Marino said, "So that's why they went to see Bonaventura."

The cardinal nodded.

"He wasn't a man they could have found easily, so someone told them where to look." Marino couldn't keep the accusatory tone out of his voice.

"They threatened to leak the contents of that file to the press if I didn't produce him. I cannot afford that kind of publicity." The old man hung his head, put his hands together, and slowly turned his heavy gold ring. "They gave me their word. No harm was to come to Ignazio. I took the extra precaution of warning him about their visit and implored him to cooperate. Never once have I doubted the innocence of The Holy Hand in this affair. It was a matter of convincing the Americans."

Marino understood leverage. The Americans had been smart to use the file. It's exactly what he would have done.

The cardinal sighed heavily. "Ignazio was a misguided sinner. A stray at times, I'll admit. He was true to the faith, however, and a key member of my flock. You must find justice for him, Colonel. I'd consider it a personal favor."

Marino stood. "I have two of my best detectives on the case, Your Eminence. I am confident we'll make an arrest soon."

Chapter Thirty

The Arsenale

It was dark, and the chilly wind had teeth.

Nabeel Haddad shivered under his thin thobe as he steered the package delivery motorboat toward the matching towers looming on opposite sides of the canal. They looked like rooks on a chessboard fit for giants.

The address surprised him.

The Arsenale, as the shipyard was called, was not open to visitors unless Venice was hosting La Biennale di Venezia art exhibition. But, it was open tonight.

Tired and hungry, a hot tea would do him good. He was ambivalent about delaying Isha, the evening prayer, to deliver the last package of the day, yet, he couldn't be happier. Dalia had called earlier and told him that Amir would be admitted to the new hospital by the end of the week. It was the first good news in a long time and made him smile inside. His outside smile never faded, but it had no beating heart behind it. Today, it did.

His conscience was also clear; he had placed the call to the police.

If there was something troubling about the hidden man in the room or the Armenian with the drifting eye who had given him the mysterious package to deliver in the middle of the night, it was now up to the police to discover. He told them everything. Everything, that is, except his identity. The police officer who took his call had transferred him to a trickster who tried to get his name. Nabeel said nothing on that account. Dalia would be proud.

Passing the towers, Nabeel negotiated a right turn in the widening canal and steered into a large expanse of water that was the heart of the shipyard.

For centuries, the Arsenale was where they'd built the vessels that had given Venice its military and economic power. It was a chapter of history he often liked to share piecemeal with Amir and Dalia. History he'd learned at one of the many museums in the city.

He'd also learned a great deal about gondolas, like the fact that eight different kinds of woods are used in their construction, selected for weight, strength, flexibility, and water resistance. The port side (or left side when facing forward, as he often had to remind Amir) was made longer than the starboard side to resist a left-turning tendency when the gondolier applied the forward stroke of the oar. He had fallen in love with the flat-bottom Venetian rowing boat and dreamt of becoming a gondolier. He'd asked every gondolier he came across how he could become one of them. The few who would talk said a gondolier to teach and a gondola for practice were required. Then a school, the academy of gondoliers. And finally, a license from the guild if he passed the test. But no gondolier was willing to take him on as an apprentice. They all said it was a centuries-old tradition passed down from father to son. Those with no sons insisted they only took on family members. A few were unkind, mocking his devotion to Islam. Still, Nabeel was determined. God willing, he would show them he could be one of the four hundred gondoliers who carried on the noble trade.

In the light of the streetlamps on the wide walkways lining the shipyard, Nabeel eyed the package. Anchored in place by a net, the plain square cardboard box looked insignificant on the long deck of the motorboat. Its dimensions were similar, he realized, to the box he'd used to ship an authentic European football to Amir, a ball his son had yet to play with. When he heaved a heavy sigh that threatened to spoil his mood, he reminded himself that now there was hope Amir would someday use it. God willing, he might even score goals like the great Lionel Messi!

Piloting from the stern of the motorboat, he worked the rudder to navigate an elongated S course. He passed rows of buildings set far back on the quays. Each of them had once served a specific purpose in the process of shipbuilding: manufacturing parts, assembling ships, making munitions. He didn't know what they were currently used for. Perhaps some of those buildings still made ships. Or gondolas! Until that moment, it had never occurred to him where the gondolas were made or serviced. The more thought he gave it, the more convinced he became that this was the place.

Minutes later, he slowed the motorboat to scan the buildings on the port side of the craft. The delivery instructions did not specify a building number. They simply pointed to the building directly in front of the last pier before the shipyard emptied into the Venetian Lagoon. When that pier came into view, he cut the engine and steered toward it, aiming for an empty spot behind another motorboat. Once he'd securely moored the boat, he detached the net from a set of hooks and picked up the package. Its weight surprised him. He estimated five kilos. Whatever it was, it was heavier than a soccer ball. A gift from Murano, perhaps? A set of those multicolored glass balls Dalia loved so much?

With the box firmly under his arm, he stepped off the boat and onto the pier. He checked his watch. The instructions were explicit regarding the delivery time. His employer offered that option, within a ten-minute window, to anyone willing to pay a premium. Few did.

He ambled over to a set of stucco buildings, aiming for the one directly in front of the pier. The two nearest streetlamps were out. In the dusk, Nabeel could see the building was tall and wide and industrial with large front doors and no windows. He approached the wicket in one of the doors and knocked. All he got was a hollow report.

In the wind, he picked up the scents of charred wood and iron. Not unpleasant, just unexpected. Ghosts of the past? After his second knock went unanswered, he stepped back to look around. The place seemed abandoned.

Did he have the exact address? The right time? He rechecked, and both were correct. What to do? He pulled out his phone to call his employer. Before he hit speed dial, the package he held vibrated and rang. He put an ear to the box and pulled back when it rang again. It sounded like a phone. Why would a ringing phone be inside a sealed package? Who would call it? The box was too big and heavy for just a phone. What else could ring like that? He studied the packaging. There was nothing special about it, just a strip of clear packing tape running along the top and bottom. He could cut it, look inside, and reseal it. He had tape on the boat.

Jabbing the tip of his tongue at the hole of his missing front tooth, he put the box down on the quay and crouched. With a sharp thumbnail, he split the tape and opened the box. Inside was a phone lying on a bed of packing peanuts, whining like a baby. He grabbed it.

"Nabeel Haddad?"

He knew that voice! Deep and commanding, the Arabic pronunciation flawless.

"Yes," Nabeel croaked, "it is I."

"Do you know who I am?"

Licking his dry lips, Nabeel replied, "You are the man who knew of my son's illness ... may the peace and mercy of Allah be with you."

"I am also the man who paid handsomely for your services, Nabeel Haddad. Services you failed to render."

"Sir? I-I delivered the package—a suitcase—to the address the man you instructed me to see had given me—at the specified hour."

"That much is true. But you were also paid to keep a tight tongue."

Nabeel felt nauseous. He became aware of his rapidly beating heart. "Sir? I-I told no one."

"You are a good Muslim, Nabeel Haddad, but a bad liar."

"Sir, I-I—"

"Beware that your tongue might cut your throat."

Nabeel shifted his weight from one foot to the other, the phone heavy in his hand. "Sir, please. I-I never—"

"Look inside the box." The man's voice seemed to grow louder. Closer.

Nabeel's mind was moving faster than his heart was beating.

How did the man know he told someone? Did he know it was the police? Was that possible? Even so, Nabeel never identified himself or offered a clue as to who he was.

"Are you listening, Nabeel Haddad? Look inside the box!"

Nabeel winced.

Still holding the phone to his ear with one hand, he scooped out a layer of packing peanuts with the other. He was immediately assaulted by the pungent odor of rotting fruit. The smell of iron he'd caught in the wind earlier was much stronger. His hand shook so badly he made a tight fist in a vain attempt to steady it. He scooped out another layer of packing peanuts and froze when his fingers brushed against something cold and clammy.

"Sir, p-please … I'm just a humble—" Nabeel dropped the phone.

The top half of a human face jutted from the packing peanuts. Both eyes—as independent from one another as those of a chameleon—were open wide. One was grotesquely turned to the outer edge of its eye socket. The other stared directly at him. He sprang to his feet but couldn't run. His legs were rooted. His eyes fixed. The box held a morbid fascination.

Nabeel never saw the approaching shadow. He never heard the unsheathing of the dagger or the light footsteps. Nor did his nose catch the whiff of hand-rolled cigarettes, even as it drew intimately close. He did feel the raw power of a muscular arm seizing him from behind, wrapping itself quickly around his neck and squeezing.

Before he could muster a cry or a word of protest, he was paralyzed by a flash of pain. The long dagger, passing easily through his thobe, pierced his kidney.

His final vision, flashing fast and bright in his mind, was of Amir running past a row of defenders on a lush European football field, dribbling the ball Nabeel had sent him between nimble feet. In the stands stood sweet Dalia, cheering as their son managed a maneuver only the best players could match. And as the ball lifted off Amir's foot, curving at an impossible angle toward the corner of the goal post, darkness came.

Chapter Thirty-One

When in Venice

When in Venice, you eat like the Venetians. That means seafood.

Kamaria and I waited for a table at Il Ostrica, a small seafood restaurant near my hotel. We had an eight o'clock reservation, but it didn't seem to matter. The place had only nine tables, and no one was in a rush to leave. At the bar, I milked a beer while Kamaria enjoyed a glass of white wine.

"I am sorry this has happened to you, Miles. I did not expect it. Marino is difficult, this is true, but I did not think of him as vengeful."

"Is that what it was?"

Kamaria bit her lower lip. "I do not know for certain, but what else could it be? You did … how to say? Challenge him? Superiors are quick to anger over insubordination."

I knew it was payback. You don't show up the brass and walk away unscathed. But I was curious what she thought and hoped she'd share the gossip circulating in the ranks of the Carabinieri. Instead, she'd summed me up accurately as insubordinate.

She put her hand on my shoulder. "When will you leave?"

"Tomorrow night."

"Are you upset?"

I finished my beer and set the empty bottle on the counter. "I'll get over it."

"What will happen when you are in New York? Will you still be a policeman?"

"Technically, yes. I'll be handcuffed to a desk, pushing paper until my union and the brass work things out. My guess is they'll add a naughty-cop letter to my file and officially pull me from the task force. I doubt it'll get any worse than that. Homicide always needs good, experienced detectives to clear cases."

She nodded. "You will miss Venice?"

I glanced at her. "You mean will I miss you?"

She laughed. "Oh, I know you will miss me."

I smiled. "You'll come to New York for a Broadway show and dinner. I cook a mean Creole gumbo and jambalaya."

"You can cook too?"

"On the dance floor, I'm James Brown, and in the kitchen, Emeril Lagasse."

"Is that so? And who are you in the bedroom?" she asked with a lopsided grin.

As a good rejoinder was coming to mind, the bartender interrupted with another round of beer and white wine. In good English, he struck up a random conversation, which morphed into griping about the giant cruise ships jamming up the Grand Canal and dumping disaster on St. Mark's Square. When I asked what he meant, he explained that the ships were an environmental disaster for the Venetian Lagoon, a traffic disaster in the canal, and the tourist influx they brought was a cultural disaster for the residents. He then bemoaned the disaster of politicians too weak and corrupt to do what was needed. And all of this was compounded by the disaster of the water gate construction project, which was meant to keep Venice above water. He ended by recommending the sea bass tartare and pointing out what a disaster it was when served without prawns carpaccio.

I was about to pick up where we left off when Kamaria asked, "When will you tell me about your meeting with the CIA? No one is talking about it."

That topic, as the bartender would have succinctly put it, was a disaster.

"My meeting with the CIA? Oh, big waste of time. The spooks denied everything."

The stools we sat on were uncomfortably tall, and skimped on back support. To boot, the leather was slippery. None of that seemed to bother Kamaria. She crossed her arms and legs and leaned back, not sliding an inch. I kept my eyes on my beer bottle, turning it slowly, feeling her frown boring into the side of my skull.

"You must do better than that. I detect deception. You did not make eye contact, and you repeated my question." She paused, which underscored the restaurant's soft acoustic music and din of animated conversation. "Have I done something wrong to betray the team's trust?"

Damn.

Struggling to keep from sliding off the stool, I turned to her. She looked smoking in a short, formfitting red dress and black stiletto heels sharp enough to puncture Kevlar. Her hair hung in tight cornrows, each braid ending in a trio of gold beads. She could have passed for the Queen of the Nile.

"Tell me," she said.

I blinked a couple of times to jumpstart the higher order functions of my brain. "There's no lack of trust. You've proven yourself. You're one of us. It's just that O'Neil felt ... well, the information is—"

"Is what? You are upsetting me, Detective Jordan."

Detective Jordan? Ouch!

I sighed and raised my hands in surrender. "You're right, you're absolutely right. You're an active member of the team and you should know."

Being a free agent made it easy to disregard orders. I told Kamaria about my meeting with CIA Field Supervisor Franklin Shears. I didn't mention the mole or give any details regarding the debriefing with O'Neil. I also left out the amateur shooter angle and how that strengthened the CIA's claim of innocence. As I talked, her frown melted away and her arms unfolded. She listened without interruption, occasionally nodding to let me know she was actively listening.

When I was done, we sat quietly.

Kamaria put her hand on my forearm. "I understand why O'Neil did not wish to share this information. I cannot blame him. It is smart. I have heard of The Holy Hand. People say they have powerful members."

"Like who?"

"No one knows for certain. Only rumors. It would not surprise me if some of their members are Carabinieri."

"And why is that?"

"Many are religious, and most feel threatened by Islam."

"They ever been investigated? The Holy Hand, I mean."

"Yes. Most recently, with regard to the bombing in Rome. The investigations do not grow fruit."

Maybe because their infiltrators in the Carabinieri are burying them?

She added, "I believe this is a good lead, Miles. The involvement of The Holy Hand must be investigated."

"I guess you're right. It's a lead, and it's all we've got anyway. The CIA won't talk to us again."

Kamaria sighed. "I envy you. You are in a good place in the investigation."

A good place? She forgot I just got kicked off. Still, I saw her point.

She'd volunteered to drive firearm analysis from the start as something of a training exercise. It was a bum assignment. Tracking down the registered owner of a gun in hopes that the perpetrator who used that weapon in a crime and the owner are one and the same was usually a waste of time. Guns are often sold without paperwork. Guns are also reported lost or stolen.

"Any luck with the rifle?" I asked.

Kamaria looked down at her empty hands. "I found the American gun collector who owned it. The lab was able to recover enough of the serial number—you remember it was filed. The man knew the Walther gun well. It was his favorite. He was very happy to learn we found it after seven years of theft." She scratched her eyebrow. "When I told him it had been used in a crime, he was very upset."

"Was that the only gun stolen from his collection?"

"He said four guns were taken from his home. He believes the thief is a rival gun collector but has no evidence. The rival was investigated and never charged. Good alibi for the day of the theft. So, I am in the mud, stuck."

"A rare rifle like that has got to draw a hit somewhere," I said.

Between her fingers, she rotated a couple of napkins on the varnished bar counter. "This is true. I found three purchased at gun shows and one in a large gun shop. The owners have them still."

She made no mention of Marino's attempt to sidetrack her, as O'Neil had suggested. She was obviously putting in the overtime needed to satisfy Marino and still move her side of the investigation forward. That's what good cops do, which made her temporary exclusion from the team all the more unfair.

"What do you think, Miles? Am I wasting time?"

I rubbed my goatee, thinking that, among criminals, the rifle could have changed hands a half dozen times.

"Conducting an investigation is like baking a cake," I told her. "You can get away with adding a bit too much of this or not enough of that. But if you skip a step in the process, you run the risk of ruining the entire confection. So even though I think walking this gun is a likely dead end, it has to be done."

Kamaria nodded.

"What does Ruiz think?"

Kamaria rolled her eyes. "He tells me to keep looking but does not suggest where. He is never in the office to help. Oh! This reminds me. The firearm analysis gave confirmation. The bullet that killed El-Hashem was fired from the Walther rifle you found."

"When did they confirm it?"

"Today, early evening."

The news was expected but still a relief. "How about we take a break from the case?"

She pushed the napkins aside and reached for her wineglass. "I like your suit. Blue is a good color. You should wear it often."

Good thing I'd brought extra suits to Venice. The one I'd worn in the morning was out of commission. Damp, rumpled, and stinking of the day's unpleasant events.

"Been wearing a suit to work every day for ten years. It was nice to take a break from it while being undercover. By the way, did I tell you that you look more stunning than St. Mark's Square lit up at night?"

She smiled. "Three times."

"Only three?"

She pinned her eyes on mine. "You are a sweet man. And a poet!"

"You're too kind. What I have is a runaway sweet tooth, and I write poetry like Dr. Seuss."

She scrunched her lips. "Dr. Seuss? I do not know him."

"A famous American writer. Children's books."

"Tell me his poetry."

"His poetry? I guess you can call it that. Okay, ready?"

She leaned in a little closer. *Lilac and freesia.*

In my best James Earl Jones imitation, I quoted a few of my favorite Dr. Seuss lines.

Kamaria laughed, covering her mouth with her hand. "I understand nothing you said. But it is funny, like a funny song."

"It was my favorite book growing up. Knew it by heart. Still do."

"How do you make green eggs with ham?"

I paused. "Never thought about it. Food coloring? Veggies?"

"What is veggies?"

The hostess approached us with two leather-bound menus in hand. "This way, *signore*."

Instead of taking our drinks, we clinked glasses and chugged them down on the count of three. I slid off the high stool and took Kamaria by the hand.

The lanky hostess weaved through the tight spaces between the tables with ease, and with the exception of one particularly narrow spot, so did Kamaria. I, on the other hand, was a tornado. My belly and ass conspired to squeeze, shove, and dislodge unwary diners along the way. I couldn't say "excuse me" or "sorry" fast enough. Most of the diners were British and seemed to take the onslaught in stride.

"It's quite all right, old chap!"

"Nary a scratch. Didn't fall arse over tit!"

"Everything is tickety-boo!"

After knocking a French tourist off his chair—a shrieked "*monsieur*" and an "*excusez-moi*" giving him away—the other diners sitting in the tornado's path quickly made room by dragging their chairs and tables aside as many inches as they could. When we made it to our table and I sat, everyone cheered. Kamaria pretended not to notice. I was flustered, feeling like a complete fool. I should have picked a bigger restaurant.

The hostess handed us the menus, which were engraved with the Italian words "Il Ostrica" and a dubious drawing of an oyster.

At the bar, I'd been too distracted by Kamaria and the case to give the place much notice. Now seated against the wall, I took stock. The restaurant had a contemporary décor. The walls were plaster and bare of artwork. Foot-long cylindrical chrome spotlights dangled over each table on electrical cords snaked from the ceiling. The tables and chairs were wood and chrome, with boxy shapes and smooth surfaces. The sweet aromas of sautéed onions, rosemary, garlic, and Parmesan cheese wafted through the air. Our table was set with wild-colored glasses and a glass candleholder. The silverware was flat and boring, but went well with the fluted chrome vase propping up a sunflower. Everything was carefully arranged over a cream-colored tablecloth.

I was still pretty embarrassed and couldn't look Kamaria in the eye. But when she reached over and held my hand I couldn't help myself. Her hazel eyes were beautiful to look at. We smiled at each other.

"I like this place," she said.

"I Googled the five best restaurants in Venice."

Her eyes widened. "This is among the five best?"

"No, but I liked the reviews anyway."

She punched my hand playfully.

"Oh, I love this candleholder." Turning it between her fingers, she added, "I must have it. I have so many candles in my apartment. The light … how to say? Softens the mind?"

"Soothes?"

"Yes, soothes the mind."

The problem with fine dining in Venice is that you can order a five-course meal and still leave the restaurant hungry. The portions were sized for elves. I'd snacked on a bowl of seafood risotto from a nearby trattoria about an hour before picking up Kamaria and figured that would hold me. I was wrong. My stomach growled as I read the menu: roast pilgrim scallops, black spaghetti with anchovies, grilled octopus, braised short rib ravioli, roasted branzino with caper butter, guinea hen with truffles, poached halibut.

A few minutes after I'd selected a Pinot Grigio, the waiter was skillfully pouring it into our wineglasses. He then asked if we were ready to order. We nodded. Kamaria ordered the fish soup with pasta and green lemon to start and the guinea hen with truffles for her entrée. I ordered a sardine sandwich with ricotta cheese and candied capers for my appetizer (it sounded tastier than the sea bass tartare the bartender had recommended) and the grilled octopus with fava beans and turnip tops for the main event.

When our appetizers were served, Kamaria asked, "What do you know about your ancestors?"

I took a quick bite of my sardine sandwich. It was a joy. The candied capers were an entirely new taste experience for me—tangy, briny, sweet. Too bad the sandwich was the size of a Twinkie.

"My ancestors? They were slaves, Kamaria."

She salted her soup. "Yes, but where in Africa did they come from?"

Another two bites and my sandwich would be a fond memory. *How would it look if I ordered another?*

"Hold that thought." I waved the waiter over and ordered another sardine sandwich, asking Kamaria if she wanted to try one. She declined, saying she needed to leave room for the guinea hen.

"I am still holding my thought." Kamaria skimmed the surface of her soup with a spoon and tasted it. "This soup is very good."

"Your thought?"

"Yes. Your African ancestors. Where did they come from?"

"Oh, that." I finished my first sandwich. "My grandmother has always insisted our ancestors came from Sierra Leone or that area of West Africa before the country was founded. Where she got that notion is a mystery, but she's been waiting on me to come up with the proof."

"Because you are a detective?"

I nodded. "She thinks I can find out anything."

The waiter arrived with my second sandwich and poured more wine before dashing off. A busboy brought more bread, which seemed to be the only food staple in abundance.

Kamaria buttered a slice of bread. "Did you?"

"Did I what?"

"Did you investigate for your grandmama?"

I shook my head. "I hated the idea of poring over a slave ship manifest. Besides, without a ship name, how would I locate the right manifest if it even existed? I did do some research on Sierra Leone. Do you know about the cotton tree?"

She shook her head and sipped another spoonful of soup.

I said, "It's the symbol of Freetown, the capital. The city was built around this enormous cotton tree."

She put down the spoon and wiped her mouth with a cloth napkin. "I remember now. It is many, many meters tall, and very, very wide."

I sipped some wine; it was too light and a bit more fruity than oaky, but it still worked with the candied capers and sardines. "It's ironic."

"What is?"

"Calling it Freetown. It used to be a slave-trading port."

"It is not ironic. It is healing. Mother Africa reunited with her children."

While I reflected on that optimistic view of one of history's darkest chapters, our appetizer plates were cleared, our wineglasses topped off, and our entrées served. Before me lay a work of culinary art: grilled tentacles in a spiral arrangement garnished with parsley and a light wine sauce over a puree that had to be the fava beans and turnip tops. Kamaria's dish looked just as appetizing, the guinea hen wrapped as a wheel with truffle stuffing in the middle and garnished with nuts, fingerling potatoes, and a honey-brown sauce.

I reached for my wineglass and held it up. "To good company."

We clinked glasses.

"This octopus is amazing," I said between chews. "Would you like to try it?"

We tasted each other's food, comfortably passing loaded forks between us. To me, that's about as intimate as a couple can get in a public place without risking arrest for lewdness.

"Will you dance with me again?" Kamaria's eyes had wine in them.

"Just name the place."

"Under the cotton tree, in Sierra Leone."

I was overcome by a sudden urge to board a plane to Africa with Kamaria by my side. Our eyes flirted across the small table that separated us. Rum and coke, gin and tonic. That was us. A beautiful woman and a handsome fat man. What a pair we must've made.

Chapter Thirty-Two

Ponte dei Sospiri

After dinner, we made our way down narrow, winding streets until we reached a canal. Converted gas streetlights and lanterns affixed to brackets bolted into the building exteriors provided a warm, golden illumination. In the water, the lights shimmered like moons. Kamaria took my hand and dragged me across a short bridge. On the other side, a gondolier wearing the traditional black-and-white-striped shirt and straw hat smoked a cigarette. He stood on the jetty where his handsome boat was docked.

"Come, Miles. We will ride a gondola."

I don't like boats. They shift under my weight the moment I set foot in them, making me feel I'll lose my balance, tip over, and bounce into the water. Humpty Dumpty. The humiliation of the fall would pale in comparison to having the incident recorded on someone's phone and posted on the Internet for the world to see. This is the age we live in, where the eye of the camera was omnipresent. As a cop, I was sharply attuned to it, knowing every action I took, every word I said was material for someone's camera phone. It was a harrowing way to do the job.

As we approached, I eyed the gondola's black lacquer finish and sleek, elegant body with suspicion. It looked too small and filled me with a sense of foreboding. I stopped. Kamaria turned around and put her hands on her hips.

"The big man is afraid of a little boat?" Her smile turned into that lopsided grin that always made her look mischievous and sexy.

"Of course not," I lied.

"You first." She pointed to the boat and turned to talk to the gondolier.

I took a deep breath, grasped the jetty railing, and boarded.

The gondola rocked as all boats do, but boxed in by two red-and-white-striped poles, and perhaps because of its unusual design (curvier and bulkier on one side), it was stabler than I expected. I staggered into its lavish passenger cabin without incident, landing in a loveseat with ornate framing and a tufted back; the walls of the cabin had elaborate wood carvings, including one of the winged lion.

Kamaria sat next to me. It was a snug and cozy fit.

The gondolier assumed his position behind us, standing on the stern. He worked the oar, which rested on a wooden fulcrum projecting from the side of the boat. Soon, we were underway.

"He is Luigi," Kamaria said. "The gondolier."

I turned and nodded at Luigi.

Under his straw hat, I glimpsed a brushstroke of silver and a craggy face. He was older than I expected, perhaps early sixties, and showed no signs of exertion despite the heavy cargo. He rowed the boat with ease, so he was either a lot stronger than he looked, or the gondola was a highly efficient craft. We glided along the dark water as gracefully as a duck in a pond. I felt like a kid on a waterpark ride.

"This is great." I put my arm around Kamaria. "Now I really feel like I'm in Venice!"

"*Fantastico.*"

We kissed.

Kamaria reached in her purse for her phone. "I want a picture." She held the phone at arm's length while pressing her smooth face against mine.

"Hold on, I'll do it." I took the phone and held it out so I could frame the gondolier and the canal in the background. "Smile."

I snapped the photo. The flash was blinding.

"Another," she said.

I took another photo. "Perfect!" I quickly stashed her phone in my suit jacket, fearing a third photo would burn a hole in my retina.

"How do you know it is perfect?"

"I'm a trained professional."

"I want to see."

I pulled out her phone and held it out so she could unlock it. Then, I scrolled to the first photo, where I was squinting and smiling stiffly. In the second, I looked like a thief caught in a patrol car spotlight.

"See? Perfect." I smiled.

Kamaria looked unsure. "We will do another when we reach the piazza."

"Fair enough."

"May I have back my phone?"

The sound of the gondolier's oar dipping in and out of the water was soothing. Muffled conversation flowed from open windows, and laughter and gaiety issued from a nearby marketplace. The buildings we passed were stained with a foot-wide band of algae created by the rising waters that threatened to destroy the fabled city.

I asked, "How bad is the flooding?"

"It is bad in winter—*acqua alta.* Streets and piazzas flood. The water can rise to sixty centimeters for three or four hours per day. Then the … how to say? Tide?"

I nodded.

"The tide is less, and the water returns to the canals."

The bartender had explained that the disaster of MOSE—Modulo Sperimentale Elettromeccanico, or Experimental Electromechanical Module, the water gate construction project meant to protect Venice from flooding—was making the flooding worse by redirecting and disrupting the water flow.

"At least the MOSE project is underway," I said.

"It is worse for the *acqua alta.*"

"Sometimes things have to get worse before they get better."

The bow of the gondola, which tapered to the metal prow that cut the water, pointed to a bridge high above the canal.

"What's that?" I pointed.

"This is the Ponte dei Sospiri. I do not know how to translate. It joins the Doge's Palace to the prison."

"The Bridge of Sighs."

"Size?"

I demonstrated a sigh.

"Ah, *sospiri.*"

The bridge was enclosed and made entirely of white stone with sculpted figurines, scrolls, and pilasters. Two latticework windows looking out like a pair of square eyes were probably meant to tease the doomed headed for the prison with splintered views of freedom, back in the days when the powerful doges ruled Venice.

I had my arm around Kamaria, her head resting on my shoulder. As the gondola approached, I could see that the bridge rose at least two stories above the waterline. Beyond it was a pedestrian bridge, looking suddenly small and ordinary against the backdrop of the Grand Canal.

Kamaria said, "When a couple kisses under the bridge…"

She lifted her head from my shoulder and crossed her arms.

"Something wrong?"

She stared into space.

"Kamaria? What's wrong?"

"I cannot do this." A frown creased her forehead.

"Do what? What can't you do?"

"You cannot understand."

"Try me."

She craned her head upward toward the bridge. "It is said, when a couple kisses under the Ponte dei Sospiri at sunrise, they will have eternal love."

"Is that what you're upset about?" I tried injecting humor into my voice. "We'll just come back at sunrise. I'll even spring for the ride."

"You are a sweet man, a good man. I … you do not deserve this."

The arm I had around her suddenly felt heavy and intrusive. I pulled it back and reached for her hand. "I'm not trying to force anything. Whatever happens, happens. I'm just happy to be here with you."

"My parents. The war. I am broken. I am not like other women."

"That makes you special."

"Special?" She tittered. "Oh, I am so very special."

"You *are* special."

"I live. My parents do not. Their spirits visit me at night in terrible dreams. And they accuse me. Not with words. With their eyes, with sad faces. They blame me for living. They blame me for inviting death into our home."

I squeezed her hand. "We talked about this. You had no reason to suspect your family was in any danger. And you were just a kid."

"I ignored Mother's scream. I moved faster when Father rushed to stop me. I killed them! Do you not see?"

"Don't do this."

"I cannot love."

Love?

We had shared an intense but brief connection, one counted in days. *Why is she telling me this? Does she see something in me, a future perhaps?*

I wanted to soothe her, remind her that we were just two lonely people out on a nice date. There was no past or future. There was only the moment.

But the mood had changed.

She had changed.

Chapter Thirty-Three

Gun Collector

Day 4

Thursday, 0005 hours

At St. Mark's Square, Kamaria drifted away alone in the gondola.

I limped across the promenade and past the Doge's Palace. Lights blazed from every window of the Procuraties, creating a Christmas-light effect that rivaled Rockefeller Center in December, and the basilica glittered like a gold crown under strategically placed spotlights.

Kamaria's presence still lingered: her touch, her scent, the soul in her voice. Nothing is more distracting or consuming to a man than a special lady occupying choice real estate in his mind. *What did she mean when she said she couldn't do this? That I didn't deserve it?* It was just a date. Our second date, really. She said she was broken. Is that what I didn't deserve, her broken self?

Well, I was broken too.

Perhaps she was the glue that could fix me.

Perhaps I could fix her.

I wanted to tell her that. I wanted to reach for my phone and tell her to give me a chance to fix her—one date at a time. But I knew I wouldn't.

I learned a long time ago that a woman's mind is a complex

apparatus, as foreign to me as it was appealing. I'd stopped trying to figure it out. Instead, I relied on scant clues to piece together the messages and unlock the mysteries. And I always seemed to fall short, either by correctly deciphering the message and drawing the wrong conclusion or by missing it entirely. Sometimes I wondered if the clues were not scant at all, but instead solid leads I just didn't know how to follow. Regardless, this flaw was the reason for my two failed marriages.

Operating on autopilot, I limped halfway across the square and stopped in front of the Procuratie Vecchie. The window where it had all started was as brightly lit as the rest. There was nothing ominous or telling about it. No one would suspect that a high-powered rifle had been fired from it—and killed a man—simply by looking at it. Still, it had happened. A shooter working behind that window, behind those venetian blinds.

A man behind a blind is like a lion in the grass.

Staring at the window took me back to the day of the shooting…

The shooter loomed at the window, a dark, menacing figure behind the blinds. His featureless face watching the unfolding chaos in the square … no … not the square.

He was watching me!

He made me. He knew I'd seen him.

What did that mean? Did he…?

Fearful that the slightest movement would erase the idea taking shape in my mind, I stood very still. A moment later, I texted Vincent to ask him to check if anyone had taken more than one radio on the day of the shooting.

My phone rang.

"Yo, talk to me," I said.

"No cigar. I know a chick down in the equipment room. Had her look. No one checked out more than one radio, and all radios were accounted for. Not a bad idea to check. Though really all the shooter needed was the frequency and the encryption code, so any radio would do. And everybody had that info."

I hung my head. "Knew it was a long shot."

"You heading back to the hotel, I hope."

"I'm halfway there, man."

"Right, and I'm Cinderella getting ready to hit the town with the seven dwarfs."

"Snow White."

"What?"

"Snow White was the one with the dwarfs."

Vincent blew out a deep breath. "Don't fuck up, Miles. O'Neil is going out on a limb for you. Sit tight, follow orders. We'll get something soon O'Neil can work with and get you reinstated."

We ended the call.

Sit tight, follow orders. I never had a problem following orders, so long as those orders didn't interfere with the momentum of an ongoing investigation. When they did, I couldn't help but succumb to rebellion and deceit.

Before I turned to leave, I glanced at the night owls with camera phones roaming the square. Here was one of the most romantic and inspiring places on the planet, and instead of engaging each other, people were busy with their phones.

I missed Kamaria.

What olive branch could I offer her? A new lead, perhaps? She'd walked the rifle to a dead end. Since other guns were also lifted from the same collection, she'd logically followed that line to other gun collectors. Those too had been dead ends.

Did she check the buyers and sellers with whom the original collector had done business?

Being the thorough investigator she was, I assumed she had. However, she hadn't mentioned it, and only now had it occurred to me. Maybe she hadn't gotten around to it. I reached for my phone and hesitated. It was too late to call, and she might get annoyed at me for asking anyway. Besides, the point was to surprise her with a new lead.

I glanced at my phone clock. It was still early enough in the

States. I could call the gun collector and ask him myself.

* * *

The Carabinieri headquarters was a spooky place at night. Poorly lit, the stone entryway and garden beyond had the warmth and charm of a graveyard. Even the sound of the fountain had the eerie undertone of setting the stage for the dead to rise.

I opened the double doors of the building and hesitated. The night sergeant sat behind the hallway desk, reading a newspaper. The word was out that I was off the case, and desk personnel had likely been advised that I was no longer welcome in the building, let alone the task force squad room. For a moment, I considered calling it a night. But I'd made it that far and was too wired to sleep anyway. Then I got an idea.

Cops, regardless of locale or jurisdiction, share a common love of baked goods. It begins innocently enough with a cookie here, a slice of cake there. Gradually, that love nurtures a greedy sweet tooth as they accumulate years on the job. It gets to the point where a box of donuts will trigger a feeding frenzy among the veterans, not unlike a school of hungry piranhas. I called a nearby café that caters to night owls and ordered a half dozen pastries. I told them to deliver them to the desk sergeant under the patronage of an anonymous citizen.

I lurked in the shadows of the garden until the delivery boy arrived a few minutes later. The sweet aroma of fried dough from the greasy paper bag he carried wafted in the cool air. When he had the desk sergeant's undivided attention, I snuck through the doors and climbed the stairs to the task force squad room.

The room was empty. A part of me was disappointed that Vincent wasn't there to give me the third degree. I guess I was feeling a little lonely and sorry for myself. Strumming tiny violins wasn't how I rolled, but even I have tender cuts of heart that sometimes hurt.

The smell of espresso and cigarettes was fresh, a telltale sign that the team had put in another late night. A couple of desk lamps cast faint spots of light. The paperwork on each desk had doubled since the shooting. Everyone was busy chasing public tips and old leads and trying to develop new ones. Even my desk was stacked with folders, most likely items other investigators thought I might find interesting.

I walked over to Kamaria's desk—the least cluttered in the office—and turned on her light. I grabbed her investigative work binder and flipped through it until I found the firearm analysis report. In plain Italian, it confirmed the match between the bullets recovered from the wood panels of the maize cart at the square and the Walther rifle I'd found. I flipped through more pages until I found an investigation call form. There were only two names on it: Hank Robin and Wendell Givens. From Kamaria's notes, Robin, age sixty-four, was the original owner of the rifle, an avid gun collector who owned and operated a midsize ranch in Whitefish, Montana. Givens, forty-six, the man Robin had fingered as a suspect in the burglary, was listed as a furniture manufacturer and small arms collector, also a resident of Montana.

I sat, frowning at the call form. Only two names? I would expect at least a dozen, starting with the original case investigators, followed by other collectors, witnesses to the burglary, if any, neighbors, and family, friends, and acquaintances of the two men listed. Kamaria said Givens had a solid alibi. Who? Why wasn't that name listed? References to the original investigators, or even a case number, were nowhere to be found.

Was Kamaria keeping another binder? If so, where? Those binders never left the squad room.

I picked up the phone and dialed the first number. On the third ring, a man with a gruff voice answered.

"Hank Robin speaking."

"Mr. Robin, this is Detective Miles Jordan with the New York Police Department and the FBI."

"FBI? Well now, ain't that a surprise."

Shit, I forgot.

Being from Montana and a rancher, Mr. Robin was likely not a fan of the federal government. He might also be a member of the local militia and dislike minorities. Changing my voice wasn't an option, but at least I could have left the Feds out of my fancy introduction.

"Sorry to bother you at this time."

"Ain't no bother, even if you're government. Just me and my rig cruising around the ranch. Have a wolf problem."

I heard the creaky complaints of a vehicle forced to roll over rough terrain.

"Perhaps you can pull over?"

"Sure. Just give me a minute till I get my rig over a stubborn hump."

I waited out the roar of a big engine and the slip and catch of spinning tires over dirt or gravel. I imagined a rusty pickup struggling uphill and Mr. Robin executing the tricky maneuver with one experienced hand on the steering wheel and a half-eaten stick of beef jerky in the other. A few seconds later, the engine noise leveled out and died, the tires went silent.

"Ain't nothing reliable as a Ford. Can't imagine what possessed my neighbor to buy Japanese. Must be catching Alzheimer's. You drive a Ford, sir?"

"My G-ride was a Ford."

"Beg your pardon?"

"My government ride, or government-issued law enforcement vehicle."

"G-ride … I like that. Maybe I'll start calling my rig the H-ride, as in Hank issued." He let out a throaty laugh.

"Mr. Robin, the—"

"Call me Hank. Mr. Robin is for swindling lawyers and ranch hands. I didn't catch your name."

"Detective Miles Jordan."

"Detective? I thought you FBI types were agents. At least you are on TV."

"I'm a detective assigned to an FBI task force."

"A New York detective. That right?"

"Yes, sir."

"Hmmm. Quite confusing, if I may say so. Why don't you just say you're the law and save yourself the trouble? I'm sure a young-sounding fellow like yourself has better things to do than prattle with an old coot like me."

A young-sounding fellow. I smiled. It seems I was wrong about Hank.

"Hank, I understand one of my colleagues contacted you regarding a rifle you used to own."

"A colleague, you say? Only call I got was from a young-sounding lady, called from Venice, Italy, of all places. She had the dandiest accent, no spaghetti in it. Couldn't place it. You calling from Venice as well? Saw a number with too many digits on the caller ID."

"Yes, sir, I am. And that sounds like my colleague, Officer Kamaria Uba. That's the lady you spoke to, correct?"

"Well, I don't quite recollect, but that's something close. She didn't say she was FBI or nothing like that. She said she was Italian police. The Carbine-eerie or Cabin-airy. You sure she's your colleague?"

"The FBI often works with different agencies and police departments, both foreign and domestic. Officer Uba and I work together on the same task force."

"Different departments, foreign and domestic? Don't quite see how an arrangement like that can work. What can I do for you, sir?"

"I'm making a follow-up call. I might ask you the same questions Officer Uba asked or along the same lines. Sometimes that helps jog a person's memory and they'll recall new details or cover something that might have been missed. It's strictly routine. Do you have a few minutes?"

"We can talk as long as you like. Unless I spot my wolf problem."

"Great, I appreciate it. I understand you owned a Walther WA 2000 semiautomatic rifle that was stolen from your home?"

"That's right. Was my favorite. Rare iron, too good for shooting wolves."

"Can you describe the burglary?"

"Ain't much to describe. Came home from a hunting trip to find my gun room in tatters. The Walther gone missing was the first thing I noticed. Had it in a custom-made glass case that was smashed to smithereens. A Springfield model 1861 rifle musket, an American Luger, and a LeMat revolver were also stolen. Hell, those four were the pick of my collection."

"How did the burglar enter your house?"

"Front door, I suppose. We don't lock our doors out here."

"So there was no evidence of forced entry?"

"None that anyone could find, no, sir."

"You gave the police a name at the time, someone you suspected?"

"That's right. I told them it had to be Weasel Givens."

"Weasel? You mean Wendell?"

"One and the same, sir."

I chuckled. "And why did you suspect Mr. Givens?"

"Simple arithmetic."

"Can you be more specific?"

Hank's voice had turned hoarse. He tried clearing his throat. When that didn't work, he coughed and hacked up something from the deep reaches of his lungs. I held the phone away from my ear and waited, feeling that the man deserved some privacy to sort himself out.

"Pardon me. That's what I get for not quitting those Marlboros sooner." He took a deep breath and cleared his throat once more. "Now, where were we? Oh, Givens. Well, for the better part of a year, the man had been harassing me to sell him the Walther and the LeMat. Kept upping the ante, wouldn't take 'not in your lifetime' for an answer."

"Did Mr. Givens show an interest in the other two firearms?"

"No, not particularly. Whenever he'd mentioned the Walther or the LeMat, I'd tell him they were part of the four amigos. See, they all had serial numbers ending in eight-eight-five, like they was meant to be together. The damnedest thing. I would never part with them. So out of spite, I suppose, he took the other two."

I glanced at Kamaria's notes. Her cursive was neat and compact, which made the meager material seem all the more insubstantial. "The police talked to Mr. Givens, correct?"

"That's right. They said he had a solid alibi and dropped him from their suspect list."

"There were other suspects?"

"To my knowledge, Givens was the list."

"The police ended their investigation after clearing Givens?"

"That's how I would describe it. Though they said it was an ongoing investigation, I never saw much ongoing after that."

It was a common misperception that never failed to irritate me. "No news" was automatically assumed to mean the investigation had been dropped. People just didn't understand the nature of investigative work. A case could move at blazing speed: the right interviews, clear evidence, a willing witness, a perp, an address, and a quick pickup. Case solved before lunchtime. High fives, fist pumps. Or it could drag on for days, weeks, even years. Often, a lot of those cases were hobby cases, worked on weekends, holidays, and comp days long after they'd gone cold—particularly homicides. Such was the dedication of the professionals who worked them. Regarding this particular case, my guess was that the statute of limitations had run out. The average for burglary ran five years, though it varied by state. So Hank was probably right. His case had been shelved for good.

I asked, "Do you recall who the investigators assigned to your case were?"

"Be pretty surprised if they aren't retired. Both of 'em

looked five years past their expiration dates back then. But I might still have their cards down at the house someplace."

"Don't worry about it. I'll call the local police department in—" I checked Kamaria's notes "—in Whitefish and give them your name. They'll provide the case details."

I kept flipping through Kamaria's binder, cover to cover, hoping in vain that missing pieces of investigative documentation would suddenly turn up.

"Hank, did the police give you details regarding the alibi they used to clear Givens?"

"They said it was his mother and some story about a family gathering."

"So, multiple people could vouch for his whereabouts at the time of the burglary?"

"I suppose."

I pictured Hank as a disheveled reed of a man under a beat-up Stetson, pressing his thin lips into a line and shrugging his bony shoulders.

"What about buyers and sellers you've done business with?" I asked. "I'm sure you gave names to the investigators. Did you give any to my colleague, Officer Uba?"

"I suppose. But it's been a long time. Memory ain't what it used to be."

I pressed the phone closer to my ear. "It's been a long time? What do you mean?"

"Long time since I spoke to your lady colleague, is what I mean."

"You mean longer than a day or two?"

Hank paused. "I'm not catching you, sir."

The room felt hot, the air thicker. "Hank, are we talking about the same gun? A sniper rifle, short with a walnut stock and the clip—"

"You said a Walther WA 2000, didn't you? Ain't too many of those exist and even fewer with a serial number ending in eight-eight-five and tracing back to me. Your lady colleague read out the meat of that number, and it matched my paperwork to a tee. I right suppose it's the same rifle."

"When did you speak to my colleague, Officer Uba?"

Hank paused. "Is this some kind of joke, sir? Left hand not knowing what the right hand is up to? Didn't you say you two work together?"

"Hank, please, stay with me. When did you speak to Officer Uba?"

"Well, let's see now. Had to be about ... two years ago."

"Two years? Did you say two years?"

"I said *about* two years ago. Your lady colleague called after the Italian police had caught a fellow with my rifle, supposedly after he shot a mafioso. She promised I could...."

Hank Robin's voice faded. I thanked him in midsentence and disconnected as he tried to ask about his rifle. I leaned back in Kamaria's chair and squeezed the armrests until my fingers hurt.

Chapter Thirty-Four

Firelight

Marino locked himself in his office.

He sat in one of two wingback chairs facing the fireplace. The three logs stacked on the wrought iron grate were fully engulfed. Still, he shivered. He grabbed a bottle beside the chair and poured another finger's worth into the snifter, careful not to spill a drop. He rested the bottle on his knee and eyed the label. Here was one of the finest cognacs in the world, a truly rare French delicacy, and he could barely taste it.

Worry does that to a man. It dulls his sense of taste. *Does it dull his thinking?*

He set the bottle back on the marble floor. Cupping the bowl of the snifter, he swirled the cognac. In the firelight, the gold-brown liquid chased itself around the bowl. The light passing through the glass cut golden beams across his uniform. One spotlighted his ribbons. The effect seemed suitable, like a divine nod to his accomplishments. Accomplishments that could go up in flames as quickly as those logs in the hearth.

He brought the rim of the snifter to his nose. The aroma had improved, with hints of fruit and flowers. To his disappointment, however, the taste still eluded him. All he got was the burn.

The Americans had a finger pointed at The Holy Hand. That was troubling. Worse, this wasn't the work of the rabble of Americans he already endured and could, to some degree, manipulate. An entirely different entity had spent the time and manpower required to build a file linking the cardinal to Bonaventura and, by association, to The Holy Hand. That entity had to be the CIA.

Less than forty-eight hours ago, Officer Kamaria Uba had reported that the Americans had identified the alleged shooter as a CIA operative. Assuming that was true, it was an explosive revelation with far-reaching political implications. Yet, they didn't hide the information from her. O'Neil, on the other hand, had been vague when he updated Marino on the status of the task force investigation. He'd never mentioned the CIA by name. Instead, he'd referred to a sister agency, adding that the situation was politically sensitive.

Marino was sympathetic. He understood bureaucracy. It was a tangle of government offices and jurisdictions that required finesse and patience to negotiate. He didn't press O'Neil for details, agreeing to give him time to get answers. Now he saw that was a mistake.

The warmth of the fire was at last reaching his bones. He took another sip. The cognac, too, was cooperating, oiling his joints, loosening his muscles. If only he could taste it.

Now that O'Neil and his minions were in possession of this CIA file, it was easy to see how its contents shaped their underhanded strategy: blackmail the cardinal to give up Bonaventura, torture Bonaventura to give up The Holy Hand.

Why did the CIA build the file? Why give it to O'Neil?

Assuming Officer Uba's intelligence was accurate, the CIA secretly planted a man inside the Procuratie that day. He'd been careless, getting caught on camera, which led to his identification as the prime suspect in a high-profile homicide.

Why was he in the building in the first place?

Marino saw only one logical explanation. The operative was there to assassinate the Arab, El-Hashem. When the operative was later identified, the CIA executed a prearranged damage control plan. That plan was to point a finger at someone else—

The Holy Hand. Bonaventura was the key. Watch him, see who his associates are, dig for skeletons, build a file. When someone comes calling, hand over the file and walk away.

Why did the CIA target the Arab?

Perhaps the Arab was also working for the CIA and had information not fit for FBI interrogators. Or the assassination was part of a larger geopolitical plan aimed at expanding American arrogance around the globe. It could be any, or none, of multiple conspiracy theories he could come up with.

Did it matter?

Did he care?

He shook his head in answer to both questions and finished his cognac.

What did matter was Bonaventura's demise effectively dismantled the American plan. What did they have anyway? A few photos of the cardinal having an amicable lunch with a member of his church? A record of donations from a certified charitable organization? A combined nothing.

However, his theory of a CIA assassination was something—something big! It meant, to his relief, that the shooting hadn't been carried out by The Holy Hand. It also provided the excuse he needed to rid himself of the Americans forever.

How to use it?

He had no evidence. Just the cardinal's claim of the existence of a file and a lot of conjecture. But maybe he didn't need evidence. He just had to convince the spineless politicians in Rome. Not the courts. And in politics, conjecture was often fact. Still, he needed a plan and time to execute it. Which meant the Americans would have the latitude to continue their underhanded investigation. That was concerning. If there was one thing he'd come to reluctantly admire about American arrogance was its talent for turning losses into wins.

Marino had been obstructing the task force investigation from the start when he didn't know the players or the motives and couldn't gauge how the shooting would reflect on the Carabinieri or him. Even a hint of blame would ruin his shot at promotion to general. Slowing things down until he had more intel had been the right strategy. Now he knew he had to dismantle the team. Jordan had been easy to get rid of. His fate was sealed the moment he lunged at Marino himself. The audacity had been breathtaking. It took just one phone call, one incredibly short phone call to end Jordan's career with the FBI. Surprisingly—or perhaps not so surprisingly, given that Jordan was African—the Special Agent in Charge did not protest or bother to defend his man or even attempt to dissuade Marino from filing the charge.

He had nothing on Santoro until Longo had told him about the rope. If Giordana's theory panned out and the laboratory linked Santoro to the rope, Marino would have all the leverage he needed. And even if there was no match, Marino still had enough malleable circumstantial evidence to get rid of him. After that, he would quickly remove Uba from the team and pick off the rest one by one if needed.

Collecting a DNA sample from Santoro was a priority. There was no point in demanding one from Jordan now that he was gone. He made a mental note to call Longo with new instructions.

He reached for the bottle and poured another finger of cognac.

This time, he tasted notes of dried rose nectar, jasmine, nutmeg, and saffron. And he smiled.

Chapter Thirty-Five

The Courtyard

The night was an old man, growing older and frailer by the hour. Like the dead—like Nabeel Haddad—the night was cold and clammy and smelled faintly of rot, of the canals and their stagnant water. But unlike Nabeel Haddad, the night would suffer a natural death.

Nabeel Haddad's Armenian contact, the man who supplied the suitcase and whose severed head would later fester inside the courier's last package, had also been an atheist. A vile man who honored nothing but the euro. From the start, an expendable hire, a loose end to tie up quickly and professionally. However, the treachery of the courier—his reckless call to police—had brought forth a dark rage. Instead of losing his life to a merciful bullet, the Armenian lost his head to the edge of a sharp knife.

He had expected better from Nabeel Haddad. The betrayal of a good Muslim hurt. It always did. It tested his faith in man. Nevertheless, the courier had been taken care of. At the moment of death, he uttered the required words: *Verify we belong to Allah and truly to Him we shall return.* He'd also made the proper arrangements. Had it been guilt? He didn't know anymore. Guilt was an expendable emotion. What he did know was that Nabeel Haddad did not die in vain. The courier's son would be cared for. A promise made is a promise kept.

Standing next to the towering doors that sealed off Portico Foscari, the famous corridor leading to the official entrance and courtyard of the Doge's Palace, the man zipped up his jacket and blew into his cupped hands. The smell of nicotine on his fingers triggered a powerful craving. Instead of rolling a new cigarette, he checked his watch: 12:45 a.m.

Two guards usually patrolled the palace and its grounds. Tonight, there was only one. The guard entrusted with securing the courtyard was on a boat with a harlot (a dirty but necessary expense). That gave the man twenty minutes.

The locks on the massive doors were weak adversaries for his picks. He soon unlocked them and had one door ajar to slip through.

Portico Foscari was flanked by St. Mark's Basilica to the north and the palace courtyard to the south. Long past visiting hours, most of the lights were turned off. Camouflaged in his black fatigues, he crept down the corridor and stopped at the first of three arches that gave access to the rectangular courtyard.

Protected by high walls, it offered the perfect venue for the Israeli prime minister's speech. The crowd scheduled to listen to his false message was expected to be small by political standards. A stage with a podium and seating for dignitaries stood in front of the palace's Renaissance wing. Two seating areas filled with folding chairs faced the stage. Guests, staff, celebrities, and the press—what would later become the herd—were expected to fill those chairs.

He listened and scanned the darkness. Nothing was amiss.

The man moved across the courtyard and turned down the aisle in the seating area. He resisted the urge to move the chairs closer; the tighter the cattle were packed, the more they would savage one another in the ensuing panic. A clever idea that would require too much time to implement. Besides, the staffers would likely move them back and whine about it like children.

He froze.

Children!

He had forgotten about the children. No matter how they'd been reared or by whom, each was an empty vessel ripe for the goodness and wisdom of Islam if given that saving opportunity. He took great care to avoid killing children. The same could not be said of the enemy, who killed indiscriminately using drones piloted by cowards on the ground. War, by its nature, was indiscriminate. In the chaos of battle mistakes happen and innocent people are killed. He understood that. He was a soldier. To look a man in the eye, however, gave one a moment to evaluate, to reflect, before delivering death, thus minimizing those tragedies. If a mistake was made, one had to live with remorse. It was a brutal aspect of war the enemy's technology eliminated. No final, wrenching image to torment the mind, to hinder sleep and wakefulness. If the baby sleeping soundly in the adjacent room or the boy playing nearby was killed, it was an accident. They had a sanitized name for it: collateral damage. It was a despicable form of warfare.

Friday's mission would be no accident. The enemy would be looked square in the eye the moment before death was delivered in a single, brilliant flash of light.

He resumed his walk with a sag in his shoulders, a slight drag in his step. Each meter traveled brought him closer to the realization that it was too late to abort. Too much planning. Too many years waiting for the perfect opportunity; there might never be another. He decided if there were children seated on the stage, he would declare them martyrs and honor their sacrifice.

Stopping at the edge of the stage, he considered the safety glass.

A series of bulletproof partitions created a transparent wall around the stage. Cleaned thoroughly, it would stand almost invisible. Taller than a man, it offered plenty of protection from sniper fire or shrapnel to a speaker and the dignitaries seated behind him.

This was a problem, though not unexpected.

The bomb vest itself did not pack enough explosive material to defeat the barrier. Death was delivered mostly by the omnidirectional discharge of the shrapnel. The glass would stop all of it.

Then there was the problem of security. No one would get this close. A small army of Carabinieri and Israeli security would form a human shield in front of the stage and along the sides. Bomb-sniffing dogs and their handlers would patrol the aisle and the courtyard's perimeter. Perched high on the rooftops, police snipers would keep a vigilant eye on the crowd and stage.

None of this was unexpected.

The only unknown was the Americans. They had a sharp inclination to think differently, to disregard the opinions and experiences of others. This they often did at their own peril. Though grudgingly, he admitted, it also gave them an edge. Their recklessness made them unpredictable.

At least he didn't have to worry about the fat man, the one most likely to think differently. His plan for the glutton was already in motion.

He'd come to survey the venue, to see with his own eyes if his plans were wise. He saw no reason to alter them. As he'd expected, the heightened security and the bulletproof wall removed the option of a frontal assault. True, any attack would destroy large chunks of the herd. The headlines would still be there. The fear. But the herd was not the target. The prime minister was. To kill the prime minister, the vest had to be detonated behind the glass on the stage itself. And that was a problem with a solution.

He checked his watch again. Old man night was aging fast. He had to hurry. There was another loose end to tie up.

Chapter Thirty-Six

Icing

I scowled at the phone, wishing I could melt it with eye lasers as if the gadget was responsible for the ugly twist the case had taken. When I snapped out of it, I pushed back from the desk and stood. Pacing around the dim room on pins and needles, my hollow footsteps were the only sounds keeping an oppressive silence at bay.

I stopped at my desk and grabbed the largest of four unopened cookie boxes from the bottom drawer. I tore open one end of the box and ate a handful so fast I barely constructed the memory. I resumed my pacing, holding the box to my chest with one hand and pillaging the contents with the other.

Two years.

That's how long ago Kamaria had talked to Hank Robin. Not the day before. And not about the El-Hashem shooting but another case entirely! The implication was clear. The rifle had been taken out of evidence storage, either by the shooter or by an accomplice. And it didn't take an investigative genius to point the finger at Kamaria.

I can't be this wrong about her. Can I?

Resettling in Kamaria's chair, I tossed the cookie box on a stack of folders and picked up the phone.

"Santoro." Music and the din of lively conversation blared in the background.

"It's me," I said. "Where are you?"

"The Smokestack, with the Lufthansa stewardess."

"Take a rain check."

"What?"

"Tell her something's come up."

"A rain check? Are you outta your frigging mind? You don't take a rain check on a nine point five."

"Vincent, I need you to meet me at the squad room."

"Squad room? Oh, for fuck's sake, you just can't let it go, can you? On vacation, on suspension, on the commode, naked and oiled at a happy ending massage par—"

"I don't do happy ending massages, man."

"You don't? What about that gift—"

"Just meet me at the squad room!" I hung up.

I flipped again through Kamaria's case binder. There were no follow-ups for buyers and sellers Robin had done business with. The names of the investigators who'd looked into the burglary were still MIA no matter how many times I scanned the pages, and various public tips were written off as one-liners: person of interest not found, solid alibi (but no mention of who or what the alibi was), interview inconclusive.

What had Kamaria been doing since the shooting? What was her role in this entire mess?

* * *

Vincent barged into the office wearing a T-shirt and a sports jacket snug enough to draw attention to his overdeveloped upper body. He paused near the door and scanned the room. When we made eye contact, he shook his head and walked to Kamaria's desk.

"This better blow off my boxers." He wheeled over a nearby office chair. "You have no idea what I gave up to be here."

"You know I wouldn't call unless it was important."

He settled on the opposite side of Kamaria's desk. "Before I forget, I followed up on Bonaventura, and it turns out..." Vincent reached for the cookie box and shook it. "You ate the whole box? This is serious, isn't it?"

I gave Vincent the rundown of my conversation with Kamaria and the phone call with Hank Robin. At some point, my hand snuck into the cookie box and came away with a stray, which Vincent did not begrudge me. When I was done talking, we sat in silence.

"Holy shit," Vincent whispered. "Kamaria is the mole."

"We don't know that. There might still be a plausible explanation."

Vincent arched an eyebrow. "You think?"

I didn't reply.

Vincent said, "If we believe this guy Robin—and I think we do—then that rifle sat in custody for two years collecting dust and rust under lock and key. Then, all of a sudden, it's in the hands of the perp who shot our snitch."

Vincent sat forward and narrowed his eyes. "You see the flashing arrow sign here? Even without the baloney she fed you and the bum case she's putting together here, Kamaria is still the common denominator. She knew all about the snitch. And being Carabinieri, she has access to everything in the evidence room. She can drive a forklift in there and come out with a pallet full of boxes, and nobody would bat an eye … oh, come on, don't look at me like that."

"Like what?"

Vincent sat back and crossed his arms. "Like you're grinding an axe with my name on it."

"I'm not."

"Yeah, you are. Your eyebrows alone are homicidal. Look, I understand you have a thing for her, but you can't think this out with your pecker."

"That has nothing to do with it!"

"Now you're being defensive." He shrugged. "Just saying."

"You're jumping to conclusions, and that's lazy police work."

"If the shoe fits."

I swept my eyes over the top of the desk. "We're missing something. Maybe she's got notes and hasn't updated the case binder. I never looked at her binders before. Have you? Or maybe her brass is telling her what to say and do. Why lie about Robin? It doesn't make sense. What if someone checked?"

"Why would anybody check?"

Vincent was right. Nobody would double-check an investigator's case in progress unless there was a good reason. Like suspicion of wrongdoing, which I just happened to stumble upon. Kamaria's desk was suddenly repulsive. I turned to the windows.

Vincent sighed. "We gotta call O'Neil."

"No!"

Our eyes locked.

"Not yet," I said in an even tone. "Let's confirm this. We don't know what is or isn't in that evidence room."

"Lemme guess. You wanna check it out."

I pushed the chair back and stood. "Let's go."

"Now? You're not even supposed to be here. You're suspended, remember?"

I was halfway to the door when I heard Vincent groan. "You know, I hate when you get like this. Shit … hold up, I'm coming!"

* * *

Like much of Venice, the evidence room of the Carabinieri headquarters seemed suspended in the Middle Ages. We descended a steep and narrow stone staircase with lighting so poor I wondered if we were meant to have torches in hand.

The bottom step was shorter than the rest by half, and it brought me to an abrupt stop that jarred my tender knee.

"Ow, shit!"

"Watch that last step," Vincent said.

"Yeah, thanks. If I ever have to defuse a bomb, you're the guy I want directing me on the radio."

Vincent stood at the end of the short, dark corridor. When I came up behind him, he said, "Wait here."

If pain was an indicator of poor health, then my knee was clearly a sick kitty. Perhaps there was a torn ligament in there, or the stress of supporting my ever-expanding belly had finally worn away some vital cartilage. I squeezed it, rubbed it, flexed it. No matter where I touched or how much pressure I applied, it felt tender, bruised, unwilling to bend without a fight. Exactly how I felt about Kamaria.

Before I could dwell on that, Vincent was back.

"I don't know the EO," he said. "But I think she's cool. Has a smile I can work with. Just let me do the talking."

The mouth of the corridor opened onto a dark vestibule that served no obvious purpose. We walked through the vestibule and into a cavernous room with a stone floor, brick walls, and an arched ceiling also made of brick. It looked like a wine cellar, only instead of oak barrels and corks wet with aging Chianti, the air smelled of musk, cardboard, and narcotics (weed for the most part). A tall fence of iron bars capped with spear points sprouted from a brick half wall, forming a formidable barrier that divided the room roughly into one part walkway and three parts storage area, what we called The Cage.

A wooden counter, equipped with a phone and a computer, broke the continuity of the fence. Standing behind it was a young Carabinieri evidence officer. She wore a dark blue uniform with a tie and a white shirt. Silver buttons strained to keep a curvy figure in place. Her light brown hair was up in a bun, discreetly pinned and perfectly shaped. It looked like a cinnamon roll. When we approached, she gave me a sharp look.

"*Ciao, bella*," Vincent said.

She didn't return the greeting. She grabbed the phone.

Vincent reached over and put his hand over hers, urging her to hang up. He asked her name. She gave her surname, saying "Cambio" like a declaration, a line in the sand. Skipping any further introductions as it was obvious she knew who we were, Vincent and Officer Cambio engaged in an animated discussion. All in Italian. Very fast Italian. From the bits and pieces I caught, it covered my suspension, our need to tie up a loose end, and Marino's implicit orders to shoot me on sight or have me hauled off to the gallows. Vincent's guarantee of my immediate departure thereafter, and an invitation to The Smokestack, prompted Officer Cambio's thawing into Lorena.

Through it all, I gained a new appreciation for the Italian language. It's rich and mellifluous, a spontaneous song worthy of romantic strolls and long drives in the countryside. It's the kind of language that sends shivers of excitement down a lover's back when the sweet words are whispered in the ear or spoken aloud as the sun sets over a vibrant horizon. Considering my Italian was an assault on the language, I remained on the sidelines as Vincent suggested, maintaining the contrite look of a man who knows he messed up and just needs a second chance. *Pretty please, ma'am, frosting on top.* Eventually, that earned me a smile, though one with a lot less wattage than those she reserved for Vincent.

Vincent asked Lorena if she knew about the El-Hashem homicide. That set off a giddy "of course" and encouraged a gossip huddle. Vincent kept the smile on her face but told her nothing everyone didn't already know. She nodded with enthusiasm when he asked for the evidence box. Needing the case number, she set her hands on the computer keyboard and looked up at Vincent expectantly.

"Case number is November Alpha 2-0-2-0-7-4," I said to Vincent. "But before she brings the box, ask her if there's any case on file where a Walther was used."

He spoke to Lorena. She worked the keyboard with nimble fingers, made practical for the task with unpainted nails cut short.

A moment later, she confirmed what we'd already suspected: a Walther rifle had been used in a mob case. Kamaria was a member of the Carabinieri's Special Operations Group, which, along with terrorism, specialized in organized crime.

In a voice I hoped would mask the turmoil I was in, I said to Vincent, "Ask her to bring the rifle, the one from the mob case."

Lorena nodded at Vincent's request and disappeared behind a row of bookcases.

While most modern police evidence rooms had movable, space-saving floor-to-ceiling shelves, The Cage was lined with rows of massive wooden bookcases, all of which looked as old and settled as any building in the city. The rifle, however, was likely stored on a gun rack, chained or cabled.

While we waited, I put my hands on the counter to steady myself. I wanted to believe it was to relieve the pressure on my knee. It wasn't. I just couldn't hold back the doubt wolves nipping at my thoughts any longer.

"You okay?" Vincent clasped my upper arm to steady me. "You look like you're gonna faint."

"I can't be this wrong about her."

"What?" Vincent leaned in. "What was that?"

It was meant to be a thought, yet the words had escaped as a barely perceptible whisper. "Nothing, I'm fine. Just my knee."

Vincent let go of my arm. "She had me fooled too. She had everybody fooled."

"The jury is still out until I see..."

Lorena emerged from another aisle. She held the unmistakable Walther WA 2000 sniper rifle.

She approached the counter and offered the rifle to Vincent. He stepped back and pointed at me. Lorena hesitated, probably aware that the cameras in The Cage would further record her blatant disregard of Marino's orders. In that short stalemate, she must've seen something in my expression that softened her. She handed me the rifle, smiling as if saying, "Screw it."

I took the rifle by the walnut stock and eyed the folded bipod. I'd found it with the bipod in that exact position—

retracted. The shooter hadn't used it to steady his shot since he'd chosen, out of apparent inexperience, to put the barrel of the rifle out the window. The short magazine, which was curiously fed behind the pistol grip, was missing, replaced by a locking cable looped through the action. Tied to the trigger guard was the entire reason we'd come: the weapon evidence tag.

On the front of the tag, a date about twenty-six months prior—close to the two-year window Robin had claimed—was penned in sloppy handwriting. The time, entered in military units, claimed the weapon had been recovered in the early morning hours. A location I didn't know was listed. Special Operations was the investigating unit. The case number was one I'd never seen before. I skipped the make, model, and caliber to look at the serial number. It stared back at me like an old friend.

The rifle I held was the rifle used to kill El-Hashem.

I flipped the tag around to the chain of custody record. A two-column table listing "Date" and "Released To" had several entries. Most of those were dated shortly after the recovery date, with names and signatures of Special Operations personnel I didn't know. But the last entry, the only one in blue ink as opposed to black, was the icing on the cake.

It was dated the day before the shooting and released to Officer Kamaria Uba.

Chapter Thirty-Seven

Stalker

When I handed the rifle back to Lorena I saw sadness in her eyes. Maybe the sadness in my eyes was contagious, or maybe it was just how I saw the world.

Gray and gloomy.

Cruel and unfair.

"Time to go." Vincent put a hand on my arm and started pulling me away.

"Wait. Ask her what weapon was submitted for the El-Hashem case."

"Miles, I think we both—"

"Ask her!"

Vincent paused then turned to Lorena. The words between them floated around me like ashes from a smoldering fire.

"No weapon was submitted," Vincent said. "Just what's in the box."

I dropped my head and backed away. Limping along the wall of The Cage, I gripped every third bar as I went, slingshotting myself forward as my legs didn't seem to have enough power on their own.

"Kamaria's the shooter," I said.

Vincent draped his massive arm around my shoulders and got me walking with him. "Maybe. But we don't have the whole story."

"She had opportunity. The clock tower is next door to the Procuratie Vecchie. She had radio access. Knew exactly where the mark was in real time. She never submitted the rifle to ballistics since she never submitted it into evidence. And she forged the firearm analysis report I found in her binder. Why? To make it look like she was making progress by simply confirming what we already knew. She also lied to me about the gun owner. And her name is on the chain of custody for the rifle I recovered but in a completely different case. We have the story. She's the shooter!"

"Calm down. You'll give yourself another heart attack." Vincent squeezed my shoulders. "What's the motive then, if she's the shooter?"

We stopped walking.

"What's the motive?" Vincent repeated.

"I ... I don't know." I looked away, my eyes unable to focus. "I haven't gotten that far, man."

"Then we still have work to do. Let's call O'Neil, tell him everything we got, and let him decide our next move. It's a shit storm if she's the shooter, so we've got to be as close to a hundred percent sure as possible."

"Right under our noses," I muttered. "Right under mine."

The vestibule seemed gloomier than I remembered, with the edges lost to total darkness. The light trickling in from the poorly lit staircase and the evidence room could only muster enough illumination to cut a narrow path.

When I neared the staircase, a tall, dark figure stood at the top. Something about the slim, masculine build was familiar. As he started to descend, I noticed his arms were at his sides, bent like his hands were riding in the front pockets of a jacket.

Grabbing Vincent, I pulled us into the darkness.

The sound of descending footsteps continued uninterrupted. No inquiring shout was issued. Either we hadn't been spotted, or we didn't matter to this man. As the footfalls drew closer, I got the eerie sensation of being transported back to that dark alley in residential Murano.

The man came off the staircase, awkwardly negotiating that tricky last step as though expecting it but still surprised by it. And there, in the faint light of the path, I saw an orbital injury to the left eye, purpled and amorphous, the type of trauma that can come from a host of causes, including an intentional right jab skillfully delivered in a dark alley.

Here was my stalker.

I was reeling.

The shock and anger that consumed me one moment drained away the next when I recognized the face of the man walking past us. Special Agent Antonio Ruiz pushed his hands deeper into the front pockets of a light jacket.

Chapter Thirty-Eight

Thumb Drive

Watching Ruiz rush by made me realize how much I disliked the man. Smart, ambitious, and smug, he was perfect brass material, a future Special Agent in Charge of something big. He wasn't much of a team player, never missing an opportunity to one-up you. It didn't matter if it was a major break in a case or a meaningless game of darts at a bar. And he was sneaky, working leads on his own and not sharing information when he had no reason not to. All that made him the perfect errand boy for a higher-up. But who? The SAC? O'Neil?

When Ruiz was well out of earshot, I whispered in the darkness, "Son of a bitch."

"What's he doing down here? And why are we hiding?"

"He's the stalker from the other night!"

"No shit." Vincent paused. "You sure? You said you couldn't ID him."

"Same build, same body language. And his left eye is hamburger meat."

"Didn't catch that. You clocked him?"

"Right jab, before he got away."

"You never told me that. Happened Tuesday, right? Almost two days ago."

"Have you seen him since? I haven't."

Vincent shook his head. "Now that you mention it, nobody has. He's been following mysterious leads off on his own again."

We stood in the dark, watching Ruiz head toward the counter.

Vincent whispered, "He's real FBI. If he was following you around, then we really can't trust nobody."

The case had turned to candy, detective candy—exactly what I needed. Work was the therapy I could always count on to deliver me from disappointment and setbacks. The case came first. It always did. And badge or no badge, I was taking it wherever it led.

"I've been telling you that all along," I said. "We're on our own."

After a brief silence, Vincent asked, "What's the plan?"

"Ruiz first."

"Why? We got a hook on Kamaria. Nothing on Ruiz except your word against his."

"What can we do about Kamaria right now? Pick her up? Sweat her? She's no Bonaventura. She's a cop! She'll lawyer up before we get anywhere near an interview room. Besides, the minute we pick her up, we'll alert everybody, including Ruiz. Not knowing his angle is risky."

"We don't pick her up; we put her under surveillance. She's still hanging around, so her role here isn't over yet."

I hadn't thought of that. If Kamaria was the shooter, why hadn't she disappeared? Sooner or later, we would have uncovered her lies.

I scanned the vestibule's darkness. I couldn't tell where the ceiling started or the floor ended. It was the perfect metaphor for a case that kept yielding more questions than answers.

"Miles, you listening?"

"Ruiz first. Let's at least find out why he's here."

"Obviously, to sign something outta evidence."

"Sign out what? And why in the middle of the night?"

"Hmmm. Dunno."

"When he leaves, I'll follow him. You find out what he took from evidence."

"With that knee? You couldn't tail Nonna Geppina down a supermarket aisle without being made. I'll tail him. You talk to Lorena."

"How do I talk to Lorena?"

"With your mouth and your hands. Trust me, it's—here he comes."

Ruiz entered the vestibule and rushed past us with an urgency that made his sudden visit all the more perplexing. He was soon scaling the steps two at a time. When we heard the closing clang of the door at the top landing, Vincent hustled after him. I limped back into the evidence room.

Lorena was standing behind the counter, setting the lid on a cardboard file box. Scrawled across the sides of the box was the case number I knew. When she spotted me, she leaned over the counter to glance down the walkway, no doubt looking for Vincent.

"Ciao." I pointed to the box. *"Per piacere posso per questa scatola vedere La Catena Custodia."* I tried to mimic the hand choreography I'd seen Vincent do so often, hoping the visual presentation would somehow disguise my abysmal Italian. The look on Lorena's face was either hopelessly confused or utterly appalled. I pointed again. *"Scatola questa … per piacere."*

"I not to speak to you, *Signore* Jordan. Captain say."

"Oh, you speak English?"

"A small … very terrible. Like you speak *Italiano.*"

I laughed hard enough to be contagious. Lorena soon had tears in her eyes. And although I had no tears for laughter, it was a release and a relief. It reminded me that we're all just passengers on the train of life, each of us getting on and off at random. No matter what the track offered, whether it was smooth straightaways with breathtaking views or long, dark tunnels, the train kept moving relentlessly forward. Enjoying the ride was all we could do.

In addition to putting things in perspective, the laughter also served to form a bond, however brief and fragile. "Please," I said. "It's very important that I see the chain of custody sheet."

Lorena's smile faded.

"Chain of custody," I repeated. "*La catena custodia.*"

She opened the box and pulled out the chain of custody sheet. Only five items were listed. At the top was the monk's habit we'd recovered from the duplicitous Agent Kaufmann. Tufu had tried to trace it, hoping it came from a specialty shop that would help narrow the field. Instead, the garment was readily available online to anyone. The next article was the duffel bag we assumed was used to transport the rifle, also readily available in every tourist shop in Venice. It proved to be a two-time loser when forensics couldn't find any useful DNA on it. The bullets extracted from the maize cart at the square and a server hard drive were listed third and fourth. Ruiz had no interest in any of those items. He'd come in the middle of the night exclusively for a thumb drive containing a video download of my mano a mano with Agent Kaufmann.

The video came from a surveillance system inside the Procuratie Vecchie, configured to save daily footage on a local server. Since the server's hard drive was impractical to carry around or access and had to remain in evidence in case a sleazy defense attorney challenged the authenticity of a downloaded version, the techs put a copy of the video on the thumb drive Ruiz had taken. And that stuck out. Along with Colt, Ruiz had already seen the video, presumably several times while working to ID Kaufmann. Why did he need to see it again?

Chapter Thirty-Nine

The Holy Hand

Marino marched down a hidden corridor that ran beneath the Doge's Palace. Thick candles on iron sconces bolted into the walls lit the way. Against the stone floor, the clack of his footsteps seemed out of sync with his actual footfalls. Midway, he stopped and turned. No one followed. No one ever did. He had walked this corridor many times before, and it always made him uneasy. He didn't know why. It wasn't narrow or built with a low ceiling. The air shafts provided enough ventilation. The space wasn't littered with cobwebs or echoing with the scurry of small claws in the shadows. Perhaps those shadows moving at the edges of the candlelight were the source of unease or the heavy wooden door at the end of the corridor.

Marino rapped on the door. It opened with a creak. At the doorway stood a bald man with skin so dark it seemed an extension of his black robe.

"You are late, Brother." The man offered a spare robe.

They called this man the African, which was uninventive, given that he *was* African, and there was nothing unique about an African in Venice. There were many—too many. Tanzania, Nigeria, Somalia, what did it matter? All the same. The African's countenance, looming on the other side of the door like an underworld ghoul, always unnerved him.

Stepping inside, Marino took the robe. He threw it over his dress coat and loosely tied the waist cord. The robe did not have a hood; they were not a cult. It did, however, have an embroidered gold emblem on the chest: an open hand, drawn to scale, with a cross wrapped in a thorny vine centered at the palm—the symbol of The Holy Hand.

"This way, Brother."

The African led Marino to a second door. The crack of whips beyond it made Marino wince.

"Mortification of the flesh," the African said. "Is there a more pleasant sound, Brother?"

Marino silently cursed. Bonaventura's symbolic wake (his body was still cooling in the morgue) had run longer than expected. Now he was forced to witness the distasteful, archaic practice of self-flagellation.

When they crossed the wide-arched entry to the main chamber, the African bid farewell with a predictable, "The princeps will find you shortly. Enjoy the gathering, Brother. May God's hand always guide you."

The main chamber was awash with candlelight glowing from chandeliers, wall sconces, and tall candelabra, from which melted wax clung like stalactites. It was a cavernous space, cold and gloomy despite the warm light. It had none of the decor one would expect for hosting a religious gathering. The stone walls were bare. The columns supporting the vaulted ceiling were strictly functional, not a carved leaf of foliage or a decorative groove among them. The floor was as bare as the walls, though worn smooth by centuries of human foot traffic.

Despite the late hour (it was almost three in the morning), a full congregation of Holy Hand members in black robes filled rows of long wooden benches. News of their token leader's untimely demise had traveled fast. A casual observer might assume they'd come to pay their respects to Bonaventura, but Marino knew the spectacle of self-flagellation drew them.

Blood always drew crowds.

He walked down a side aisle to the front row. Directly in front was an altar, a simple square platform with a wooden table in the middle. Two large candles and a crucifix wrapped with a thorny vine stood on the tabletop. Kneeling around the table in a semicircle were thirteen select members, their robes rolled up beside them, their bare backs—torn and bloody—in full view of the congregation.

Like a macabre drill, thirteen hands swung short three-prong whips with copper wire ends over shivering shoulders. *Thwack ... thwack.* They followed the rigorous example of the only member with a red robe beside him, the robe of the princeps.

After a few more lashes, they stood, threw their robes over their bloodied backs, and turned to the congregation. The princeps—the true leader of The Holy Hand—slipped a large gold crucifix on a thick rolo chain over his neck. He kissed it and made the sign of the cross.

Marino did not participate in the silent prayer that followed. Though he was religious and believed in the cause, he reminded himself not to get sucked into the fervor. The Holy Hand was a means to an end. Nothing more.

When the prayer concluded, the congregation quietly departed. The group of thirteen did too, twelve battered brothers blending into the crowd as it exited and the princeps breaking away to join Marino.

"May God's hand always guide you, Bishop," Marino said with a slight bow.

"May God's hand always guide you, Colonel."

The cardinal red of the princeps' robe suited Bishop Tommaso Cusa well. Maybe the short silver hair, muscular jaw, and tall, slim build gave the bishop the air of power and authority that color was meant to convey. It was an effect lost on his boss, the old and shrunken Cardinal Perricone.

They waited until the congregation members dispersed. Bishop Cusa then pointed to the bench. They sat.

"Bonaventura's wake was a lovely affair, quite moving for the whole congregation," the bishop said.

"I'm sure."

"A good front man. Well-liked, respected even."

Marino looked away. "As you anticipated, he was about to betray us to the Americans. I had no choice."

"Had Bonaventura betrayed what he knew…" The bishop shuddered. "As instrumental as you are, Colonel, in helping us do God's work, you lack the power to stop the kind of investigation that would have unleashed. Why risk the downfall of The Holy Hand? Why risk His Eminence's rise to the halls of the Vatican as the father of our church? Why risk the promising future God has bestowed upon you and me? You did what had to be done, guided by God's hand, acting as his instrument."

Marino turned back to the bishop. "I've got a trusted man leading the Bonaventura investigation. He'll bury it or steer it toward the Americans."

The bishop nodded. "I believe burying the investigation is the most prudent course of action. To smear the Americans with it will only serve to prolong it."

They turned at the sound of footsteps. The African was approaching. The bishop held up a hand and said to him, "Leave us, Brother."

The African stopped. He glanced at Marino. "Princeps, the flesh is weak. I must tend to your wounds."

"I have suffered far more for far less. I endure." The bishop smiled. "Go, Brother."

Marino watched the African reluctantly leave the main chamber. "Did we have anything to do with the Arab's assassination?"

"Absolutely not. Why do you ask?"

Marino considered the bishop's indignant reply. "The file the Americans have makes a compelling case."

The bishop nodded again. It was an irritating habit.

"We are agreed; it is compelling." The bishop clenched the chain of his crucifix. "Eliminate the Arab so The Scorpion can remain free to attack Venice or the mainland. Such an attack would certainly win His Eminence a great many new supporters, while emboldening those he already has. A beneficial plan indeed. Though not one sanctioned by God, I assure you."

The bishop rolled his shoulders and shifted stiffly on the bench. Blood soaked through his robe, causing the fabric to stick in patches across his torn back.

"The African is right, Bishop. You need care." Marino pointed a thumb at his own back.

The bishop clenched and unclenched the chain. "Have you discovered the source of the file?"

"I have a theory that the CIA supplied it."

"The devil American spy agency?" The bishop made the sign of the cross. "Are you sure?"

"My confidence is high, though I have no proof."

"We did not invite spies here. We invited the FBI! How do you come by this troubling theory?"

"An officer I have inside the task force reported that the FBI had identified a CIA operative as the shooter. An accusation the CIA will surely deny."

"A CIA operative?"

"An assassin."

The bishop gasped. "You never mentioned this before, to me or the cardinal."

"The investigation was unfolding. At the time, it did not concern you, the cardinal, or The Holy Hand."

"Do you grasp the political implications of the American spy agency working in Italy?"

"I do."

"Then why—"

"There's no evidence linking the operative to the crime. And given its sensitive nature, I needed more information before raising the alarm."

The bishop let go of the chain and nodded. "Continue."

"I believe the CIA is responsible for the hit on El-Hashem."

"Really? With what motivation?"

Marino shrugged. "It was a covert operation, so we may never know. What matters is The Holy Hand was offered as a sacrificial lamb."

The bishop nodded. "To focus the investigation away from the CIA. It's logical."

"It's dirty and unscrupulous."

"Yes, that's one way to look at it. But perhaps there's another."

Marino waited.

"Perhaps this is God's will. The way he has chosen to use us."

Marino frowned. "How do you mean?"

"Do the Americans think The Scorpion will strike?"

"Yes, they are operating on that assumption."

"Under what specifics?"

"The focus is here, in Venice. During the Israeli prime minister's three-day visit."

"Mighty Father in heaven, that soon? The prime minister is due tomorrow. And he is … a logical target."

"That's what the Americans think."

"And what do you think?"

Marino jumped off the bench and began marching in front of the altar. "What do I think? I think inviting the Americans here was a mistake!"

"You've made that quite clear on numerous occasions."

"They are a meddlesome group of arrogant incompetents. The CIA fills their heads with conspiracy theories, and the idiots come chasing us!" Marino emphasized each point with violent hand gestures.

"What I want to know, Colonel, is whether you agree with them or not."

"That The Scorpion will strike here?" Marino marched back to the bishop and sat. "The Scorpion is no fool. This is a man who has outwitted the best law enforcement agencies in Europe for years. If he was anywhere near the square on the day of the Arab's shooting, then he saw the level of security I have in place. He'll assume—rightly—that after that incident, I will deploy nothing short of an army to secure the prime minister. It will be impossible to get anyone near him."

"Then the answer is no." The bishop clasped his crucifix. "His Eminence has business in Rome tomorrow. He will not be in attendance, and neither will I. But if the Americans are right and you are wrong ... if something were to happen..."

"The Americans will get the blame."

"That's not what I mean."

Marino waited.

"If something were to happen, and you were in a position to stop it, would you?"

"Of course. It's my duty."

"Knowing that the success of such an attack—an attack for which we bear no responsibility—would greatly benefit our cause, would you still stop it?"

Marino arched his eyebrows. "Are you suggesting that I not do my duty?"

"I am suggesting that you do God's will."

Marino gazed at the bishop's crucifix with sudden clarity. "As you said before, I'm God's instrument."

Bishop Tommaso Cusa nodded. "Indeed, you are."

Chapter Forty

The Play

As I left the evidence room, I got a text message from Vincent: *Ruiz lifted a laptop from squad room and rushed to hotel. What u find out? What r we doing?*

A choice lay before us.

If we went by the book, we would do nothing. I had no proof that Ruiz was my stalker. His eye injury could be explained a dozen different ways. Even if I had proof, what had he actually done other than spook me? I'm the one who attacked him. And aside from the odd hour, there was nothing fishy about Ruiz's retrieval of the thumb drive. He was an investigator working a high-profile case with a critical timeline. He was expected to work with the evidence.

Off the book, I knew Ruiz followed me that night but not why. The answer to that question could throw the case for more twists and turns. However, the optimist in me thought something might shake loose and point us in the right direction. But we needed Ruiz's cooperation. A tall order. A cop won't fall for the verbal judo of an interrogation.

Vincent texted me again: *Hello??? u there???*

I texted him back: *On my way.*

I snuck out of the Carabinieri headquarters and limped along three alleyways connected at crooked angles. The one to Ruiz's hotel was so narrow my elbows scraped the brick walls when I wasn't careful. The city planners had not counted on the

generous girth of well-fed Americans. Luckily, it was late, and no one was coming in the opposite direction.

The hotel's glass entrance offered a reprieve from the alley's claustrophobia. It receded four feet into the building and stretched at least six feet wide. The lobby inside was small but tastefully decorated with wood trim and oil paintings. Two small neoclassical couches led the way to an enclosed reception desk that looked like a fancy ticket booth. A kid in an oversized suit sat behind the glass window, reading a paperback.

There were two ways to get past a reception desk at a hotel. One was to flash a badge, which I didn't have. The other was to keep walking as though you belonged there. A suit helped. Taking the second option, I nodded at the kid as I walked past. That seemed to work for him. He went back to his book.

I took the stairs. At the landing, I met Vincent.

"Took you long enough," he said.

"Knee feels better, thanks for asking."

"You gonna tell me what you found out or what?"

"He took the thumb drive."

Vincent snapped his fingers. "Explains the laptop. Must be watching it right now. But … why? Didn't he go over that video a thousand times?"

"That's one of the things we're here to find out."

He scoffed. "And how are we gonna make him talk?"

My head throbbed with dark thoughts coming to me in waves. "What choice do we have?"

Vincent crossed his arms. "Oh, so we're gonna squeeze Kamaria too when the time comes?"

I turned away, feeling my face flush.

"We're not squeezing a Fed." He shook his head. "We bend the rules, bend them as far as they'll bend, but we don't break 'em, Miles. We *won't* break 'em."

"Squeezing Bonaventura wasn't breaking the rules?"

"That was different. He wasn't a Fed or even a US citizen."

"Still wasn't right. We crossed a line."

"Not about right and wrong. It's about the rules."

I studied the plush blue runner that covered the marble stairs and most of the landing. It was easier than staring at the ice in Vincent's eyes.

"You're right," I said. "We're not breaking the rules. I am."

He stepped back and pointed a finger at me. "You're outta your frigging mind, you know that?"

I fished my phone out of my suit jacket and held it up to Vincent: Thursday, 3:07 a.m.

He looked away. "I know the score."

"The prime minister is set to give his speech tomorrow at 0900 hours. That's less than thirty hours away."

Vincent ran his hands through his hair and took a deep breath. "There's gotta be another way."

A minute later a dim light went on in my head. "There is another way."

"What is it?"

"Leverage. But what can we leverage?"

Vincent smiled. "Shit, that's easy!"

"It is?"

"What does he value most? What'd he waste a fancy Harvard education on?"

I scratched my goatee. "The FBI?"

"Right!"

"And how does that help us?"

He put a heavy hand on my shoulder and shook it. "Think! Who ran firearm analysis?"

"Kamaria."

"And she's dirty, right? Where does that leave Ruiz?"

It took a moment to register only because the beauty and simplicity of what Vincent was implying deserved reflection and appreciation.

"In a bad spot." I grinned.

"Right! He was her mentor, supervisor—whatever—on firearm analysis, and he failed to see the con job she was pulling. Either he's not as smart as everybody thinks, or he's in on it."

"But if he's in on it, he won't tell us shit, and we're back to plan B. *I'm* back to plan B."

"Oh, he's not in on it." Vincent let go of my shoulder. "He'll sell his mother and throw in his aunts and uncles for free if it means a promotion. But he's not doing *anything* that'll hurt his career. He's got a thirteen-year calendar in his locker full of notes and timelines laying out his rise to director, for crying out loud. This guy's on a mission."

I wasn't convinced.

"Look, I have no idea what he was doing the night he was following you around. But with this thing, this … Kamaria thing, he just got the wool pulled over his eyes."

He wasn't the only one.

"So, what do you think?"

I pushed off the wall and forced my knee to bear its share of the weight. "Let's run with it and see. Like we do in Brooklyn."

Chapter Forty-One

Past the Midnight Oil

I rapped on the hotel room door. Vincent stood behind me like a wall, blocking out most of the warm hallway lighting.

"It's the middle of the night," Ruiz said from beyond. "Who the hell is it?"

"NYPD," I said.

The pause that followed was a little too long and obvious to be mistaken for anything other than surprise and caution. Ruiz turned the lock and opened the door.

The man standing on the other side of the threshold couldn't claim we'd woken him from a deep slumber. Dressed in his everyday uniform of polo shirt and chinos, Ruiz looked like he'd just returned from a day in the office—a long day, given the 3:00 a.m. shadow marring his otherwise clean-shaven face, and a rough day, considering his swollen black eye.

"Burning past the midnight oil?" I asked.

"Aren't we all?" he replied.

I nodded. He nodded. I'm pretty sure Vincent nodded. He didn't move. We didn't either. The standoff should have been awkward. Instead, it seemed quite natural. For Ruiz's part, I figured his mind was busy processing a half dozen thoughts. For us, it just meant we were content to let the man simmer.

"You gonna ask us in?" Vincent said eventually. "Or what?"

Leaving the door open, Ruiz retreated down a short hallway. We followed. The hallway emptied into a small IKEA furniture showroom—a lot of squares and rectangles built of cheap particleboard. The walls were dark gray, so the walnut veneer of the furniture contrasted well enough. On the night table, wedged between the wall and the double bed, lay a closed laptop with a task force sticker on the cover and a thumb drive conspicuously protruding from a USB port.

I approached the nightstand. "Writing a report?"

Ruiz stood near the end of the bed, looking confused. When he saw I was pointing at the laptop, he said, "Research."

"Research?" Vincent moved in behind him. "What kind of research?"

Ruiz turned to Vincent. "Stuff… stuff I'm following up on."

"Yeah?" Vincent tilted his head. "Like what? How to treat a black eye?"

He turned back to me. "What've you got?"

Ruiz had made his calculations and come to the right conclusion. We knew something he didn't. That gave us a tactical advantage. His only course of action was to cut to the chase and hope to recover in the process. He didn't strike me as the type to stash his service weapon under his pillow, so I opened the nightstand drawer and reached for his compact Glock 26. I removed the magazine and the chambered round, pocketed those, and put the empty gun next to the laptop. Pointing to the end of the bed, I said to Ruiz, "Sit."

He didn't move. I suspected he was recalculating. Should he cooperate, see where this goes? Should he take the initiative? His waistband was clear of other weapons, but we knew he carried a small hammerless Smith & Wesson revolver in an ankle holster. We also knew he had the muscle memory to reach for it fast enough to give himself a good chance.

Vincent put the muzzle of his much larger Glock 17 against the back of Ruiz's head. "Don't even think about it. I'll blow that big Harvard brain all over this room if you don't sit the fuck down in the next five seconds."

"Stand down, Officer!" Ruiz spread out his arms and splayed his hands so we could clearly see them. "I'm a federal agent. Stand down!"

"You're also a Boston Red Sox fan and an arrogant prick. And I don't like you. Now sit." Vincent pressed the gun against his skull until the man had no choice but to follow the instruction.

Once Ruiz was seated on the edge of the bed, Vincent reached for the ankle holster and pulled out the agent's small backup revolver. Holding the gun upside down by the trigger guard, Vincent said, "You know what they say about the size of a man's gun and the size of his—"

"You two have just violated enough FBI regulations to get kicked off the task force."

"I've already been kicked off," I said.

"And I don't give a shit," Vincent added.

Ruiz swung his glare back and forth between us, his puffy, eggplant-colored eye overshadowing the other. "What do you want?"

I walked over to the tall media chest propping up a 40-inch flat-screen TV that stood directly in front of Ruiz and leaned against it with my arms crossed.

Vincent holstered his weapon. He pulled up a nearby chair and turned it so he could straddle it. "Sorry about the gun. Just making sure you didn't try anything stupid."

"Fuck you. Your ass is grass. When my report—"

"If I were you, Ruiz, I'd be more worried about your career than mine."

Ruiz went rigid like a man suddenly doused with a bucket of ice water. There it was. The tactical advantage. We knew something he didn't. Something that probably gave us a free pass, if not an outright obligation, to pull a gun on a federal agent.

"What are you talking about?" he demanded.

"We're talking about you flushing that thirteen-year career calendar down the crapper." Vincent raised his arms like a ringmaster. "FBI Director Antonio Ruiz! The dream that never was."

Ruiz's eyes kept bouncing between us.

"It doesn't look good," I added gravely.

"I still have no idea what you assholes are talking about."

"Now, now," Vincent said. "Name-calling is beneath a man of your education."

"Dealing with assholes is beneath my education."

"Ha, good one." Vincent clapped. "And you made it up all by yourself too."

I asked, "How'd you get that black eye?"

He maintained eye contact and replied without hesitation, "Bar altercation."

Vincent laughed. "A bar fight? You, Mr. Boy Scout, in a bar fight? Come on. Didn't Harvard teach you how to bullshit better than that?"

Ruiz paused, his brain no doubt recalculating once more. Glaring at me, he said, "I was sucker punched in a dark alley. But you already know that, don't you, Jordan?"

"Why were you following me that night?"

Smiling now, Ruiz said, "I'm not at liberty to say."

"Why didn't you ID yourself?"

"Never got the chance."

"And you ran."

"I withdrew. And only *after* I got sucker punched."

"I could have shot you."

"On what grounds? There was no use-of-force continuum. I just happened to be walking in the same dark alley as you and was attacked. I withdrew to avoid escalation. I did nothing wrong. As a matter of fact, you just admitted to perpetrating that assault."

I planted my hands on my knees and leaned forward, getting in his face. "Who put you up to it?"

"You're wasting your time."

"Was it the SAC? Marino?"

"Marino?" Ruiz snickered. "I don't work for that little shit."

"Then it was the SAC."

"It'll all be in my report along with a detailed account of the unprovoked assault I sustained at the hands of the ever-reckless NYPD."

"Talk to us, man. We're on the same team!"

"Are we?"

"What's that supposed to mean?"

"This is it?" A smug smile spread across Ruiz's face. "This is how my career goes down the toilet? I spooked you in an alley? Are you two really that obtuse? Go on, get the fuck out of here. I've got work to do."

"What're you working on?" Vincent asked. "Like *really* working on?"

Ruiz didn't reply.

I leaned in closer, close enough to smell sweat and sour breath. "We got the shooter."

He winced like I'd faked a jab at his injured eye. "Bullshit."

I straightened my aching back. "The ID is solid."

"Bullshit," he said again, eyeing me so hard his good eye seemed to bulge.

"No bullshit," Vincent added. "And it's bad news for you, considering who it is."

"What the hell is that supposed to mean? Who is it?"

"Kamaria," I said.

Ruiz's jaw dropped and his eyes drifted.

"See it now?" Vincent stood, backed away from the chair, and walked to the side of the bed. "See how fucked you are? It's Kamaria. The Kamaria who ran the firearm analysis, the same Kamaria you were supposed to supervise. What do you think the brass'll make of that? Huh?"

Ruiz's jaw began to move but not enough to form words. His gaze was somewhere between the floor and his knees.

"I'll tell you what they'll make of it. They'll say you're either an idiot or an accomplice."

I let Vincent's words sink in before adding, "Tell us why you followed me that night."

"How do you know Kamaria is the shooter?"

"Why'd you pull the thumb drive out of evidence?" I asked. "What are you hoping to see now that you didn't see before?"

"You've been following me?"

"No. We saw you coming out of evidence."

"You were there? I didn't see you. Why? Why were you there?"

"Following up on Kamaria's firearm analysis report," I replied. "That's how we put it together."

He said after a long pause, "Tell me what you found. I'll tell you what you want to know."

I reached for the chair Vincent had vacated and turned it around so I could sit properly. For the next ten minutes, I walked Ruiz through my interview with Hank Robin and up to the moment we knocked on his door.

"All points to Kamaria as the shooter," I said in conclusion.

The entire time Ruiz had been sitting on the edge of the bed, there had been a rigidness about him, a physical manifestation of his unwillingness to talk to us. The only evidence that he was not in a sitting coma was his constant turning of the bezel on his huge diving watch. After my debriefing, that rigidness was gone, his watch forgotten.

He leaned forward, his elbows on his knees, his head in his hands. "How could I miss all that?" he said. "She asked the right questions, made the rookie mistakes you'd expect."

Vincent said, "She played you."

Ruiz lifted his head. "This doesn't make sense. If she's the shooter, why hasn't she fled? That entire gun swap was fragile. It wasn't going to cover her tracks forever."

Vincent shrugged. "We don't know."

"What's her motive, then?"

I replied, "We don't know that either."

"Did you pick her up?"

I shook my head.

"Why not?"

I explained the reasoning.

Ruiz said, "She's at least under surveillance, right?"

Vincent and I exchanged looks.

"No," I said. "Not yet."

"Not yet? Why the hell not yet? What are you waiting for?"

"You," I said.

Ruiz paused. "You don't know who to trust."

"That big Harvard brain is truly impressive."

Ruiz ignored Vincent and shot me a hard look. "I suspected you were the shooter."

I reeled back and pointed a finger at my chest. "Me?"

"Yes, you."

Vincent said, "Why the fuck would you think that?"

"Why wouldn't I? Why didn't you, Vinny? Why didn't anyone?" He sat up and said to me, "Everyone knew you had a hard-on for El-Hashem. You wanted him so bad you pulled high-level strings just so you could get on the task force and stay on the SOB. You were hell-bent on nailing his ass for that triple homicide. You never let it go. If anyone wanted him dead, it was you."

He paused, either for effect or to study my reaction. "And then at the square, you don't fall in behind the ground team. You go off script. Even then, before the shit hit the fan, it struck me as odd. But I was doing my job. I couldn't watch you and El-Hashem at the same time. I stuck with the subject. Next thing I know, shots fired. The snitch goes down, and you're MIA, calling in a shooter no one else saw. See what I mean? You were a prime suspect. You had motive. You had opportunity."

Vincent whistled. "If I didn't know you like I know you, Miles..."

I laughed. But unlike the laughter I'd shared with Officer Cambio back in the evidence room, this release of nervous energy was anything but calming. To know I'd been that transparent was unnerving. Anyone listening to Ruiz would conclude I'd been obsessed with El-Hashem and had lost all sense of perspective and professionalism. Was that the case? If I wanted to be brutally honest with myself, I would have to admit it was, at least partially. Crime scenes involving kids always did something to me. The heartbreaking images, the reek of innocent blood, were like hands reaching into my soul and unlocking something dark and relentless.

Ruiz crossed his arms and tapped his heels on the floor. "I fail to see what's so fucking funny."

I composed myself. "It's ... it's just so ... absurd and logical. I do make a good suspect. I bet my reaction to Marino's accusations back at the squad room didn't help."

Ruiz puckered his lips and nodded. "That sealed it for me. Smelled of guilt. I'd never seen you disrespect the brass, let alone lose your shit like that. I read it as a good deflection."

Vincent sat on the bed next to Ruiz. "Let me guess. You didn't tell anybody what was going through that big brain of yours because you were gonna crack the case all by yourself, right?"

Ruiz shook his head. "Who was *I* going to trust? We had a mole and we all knew it."

"What, you don't trust any of your FBI buddies?" Vincent asked. "Find that hard to believe." Vincent was making the point all three of us knew: it was just classic Ruiz, trying to one-up everyone else.

I said, "What about Kaufmann? He was proof that someone else was there."

"What could I make of that? I see you in that video wrestling a disguised perp who later turns out to be a CIA operative. I barely get a chance to process that when I hear you're meeting with the CIA—alone."

"And you thought ... what?" I asked.

"I just told you, I didn't know what to make of it. Maybe it was legit. Maybe it was all a smoke screen. Maybe you were working for the CIA. Maybe they were there on something else, and you just happened to stumble on it."

Ruiz's explanation was plausible. There was nothing in his body language that hinted at deception. Of course, a professional interviewer himself, Ruiz could be a professional liar when he needed to be. But my gut told me he was playing ball.

"So you followed me to that meet to get answers," I said.

"I wanted to see who you were meeting and what was being discussed. I couldn't get close enough, though. Those agents were watchful. After the meet I kept following you, trying to see if I could piece something together."

"Instead, all you got was a knuckle calzone." Vincent laughed.

Ruiz glowered at Vincent but said nothing.

I asked, "Where was your partner on all this?"

"Colt?" Ruiz shrugged. "He was rolling with the team directive. Find the benefactor, find the shooter, find The Scorpion, save the day. Like everyone else, the CIA angle threw him for a loop. But Colt has a vivid imagination. He was speculating a Russian or Iranian plot to explain the CIA involvement."

"*Marone*, how'd he ever graduate from FBI school?"

"Tell me about the video," I said.

Ruiz turned the bezel of his watch a couple of times. "After our incident in the alley, I kept trying to make sense of your meeting with the CIA. You in bed with them was all I could come up with, so I wanted to bring you in for questioning. But I needed a hook. I thought maybe there was something in that video that we missed and I could use."

"Like what?" I asked.

Ruiz shrugged. "Maybe your fight with Kaufmann was staged, and we just didn't see it."

"So that's all you focused on?"

"That's all I had time for before you characters showed up."

"And?"

"And what?"

"Did you see anything new?"

He shook his head.

"But you did miss something," I said.

"What do you mean?"

"You missed Kamaria."

Ruiz shook his head emphatically. "No way. We watched all the video recorded before the shooting—several times. We would have spotted her. The video quality is good and covers the only stairwell on that floor."

"If a disguise almost worked for Kaufmann, why wouldn't one work for her?"

His mouth fell open. "Didn't think of that. Then again, we weren't looking for that—for her."

I walked over to the nightstand and picked up the laptop. "Let's watch the video."

Chapter Forty-Two

Video

I put the laptop on the media chest and connected it via Bluetooth to the 40-inch flat screen. Vincent, Ruiz, and I huddled around it.

"What was the camera setup?" I asked.

Ruiz logged in. "One high-definition IP camera streaming video to a local server. It's hardwired to a LAN, set to record twenty-four seven. The server holds about a month of video before it starts overwriting the oldest files."

The machine came out of login to display a frozen frame of video, which was projected onto the TV. Ruiz was right; the quality was good. The focal point of the ceiling camera was the stairwell. Its wide-angle lens captured the left end of the hallway and a portion of the hallway to the right of the stairwell on the second floor of the Procuratie Vecchie. As I'd seen when I was there, that put the shooter's room behind the eye of the camera. To the right of the stairwell hung a large gold-framed mirror, followed by the room Kaufmann had used to make his escape. Several feet after that was me pressed against the wall, grimacing at a punch in the kidney from Kaufmann. As if to underscore the effectiveness of that blow, one of the smoke detectors mounted high on the wall was caught with its intermittent bright red power light on.

"Why only one camera?" I asked. "You lose half the hallway."

"The building caretaker told us they had a couple of burglaries in the offices on that side of the floor." Ruiz shrugged.

"Maybe they're waiting for the burglars to visit the other side before putting a camera there."

He hovered the cursor over the video software's rewind button. "How far back?"

I turned to Vincent. "What time did we get to the square that morning?"

"About eight," Vincent replied.

"What about Kamaria?"

"Dunno. She left op plan with one of the Carabinieri units. Didn't see her again until after the shooting."

Kamaria had attended the operation plan meeting that morning at dawn, hours before the shooting. We all did. And like Vincent, the next time I saw her was after the shooting when I was stinging from the beating Kaufmann had administered.

"Start there," I said to Ruiz. "At 0800 hours."

The smoke detector power light was a steady red as the video rewound fast enough to eliminate its intermittent blinking, an effect similar to the spokes on a wheel blurring together to appear as a solid disk when a car is cruising. Then for an instant, it wasn't, and I thought it was my imagination. When it happened again, I pointed at the TV. "What was that?"

Ruiz paused the video. "What was what?"

"The smoke detector there, it has a red power light. And it just blinked."

"So?"

"Those lights are set to blink at steady intervals of about three seconds. I saw that when I was there. When the video moves fast enough it's a steady red. But it just blinked, so the video must've skipped."

"Oh, that. Dropped frames. Happens with network cameras. The techs confirmed it."

"Back up a little and play it."

Ruiz backed up a minute and played the video at normal speed. This time, I watched the twenty-four-hour clock display at the top of the screen. A perceptible wobble in the image occurred at the moment the time skipped from 10:15:20 to 10:15:32.

"Shit, man, you sure the techs okayed this?" I pressed Ruiz. "Twelve seconds is more than a few frames."

"I didn't say they okayed anything. They gave us a plausible explanation for dropped frames, which we accepted. Our objective was to ID the perp, and the dropped frames did not interfere with that objective."

"Does it happen again?"

Ruiz shrugged. "I just told you that's not what we focused on."

I pulled at my goatee. "Okay, instead of rewinding this time, can you just jump to 0800?"

Ruiz moved the cursor and tapped a few keys on the keyboard. The progress bar at the bottom of the video jumped backward and the image changed. The time on it was 08:00:00. We started our review from there.

Between 08:44:03 and 09:54:02, over a dozen people stepped off the stairs and walked down the left end of the hallway. We scrutinized them all and for various reasons decided that no one was a person of interest.

At 09:58:06, two men in monk habits stepped off the stairs. Both were bald and pink under their brown skullcaps and as thin as the cinctures tied around their waists. They too, headed down the left end of the hallway, absorbed in conversation. Less than a minute later, another man dressed in a habit (the hood drawn over his head) stood at the top of the stairs. Unlike the first two, you could balance a pitcher of beer on each of his shoulders.

"That's the spook, isn't it?" Vincent leaned into the TV for a closer look.

Kaufmann had presumably followed close enough behind the two monks to appear as just another monk going wherever monks went at that time of the day but not so close as to attract their attention. Peeking into the hallway, he waited until they disappeared behind an office door before emerging from the stairwell. With his head down, he turned right and walked under the camera and out of view.

Ruiz fast-forwarded until the video put me at the stairwell. The red power light on the smoke detector had clearly blinked once more. That gnawed at me. It was lost information.

Playing at normal speed, the video showed me leaning on the railing post and breathing like I'd just run the forty. At first glance, I refused to recognize the fat guy on the screen. Pictures made me look huge; video did too. I expected a barb from Vincent, but he was too engrossed with the video to care.

With professional detachment, I watched my chance encounter with Kaufmann unfold. Staring at the gun I had in his face, he removed the hood and slowly circled. Then, lightning fast, he ducked and charged.

"Jesus. You got your ass handed to you," Vincent said. "You sure you don't want payback?"

I didn't reply.

In the video, Kaufmann shook off my feeble tackle and made a beeline for the room near the stairwell. Responding Carabinieri soldiers gave chase. Seconds later, Kamaria came off the stairs and rushed toward me. It was the first time she appeared. No one we observed coming out of that stairwell—the only public ingress or egress to that floor—remotely matched her physical description. Unless she'd had a Hollywood FX makeover, Kamaria had not been on that floor at any point prior to the shooting.

"She can't be the shooter," I muttered.

"Looks that way." Vincent stretched his neck sideways until it cracked. "If it's not her or that meathead spook, then who?"

"An accomplice," Ruiz said.

"No shit. That big Harvard brain strikes again."

Ruiz flipped Vincent the bird. Vincent blew him a kiss.

"Can we eliminate Kaufmann?" I asked. "He was the only one who turned to the right of that hallway, where the shooter's room is located."

Vincent said, "If we don't eliminate him, then it means Kamaria supplied the rifle to the CIA. And that doesn't make sense, does it? Why would they operate like that? They got tons of resources."

For a long moment, no one said anything.

"Maybe the shooter was already there. In that room," Ruiz offered. "Went in overnight or the day before. We didn't look at video prior to the morning of the shooting."

"How much video is on that thumb drive?"

"Forty-eight hours."

"Let's see it. But rewind instead of jump. Twelve hours, to start with," I said.

Ruiz rewound through twelve hours of video. I kept a close watch on the smoke detector light. When Ruiz stopped it, the date was the day before the shooting, and the time was 23:15:17 or 11:15 p.m.

"Nada." He exhaled sharply. "Go back another twelve?"

I took a step back. "Wait. You missed it? You both missed it?"

Vincent and Ruiz shot me puzzled looks.

"Missed what? The boring movie of the week?" Vincent said. "Nobody came up those stairs all night."

"The smoke detector light. It never blinked."

Like a moment of time captured in a frame of video, we all froze.

Snapping out of it, Ruiz asked, "How many times did it blink before?"

"Twice," I said.

"You sure?" Without waiting for a response, Vincent added, "We better go through the video again."

Ruiz fast-forwarded through the same twelve hours of video and then a little more, stopping where Kamaria came out of the stairwell. "You're right; it blinked twice."

"*Only* twice, in twelve hours," I said. "Either both are legit and very convenient network glitches that occur before and after the shooting, or—"

"Are evidence of tampering ... shit."

"Shit is right. Looks like you guys dropped the ball."

"Shut up, Vinny." Ruiz looked down at his watch and spun the bezel.

I asked Ruiz, "Did the techs watch any of this video?"

He didn't reply.

"Ruiz!"

"I don't know! I didn't work with them; Colt did. But no, I don't think so. Like I said before, the spook was the focus, and there were no video issues there."

"Was that local server backed up?"

"No. It wasn't backed up. Not recently. Not for the last three months. There was an external hard drive, but it wasn't connected to the server. The techs said the last file on it was dated three months ago."

Probably fed up with aching, my knee had gone numb. I turned away from the TV and sat on the corner of the bed. The mattress sagged and the box spring creaked. "How often was the video on the external drive backed up?"

"Every day."

"They did a daily backup and then just stopped? Why? Did you ask the caretaker?"

Ruiz kneaded his forehead supposedly trying to ward off a migraine. "We did after the techs told us the external drive was useless. The caretaker didn't know why it was disconnected. He said the night caretaker handled that stuff. We were supposed to do a follow-up, but after ID'ing the spook, it wasn't necessary."

"It is now."

Vincent said, "What does it matter why they disconnected the external drive three months ago? That *was* the backup, and now it's lost forever."

"Maybe … maybe not," I said.

Vincent cocked his head. "'Maybe not' how?"

"A cloud backup. That would explain why they don't use the external drive anymore."

Ruiz puckered his lips and nodded. "Makes sense."

I got up and limped for the door. "Let's go."

"Where?" Vincent asked.

"To see the night caretaker."

Chapter Forty-Three

The Face

We waited for the night caretaker at the Procuratie Vecchie in the corridor where I'd been shot at with a submachine gun. I hadn't set foot inside it since the incident. The chunks of plaster chiseled off the ceiling by the spray of gunfire had been swept off the marble floor, but the ceiling remained conspicuously pockmarked.

It was almost four in the morning, and the square was still lit up like a chandelier. The wind swirling in the dark sky pinched with chilly fingers.

A man with an enviable shock of jet-black hair approached. He was outfitted in a black dress shirt and a black suit that left no room for those last ten pounds fit folks are obsessed with losing. He wore a bloodred tie that stood out against the black like an exclamation point. His pale skin seemed translucent, revealing webs of blue veins in his neck and forehead. When he introduced himself as Mr. Ricci, he didn't smile or offer his hand. He stood motionless with his arms pinned at his sides.

Vincent leaned into my ear and whispered, "First we interview Jesus Christ, now we're gonna talk to Dracula."

Hasty introductions followed, though Ricci did eye Ruiz's and Vincent's credentials carefully.

In Italian, Vincent told Ricci about the video and asked why the external drive had been disconnected. Ricci spoke in a deep, raspy voice that gave me the willies.

Maybe Vincent was right. Maybe this guy is Dracula. Is there a more appropriate place for a vampire than a five-hundred-year-old European building?

I caught the Italian word for cloud: *nube*.

Vincent spun around. "They do a cloud backup." He traded more words with Ricci. "Okay, he said he can't show us the cloud stuff on the server since we took the hard drive, but he has a laptop in his office. He offered his phone, but I said we need a bigger screen."

Ricci led us into the building through the entrance reserved for tenants. On the day of the shooting, in the middle of so much commotion, I hadn't noticed how opulent the small lobby was. Just like the second floor, the ceiling had intricate moldings and fading frescos. There was no shortage of marble spread across the floor and stairs, which we had to climb quickly to keep up with the agile vampire.

Trailing the group, I paused at the landing and glanced at the shooter's room. *Is the secret about to be revealed?* I turned away and limped past a row of offices for a large insurance carrier.

Ricci's office was at the end of the hallway. He stood by the door, scrolling through a fully stocked key ring that probably held a copy of every key in Venice. It was at least the diameter of a grapefruit. *Where had he been keeping that?* I hadn't spotted the slightest bulge, crease, or ripple in the man's attire. I also didn't see how he eventually found the key he needed; they all looked exactly the same.

The office was barely lit by a desk lamp and smelled of bleach. A heavy drape with no split or visible means of drawing it covered the window. I suspected its sole purpose was to block out every photon of sunlight so Ricci wouldn't burst into flames.

A large flat monitor and a computer tower turned on its side were spread across two stubby filing cabinets. The monitor was off. The tower's side panel stood propped against the wall, leaving the electronic guts exposed. A dangling cable ribbon and a gap in that tight arrangement marked the spot for the hard drive I'd seen in the evidence room. On the nearby metal desk, next to the lamp, was a large laptop tethered to a network cable.

Ricci settled into a desk chair and opened the laptop. We crowded around. After a couple of swipes and clicks on the trackpad, he'd accessed the remote cloud backup drive. Following Vincent's instructions, Ricci located the video file for the day of the shooting and fast-forwarded a little past the point where the camera first captured Agent Kaufmann at the stairwell.

We watched the video from there in real time.

The minutes ticked away.

No evidence of a wobble materialized, just a smooth image composed of a steady stream of video frames.

Ruiz stood transfixed. "No glitches. Not a fucking thing wrong with the network."

A man we hadn't seen before suddenly appeared at the stairwell.

"Look!" I pointed.

He turned down the right side of the hallway with haste and purpose. A cap with the Lion of Venice stamped across the front panels hid his face, but the skin I could see on his neck was white. He was slim in a way that suggested fitness and wore the overalls of a building maintenance worker.

Ricci stopped the video. He turned to Vincent and said something too urgent and quick for me to catch.

Vincent said, "He's saying that's not one of his guys. That's their uniform, but he's never seen this guy before."

My heart beat faster. "How can he tell? You can't see his face."

Vincent spoke to Ricci then answered me. "They got only one employee with short blond hair, and he's got a hundred pounds over this guy."

I hadn't noticed the buzz cut of sandy blond hair under the cap. "What about the day crew? He's the night caretaker."

"Didn't you hear me ask him that? He says he knows everybody."

No, I hadn't heard that. I'd stopped listening to Ricci altogether. My attention was riveted on what the man in the video was carrying. "He has a duffel bag. Can we zoom in?"

A moment later, we were staring at a solid navy canvas duffel bag with the word "Venezia" embroidered in gold letters along the sides.

"That looks like the bag we have in evidence." Ruiz pointed. "And there's something rigid in it."

"Something like a short sniper rifle," I said.

Reaching over Ricci's shoulder for the trackpad, I zoomed out and played the video. The twenty-four-hour clock read 10:15:27, approximately fifteen minutes before the shooting. I let it play until the man disappeared under the camera and then reappeared hustling toward the stairwell. He wasn't carrying the duffel bag anymore. There was something familiar about his gait, a slight swinging out of each leg as it went forward. I stopped the video with the man in midstride, his back to the camera. I zoomed in, not on the man, but on the gold-framed mirror that hung a few feet to the right of the stairwell. Reflected there was a white face with a horseshoe mustache.

The face of the shooter.

The face of Special Agent Maxwell Colt.

Chapter Forty-Four

Loose End

We left the Procuratie Vecchie in glum silence and walked across the empty square to a marble bench built into the side of the basilica and sat.

Vincent said, “Holy shit. If I hadn't seen it with my own eyes.”

Ruiz kneaded his forehead. “Why would Colt…?”

“Before we even get into the why,” Vincent said, “let’s put together the how.”

I nodded. “More pieces fit.”

“Yeah, like the extra hat.”

Ruiz frowned. “What?”

I turned to Ruiz, who sat slouched between us. “After El-Hashem was shot, I saw Colt’s hat trampled in the mayhem. At some point prior to the shooting, he ditched it. He couldn’t enter the building wearing a red flag like that. In the video, he’s wearing a cap.”

Ruiz shook his head. “He had that hat on when we went looking for video, and it looked new. Like it always does.”

“That’s another hat,” Vincent said.

“Another hat?”

“We asked him about it at the bar the other night.” Vincent shrugged. “He said he travels with a backup.”

Ruiz dropped his head like the weight of his thoughts was too much for his neck muscles to bear. “Go on, Jordan.”

"Colt's position was just a few yards shy of the Procuratie Vecchie. So he ditched the hat, blended in with the crowd, and met up with Kamaria somewhere inside the building. The open arcade or the square itself would've been too risky."

"She was at the clock tower, right?" Vincent asked.

"That's what she said on the radio, but she could've been anywhere."

Ruiz lifted his head. "Why meet there?"

"She supplied the weapon," I said. "Remember?"

"I know. What I mean is, she could've given it to him at any point prior to the operation."

"He didn't have a bag at the operation plan meeting or on the walk to the square."

"Maybe he stashed it somewhere."

"Maybe. But that's risky, isn't it? What if it was found?"

"True." Ruiz sat back and stretched out his legs. "Kamaria didn't walk to the square with us that morning. She could've easily picked up the bag along the way."

"Right. I also think she supplied the building maintenance uniform he had on. Colt first appears in the video about fifteen minutes before the shooting. Like the rifle, it had to be delivered quickly. There was enough room in the duffel bag for both."

"So he gets the duffel bag and changes somewhere?"

"Could've been in the small lobby of the tenants' entrance. The uniform was just a pair of overalls and a cap. Easy to throw on. Once disguised, he climbed the stairs to the second floor and headed for the shooter's room."

"And he knew exactly where to go," Vincent added. "Zero hesitation. That room was picked out in advance."

Ruiz said, "We don't know if he actually went into that room or how he got inside if he did. The video doesn't show that."

I said, "I think it's safe to assume he did. To get inside, he had a key. Picking the lock is a gamble. There's no telling how long it'll take. Then he had to unpack the rifle and set up to take the shot. Which he did like an amateur."

"What do you mean 'like an amateur'?"

"He stuck the barrel of the rifle out the window." I told him about my conversation with M&M, our NYPD SWAT guy.

Ruiz raised his voice. "You knew the shooter was an amateur all along, and you never mentioned it?"

"We had a mole, remember?"

"You held that back, just in case it was somebody on the task force? Namely, one of us?"

I didn't say anything.

"What were you thinking when we thought the shooter was CIA?"

"It didn't seem to fit. I expected the CIA to use professionals."

Vincent said, "I did too, but I kinda entertained the possibility. Like maybe they sent somebody expendable, not really qualified for that kind of mission. I know. It sounds stupid."

Ruiz said to Vincent, "You knew too?"

Vincent didn't reply.

Ruiz said, "Well, amateur or not, Colt got the job done."

"He had an ace," I said. "Having radio access, he knew every move the target made in real time."

"Still, he hit a moving target."

"No, he didn't. Right before El-Hashem was shot, he received another text message."

Vincent snapped his fingers. "I remember that. Made him turn around and wait by the maize cart."

"Right," I said. "And Colt knew the number of the phone we gave El-Hashem to use. We all did. He sent that text message—maybe from a burner he'd been using all along, posing as The Scorpion—to put El-Hashem in his crosshairs."

Vincent stood. "That means we have no link to The Scorpion."

We paused.

"We don't know that for sure," I said.

"There's a lot we don't know for sure," Vincent countered.

"I know Colt panicked. After shooting El-Hashem, he spotted me approaching the window from the square. He took off and forgot the rifle or figured it was better to leave it behind than to run into me while having it in his possession. He did have enough sense to take the shell casings."

Vincent clenched his fists. "When are we picking up the dirty son of a bitch?"

"But what's the motive?" Ruiz's voice dropped a few decibels. "Why do this?"

"Has to be The Holy Hand," Vincent said. "We know they have a mole inside, and we can be sure it's Kamaria. She's gotta be a member or on the payroll."

"She's Muslim," I said. "She can't be a member. But she could work for them."

"And Colt?" Ruiz asked.

"She recruited him," Vincent said.

"Recruited Colt? How?"

Vincent shot me a look. "They're lovers."

Now it was my turn to hang my head. I didn't want Vincent or Ruiz to see the expression on my face. I wasn't sure what it was showing since I wasn't sure what I was feeling. Kamaria told me they'd had a relationship but made it clear it was over. Vincent was suggesting they were still involved. You stood a better chance of manipulating a lover to commit murder than you did an ex. If I accepted that, I had to accept my brief, budding relationship with her was a sham.

"Lovers?" Ruiz leaned forward and propped his elbows on his knees. "Until a couple of months ago, I suspected something was going on between them. I broke Colt's balls about it, but he always denied it."

"What changed?" Vincent asked.

"They just stopped being so chummy, like a wall went up between them," Ruiz said.

"Like they broke it off?"

"Yeah, maybe. Or maybe they just decided to be discreet, given what they were planning to do."

Vincent held up his arms. "How's this for a motive? Kamaria tells The Holy Hand about the snitch and his connection to The Scorpion. The Holy Hand sees an opportunity to boost the cardinal's ratings—same old theory we've had all along. They plot to take out our snitch, and Kamaria is given the job because of her access. She recruits Colt as the triggerman."

Ruiz pursed his lips and nodded. "It's a start. What do you think, Jordan?"

Though it was still dark, a vendor arrived at his cart and set to open for business. Others would soon follow, along with the tide of irritating, selfie-snapping tourists.

"Well, what do you think?" he asked again.

"It's plausible," I said. "But something is bothering me. By taking a rifle out of evidence to use in another crime, Kamaria took a huge risk. It's not the kind of thing that would go unnoticed. Sooner rather than later, someone would have caught it. A subsequent investigation would start with her. It's almost as if … as if she didn't care. Or needed the charade to hold up only temporarily."

"For what reason?" Vincent asked.

I looked around without focusing. "I don't know. And why recruit Colt at all? Why not do the hit herself?"

Ruiz said, "Maybe she needed someone expendable."

"Oh shit! Colt is a loose end."

Chapter Forty-Five

Heart in Two

We were too late.

The walls around the alcove bathtub were splattered with blood, skull, and brain matter. Colt lay naked and partially submerged in the crimson bathwater. His head drooped awkwardly to his right, away from the wall and toward the edge of the tub. A gaping hole in the side of his head marked the violent egress of an expanding bullet. The round had ended its trajectory as a fragmented star-shaped mark on the white marble tile of the adjacent wall. On the floor next to the bathtub lay a Glock .40 caliber pistol.

In the small bathroom, Ruiz squeezed between us to take in the scene. "Oh, fuck." He stumbled backward and sat hard on the toilet seat. "Fuck, fuck."

"Poor bastard." Vincent took a deep breath. "Did himself a favor."

"No, he didn't." Ruiz's voice cracked and his eyes moistened. "Colt was left-handed."

I took a closer look and understood.

The gory exit wound on the left side of the skull suggested Colt had shot himself on the right side with his right hand. The chances of that were between slim and none. Putting a gun to the side of your head and pulling the trigger isn't a guarantee of death, let alone instant death. If you failed to keep the gun steady and at the right angle to hit the brain stem, you risked a slow, conscious death by intracranial hemorrhaging. Worse, you could survive with permanent disfigurement, blindness, or severe brain damage. It was a task you trusted to your dominant hand.

I slipped on a fresh surgical glove from my suit pocket and felt Colt's neck muscles. "Rigor hasn't set in."

Vincent said, "That gives us a few hours' kill window to work with."

Ruiz whispered, "Kamaria did this."

I peeled off the glove. "They were lovers. Kamaria didn't know Colt was left-handed?"

"She caught him like this." Vincent pointed at the water spout on the other end of the tub. "This is the only way to take a bath. Would've been very difficult to get it right."

"Then why bother?" I asked. "Colt's prints will be all over that gun"—I pointed to it—"if it turns out to be his service weapon. But the techs won't find any gunshot residue on his right hand. What does a sloppy crime scene buy?"

"Time," Vincent offered.

"Time for what?"

"Seems obvious," Ruiz replied.

I turned to Ruiz.

"To flee," he said.

The bathroom was shrinking, the air in it quickly thinning.

Kamaria is a killer. A black widow.

I staggered out of the bathroom to breathe.

The rest of Colt's apartment was a square of space barely large enough to fit a kitchen, a bed, and a desk. Landscape oil paintings of the American West were displayed on a couple of walls. On top of the desk, a bottle of Jim Beam and an empty shot glass beckoned me. I walked over, rolled out the desk chair with my foot, and sat. I considered the bottle. Kamaria was a wine drinker. Even if her duplicitous nature had prompted her to hide a love of bourbon, her cop smarts guaranteed she hadn't left behind prints or DNA on a bottle of Jim Beam or Colt's personal shot glass.

I poured two fingers' worth of bourbon and drank. The hot rush of liquor did little to wash away the tension or give me a much-needed boost of energy. I felt so tired I could barely think. I was pouring another round when my cellphone rang.

"Why isn't Ruiz picking up his goddamn phone?" O'Neil shouted over the line. "What's the status on Colt?"

"We're at his apartment. He checked out—permanently."

O'Neil paused. "He ate his gun?"

"Large exit wound on the side of the head. We think they staged it."

"They?"

I closed my eyes. A headache was brewing.

"Miles, still there? Who's 'they'?"

"I meant Kamaria. She's our prime suspect. Do the Carabinieri have her in custody?"

"Negative."

"What?"

"She's in the wind."

After we realized that Colt was a liability in danger of extinction, Ruiz called O'Neil to brief him. O'Neil instructed him and Vincent to apprehend Colt. I was allowed to tag along but only as a civilian. A team of Carabinieri had been dispatched to pick up Kamaria.

O'Neil continued, "No luggage, ID, or paperwork of any kind was found in her apartment. The Carabinieri issued an APB. Interpol has been alerted."

What Vincent and Ruiz had suggested about using a sloppy crime scene to buy time to flee was beginning to fit.

I said, "Colt's kill window is a few hours. She's got a head start."

"Tracking her down is not our job." O'Neil let that sink in for a moment. "We're handing that over to the Carabinieri along with Colt's homicide."

"But, Top, Colt was one of us."

"He stopped being one of us the moment he took that shot. And don't get me started on Kamaria. I respected her. I trusted her, goddammit!"

A dwindling part of me still clung to the hope that Kamaria's role in this mess could somehow be explained.

O'Neil cleared his throat. "Our top priority now is the Israeli prime minister's safety."

It took a moment to register. "Our? Does that mean I'm—"

"What did I tell you when we last spoke?"

"To … uh … lay low."

"And did you?"

"No."

"Goddamn right you didn't. You disobeyed an order, one I issued after sticking my neck out for you. Don't ever do that to me again—ever."

I felt my face flush. I didn't say anything.

"Lucky for you, you hit pay dirt. So as of right now, you're reinstated."

Relief coursed through me like a shot of adrenaline. "And Marino?"

"He's got bigger problems to worry about than you. His handpicked Special Operations star detective turns out to be a murderer and a conspirator."

I buried a reflex to defend her, which was, to my disbelief, still there despite all we'd uncovered.

O'Neil added, "After you hand things over to the Italians, make sure you all get some shut-eye. The Israeli delegation is scheduled to arrive tomorrow at 0600 hours. I need everybody tip-top when the prime minister gives his speech at the Doge's Palace."

O'Neil terminated the call.

I tossed my phone on the table and poured another shot of Jim Beam.

And then another.

The night had started out with the promise of romantic intrigue. It ended in a nightmare. Not the kind that keeps you up at night in a cold sweat. That I could handle. It was the kind that breaks your heart in two.

Chapter Forty-Six

Still Want Answers

The snoring woke me.

I was parched. My lower back was a jumble of knots. To boot, the remnants of a headache were quickly regrouping.

I could pin the headache on too much Jim Beam and his famous Kentucky bourbon. Perhaps the thirst too. The cause of the lower back pain, however, was a mystery. White crown molding and a dark ceiling stared back at me. I turned my head. In the semidarkness, I glimpsed the silhouette of a couch. Vincent and Ruiz sat at the ends of it, slumped against bulky armrests. Both were fast asleep. At least one snored up a tropical storm. Above them hung two rows of portraits.

Old men in uniform.

Armed with that clue and a grimace, I knew I'd fallen asleep on one of the overstuffed, marshmallow-soft couches in the hallway leading to the task force office. I was still in my suit, with my shirt collar unbuttoned, tie loosened, and jacket subbing for a pillow. Through the thin fabric, the hard case of my phone pressed against the back of my head.

I rolled sideways. A bolt of pain lit up my lower back. I yelped.

"You okay, Jordan?"

In the gloom, Ruiz's eyes looked unusually white and creepy. I half expected him to hoot.

"Hell no," I whined. "Why did I lie on this shit couch? Now my back is killing me."

"You crashed on it. Happens when you go sleepless for thirty hours."

Biting my lower lip, I pushed off the doughy seat cushions with my hands and elbows. Then I lowered my legs over the edge until my feet were on the floor and I was in a rigid sitting position. I groaned. "What time is it?"

Ruiz checked his fancy diving watch, which apparently told time in the dark. "It's 2100 hours."

Three hours before midnight.

Where had the day gone? After my call with O'Neil, we stayed around while the Italians processed Colt's crime scene. After that, we were too wired to sleep and headed to the office. I now remember taking my gun and shield from O'Neil, feeling grateful and whole again, and sitting on the couch.

"I've been lying here for six hours?" I said.

Vincent giggled in his sleep and mumbled something. I caught the words "Lufthansa" and "cockpit." He then resumed his thunderous snoring.

Ruiz eyed Vincent. "Does he always snore like that?"

"I wouldn't know; I don't sleep with the guy."

"Never dozed off on a surveillance?"

"No, Ruiz, we don't fucking doze off on surveillance."

Ruiz's face was suddenly bright and ghostly, illuminated by the backlight of his phone. "You got any updates?"

Fearful of another back spasm, I carefully unwrapped my suit jacket and grabbed my phone. It took me a moment to adjust to the sudden brightness of the screen.

"No," I said. "Kamaria must still be in the wind."

Ruiz nodded.

"If you had to guess, where do you think she went?" I asked.

He put away his phone. "Assuming she acted on behalf of The Holy Hand, she would likely be holed up somewhere in Europe. It's the only continent they operate in."

"You don't think she's still in Venice?"

"Highly doubt it. No reason to stick around. Like you said, taking that rifle out of storage was risky, so her charade was short-term."

"Why did she hang around at all?"

Ruiz took a moment to answer. "Maybe waiting for the right time to kill Colt."

I considered that while trying to massage the tension from my lower back. Why did she wait three days to hit Colt if her intention was to disappear anyway?

A couple of minutes later, Ruiz said, "Though I'm having a hard time believing she's working for The Holy Hand. How do you guys make that connection?"

Still rubbing my back, I said, "You know how she ended up here, in Italy?"

He shook his head.

"She was brought over by the church. Some sort of program for orphans of the civil war in Somalia back in the early nineties. Maybe she felt indebted and sees The Holy Hand as a way to repay."

"How do you know this?" When I didn't reply, Ruiz said, "You got involved with her?"

I hesitated. "A few drinks. Didn't go anywhere."

"Does O'Neil know? This can be construed as a conflict of—"

"She's going down for whatever crimes she's committed, and I'll do my part to see that happens. Nobody gets a free lunch on my watch."

"That's all well and good, but I don't think—"

"Frankly, I don't give a shit what you think." Bracing against my knees, I slowly stood.

Ruiz sat up. "Where are you going?"

Keeping my back as straight as I could, I bent my knees to get my phone and suit jacket off the couch. That's when my bum knee decided to lock up. I stood frozen and precariously unbalanced. Ruiz rushed over and grabbed me before I toppled over.

"Sit down. You're an orthopedic basket case." He picked up my phone and jacket.

I snatched my stuff when he offered it and started down the hallway.

Ruiz said, "Where the hell are you going?"

"To check out Kamaria's apartment."

"What for? The Carabinieri cleared it."

"I haven't cleared it."

"Uh … you want company? Hey, Jordan!"

I flipped him the bird over my shoulder and limped on.

Chapter Forty-Seven

Eleven Hours

The man stood in the cramped room with his arms folded, cupping his elbows. Resisting the urge to roll and smoke another cigarette, he studied the items he'd unpacked from the suitcase Nabeel Haddad had delivered.

Neatly assembled on the bed were bundles of multicolored wire, tightly packed hardware in clear plastic bags, wire caps, electrical tape, one dead man's switch (battery pack included), a roll-down tool case, plastic explosives carefully shaped as square and rectangular panels, and most importantly, the uniform.

Delivered that morning, the tactical uniform—similar to the combat fatigues he'd once worn in battle—was the perfect disguise. Its most convenient accessory was the bulletproof vest worn as an outer layer. The small but prominent patch on the top chest panel reading "Carabinieri" and the much larger patch spanning the back guaranteed access to the stage.

Access to the stage meant death to the Israeli prime minister and his dogs.

He dragged a chair to the side of the bed and sat. He unrolled the tool case along the edge of the mattress. All the necessary tools were there. Each made for a specific purpose, designed to reliably execute that purpose with precision.

Why didn't human tools work the same way?

Why were they so unpredictable?

So flawed?

Next to the neatly folded uniform were several ammo pouches he intended to pack with the hardware.

Nuts. Bolts. Ball bearings.

Once fixed to loops on the outside of the vest in a near circular arrangement, the pouches would simply appear to hold extra magazines. Nothing out of the ordinary. Carabinieri personnel were expected to carry extra ammo for their submachine guns.

He grabbed the vest and draped it over his lap. With the Kevlar plates removed, it was lightweight, almost insubstantial. Panels of plastic explosives would soon replace the Kevlar and provide a solid framework behind the ammo pouches, ensuring the maximum omnidirectional discharge of the hardware.

The cheap wall clock above the bed chimed: 10:00 p.m.

Eleven hours.

He reached for a bundle of wire, a fine-gauge wire stripper, and set to work.

Chapter Forty-Eight

The Photo

The boat ride and walk to Kamaria's apartment lessened my lower back pain from near paralysis to a dull ache. My bum knee was another story. By the time I reached the three-story building where she had supposedly lived for a number of years, I was limping again.

A Carabinieri unit had the building under surveillance in the unlikely case Kamaria had unfinished business there. This was not a movie stakeout, where the noble crime fighters pull an all-nighter in a cramped unmarked car. A pair of undercovers on foot was doing a bad job of blending in. One walked the perimeter on the balls of his feet; the other stood guard near the entrance, sucking on a cigarette. Both wore rumpled dark suits, white shirts, and loose ties. They might as well have been wearing uniforms and holding bullhorns.

Catching them completely unawares, I flashed my creds and told them in broken Italian that I was there to check out the apartment. They had every right to tell me to piss off. It was their job to find and apprehend Kamaria, not mine. Instead, they asked if I would mind the store while they took a short break. No problem.

I entered the cramped lobby, hoping to find an elevator. Instead, I got more stairs. Luckily, there was only one flight to climb.

Kamaria's apartment door was sealed off with crime scene tape. The Italian version of a no-knock warrant had been executed and the door forcibly compromised. The doorjamb was splintered where the locks made contact, the telltale sign of caving to a Halligan tool, a bigger, badder version of your average crowbar. I broke the tape and pushed the door open.

Inside, I groped the wall for the light switch and flipped it. A teardrop-shaped Moroccan lantern hanging from a chain lit a morsel of heaven. White was everywhere. On the walls, in the carpeting, splashed all over the furniture. It was a warm white, with touches of silver, gray, and aqua. The living room was lined on three sides with connecting floor seating, about a foot high, backed by neat rows of overlapping cushions of various shapes and sizes. A square of four picture frames forming a collage of geometric patterns and Islamic calligraphy hung on the wall.

I limped over to the floor seating and carefully settled on the nearest cushion. It was firm and comfortable. Sitting back and stretching my legs, I caught a faint but unmistakable scent.

Lilac and freesia.

Who was Kamaria? Who was she really? No matter how I turned it, I couldn't reconcile the two versions: the witty, sweet lover and the calculating black widow. A piece was missing, something that either bridged the gap or cast an entirely different light on things. She was a casualty of war, orphaned in a terrible attack so close and personal her survival had been a miracle. How does that shape a person? What demons does it nurture?

I am broken.

On the gondola ride that now seemed more a figment of my imagination than an actual memory, she had uttered those words. Broken because she had invited into her house a killer disguised as a smiling boy. A killer who mercilessly gunned down her parents. She carried the curse of survivor's guilt and all the second-guessing and nightmares that go with it.

The rattle of a nearby window shade resisting a sudden gust of wind pulled me out of my reverie. A few feet away stood a white table with four chairs. Next to it was a prayer rug with an arch-shaped design at one end whose point, no doubt, faced Mecca. The kitchen, not far from where I sat, was a tight arrangement of white cabinets and appliances.

Suddenly, the whiteness of the apartment bothered me. Not the color itself, but what it seemed to be telling me: generic, impersonal. In the entire spread of living room and dining room space, there wasn't a single item I could connect to a specific occupant. No pictures. No books or magazines. No evidence of mail. The dining table was bare. No place mats or tablecloth. No salt and pepper shakers. No napkin holder. And not a single candle anywhere. At the restaurant, hadn't Kamaria said that she loved candles and had many?

I knew I had a problem when I tried to get up from the floor seating. I couldn't float like a butterfly or spring to my feet. Gravity doesn't pinch an ass like mine; it grabs greedy handfuls. After a couple of failed attempts, I managed to roll off the cushion on all fours and eventually get on my feet. The effort took a toll; something shifted awkwardly in my bum knee.

In the kitchen, the lighting was fluorescent. Unlike the Moroccan lantern, it cast a blinding glare over everything. The stove and sink were spotless. So was the countertop. The refrigerator contained a six-pack of fat-free yogurt and a bottle of sparkling water. Two cabinet drawers housed a fork, three spoons, and a lonely knife. The bottom cabinet was empty.

I left the kitchen to look for other rooms and hobbled down a hallway. The first door to my left was the bathroom the techs had collected Kamaria's DNA from as part of Colt's murder investigation. A laundry room with a stackable washer and dryer followed on the right. At the end of the hallway, the ubiquitous white carpeting ended at the bedroom doorsill. Inside, the floor was bare. Dark hardwood planks ran parallel to a neatly made bed. A set of shutter doors opened to an empty closet. No errant clothes or shoes. Just a row of hangers left behind as mute witnesses.

I turned around to take in the room as a whole.

My eye was drawn to a large framed photo hanging on the opposite wall, a high-resolution shot of a stunning African landscape. A jagged mountain range loomed in the background. Tall yellow grass filled the foreground. Hidden in the grass, spying on a herd of antelope, lurked a lion.

A man behind a blind is like a lion in the grass.

The lion was a female. A huntress. Her ears were pricked, her muscles taut. She was poised to strike. The antelope were oblivious to the danger. The photo was so vivid I could feel the heat of the unseen sun. I could smell the moist earth, the wild basil, the dew coming off the mountains in the breeze. I approached the photo and reached for it.

No, leave it! The voice in my head grew loud and desperate. My heart beat faster.

Her scent was there too, sudden and overpowering. Had the antelope caught the scent of the lioness the moment after the photo was taken, or a moment later, a moment too late? Was Kamaria a lioness?

I snatched the photo off the wall. The frame was heavier than it looked and almost flew from my hand. I examined it closely and saw what I couldn't from afar: fear. The antelope were not oblivious. Ears pricked, ranks tight, eyes everywhere.

Something on the back of the frame curled under my fingers. I turned it over. A photo much smaller than the frame was taped there, and one strip of tape had come loose. Facedown, bright white. Beckoning me. I peeled the photograph off and turned it over.

A girl and a boy stood side by side. The girl wore a white hijab, the boy a white skullcap. Both were clad in black thobes. I recognized the girl. Same face. Same flawless skin. Unchanging hazel eyes.

Kamaria.

The boy was harder to ID. He had changed over the years, filling out, toning up, facial hair disguising deep acne scars. But like Kamaria, his eyes hadn't changed. Black and lifeless, peering out from under a shock of unruly black hair.

Aarzam El-Hashem.

My mind went blank as if disconnected from the world it knew. When it came back online, the confusion was stifling. What the fuck was this? I wanted to scream. Then came another jolt.

The camera had caught a man in the background, standing near the young Kamaria and the future Park Slope killer El-Hashem. Cut off at midchest, the man's face was not visible, but that didn't stop me from knowing who he was. He wore black fatigues with the sleeves rolled up. On his forearm was a large tattoo of the deathstalker scorpion.

It all came together. Every piece of the El-Hashem puzzle and Kamaria's role in it was now in place. I felt a strange sense of calm. Maybe relief was the right word. I knew where things stood.

I dropped the photo in my pocket and left the lioness and the antelope to their fate on the bed Kamaria had probably used. I hobbled from the bedroom to the door, where I reached for my phone.

On the second ring, Vincent picked up. "Where are you?"

"Kamaria's apartment. Didn't Ruiz tell you?"

"Kamaria's apartment? What the fuck are you doing there?"

"Where's O'Neil?"

"Here, somewhere in the office."

"Find him, I'll hold."

Two minutes later, Vincent was back on the line.

"I'm back, with O'Neil."

"Put me on speaker," I said.

"Hold on … there, go ahead."

"Top?"

"I'm here."

"The Holy Hand had nothing to do with the El-Hashem hit."

"*Marone*, really? I just bet Tufu fifty bucks it was all on them."

"Goddammit, Vinny, shut the hell up!" O'Neil exhaled. "Are you sure?"

"El-Hashem was hit by The Scorpion, but not for payback or turning snitch. He was hit to protect the identity of the sleeper agent."

"Slow down," O'Neil said. "You're confirming we have a sleeper agent?"

"El-Hashem and Kamaria knew each other. They trained together as kids in at least one of The Scorpion's camps. I found a photo in Kamaria's apartment that links the three of them."

"Holy shit," Vincent said.

"Wait a minute," O'Neil said. "You just said El-Hashem was killed to … so you're saying—"

"Exactly what you think I'm saying!"

Chapter Forty-Nine

A Weapon of War

Day 5

Friday, 0100 hours

Just as the man expected, the uniform fit her perfectly. After all, she was the loyal soldier who'd delivered it, the same soldier who had provided the uniform that enabled his easy escape from the bell tower on the day of the assassination.

It was the perfect disguise for a perfect weapon of war.

But was she a perfect weapon of war? Her expression was odd: solemn and withdrawn. He expected pride and joy to radiate from her. No honor was greater than to give one's life for Allah.

"You are sparse of words, Kamaria Uba," he said. "Are you steadfast of mind and purpose?"

For a moment, he saw the starving girl struggling to survive on the streets of Mogadishu. The girl with a fire in her eyes and a deep-rooted hate festering in her heart. It was that fire and hatred that bound them.

"I have few words left for this world." Kamaria's gaze dropped to the vest in his hands. "God willing, I will soon be in paradise."

The vest was substantial now, laden with hidden wires and explosives. He held it open and walked behind her. She carefully slipped her arms through the openings. She waited patiently as he snaked the orange wire from the inside of the vest through the front of her shirt and down the left sleeve.

"Will I see my parents in paradise?"

"One cannot say for sure." He zipped the vest. "But if you do not, you can intercede on their behalf for admittance into paradise in your honor. Why do you ask? You are well aware of the seven special favors of martyrdom."

He reminded himself that she was a tool, unpredictable and flawed.

The shooting at the square had been an example of that flaw. Eliminate the target with the weapon provided and vanish in plain sight. Leave no trace. Those were the simple instructions. Yet, the tool on that mission had panicked and left behind the weapon. Instead of returning it to evidence and focusing on other details, they had to work around its dangerous discovery. That mistake cost the tool his life.

Might she succumb to the same flaw?

He studied her in silence while he taped the orange wire to the side of the dead man's switch. Her Arabic was clear and steady. No restlessness in her movements or sweat on her brow. She was breathing normally. Her eyes were focused. The bottle of water she had brought along was almost full, so there was no dryness of the mouth. She displayed the calm and readiness of a true *mujahid* on the verge of greatness.

Was his concern misplaced?

"Keep the switch in the palm of your hand. It's small enough to go unnoticed. Once armed, it cannot be undone, so choose the moment wisely."

After showing her how to arm the switch—inserting the end of the orange wire, which was stripped of insulation, into the quick connector at the bottom of the unit—he took two steps back and gave her a final inspection. "You will blend in well. Like a snake in the sand."

She looked down at his handiwork and nodded approvingly.

"Now, recite the verses," he told her. "They will give you strength and inspiration."

While she recited the verses he had suggested from the Qur'an, he sat on the creaky bed and rolled a fresh cigarette. As he worked, he glanced at the tattoo on his forearm, acutely aware of the scar where he had instructed the artist to place the tip of the stinger. The real sting had nearly killed him, the neurotoxins bringing about a severe allergic reaction. But he'd survived. And since that day, to friend and foe alike, he'd been known as The Scorpion.

He lit his cigarette and took a drag. He flicked the ash on the floor, not bothering with the rice paper square on the nightstand he'd been using as a makeshift ashtray.

As he blew out the smoke, he watched her. "You look ready, Kamaria Uba."

Chapter Fifty

Fort Knox

Security in and around the Doge's Palace was tight. The palace interior, the prison, and the Bridge of Sighs that connected the two were all closed to the public. Only Carabinieri patrol boats were allowed in the canal that ran beneath the famous bridge. The basilica next door was also closed. The top of the bell tower had been turned into a makeshift command center for a half dozen video surveillance drones. Sweeping swathes of the square and promenade approaching the palace from the waterfront were also sealed off. Heavily armed Carabinieri units guarded a fortress wall of police barricades. Sharpshooters were posted on the palace rooftops. Bomb-sniffing K-9 units worked the checkpoints.

It took us several minutes to get past one of those checkpoints, even with our fresh suits, tactical shades, and FBI credentials. Vincent, Ruiz, and I went in together. Tufu and O'Neil were nearby.

Like the morning of the El-Hashem shooting, it was a perfect September day. Sunny and room temperature.

O'Neil said over the radio, "Shadow Team, from Top, how do you read this unit?"

Protection for the Israeli prime minister was the responsibility of the Israeli Security Agency and the Carabinieri. This was their show. We were just a sister law enforcement agency helping to beef up security. For this operation, O'Neil had code-named our group "Shadow Team."

I pressed the small push-to-talk microphone clipped to the inside of my dress shirt collar and replied, "Top, from Echo One. Read you loud and clear."

Vincent, Ruiz, and Tufu followed suit.

"Shadow Team, from Top, make your way to the Renaissance wing," O'Neil said. "We're two minutes out."

We followed a crowd of slow-moving VIPs and the media gnats who pestered them into the Portico Foscari. Carabinieri units cordoned off the end of the portico, which led to the palace staircase and its imposing statues. To the right, the portico opened to the palace courtyard with three narrow archways. The courtyard, with its Gothic architecture, was a work of art. But the arches, columns, and carved statues designed to awe were now suspect and vulnerable. At the foot of the palace's eastern wing—or Renaissance wing, as it was known—a stage overlooked two sections of folding chairs separated by an aisle. Carabinieri personnel posted along that aisle were ushering the VIPs to their assigned seats while the helicopter media continued to harass them with cameras and microphones. The courtyard was easier to maneuver. Vincent and Ruiz went ahead. I lagged behind. Soon, Tufu and O'Neil had caught up. O'Neil hurried past me. Tufu hung back.

"You should be on a knee scooter," Tufu said as he came up on my flank. He also wore a sharp suit and sunglasses. Even trimmed his scraggy beard for the occasion.

I cracked a smile. "Then I could be on the quick response team."

"Roger that." Tufu slowed to match the pace of my limping. "Help me digest all this. Colt was a bad guy? Now that's something nasty. And she's the sleeper agent? Shit, never saw that coming. I always thought she was a good piece of gear."

I scanned the third- and fourth-story windows. No dark shadows lurked. On the ground, Carabinieri blue overwhelmed. Same on the second-floor balconies and the rooftops. Marino had deployed an army. I half expected to hear tanks rolling in and helicopters hovering overhead.

"That was good detective work you did there," Tufu said. "Though that little stroke of luck didn't hurt."

"Stroke of luck?"

"Yeah, finding that pretty compromising picture in her apartment. Nobody thought to look behind the wall art."

I stopped to massage my knee. The pain had spread to the back. Maybe I should've worn a brace or really ridden in on a knee scooter.

"Now, all we gotta do is wait for her, right?" Tufu shaped his hand into a gun. "And put a bullet between her eyes."

I glowered at Tufu.

"What?" he said.

After a brief standoff, I shook my head. "Nothing. Go, catch up. O'Neil is waiting."

Tufu headed toward the Renaissance wing.

The stage was a rectangle, about four feet high, accommodating two rows of chairs and a podium, with room to spare for plenty of security. Connecting sheets of bulletproof glass were erected around the stage. Guarding the approach was a phalanx of Carabinieri soldiers in full combat gear.

"Okay, listen up, people," O'Neil said the moment I joined them. "Despite credible intel and a lot of last-minute pressure from the Italian government, the Israeli prime minister has refused to postpone or cancel. He insists it would be giving in to terrorists. Hence, this thing is a go." O'Neil looked at each of us in turn. "No mention of the sleeper over the encrypted radio channel unless you have a positive ID. Despite the last-minute change in frequency and encryption codes, we have to assume she has radio access."

Since dropping the bomb on O'Neil that Kamaria was the sleeper agent, he hadn't spoken her name. None of us had. We couldn't think of her as a former colleague or a friend. She was a threat who had to be contained by any means necessary. We all understood that, but it didn't make it any easier.

O'Neil added, "Just because every goddamn soldier, cop, and field agent within a ten-mile radius of this place is on high alert doesn't mean this area is secure. Stay sharp, people."

We dispersed.

Noticeably absent from the plea to postpone or cancel was the US government. That bolstered my suspicion that the CIA's true objective had been to assassinate El-Hashem to prevent The Scorpion's capture. With The Scorpion in the wind, the chances were good—or so they hoped—that a successful terrorist attack would result in an Israeli regime change favorable to the current White House administration. But Colt had conveniently done the job for them, and all they had left to do was walk away.

Our job here in Venice is done. Luck to you, Detective.

Those were Agent Shears' parting words. Had the smug bastard admitted it?

I patrolled, stopping frequently to rest my knee. After about thirty minutes, I met up with Vincent at the back of the stage, inside the arcade of the Renaissance wing. Security there was tighter, with access restricted to authorized personnel only.

"Anybody who's not supposed to be here is getting made," Vincent said. "I think we're barking up the wrong tree."

"What do you mean?"

"Look at this place. It's Fort Knox. The sleeper is expecting that, don't you think? Smarter to hit the PM on his way outta here or at his hotel in the wee hours of the night."

"No. This isn't personal. It's political. A huge public statement. You know a better place and time to make that kind of statement? Every major network from anywhere that matters is here. So she's going to strike here."

Vincent ran his fingers through his hair. "Yeah? Tell me how. She's gotta make it past three lines of barricades and checkpoints, six surveillance drones, four K-9 units, and three hundred armed and paranoid law enforcement personnel who can ID her tits a mile away."

I chewed on that for a moment. "You left out the glass."

"And then there's the frigging glass!"

"Echo Two, from Top," O'Neil said over the radio.

"Go, Top," Vincent said into his mic.

"What's your location?"

"Behind the stage."

"Roger, Echo Two. We need more coverage in the west wing."

"Copy that, Top. Heading over now."

Vincent gave me a see-you-later nod and left.

"Echo One, from Top."

"Go, Top," I said.

"Can you cover the south wing? That knee holding up?"

"Affirmative."

"Roger, Echo One."

O'Neil checked on Tufu and Ruiz. More routine radio traffic from other units followed.

I glanced at my phone clock. The PM and his entourage were set to head over to the stage in less than thirty minutes.

How was she planning to pull it off? Vincent was right; the place was sealed up like Fort Knox. The likely method of attack was a suicide bomb. She would have to conceal her identity—not to mention a suicide vest loaded with explosives—to get past the outer barricades. Then walk halfway across the courtyard and turn down the aisle between the two crowded sections of folding chairs to get to the stage. If she somehow made it that far (assuming she had a plan for dealing with the soldiers guarding the approach), the glass protecting the stage was rated to withstand that kind of bomb blast. She needed to be behind the glass to be successful, and that meant gaining access to an area with virtually impenetrable security.

The math for success wasn't good. That worried me. What were we missing?

CHAPTER FIFTY-ONE

DAMAGE CONTROL

Colonel Giuseppe Marino stood tall at the top of the Giants' Staircase, next to the imposing statue of Neptune, exactly where the doges had made public appearances when they ruled Venice. Since that was the official entrance of the Doge's Palace, it was cordoned off and heavily guarded. He listened to the banter of a small armed unit huddled behind him as they reviewed last-minute orders. Their job was simple: protect, kill. Clear parameters. For a moment he envied them. His job, on the other hand, had become a shitshow.

In the past week, he had dealt with one clusterfuck after another. Now his career stood on the tip of a dagger. Even his best dress uniform, adorned with all the fanfare of achievement, couldn't disguise the growing tension in his shoulders. Damage control alone would not save him. Not this time.

Officer Kamaria Uba had been his choice and his alone. Because she was an Arabic-speaking African and a woman, she was the perfect political candidate and spy. An ace up his sleeve whenever he sat down to play his power games with Rome or the Americans. Or so he'd thought. Not only had she been part of a conspiracy but allegedly a terrorist too!

After being informed, the bishop reminded Marino that The Holy Hand had to be protected at all cost. "We're all in this together," Cusa had told him. The bishop gave him assurances he would always have a place in the organization. It was an empty promise. The bishop was well aware of Marino's ambitions. Being just an enforcer for the organization would never make up for his losses. He would also be extremely limited in how he could help the organization, which would further lower his standing. Eventually, he would become expendable.

He removed his peaked cap and polished the gleaming visor with his handkerchief. He caught his reflection, not liking what he saw. *Is that doubt?* His gaze drifted to the exploding grenade and the rising flame insignia of the Carabinieri centered above the visor. He suddenly didn't like that either. It stared back at him like a harbinger of doom.

Nonsense! All is not lost.

He put the cap back on and marched to the edge of the stone landing. From his vantage point, he could see the entire courtyard. Most of the insufferable politicians Rome had spewed forth for the occasion sat close to the stage. Their minions and other guests settled in behind them. The press corps crowded the west end, where the vast arrangement of white chairs ended. Everywhere he looked, there was a well-armed Carabinieri officer manning a post or patrolling.

The few suits with earpieces loitering about were mainly the meddlesome FBI, now hailed as heroes for breaking the El-Hashem case.

How outrageous!

The entire episode had been orchestrated by them. He had been the only one to see it. Yes, he'd made mistakes. Jordan, for example, whom he'd first suspected and managed to get kicked off the task force. Later, he became convinced the CIA was guilty after they tried to implicate The Holy Hand. (Their recklessness cost Ignacio Bonaventura his life.) Two mistakes of fact but not of substance. The shooter had indeed been an American. He'd been right about that all along.

He laughed aloud. *Oh, the irony of it all!* That should have been a gift from heaven, but it quickly soured when Officer Uba's involvement was revealed by none other than the FBI. After all he'd done to derail them, the Americans had still come out on top.

Their resiliency is to be admired. That thought struck him like a punch in the gut. Marino groaned. Perhaps he'd made another mistake. Perhaps the key was not in derailing them but in using them. What if they still had a role to play?

He pulled out his cellphone and made a call to his most trusted asset on the ground. If he was wrong, it was only one fewer pair of eyes focused on the courtyard's security. If he was right, he might find salvation.

Chapter Fifty-Two

In Plain Sight

I limped along the south wing arcade, keeping a vigilant watch on the VIPs and the media people who never seemed to tire of covering them. Carabinieri blue was making me dizzy. Anyone wearing that shade of blue, or something close to it, could hide in plain sight. As Vincent had put it, there was no way anyone who didn't belong was going unnoticed. The question was, who could go unnoticed?

At the operation meeting with the Carabinieri and Israeli security hours before, the possibility of Kamaria wearing a uniform to gain access was discussed. Special Operations was a plainclothes unit, but its members still had uniforms. However, that wouldn't get her past a single checkpoint; there were less than a handful of black female officers in the Carabinieri. On the other hand, they expected many more black women in the audience and media ranks, so civilian gear seemed the logical choice. Still, my gut feeling didn't jibe with that line of reasoning. Nothing blended in better than a uniform. A tactical uniform—it occurred to me—offered the advantage of being equipped with an external vest. But whether she wore a uniform or civilian clothing, she would never get explosives past the K-9 units manning the checkpoints without a miracle or a stroke of luck.

Luck? What had Tufu said about luck?

I pulled out my phone.

"Miles, what's up?"

"What was it you said about luck?"

"Come again?"

"When we got here today, you said something about a stroke of luck."

"About you finding that hidden picture? Look, I wasn't insinuating—"

I hung up.

The photo she left behind. Why hadn't I thought about it before? She scrubs that apartment clean to leave us nothing but forgets to take or destroy an incriminating piece of evidence? It was hanging like a billboard on the fucking wall!

She left it there on purpose.

I listened to the ongoing radio traffic with sudden unease. My cellphone clock read 8:45 a.m. The ceremony was set to start in fifteen minutes.

Did she leave the picture for me? Who else knew about the lion in the grass?

Fit bodies in suits, white shirts, dark ties, and wraparound shades flooded the second-floor balcony in the Renaissance wing. They were the spear of the Israeli security detail.

The radio traffic was incessant. Unit after unit gave updated reports, called in security gaps, made adjustments. The tension was palpable.

Kamaria and I had danced together like no one else existed. We'd laughed without restraint. We'd made love like seasoned lovers, never a hesitation or a careless touch. When our eyes connected, we saw a nakedness that went beyond our physical bodies—we saw the essence of who we were.

At least that's what I'd thought.

A cheer and a round of applause greeted the Israeli prime minister as he stopped to wave at the crowd from the second-floor balcony. His security detail ushered him to the Censors' Staircase and down to the ground floor. The media turned the courtyard into a nightclub with their flashing cameras. I doubted anyone got a good shot of the short, paunchy prime minister. He wore his security detail like a cape.

Now I understand what Kamaria meant when she told me she couldn't do this. She was on a lethal mission. I was a distraction, a conflict of interest.

The Israeli entourage headed down the arcade of the Renaissance wing, moving like an armored column. A moment later, the prime minister sauntered onto the stage, shaking hands with the Venice bigwigs behind the safety of bulletproof glass.

It is said when a couple kisses under the Ponte dei Sospiri at sunrise, they will have eternal love.

We would never kiss under the Bridge of Sighs at sunrise or at any other time. We would never walk hand in hand across the Brooklyn Bridge or share a porterhouse steak at Peter Luger. We would never be anything together again.

Two video drones moved in to hover directly above the courtyard. The phalanx of Carabinieri at the foot of the stage seemed to harden. With his security detail calling the shots, the prime minister was seated on the stage. The Venice bigwigs followed suit.

When this is over, I'll walk alone across the Bridge of Sighs. A fitting way to say goodbye to Venice. A sigh on the way to the prison but not one for the loss of freedom. A sigh for what could have been. And then on the way back … wait a minute. What was on the other side of that bridge?

An image of the Bridge of Sighs seen from the canal in a gondola traveling south flashed like police lights in my mind's eye. The prison was to the left of the famous bridge, and to the right was the back of the Doge's Palace.

My heart rate shot up. My hands got clammy.

I could barely process the thoughts churning through my mind.

All of the calculus—Carabinieri blue uniforms, checkpoints, K-9 units, video drones, Kamaria's darkening mood as we neared the bridge on our last night together, her words, the accessibility the bridge route offered to the courtyard—added up to one conclusion.

I moved westward to find Vincent. By the time we made eye contact, I was close to jogging.

Vincent said, “What’s going on? You look ready to burst.”

I grasped his shoulder. It felt like a stone pillar.

“She’s coming here through the Bridge of Sighs. Wearing a tactical uniform.”

“What? You sure?”

“No, but it adds up. The bridge puts her square in the back of the palace, where she has room to maneuver and make her way to the stage.”

“With everybody looking for her?”

“She might not know that; she’s been MIA for well over twenty-four hours. And even if she does, it's still the only realistic chance she has.”

Vincent clenched his jaw. “You think she’s holed up in the prison, right? And crossing the bridge from there?”

I nodded.

“But how could she get there in the first place? She’d have to bypass all this shit.” Vincent spread out his arms.

“I don’t know. I haven’t gotten that far. Maybe she got in before the barricades went up. She’s in uniform, remember? Or maybe she spent the night hidden in one of the prison cells. Don’t know, and it doesn’t matter right now.”

“And why the prison? Why not the palace somewhere?”

“Something about our last date. That bridge plays a role, it— Shit, man, we don’t have time for this.”

“Okay, okay.” Vincent shot surreptitious glances at the crowd. “What do you wanna do?”

“Check out the bridge. Maybe wait there.”

“You don’t think somebody’s got that covered?”

"Probably, yes, but they'll be mobile. There's no reason to stand guard there. She can slip past or just blindside them. She'll have the advantage. No one is expecting her to come from *inside* the palace."

Vincent paused. "Shit."

"You know how to get there, to the bridge?"

"Never been in there, but we can get a map by the stairs." Vincent pointed to the Censors' Staircase.

"Let's go."

"Wait. We have to tell O'Neil," Vincent said.

"Text him."

I made a beeline for the staircase entrance, from where the Israeli entourage had emerged just minutes before.

On the stage, the mayor of Venice had wrapped up a welcome speech. The Israeli prime minister was next.

I shouted over my shoulder, "Vincent, move it!"

"I'm here. Go, go."

As we approached the staircase, I winced. One of the four soldiers on guard was none other than trigger-happy Officer Lorenzo. I braced for another spray of gunfire. Instead, Lorenzo snapped to attention and saluted me as though I were a field general. The other soldiers followed suit.

"Why are these balloon heads saluting us?" Vincent asked as we reached the foot of the stairs.

I took off my shades and snatched a map from a nearby rack. Vincent looked over my shoulder. The ground-floor diagram only showed a museum in the west wing, the courtyard, and the Censors' Staircase. The second-floor diagram, however, had what we were looking for.

"There's the bridge." Vincent tapped the map. "Running from the prison here to the palace."

"Hmm … two passageways. The one on the right is…" I checked the map key. "…the visitors' passageway and the other … the prisoners' passageway."

"What's that broken line there?"

I studied the diagram. "It's not clear, but I think it means the prisoners' passageway is connected to some other level in the palace not shown here."

Vincent scratched his head. "Fucking confusing." He traced the visitors' passageway to the palace. "And that room?"

"That's … the Chamber of Censors."

"This map really sucks. Either way, we should wait here." Vincent jabbed his finger at the vestibule in the prison that both passageways opened onto. "Assuming you're right and she's there, it cuts her off from the bridge and confines her to the prison."

"That's a plan."

A few steps up the stairs, Vincent grabbed my arm. "Miles, if she's there … how are we gonna stop her?"

Chapter Fifty-Three

The Tail

Marino left the seat on the stage reserved for him vacant. Given his precarious position, he chose to forgo the customary elbow rubbing with insufferable politicians to personally oversee security. So far, nothing out of the ordinary or unexpected had been reported. He listened to the radio carefully, issuing orders, questioning unit deployment and movement, pouncing on anything inefficient or shortsighted. Through it all, the dilemma he faced weighed heavily on him.

A few hours earlier, he'd signed the order for the immediate termination of Officer Kamaria Uba from the ranks of his beloved Carabinieri. A formality because the termination was technically effective the moment her fraud in the evidence room was uncovered. Since then, charges of conspiracy and murder have been leveled against her. If the Americans were right and she was indeed a terrorist on a mission, those charges would pale in comparison to what was to come.

And there was his dilemma.

If former Officer Uba somehow managed to breach his security and carry out a successful attack, it would mean the end of his career. On the other hand, if his men managed to capture her or stop the attack, it would be a loss for The Holy Hand. The bishop—the princeps—would be most unhappy; he was a dangerous man to upset.

From the top of the Giants' Staircase, Marino marched the length of the landing in back-and-forth sweeps. What should he do? His men were under strict orders to stop the threat at all costs, so allowing her to succeed, as the bishop had suggested, wasn't an option. How could he accomplish that without issuing explicit orders to his men to turn a blind eye? The idea was absurd. Yet, the bishop was not a man who dealt in the absurd. He must've meant something else, something figurative that was not clear to Marino at the moment.

The best outcome hinged on the Americans being wrong. No terrorist attack meant the vultures in Rome would heave a collective sigh of relief, shake their crooked fingers at him, and forget the entire episode within a month's time. The bishop, too, would fall in line, not faulting Marino for the organization's lost opportunity.

His cellphone vibrated against his chest. He winced at the caller ID. It was Detective Fredo Longo, the ground asset he'd diverted away from courtyard security to monitor the Americans. Longo had strict orders to call him only if the Americans did anything unusual.

Marino answered. "I'm listening."

"The Americans are on the move, sir—Jordan and Santoro. They're entering the palace now through the Censors' Staircase."

As second-in-command of security (sharing the responsibility with the tiresome Israelis), Marino had been given every unit's operational plan. He knew the Americans were to stay in the courtyard at all times. He had shared that information with Longo.

"Is that so? They didn't radio it in, did they?"

"No, sir."

Marino's heart rate surged. "Quick! Follow them. Don't let them spot the tail. Keep me posted on everything they do. Understood?"

"Yes, sir."

Chapter Fifty-Four

Narrow Passageway

Vincent and I took the Censors' Staircase to the second-floor balcony, which offered a sprawling view of the courtyard. The stage was directly in front of us and just one floor below. The prime minister started his speech.

"Gift shop?" Vincent asked.

"To the right." I pointed to the north end of the balcony. "From there, it's a straight line to the Chamber of Censors."

We hustled, trying not to arouse the suspicion of the Carabinieri personnel posted along the balcony. We didn't want any of them to report on us over the radio in case I was wrong.

I cut through the palace gift shop and headed toward the back. Vincent was hard on my six. We crossed a short, nondescript hallway and entered the first chamber. Without breaking stride, we flashed our credentials at two Carabinieri officers posted there. Vincent gave curt replies in Italian to their questions as we went by. From there, it wasn't exactly a straight line to our destination. It was more like a jagged line running through four connecting rooms. Aside from being empty of both furnishings and guards, the details of the chambers were a blur of wood and color.

When we reached the fourth room, I stopped. A standing floor sign confirmed that the small room was the Chamber of Censors. Dark wood paneling rose halfway up the walls toward the vaulted ceiling, and oil paintings of dour white men in robes covered the rest. To my left was another set of stairs, only this set was narrow and short and made of steel. It rose about a half story into a narrow passageway.

"That's the bridge," I said.

I climbed the stairs and entered the passageway. It was gloomy and oppressive. The walls were rough-hewn. The floor was off-white marble and somehow felt cold underfoot. In the confines of the passageway, all the comfort and opulence of the palace seemed a mile behind us. I stopped at the first window to my right. It had no glass, just the tight latticework of stone I'd seen on the gondola ride with Kamaria, offering a splintered view of the outside world.

Soft footfalls caught my attention.

I drew my weapon. Vincent, who was two steps behind me, had already drawn his.

We waited.

"I hope you got a plan," Vincent whispered. "Because if that's—"

A figure in a Carabinieri uniform in full combat gear appeared at the other end of the passageway. Long pouches seemed to cover every inch of the vest—plenty of ammo to feed the submachine hanging from the shoulder. Beneath a beret, Kamaria's hazel eyes stared at the business end of my SIG Sauer P226.

Chapter Fifty-Five

Update

Marino grew tired of marching back and forth on the stone landing of the Giants' Staircase. Lack of initiative wore him down, not exercise. What else could he do? Without additional intel, he was reduced to issuing routine orders on the radio and pacing like a nervous nanny. The Israeli prime minister was ten minutes into his tedious speech, and nothing unexpected had been reported.

Maybe the Americans were wrong, and no attack had been set in motion.

Oh God, if my luck will hold!

He prayed with a sudden fervor that surprised him. When he was done, he glanced at the giant statues of Neptune and Mars. *What do the ancient Roman gods of sea and war have to say?* He shrugged and prayed to them too. What did it hurt?

Just as he was beginning to believe his luck might actually hold, his phone rang.

Longo!

Marino pressed his lips together and hesitated before answering. "I'm listening."

"Sir," Longo whispered, "I've followed the Americans into the Renaissance wing, through the gift shop. They are in the Chamber of Censors."

"The Chamber of Censors? What are they doing there?"

"Well, they're actually not *in* the chamber, sir. They've taken the short stairs to the Bridge of Sighs. They are preparing to cross."

Marino turned that over quickly in his mind. "They're headed for the prison. What could they be—"

"Sir, there is someone else on the bridge, someone on the opposite side. I can't see who. The fat one is blocking most of the corridor. I do see a pair of dark blue fatigues. I believe it's a Carabinieri soldier."

Marino paused. "Are you sure? I don't have anyone stationed there. No one should be coming from that direction. You must get a visual! I need to know who's on the other side."

"Sir, I'm on the chamber floor. If I climb the stairs to get a better look, the Americans will know I'm here— Wait … they've drawn their weapons."

Marino stopped pacing. His body went rigid. Heat flashes flared on his face and neck.

"That is highly irregular, isn't it, sir? They shouldn't be pointing guns at our men."

Longo was truly a half-wit. The man was like a reliable horse, good to pull and carry so long as you held the reins to guide it. There was no point in making him see the obvious.

The Americans had struck again. This time, confirming his deepest fear. They wouldn't have drawn their weapons otherwise.

Speaking quickly, Marino said, "The bridge has two corridors; are you familiar with it?"

"Yes, sir."

"Then you know there's a cutout in the wall between the corridors. The opposite corridor will give you both the cover and the visual we need. Do you know how to get there?"

"Yes, sir, through the Quarantia Criminal. I know the way."

"Go there now. And hurry!"

Chapter Fifty-Six

The Lion in the Grass

She wore a tactical uniform like a leopard wears fur. Beauty and danger coexisting in perfect harmony.

Under the beret, her hair was cut short. Not a single cornrow fell around her shoulders. An electric-blue ascot covered her long neck like a satin sheet.

"Miles? Vincent? It is me, Kamaria." Her eyes bounced between us. "Why do you point your guns at me? This is wrong. I am an officer of Special Operations, an officer of the FBI task force. We work together, do we not?"

"Not anymore, sister," Vincent spat. "Your contract's been canceled. We know all about the rifle, about you and Colt."

I stood spellbound, my emotions mired in a pit of mental quicksand.

"And we know you're The Scorpion's sleeper agent," Vincent added, his voice thick with disgust.

Unfazed, she said, "Then you must know I come prepared."

The lines around her mouth hardened. A deep scowl disfigured her face. She raised her arm to reveal the detonator she held in her left hand. The stretch of orange wire, running out from under her sleeve to the device, broke the spell.

"Make way," she demanded.

"You know we can't do that." I kept my gun pointed at center mass. I couldn't bring myself to set up for a head shot.

Put a bullet between her eyes.

She stared at me with the same haunting detachment I'd seen in the homeless combat vets I used to serve in the Brooklyn soup kitchens. It was resignation to one's fate. And it scared the shit out of me.

In a blur of movement, she shouldered the submachine gun. Before Vincent or I could react, she had it trained on us. She held the weapon with the stock pressed firmly against her shoulder, her right hand wrapped around the pistol grip, and the long, thick barrel of the suppressor propped awkwardly on top of her left wrist. The barrel aimed at my face wasn't half as unnerving as her tightly balled fist. From the way she held the detonator, her thumb was either pressing on a push button, or her fingers were squeezing a spring-loaded lever—a dead man's switch, designed to juice the payload when the grip was released.

Over my shoulder, I whispered to Vincent, "She's got a dead man's."

"Shit." Vincent mumbled something about not having a plan.

My heart was redlining.

"You will both make way and alert no one," she said in a steady voice. "I have a radio"—she turned her head sideways just enough to reveal the coiled wire of an earpiece—"so I will know. Do not give me a reason to shoot."

"You don't have to do this. It's not too late to stop. Just put the gun—"

She swung to her left a few degrees and released a short burst. The spent shell casings ejected in a steady stream from the side of the submachine gun. With the suppressor, it sounded like a muffled rattle. Live bullets missed my right shoulder by a foot. For the second time in a week I'd been exposed to submachine gun fire and stood unscathed.

But unlike the reckless burst from Officer Lorenzo, this one was deliberately off target, which made it even more unnerving.

With every ounce of willpower, we went against our training and held our fire. Instinctively, we knew a firefight, no matter how brief, would kill us all.

"Okay, okay!" I shouted, raising my arms and pointing my gun at the ceiling.

Vincent followed suit, lifting his arms in surrender. "Hold your fire, Officer. Hold your fire!"

"Guns on the ground." She gestured at a spot on the floor with the smoky end of her weapon.

I bent over and tossed my gun. Vincent crouched and did the same.

Kamaria said, "Now, go back into the palace."

I turned to Vincent. "Back up, go down the stairs."

Vincent's eyes were fixed on Kamaria.

"Vincent, go! I'll be right behind you."

Vincent slowly withdrew, never turning his back. When I heard the steps behind me creak, I said to Kamaria, "Help me here. Help me understand what's going on. You and I, we spent time together, we … I never suspected—"

"Suspected what? That I am mad? That I am a devil?" She scoffed. "Infidels will never understand."

"I'm trying to. I want to."

"You must move."

"Tell me why you're doing this!"

"Why? Because I am a soldier."

"A soldier?"

"Do you think the war in Somalia is over?"

I frowned.

"Do you?"

"That … that was over twenty years ago."

She shook her head. "For victims, war is never over."

"What victims? What does Somalia have to do with this?"

"Everything and nothing."

I waited.

"It is about who I was, who I became, and who I am now."

"And who are you now?"

"You know who I am, Miles Jordan. You are here, are you not?"

"The photo."

She nodded. "I am the lion in the grass."

The sweat trickling from my forehead stung my eyes. I wiped it away with my sleeve. "Like the boy you mean, the boy who killed your parents?"

She looked up from the gunsight. "A boy did not kill my parents. A soldier did. An American soldier."

Chapter Fifty-Seven

Confirmation

Carabinieri Detective Fredo Longo adjusted the mouthpiece of his Bluetooth headset and made sure his phone had a solid link to it. When satisfied, he pulled his Beretta 92 from the shoulder holster under his suit jacket and stepped into the dingy corridor of the Bridge of Sighs.

He had been there before on a couple of occasions as a visitor, and it had never occurred to him how dungeon-like and depressing it was. In Renaissance times, prisoners were escorted from their sentencing trials in the Quarantia Criminal to a prison cell via that corridor. He thought he could actually feel the hopelessness of all those condemned men. The two windows to the left worsened the gloom by filtering the sunlight.

He heard voices speaking English, which he expected. What he didn't expect was a woman's voice.

Could it be?

He pressed his back against the wall to the right of the corridor, the same wall that split the bridge, and held his firearm pointed upward. This was the second time in his seventeen-year career that he had drawn his firearm while on duty. It felt both exhilarating and frightening.

He crept toward the cutout.

From his last visit, he knew the bars there were thick but spaced far apart for good visibility. When he was close enough, he peered around the side of the cutout. At first, he thought the

Carabinieri soldier was male—short hair under a snug beret. After closer scrutiny, he saw it was a woman, an African woman with light eyes. To the rank and file, she was now the infamous Officer Kamaria Uba—the most wanted woman in Venice!

At that moment, she raised her hand and showcased what she was holding.

Dear God in heaven, the woman is insane!

He was about to sound the alarm over the radio when he remembered the colonel's instructions. He stood cemented in place, listening to the American plead with Officer Uba. Abruptly, the maniac reached for her submachine gun and unleashed a torrent of fire. Longo pulled back. He tore off his fedora and held it over his pounding chest. He whispered ten Hail Marys and ten Our Fathers in quick succession.

Chapter Fifty-Eight

The Order

Every Carabinieri officer and soldier stationed in the arcade of the Renaissance wing saluted Marino as he marched by. He relished the respect his rank afforded him wherever he went, not to mention the power it permitted him to wield. To lose that would be unbearable. He'd grown so confident of his promotion to brigadier general; now all he could think of was holding on to what he had. So far, his luck was holding. No news was good news.

He marched with no destination in mind. Forward movement was a coping mechanism.

To his right, the Israeli prime minister was still regurgitating catchphrases about peace and security in the Middle East. There was still time to take that empty seat on the stage and play along as his role required.

His phone vibrated. He stopped short and pulled it out. A numbness crept into his fingers as he swiped the caller ID banner to answer.

"I'm listening."

"Sir, it-it's me, Detective Longo! I-I have an urgent—"

"Speak up. I can barely hear you."

"I-I can't, sir. Have to whisper."

"Give me a moment. Don't hang up."

Marino marched toward a palace service entrance and found a nook inside that dampened most of the event's noise.

"Longo, are you still there?"

"Yes, sir, I-I'm in the palace. In the prisoner's corridor. On-on the Bridge of Sighs—and, and she's here! She's here! The raving lunatic is here, and she just—"

"Slow down, you idiot! *You* sound like a raving lunatic. Now glue yourself together and speak like a proper officer of the Carabinieri."

He waited while Longo collected himself. The half-wit was terrified. That much was obvious. Something bad had happened or was about to. *She's here.* Is that what Longo had said?

"Sir, I apologize, I was—"

"Just give me the fucking report!"

"Officer Uba is on the bridge, in the other corridor. She's dressed as a soldier. Has a submachine gun and a detonator of some sort. I-I assume explosives are on her, beneath the tactical vest. The Americans have intercepted her. She ordered them to stand down and withdraw into the palace and maintain radio silence. Then she shot at them, sir! The maniac shot at them!"

"She shot the Americans, you say?"

"No, she shot *at* them. A warning. The fat one is still talking to her. I recognize his deep voice. His partner was told to withdraw. I believe he did."

"Jordan is in the corridor with her? Right now?"

"Yes, sir."

"What are they doing?"

"I retreated, sir, so they wouldn't hear me whispering."

"You *lost* visual?" Marino considered reprimanding the half-wit.

"Shouldn't we sound the alarm?"

Sounding the alarm would certainly contain the threat but limit Marino's options. "No, not yet. Stay on the line and await my orders."

Marino dropped his arm and held the phone at his side. He marched.

With the best possible outcome now off the table, Marino was left with one option: order his men to move in and personally see to the prime minister's safe evacuation. The bishop might understand that was Marino's only choice and still see it as a win for The Holy Hand since an attack was attempted. The insatiable news media would feast on it for days.

But what if his men managed to take her alive? Or worse, what if Jordan managed to talk her out of it? Either of those two scenarios would undermine the seriousness of the attempted attack and put the media focus on former Officer Uba and the compromised Carabinieri. That wouldn't help the cardinal, please the bishop, or save him.

That's when an idea struck him.

A brilliant solution.

He put the phone to his ear. "Longo."

"Yes, sir, I'm here."

"Shoot Officer Uba."

Chapter Fifty-Nine

Young Soldier

An American soldier!

Kamaria had told me that a Somali boy high on khat had gunned down her parents. Now she claimed that a US serviceman had been the perpetrator. Another lie? I didn't think so. The moment she said it, the puzzle piece for motive fell into place.

"You let a soldier into the house?"

She looked at me as though a vast field separated us. "It was during the great battle in Mogadishu." She relaxed her stance. "We trusted the Americans. I did not see the harm when I saw the white soldier. He was fighting. He was bleeding. I … I opened the door."

As a cop, I knew the prism of perception refracts and reshapes every story. What happened next could have played out multiple ways. In the heat of combat, a soldier desperate for cover presses up against a door that's abruptly opened. He falls on his back into a dim room. He panics and shoots at the first sign of movement. In another scenario, one or both of her parents are active participants in the swelling mob that attacks US forces that day, and the soldier's action is justified. Regardless of how it actually played out, to the impressionable mind of a nine-year-old, the soldier is guilty of cold-blooded murder.

The submachine gun hung loosely at her side and the detonator against her chest. She looked like a lost child, torn and forever changed by a terrible event that brought us to that moment.

It is about who I was, who I became, and who I am now.

I said softly, "That's what this is about? Revenge?"

"I will avenge my parents."

"Why an Israeli target, then? Why civilians?"

"America, Israel … it is all the same. And in war, we are all the same."

"Is that what The Scorpion taught you?"

She nodded. "He has enlightened me to a great many things."

"Like killing innocent people?"

"No one is innocent!"

"You are."

She tilted her head sideways.

"You're an innocent victim, Kamaria."

She looked away for a moment. "I lived as an orphan in the streets of Mogadishu. The hunger I could endure, but the guilt I could not. Yet something gave me strength to survive one more rising of the sun and then again the next day. I did not know what it was until Zafar said it was hate—hate for the soldier who killed my parents and the government who sent him. He said hate is a useful tool. It gave him strength and purpose, and it would give me strength and purpose too. I am not a victim anymore."

Zafar? Is that his real name?

"So you became a soldier for him."

"He fed me, clothed me, trained me. When the Catholics came to Somalia to rescue the orphans of the war, it was Zafar who made sure they took his young soldier. He said he was sending me on a great mission that one day he would call upon me to complete."

Footsteps crept behind me.

Chapter Sixty

The Longest Breath

Longo couldn't believe what he'd just been ordered to do: shoot a suicide bomber at near point-blank range.

The colonel had pointed out that the bridge was made of stone and built to stand a thousand years. The wall between the corridors was of the same stone and would protect Longo from the blast. The colonel had also argued that explosive vests worn by suicide bombers were designed to kill by shrapnel rather than concussive blast. When Longo asked about the Americans, the colonel reminded him of poor Ignazio Bonaventura—a fellow Venetian—dead at the hands of those same Americans. If they fell, it was justice served.

"Carry out this order and you'll be hailed a hero," the colonel had said. "Heroes are elevated to high places in the Carabinieri."

There was the payoff: a prosperous career. That, he expected. What he didn't expect was the moral spin the colonel had put on the mission. He claimed to issue the order as God's instrument. God's instrument? What did that mean?

Longo crept forward, his back sliding along the wall that divided the bridge. The cutout in the wall now loomed like a surreal portal from which there was no return. His heart was in his throat. Breathing had become labored. His clammy grip on the Beretta was crushing. That would spoil his aim, wouldn't it?

Squeeze the trigger. Don't pull it. He kept repeating that to himself while trying not to dwell on the fact that he'd never fired a single round while on duty in his entire seventeen-year career. He'd never killed anyone either. Now he was about to kill three human beings!

The conversation between Officer Uba and the fat American had taken a strange turn. Lion in the grass? Parents killed by boys and soldiers? It was obvious they shared a history, which explained why the lunatic hadn't killed him yet. Wouldn't she have to do that anyway to get into the palace? Why was she stalling? She was stalling, wasn't she? He wanted to call the colonel to get his insight, but he was too close to the cutout and risked being overheard. Quiet as a mouse, the colonel had ordered.

The sweat building up on his forehead caused the fedora to slide over his eyes. Longo panicked. He tore the hat off and tossed it aside. Somehow, he managed to hold the scream in his throat long enough to whittle it down to a whimper.

Quiet as a mouse.

A moment later, he eyed the cutout just two meters away. He kept the firearm pointed upward. The space between the bars in the cutout widened as he got closer.

At a meter away, he pressed himself tighter against the wall. His arm felt like a foreign appendage. The gun was so close to his face he could smell the rotten banana and alcohol aroma of the cleaning oil.

At six centimeters, he pulled his head off the wall and peered around the edge of the cutout. Officer Uba no longer had the submachine gun trained on the Americans.

He planned to take aim, squeeze off an accurate shot, and dive as far from the blast as he could. In theory, it worked perfectly. Like a carefully choreographed Hollywood stunt. He had to believe it would work as perfectly in real life.

He prayed that the colonel was right about the blast and the bridge.

He prayed that his aim would be true.
He asked God for forgiveness.
Longo took the longest breath of his life and braced himself.

Chapter Sixty-One

Any Moment Now

All he could do now was wait.

Marino had given Longo a decisive order that would set in motion a great many wheels. Those wheels would lift the winners and crush the losers.

Along with the terrorist, Officer Longo and the Americans were likely losers. The pep talk Marino had given Longo was just talk. He had no idea what damage a bomb carried by a suicide bomber could inflict, let alone know if a four-hundred-year-old stone bridge and people in close proximity could survive that kind of blast.

Sitting in the chair reserved for him on the stage, Marino felt forced to go along with the crowd and laugh politely at a bad joke the prime minister had shared. As the Israeli leader rambled on, Marino's story took shape.

He would start by claiming to have sent Longo on a covert reconnaissance mission based on a hunch. That hunch subsequently paid off but led to unavoidable tragedy and sacrifice. Whether Longo lived or fell, Marino would hail him as a hero for stopping a terrorist. He was better served, however, by smearing the Americans. Perhaps they had insisted on breaking the radio silence the terrorist had demanded, pushing her over the edge and forcing Longo to take action. Or they'd cowered in the face of danger, relinquished their weapons, and given the terrorist unrestricted access to the palace—a security breach

Longo could not allow. Could he paint them as conspirators? Everyone who mattered knew one American had been in alliance with the terrorist, so why not a few more?

Marino smiled. The cardinal would get his terrorist attack and the huge media spotlight that went with it. The bishop would be pleased. The politicians in Rome would praise Marino and the Carabinieri for having saved countless lives and securing the safety of an important foreign dignitary. They would make a big show of promoting him to brigadier general.

Venice would lose too, he reminded himself.

He envisioned the bridge as a sad heap of rubble spread out across the canal. Like the palace, it was one of the city's architectural treasures. That saddened him but also gave him pride. One defining characteristic of his great city was its knack for rebirth. Throughout the centuries, its great buildings had often fallen to fire and destruction. The bell tower alone had been rebuilt three times.

The bridge would simply be rebuilt and reborn.

Marino glanced at the clock on his activity tracker. Two minutes had passed since he'd given Longo the order. His pulse quickened.

Any moment now.

Chapter Sixty-Two

Out of Reach

The footsteps behind me had to be the cavalry. I couldn't turn around to see who it was without giving them away. What were they planning to do?

The bridge was enclosed, so sharpshooters were not an option. An assault team could quietly deploy along the second bridge corridor, but shooting her at close quarters was suicide while she held the dead man's switch. They could outflank and ambush her from behind, with the goal of simultaneously taking her down and securing the detonator.

What were the chances of that succeeding?

I saw only two options: containment or surrender. The former meant the use of deadly force. The latter—talking a trained terrorist out of honoring Allah with her life—was a tall order. But this was Kamaria. I still believed I wasn't wrong about her. Now was the time to put that stubborn, if not foolish, belief to the test.

"Was any of it real? Us, I mean?"

She didn't reply.

"Was there anything good between us, or was it all a lie?"

Again she remained silent, her eyes furtive.

"Answer me!"

"A lie!" She pressed her lips together. "A plan."

"A plan?"

"You needed to be distracted. Zafar believed you were a threat to the mission; the one who could unravel it. I was sent to blind you."

"Blind me? You mean manipulate me like you did Colt?"

"Colt was a needy, emotional man—easy to deceive. He believed it was El-Hashem who killed my parents."

So that's how she'd recruited Colt to kill El-Hashem. She seduced him then played the victim-lover seeking justice.

"Then I was a fool too. And so were you, Kamaria. You have feelings for me. I know you do. And that wasn't supposed to happen, right? That wasn't part of the plan."

"I feel nothing for you. You were simply a river to cross, a hillside to climb."

"I don't believe that."

"This is true."

"Then why leave behind a photo of you, El-Hashem, and the man I suspect you call Zafar? Why leave such a critical clue for me to find?"

"I left in haste and—"

"Scrubbed the apartment spotless of anything connected to you, except that photo?" I shook my head. "You left it behind, hoping I would find it. You probably didn't think it was enough for me to put it all together in the time frame we had and convinced yourself you were still true to the mission. But deep down, you wanted me here. Your total lack of surprise when you found me standing on this bridge gave you away."

"Who is there?" She quickly assumed a shooting stance. "Ruiz, Tufu, you should not be here."

She squeezed off another burst of warning shots.

"Hold your fire! Hold your fire!" Vincent screamed.

Who is Vincent talking to? Kamaria? Ruiz and Tufu? The rest of the cavalry?

I positioned myself to block as much of the corridor with my girth as I could. Bullets flying in either direction was bad.

Getting struck with one was bad too. Better me than my team or Kamaria and then all of us.

Kamaria put me in her gunsight. "Move!"

The sudden chatter over the radio indicated that the Israeli prime minister was wrapping up his speech.

"I must pass!" She angled her weapon upward and fired again, striking the ceiling.

"Miles, get outta there!"

Unsure if that was a knee-jerk outburst from Vincent or a warning that something was about to go down, I yelled, "Everybody stand down! Stand down!"

Without giving any thought to what I intended to do, I took a step forward and then another.

Voices carried.

"What the fuck is he doing?"

"Miles!"

I closed the gap.

"You must stop or"—she grimaced—"I will kill you!"

"This isn't who you are."

Tears streamed down her face. The end of the submachine gun trembled. "Miles ... please."

I reached out. "Walk out of here with me. Let's watch another rising of the sun together."

The tips of my fingers brushed against the soft hand that clenched the detonator. For a fleeting moment, it was within reach.

Then the side of Kamaria's neck exploded.

She reeled back in a spray of crimson. The submachine gun came loose.

I lunged at the detonator still in her hand. She was falling away faster than I was closing in. I didn't hear my knee pop. The gunshot blast that set us in motion was still ringing in my ears. I felt the disconnect, my lower leg going slack—the reason my lunge fell short. And then she was out of reach.

Kamaria and I crashed seconds apart. Her arm was last to fall, smacking the marble floor. I watched helplessly as the detonator bounced out of her hand.

Chapter Sixty-Three

Last Dance

The last images I would see on earth scrolled by in slow-moving frames: the narrow passageway, faint light, a submachine gun lying on the marble floor, muzzle pointed at me, shadows, blood spraying like a geyser from Kamaria's neck.

It would be a painless death for us both. That was comforting.

In suicide bombings, the individual wearing the bomb was usually obliterated, with only the head surviving, as it tends to part company from the torso like a rocket leaving the launchpad. Those in close proximity suffer a similar fate, though usually without the added fireworks.

Gruesome but painless.

Kamaria writhed on the floor, the sprays of blood growing longer.

My earpiece hummed with activity: units on the move, prime ministers and politicians evacuated, rigid crowd control measures executed. On top of that, an army was descending on the Bridge of Sighs. A lot of good that would do me. I was already dead.

Only I wasn't.

My hearing was coming back, and my knee demanded medical attention. Even my heart tachometer was looking up, no longer redlining.

The detonator had rolled about a foot away from Kamaria, free from the orange wire. That's why we were still alive.

Alive!

I dragged myself toward her, coming up on her left side, away from the spraying wound. I knelt, putting my weight on the good knee. Working fast, I removed the bulky bomb vest, lifting her upper body as needed. I kept a wary eye on the ammo pouches, stuffed to the cover flaps with shiny new hardware that trickled out as I handled the vest. Behind the pouches, C-4 replaced the armored Kevlar plates. The fact that C-4 is a stable explosive, immune to most physical shock, did little to soothe my nerves. When I got the orange wire out of her sleeve, I slid the entire package as far away from us as I could. I then yanked off my suit jacket, balled it up, and lay next to her. Propped on one elbow, I pressed my jacket against her neck to stanch the bleeding.

"You hit?"

I turned and looked up. Vincent was fast approaching. Tufu and Ruiz were close behind.

"No, I'm not hit."

Vincent scooped up his gun from the spot he'd been ordered to dump it then kept it trained on the wall between the corridors.

"You gave me a frigging heart attack. Why were you dragging your fat ass on the floor then?"

"My bum knee. It blew out."

Tufu came up behind Vincent and shook his head. "The round clipped the carotid artery."

"You don't know that." I applied more pressure on her wound.

"The blood sprayed at intervals, right? That means with each heartbeat. And I see a lot of blood here." Tufu nodded. "Carotid for sure."

Now that he mentioned it, the stench of blood—of iron—hit me. Red was everywhere.

Tufu added, "Compression won't help. She'll bleed out before they get her into surgery."

I wanted to tell him he wasn't a doctor, that his diagnosis was shit, then make him feel like an asshole for his cocky attitude.

But arguing was pointless. Tufu was an expert, a decorated medic who had probably seen more gunshot wounds in one week of combat than most trauma doctors will see their entire careers.

"I don't care. Call a bus. Now!"

"Already did," Vincent said. "Everybody's been invited to the party."

Kamaria stopped writhing. The grimace was gone. Her features relaxed. Despite the mix of perspiration and blood on her face, she looked peaceful, as if sleeping off a wicked spell in a fairy tale. Only this was no fairy tale.

"What the fuck happened?" I wiped my stinging eyes. "I told everyone to stand down. Everyone! I was so close, so fucking close. Who shot her? Who almost killed us all?"

"This asshole over here." Vincent pointed his Glock through the bars of a square opening in the wall that separated the two corridors. I'd been so engrossed with Kamaria that I never noticed it.

"Hey, Longo! I'm gonna kick the shit out of your dumb guinea ass first chance I get," Vincent said in English and then repeated it in Italian a lot less politely. "Running's not gonna save you, asshole!"

While Vincent and Ruiz debated what exactly had happened, Kamaria opened her eyes. She seemed disoriented for a moment, then turned her head slightly toward me.

"The big man looks sad," she said in a weak voice.

"I am sad."

"There is no reason to be sad. You have won."

"I knew I wasn't wrong about you. In that regard, I *have* won."

"Then why are you sad?"

"Because I also lost."

Her eyes searched my face. "I did not arm the vest."

"I know."

"You and I … yes … I left the photo for you."

Blood seeped through my suit jacket.

"Where's the bus?" I yelled at my teammates then turned back to her without waiting for an answer.

"What if ... what if I hadn't come? What would you have done?"

She didn't reply at first. Her eyes were still searching my face.

"I am glad you came." She tried to smile but shivered instead.

I had nothing to cover her with, so I pressed against her, hoping my ample body would warm her.

"Did you kill Colt?"

She shook her head so slowly it was barely perceptible. "Max is ... dead?"

"We found him in his bathtub. Gunshot wound to the head."

She bit her lower lip. "Oh, Zafar..."

Around us, I had a vague sense of activity. Uniforms and suits stepping over us or squeezing by. Some bent over, others on their haunches. A lot of milling around. A couple of Kevlar space suits rushed by. My earpiece was just noise, so I pulled it off. The last thing I heard was a cryptic message about bomb squad personnel and containment vessels. Voices echoed in and out of the corridor. No paramedics. The bus was either held up or told to stand down for the terrorist.

I fought a sudden rage to scream into my radio mic that Kamaria wasn't a terrorist. The real terrorist was still out there. Still in the wind.

Kamaria grew pale and her lips blue. Her skin felt icy and clammy, and she sweated profusely. With my arm across her chest, I felt the panic in her heart as it worked harder to make up for the drop in pressure, the loss of oxygen.

"Miles?"

"Yes?"

"Will you ... d-dance with me again?"

"Just name the place."

Her breathing grew labored. Her voice was down to a whisper.

"Under the cotton tree … i-in Sierra Leone."

I nodded. "We'll start with salsa. Then a tango. Some hip-hop or club after that. Doesn't matter, so long as we end with Coltrane."

"What is … cold train?"

"John Coltrane, a jazz legend. On the saxophone."

"Jazz? Oh … I like jazz … this is true."

When Kamaria closed her eyes a moment later, I knew I'd never see them again. I lay my head on her chest and listened to her fading heartbeat.

And then to the silence.

Chapter Sixty-Four

Media Storm

I watched the media storm raging in earnest from the second-floor balcony of the palace. TV cameras filled the courtyard, most aimed at overzealous reporters peddling the same lie.

The lie they told was that Marino had authorized an undercover operation to track down and kill a dangerous terrorist, whose identity was being withheld due to the ongoing investigation. The operation had been a complete success, resulting in the death of the terrorist and no collateral damage. The fact that the Israeli prime minister managed to deliver his speech unscathed was being hailed as proof of the Carabinieri's complete control of the situation. And Marino, being the stand-up guy that he was, credited his fine military police force for their professionalism and courage.

The media was drunk on a loaded cocktail, one with a pinch of truth and two shots of bullshit. Someone had served it to them straight up, and it didn't take a genius to figure out who.

Marino had ordered Longo to shoot Kamaria so he could take credit for stopping her, while at the same time glossing over the fact that his police force had been compromised. Smart and well played. And if the operation had gone south, I'm sure he had a backup story that portrayed him as the grieving able leader and us the posthumous heroes.

"How did Longo know Kamaria was on the bridge with us?" Vincent adjusted his suit and tie as if prepping for an interview that would air on the six o'clock news.

"Marino had Longo tail us." I struggled to hide the tremble, the last vestige of distress. "No way they figured it out on their own."

"Why would Marino put a tail on you sad sacks?" Ruiz asked.

Vincent smiled. "Because, Ruiz, everybody knows the NYPD is the finest, baddest law enforcement agency on the planet. If you wanna steal the credit for cracking a big case, you put a tail on us."

Ruiz rolled his eyes.

The paramedics who made it to the bridge a minute too late for Kamaria had fitted me with a formidable knee brace and a pair of crutches they got from a nearby medical supply store. Against their instructions, I slouched on the crutches, letting the thick rubber pads dig into my armpits.

I added, "He probably had a hunch that we knew something and put his lapdog on us."

"You mean his fixer." Vincent patted his suit jacket where his holstered service weapon bulged. "He better watch his six. That's all I'm saying."

"Get in line, Vinny." Tufu turned his head and spat. "That mofo bushwhacked us. That demands retaliation."

In the middle of the courtyard, I spotted Marino, Longo, and O'Neil. The trio appeared to be in a heated argument. Marino's violent hand gestures suggested he was demanding something.

I asked Vincent, "What did you say about Longo?"

"I said he better watch his six."

"Before that."

"Huh? Oh, you called Longo a lapdog. I said he's a fixer."

A fixer.

"What are you thinking?" Ruiz asked me.

I told Ruiz what I suspected regarding Marino and Longo. He thought it over for a moment, then said, "You think Marino deliberately ordered Longo to shoot a suicide bomber standing a few feet away? And Longo was stupid enough to do it?"

"Yes."

Ruiz did an irritating eye roll. "Give me a break."

"How would you explain what happened on that bridge?"

"Maybe Longo saw Kamaria and panicked. Maybe he decided to play the hero and do it alone. Could be any number of reasons. What you're suggesting is Marino ordered Longo to commit suicide. That doesn't make sense."

"I doubt he sold it that way. There was a wall between Longo and Kamaria."

"But not between *you* and Kamaria."

Vincent's face darkened. "You think Marino gives a shit about us? Ordering Longo to blow her up so he could feed the media his I-saved-the-day story makes perfect sense to me. I mean, just look at them."

Reporters mobbed Marino like vultures on a fresh kill. Longo stood next to him, a huge grin plastered on his face. Not standing next to Longo was his partner, Detective Giordana. She lingered far from the spotlight, alone and excluded.

"Man knows how to wear a uniform," Tufu said. "Look at all that chest candy."

"Plays well to the cameras," Ruiz agreed.

"Even on TV"—Vincent mimicked how Marino interacted with his activity tracker— "that balloon head is checking his step count."

Tufu said, "Man must shit on the trot to keep it going."

Vincent turned to me and took an exaggerated step backward. "Jesus, Miles. Now that I get a good look … you're the Walking Dead."

That drew scrutiny from Ruiz and Tufu.

"You should go to the hospital," Ruiz said.

Tufu nodded. "You look like hell, brother."

I looked down and took stock. My suit was rumpled. My tie hung askew. The knee brace was the only thing on me that wasn't sprayed, smeared, or soaking with Kamaria's blood.

O'Neil joined us and pointed at Ruiz and Tufu. "Take a hike."

They nodded and walked off.

O'Neil turned his attention to Vincent and me. "You geniuses remember that little Bonaventura fiasco? Well, Marino and Longo just made it an issue."

Vincent and I glanced at each other.

"They found DNA on that rope that didn't match Bonaventura's," O'Neil said. "They're demanding DNA samples —today."

Vincent said, "They got results? DNA takes weeks."

"They must've pulled strings," I said.

"Goddamn right, they pulled strings." O'Neil pointed at my injured leg. "What the hell happened to you? Why aren't you in a hospital?"

I'd told the paramedics that I still had work to do there. That was a lie. What work did I have? Writing police reports? That was office work that could wait. Interviewing witnesses? I was the witness. Pursuing a perp? The only perp left to pursue was The Scorpion, and the man was a ghost. The truth? I didn't want to dwell on Kamaria in a lonely hospital room.

"Wait a minute." Vincent jabbed his finger at the courtyard below. "They're looking to hook us for Bonaventura? What about Longo? That piece of shit almost got us all killed!"

"Not a goddamn thing we can do." O'Neil took a deep breath and let it seep through clenched teeth. "We fell off the operational plan, and we ran privately by phone. Granted, so did they. But Marino's spinning it, saying we went rogue."

"Oh, for fuck's sake!" Vincent said with a rising voice. "They get away with it?"

O'Neil didn't answer.

"Longo, Longo, Longo," I said. "Notice how the man's name just keeps coming up? Longo was assigned to head the Bonaventura case. Longo shows up unexpectedly on that bridge. Longo shoots Kamaria. Now Longo is trying to pin a homicide on us."

O'Neil knitted his eyebrows.

"What are you getting at?" Vincent asked.

I grabbed the handgrips on the crutches and straightened up. My armpits hurt, and my hands were getting numb.

"I'm not sure," I replied. "I'm trying to think it through."

O'Neil and Vincent waited.

"You called Longo a fixer," I said to Vincent. "The question is what has Longo fixed? The Bonaventura homicide, maybe?"

Vincent rubbed his boxy jaw. "Fixed how?"

"Longo didn't work the crime scene. Giordana did. And he didn't give a damn what she thought or had to say. When we searched Bonaventura's room, Longo spent the entire time out on the balcony, chain-smoking and surfing his phone."

"Could just be laziness or incompetence," O'Neil offered. "Let Giordana do the heavy lifting."

"Could be. It could also be deliberate. Point is, he's not interested in finding the real killer."

Vincent crossed his arms over his chest. "But why pin this on us in the first place? Can't be just to screw us."

O'Neil reached into his suit jacket and dug out a roll of Tums. "To cover up something."

"That's what I'm thinking," I said.

Vincent looked from O'Neil to me. "Cover up what?"

"Something Bonaventura knew," I replied. "If Marino can order Longo to shoot Kamaria and blow up a bridge, then he can order Longo to shoot Bonaventura."

Vincent's eyes widened. "Whoa, you just blew off my boxers."

"That's a hell of a leap, even for you, Miles," O'Neil said. "Do we even have a connection between Marino and Bonaventura?"

"Shit!" Vincent smacked his forehead then dropped his heavy hand on my shoulder. "Remember the night you called me back to the office and blew my date with the Lufthansa stewardess?"

The memory came rushing back. "What about it?"

"I was gonna tell you that I'd followed up on your hunch. Regarding Bonaventura. But then you told me about Kamaria, and everything changed. Anyway, Bonaventura *was* ex-military." Vincent paused. "Wanna guess who he served with?"

"Marino!" O'Neil and I said at the same time.

"Bingo."

A welcome rush of adrenaline surged through me.

Talking fast, I said, "Bonaventura was shot when he was about to give us The Holy Hand's police asset. This was no ordinary asset. The Holy Hand has never been charged with a crime, despite plenty of suspicion. So it had to be someone with the power and clout to squash investigations. Someone inside the Carabinieri whose identity had to be kept secret. Who fits that description better than Marino?"

Vincent nodded with enthusiasm.

"Marino put Longo on us when we met the cardinal," I added. "And again when we visited Bonaventura. With orders to kill him if he—"

"No, that doesn't work," Vincent said.

"Why?"

"Longo's too tall. The perp I saw was shorter. Besides, whoever shot Bonaventura did it from at least twenty-five yards and scored a bullseye with a single shot. Longo can't shoot for shit. He almost missed Kamaria at five feet."

"Marino can shoot." O'Neil split open the roll with his thumbnail and popped a Tums in his mouth. "He's the Carabinieri's pistol-shooting champion. He can make that shot blindfolded."

We stood silent for a long, tense moment, and O'Neil's chewing was the only movement among us. The implication of our boss' deduction was explosive. It was almost too much to process.

Vincent spoke first, "Marino does fit the general description of the shooter I saw. He's short and lean. But would he get his hands dirty like that? Seems too risky. And how do we prove it? This isn't some trigger-happy, snot-nosed rookie. This is a high-ranking officer of the Italian National Military Police."

O'Neil said, "Goddamn right. We need proof."

Longo adjusted his fedora as he talked to reporters who jostled for his attention. His boss, standing nearby, stole another glance at his activity tracker, either to check the time or to remind himself that he hadn't moved in ten minutes.

That last thought struck me.

What if...?

I looked for Giordana. She was still in exile, standing in the same spot, tapping her foot with obvious impatience. Smart and ambitious, she was forced to play second fiddle to a fraud like Longo. I bet if given a chance to change her lot, she would jump at it. More importantly, she was an honest cop.

"There's someone we have to talk to," I said.

Chapter Sixty-Five

Brigadier General

Day 6

Saturday, 1200 hours

Marino stood in front of his French neoclassical mirror. He donned the shoulder boards of a brigadier general: black and silver with a fine red border, a star, a fleur-de-lis, and a stripe of connecting pentagons.

His office was cozy, perhaps a bit too warm. He had tossed an extra log into the fireplace, just as he had poured an extra finger's worth of fine cognac in the snifter that waited on his desk. It was a celebration. Things hadn't gone exactly as planned, but his goals had been achieved.

He'd taken a calculated risk when he'd ordered Longo to shoot. Former Officer Uba had done him a great service by expiring quietly, without the mess of collateral damage. He'd been able to keep her identity secret from the media in large part because of it. But that wouldn't last long.

In a preemptive strike, he planned to hold a news conference later in the afternoon to reveal Uba's role in the attack as a lone, deranged infiltrator. He might even suggest that pressure from Rome to diversify the Carabinieri had enabled that dangerous infiltration to occur with the lowering of recruiting standards.

A politically tricky move, one he had to consider carefully.

Bishop Cusa had been the first to congratulate him. With the media in a frenzy over the story, the cardinal's supporters were gearing up for mass demonstrations against the continued invasion of Muslim refugees into Europe. They were roused by the cardinal's fiery condemnation of the attempted terrorist attack on Venice.

The insufferable politicians had been next, showering praise for a job well-done. They beamed with national pride and positioned themselves to snatch slices of the huge media spotlight. Marino had taken the opportunity to remind those fools that he had opposed the FBI's meddling from the start. His argument, designed to exploit a resurgent nationalism, was that Italian cities were better protected by Italians. No politician could argue with that. Many were forced to concede that he had been right—the closest thing to an apology that he could expect.

Not long after came the call that mattered most. His commanding officer confirmed the promotion to brigadier general. Effective immediately. Hence, the shoulder boards had come out of hiding.

He checked his activity tracker. He had many steps to go. Where should he walk to? What would be the most satisfying venue to show off his new rank?

St. Mark's Square?

The Riva degli Schiavoni?

The basilica?

All of them?

His office phone rang. Marino marched to his desk and settled in his executive chair.

He picked up the receiver. "I'm listening."

"General, sir, Detective Alonza Giordana is here to see you," his aide said.

Marino grimaced. "I'm not expecting to see this, this woman. What does she want?"

"She's here regarding the Bonaventura case. And she's accompanied by the FBI."

"The FBI? Who? Is Detective Longo with them?"

"No, General, Detective Longo is not here. One moment please."

Marino listened as his aide put down the receiver and asked in English for credentials. Less than a minute later, the aide was back on the line.

"They are members of the task force. Supervisory Special Agent—"

"Just give me names."

"Ty O'Neil, Vincent Santoro, and … Miles Jordan."

Marino smiled.

Here were the Americans, ready to grovel at his polished boots. Perhaps bribe him. No one was better at damage control than the Americans. Whomever they couldn't bully, they simply bought. This was confirmation that the DNA on the rope belonged to Santoro or the fat one.

I have them!

Oh, how he was going to enjoy this. "Send them in."

"Yes, General."

Chapter Sixty-Six

Good Cops

The Carabinieri officer who accompanied us to Marino's office was slight of frame and at least a half foot shorter than his diminutive boss. He walked with a curious stoop as if deliberately making himself even shorter. When he stopped at a set of substantial wooden doors, he knocked once then pushed them open.

Inside was an office fit for a head of state. Even the commissioner of the thirty-five-thousand-strong NYPD didn't have an office like that. It smelled of cedarwood and oak. The floor was a checkerboard of black and white marble with enough room for leather couches and chairs, tables, suits of armor, and more. A huge stone mantel framed a working fireplace.

Without Longo to embarrass her or cast her aside, Giordana confidently led the way. O'Neil and Vincent followed. I ambled along on my crutches.

As I made my way deeper into Marino's lair, I noticed the trophy case. Glass on three sides, about the size of a standard bookcase, and filled top to bottom with medals and trophies. From a distance, it wasn't obvious what the medals were for. The trophies, however, left no doubt; all were crowned with armed figurines in competitive shooting stances.

"Check out the creepy mirror." Vincent pointed to his left. "Bet Marino kisses himself in it every day."

Against an oak-paneled wall leaned an elegant gold mirror. It was taller than I was and wide enough to give me a panoramic view of my belly if I wanted one. I visualized Marino standing in front of it, snapping off salutes and fawning all over himself.

Marino was seated at the far end of the room behind an elaborately carved wooden desk that must've weighed half a ton.

"This is most irregular," he said in Italian to Giordana. "There's a chain of command. Have you forgotten? Where's Detective Longo?"

Giordana stopped a few feet short of Marino's desk. "I apologize, sir, I—"

"You have no appointment, and you barge in here with two murder suspects. Don't apologize, woman. Explain yourself!"

Unfazed, Giordana adjusted her oversized glasses and said, "General, the American detectives are here to discuss the Bonaventura case. They want to explain the DNA we found on the rope."

Marino looked incredulous. "They will admit to wrongdoing?"

"They admit to using illegal interrogation techniques on the late Mr. Bonaventura, but they deny having anything to do with his murder. They also have new information regarding the case." She paused. "And they have a suspect."

"A suspect?"

"Yes, General. They refused to share that information with me, insisting on telling you personally."

Marino waved Giordana off but didn't seem to notice that she'd merely moved to the side of his desk. He glowered angrily at us and switching to English said, "Mr. O'Neil, your men have … *come si chiama*? Balls? Have balls to come here. They admit to torture of Italian citizen Ignazio Bonaventura but claim innocent of murder? A lie! I will see them in prison for this."

O'Neil replied, "General, please listen to what they have to say first."

Giordana was wearing a wire. The Italian prosecutor had insisted on it. The plan was simple. Give Marino a shovel, nudge him to dig his own grave, and then push the smug bastard into it. Hopefully, the Italian courts would do the rest.

Marino leaned back in his chair and held up his hand, fingers spread. "Five minutes, *cinque*."

Not expecting Marino to invite me to sit, I lumbered over to a spot between two leather chairs facing his desk. Vincent stood beside me.

"Before we begin, I'm curious about your activity tracker." I pointed to his wrist. "You wear it every day?"

Marino spread out his arms. "Five minutes ... and you ask this?"

"I'm thinking of getting one myself." I patted my belly. "I have a little bit of weight to lose."

"A little?" He laughed. "I wear this every day, every hour. But it will not help you. Nothing will. You are too fat. Too *incompetente*."

I took the insult in stride, managing a fake embarrassed smile.

"Can we get on with this?" O'Neil asked on cue.

I cleared my throat. "My partner, Vincent, and I were investigating the possible connection of The Holy Hand to the El-Hashem shooting. We believed Mr. Bonaventura had information that was vital to the case, but he was uncooperative. Given the time constraints we were under, and the stakes, we felt it was imperative to extract that information quickly. So we strung him upside down and let him hang there until he was ready to cooperate. We used the rope in question to bind his hands behind his back. At no time did we beat Mr. Bonaventura or otherwise physically harm him."

Marino's eyes narrowed. "Mr. O'Neil, you are listening to this, eh?"

O'Neil said nothing. Vincent took over, summarizing everything that happened next. When Vincent was finished, Marino stood. Without taking his eyes off us, he said, "Giordana, arrest these men for torture and murder."

I feigned surprise. "But Vincent just explained that we didn't shoot Mr. Bonaventura."

Marino growled, "Explain it to the *procuratore della repubblica*!"

Ironically, the prosecutor and his team were busy listening in on Giordana's wire from another room.

"Oh, we will, General," I said. "First, we need to know your whereabouts on Wednesday morning, between 1000 and 1030 hours—the time frame in which Mr. Bonaventura was shot."

It started as a small ripple on his cheek then quickly spread to the rest of his face, forming deep fissures. "You dare ask this?"

"My partner here has this crazy idea, sir, that you might be connected to this," I lied.

Marino glowered at Vincent. "Your arrogance is impossible. I was here, my office, all morning. With officers who will swear it."

"Are you sure, sir?"

"I am sure!"

Marino snatched up the phone, barked some orders, then slammed it back in the cradle. A moment later, four armed officers entered the office.

"Arrest them!" Marino pointed violently at Vincent and me then turned to Giordana and said, "Demoted—*degradata*! Get out!"

No one moved, including the four officers.

"I gave orders!" Marino pounded both fists on his desk.

"General," I said, "Detective Giordana secured the GPS records for your sports activity account. Along with recording your daily step count, heart rate, elevation, and other data, that activity tracker also records your exact location. The GPS coordinates, along with the elevation data, put you on the terrace of Mr. Bonaventura's building on Wednesday morning between 1000 and 1030 hours."

Marino shot a nasty look at his activity tracker as if furious at the device's stunning betrayal. His mouth moved, but no sound came out.

I continued, "We know the shooter was a marksman. A single pistol shot between the eyes at twenty-five yards, about twenty-three meters." I gestured at Marino's trophy case. "You are a marksman and a very good one."

"Absurd!"

"And I'm sure when your firearms are run through ballistics, one will fire a round that matches the one that killed Bonaventura."

"Get out!"

"You're under arrest, General, for the murder of Mr. Ignazio Bonaventura."

"You, you … cannot. You have no power here!"

I turned to Giordana. "She does."

Giordana walked around the desk and executed the arrest, assisted by the four armed officers.

When I'd approached Giordana in the courtyard with the idea of pulling the GPS records for Marino's activity tracker, she didn't hesitate. Despite knowing it could end her career (cops expect blind loyalty from other cops), she made the phone calls and worked through the legal red tape. When she had the evidence, she made her case with the prosecutor general. It didn't matter to her what uniform Marino wore or how much brass was on his shoulder boards. Justice was all she cared about.

The dedicated men and women of the Carabinieri deserved good cops to lead them, cops like Giordana. Not frauds like Marino and Longo. I hoped they would see that and let her career blossom.

Speaking of Longo, he was somewhere out in the Venetian Lagoon with Tufu and Ruiz, getting a lesson on American payback. They had agreed to deliver that lesson together. Maybe it was the start of a new friendship.

As a loud, belligerent Marino was taken away, Giordana approached Vincent and me. She told us in simple Italian that in exchange for our help with the Bonaventura case, the prosecutor would not be seeking charges against us. She issued a stiff warning, however, that a repeat offense would not be tolerated—not in Venice and not under her watch. Instead of handshakes and high fives, she gave us that barely perceptible nod of hers.

I suspected it was her way of saying thank you.

Chapter Sixty-Seven

Same Mistake

The fat man walked on crutches. He was accompanied by a man as muscular as the fat man was fat. Americans were all about excess. Excess power. Excess arrogance. Excess vanity.

As Zafar followed them, he took a call from one of his lieutenants. "How is the boy?"

"As you instructed, we had him moved to the best hospital in the city. He is doing well there, and the doctors like his prognosis."

"Good. Continue to provide for the mother. She has many months of long nights ahead with a sick child."

"As you wish."

Zafar terminated the call.

The son of Nabeel Haddad had been taken care of as promised. Nabeel Haddad, the desperate courier, was given a simple task and rewarded with a chance at a new life. Why had he thrown it away to help the enemy? If Kamaria had not taken the courier's treacherous call to the Carabinieri, perhaps he—The Scorpion—would now be a guest in one of the enemy's black site prisons.

El-Hashem was another disappointment. Zafar had sent him on a simple mission to kill a double-crossing banker. The death of the banker's wife was of no consequence. The death of his child, however, was another matter entirely. Zafar demanded that all his soldiers follow a simple rule: never deliberately kill the children of the infidels. El-Hashem had committed treachery by breaking that rule. To make matters worse, he was apprehended by American agents!

Up ahead was the Rialto Bridge, one of four that spanned the Grand Canal. Zafar put away his phone and pulled ahead of the fat man and his companion. As he walked, the herd was forced to make way. The few who didn't got a shoulder clip or an outright shove. He ignored their protests. Who has time for cattle?

How long had the American agents followed El-Hashem?

Getting caught by foreign agents was always a risk. Zafar was never quite sure how well hidden or discreet his soldiers were, so he activated them for lesser missions first. In the event of a setback, it gave him room to maneuver. When El-Hashem was taken into custody, Zafar set a plan in motion. Through intermediaries, he'd instructed El-Hashem to cooperate with the American agents and lure them to Venice under the pretense of a meeting with The Scorpion. To assuage suspicion, Zafar assured him of a rescue and a divine calling. The killing of El-Hashem in the middle of a major police operation was the most satisfying achievement of his plan. It yielded the desired side effect—investigative resources were diverted away from suspicions of an attack on the Israeli prime minister.

He reached the bridge and climbed its slope. At the apex, he pulled out a freshly rolled cigarette.

Exactly which part of his plan had failed?

The time frame for killing El-Hashem was inflexible. Kamaria's identity had to be protected. El-Hashem knew her, and his reaction to her sudden appearance was unpredictable. Had that given the police too much time to work with?

The fat man was on a jetty, lumbering behind his partner, who was talking to a gondolier.

A gondola ride? A victory lap?

As Zafar lit the cigarette with a wooden match he'd struck along the stone railing, he dwelled on the fact that the police had uncovered at least part of his plan. How else had they come to intercept Kamaria on the bridge? She wore the perfect disguise. She hid in the prison all night. She had complete radio access and the encryption code of the day.

Why hadn't Kamaria armed the detonator? The question still struck him like a jab in the stomach.

Had she planned to wait until she was closer to the target?

Had she lost her resolve?

Had she betrayed him?

He would never know.

What he did know was that the fat man was somehow responsible for defeating his plan. Not the media whore colonel of the Carabinieri, who shamelessly boasted of foresight and initiative. Kamaria had warned him about the fat man. The perceptive one, she called him. Zafar had intended to kill the fat man, but she'd persuaded him not to.

That, he now knew, was a mistake.

The muscular man helped the fat man into the gondola. Zafar took a drag of his cigarette, never taking his eyes off the fat man.

If we ever meet again, I will not make the same mistake.

Chapter Sixty-Eight

Watch Their Six

I insisted on saying goodbye to Venice in a gondola, specifically, the same one I'd ridden in a couple of nights before. Vincent tracked it down for me, parked on a jetty along the Grand Canal. The gondolier, Luigi, recognized me and asked about the *bella signora.* I responded with a tight smile and a headshake. Luigi gave me a sympathetic pat on the shoulder and some encouraging words about *l'amore.*

Vincent helped me into the boat, making sure I was comfortably settled in the love seat with the tufted back and my injured leg on a cushioned stool. He took my crutches, got out of the boat, and approached Luigi on the jetty.

A couple of minutes later, Vincent said, "The gondolier's peddling a ten percent discount for broken hearts today. Says you qualify. Wanna do more than the standard forty-minute ride?"

I nodded. "It's sunny. I'll do an hour."

Vincent got down on his haunches. "You okay?"

"I will be."

He reached into his suit jacket and pulled out his shades. "I called Nonna Geppina last night. Told her about the shitty week we're having and that we're coming home. When I mentioned your upcoming surgery, she promised to cook you a feast—before and after. Three homemade pastas to start and plenty of desserts to finish." Vincent smiled. "Sometimes I think that old lady likes you more than she does me."

I had to smile. "Thanks, man."

Vincent stood and put on his sunglasses. "I'll be here when you get back. We'll get food, whatever you want, then head for the airport."

"That's a plan."

Luigi rowed the boat away from the jetty and into the Grand Canal. Sunshine shimmered on the vast expanse of water. A cool breeze picked up, giving me a slight chill. I buttoned my suit, the same suit I'd worn on my dinner date with Kamaria.

I don't know for sure what she would have done if we hadn't been on that bridge, but I believe she never intended to go through with the attack. She was incapable of carrying out the indiscriminate murder of innocent people. It wasn't her nature. That wasn't the Kamaria I knew. She was a victim. An innocent little girl honed by hate into a weapon for men with nefarious agendas. She once told me that just like the lion is a predator and the antelope is prey, people can't change their nature. I think she was right. In the end, her nature kept her from arming that detonator.

In a few hours, I would be on a plane to New York. Surgery, physical therapy, and an empty apartment in Brooklyn awaited me. Well, not so empty. My good neighbor would be dropping off Dr. Livingstone, my Siamese cat. I hadn't seen the mischievous Dr. Livingstone in almost two months. I was looking forward to his fickle company and antics.

What was next?

Vincent was taking some accumulated comp time while I was on disability. We could stay with the task force and work out of the New York office or head back to the NYPD and the Brooklyn South Precinct. O'Neil told us we could write our own tickets, blessed by both the Feds and the NYPD.

We agreed to discuss our options on the long flight home. I was leaning toward going back to the NYPD. The people of Brooklyn needed good crimefighters to watch their six. And who better than Captain America in tactical shades and a suit, on the job twenty-four seven, armed with a law degree, a gold detective's shield, and a box of cookies?

Thank you for reading *Death in the City of Bridges.*

If you've enjoyed it, please leave a quick review with your online bookstore. Every review is important and helps me reach new readers.

Acknowledgments

To my wife, Denise, for building my author's website, designing my logo, creating the map of St. Mark's Square included in the front matter of this book, and supporting me throughout this multiyear project.

To my cousin Diane Gutierrez whose keen eye for the big picture helped me avoid the disaster I was making of chapter one. *"They can't all be Andrew Dice Clay."*

To William J. Dezell Jr. (author of the Raymond Jaye series) for the eye-opening reviews and expert firearms advice, including how snipers operate and weapons to use in the story.

To L.S. Sharrow (author of *Moxie* and *Small town*) for top-notch beta reading and feedback throughout the first and second drafts.

To Allison Maruska (author of *The Fourth Descendent* and *Drake and the Fliers*) for the great reviews and publishing advice.

To Deborah Welgoss for being an excellent beta reader and early supporter.

To Julie MacKenzie (my editor) for fixing my mistakes and making this book better.

To my friends in law enforcement—namely active members of the PAPD, NYPD, and JTTF who wish to remain anonymous—for providing critical insight into the job, its personalities, and its procedures.

Additional Disclaimers

As noted on the copyright page, this novel is a work of fiction. However, taking creative freedom with verifiable facts is sometimes necessary to accommodate a given plot. There are four deliberate examples in the novel.

Maize carts are no longer a feature at St. Mark's Square. They were when I first visited in 2001. Although people still feed the pigeons with food from nearby restaurants and stores.

Some documentation shows that the bell tower in St. Mark's Square has a stairwell that leads from the ground floor to the top, which is presumably open to visitors. Conflicting articles, however, claim that the stairwell has been closed to the public for years. Not clear about its status, I visited the top of the tower on my last visit in June of 2019. I never saw the stairwell, and a spiral staircase I found only led from the top of the elevator shaft to the belfry. Therefore, what I describe in the novel is fictional.

About a dozen agents would be assigned to the ground team in an operation like the one I describe in chapter one. Since it would be impossible for the reader to keep track of a dozen active characters, I worked with a smaller number.

As noted in the novel, JTTF deals with domestic terrorism. It's possible for a case agent, and perhaps a coagent, to be deployed overseas on a big case but not an entire team. I stretched reality to fit the plot and to honor the men and women of the JTTF who work every minute of every day to keep us safe.

Everything else in the novel is as accurate as my research at the time allowed. Lingering errors of fact are unintentional and should be considered further examples of this author's use of creative freedom (envision a grammatically incorrect smiley face emoji inserted here).

About the Author

Jay (Juan) C. Ceron is a software engineer who has been writing fiction since high school. For years, he flirted with different genres, namely science fiction, horror, and literary fiction, with an emphasis on irony. After reading Thomas Harris' *Silence of The Lambs*, he knew he was meant to write police mysteries but failed to develop viable plots or protagonists. That all changed on a trip to Jamaica in 2014. While on a glass bottom boat tour, the idea for a character and a short story materialized. That character was Miles Jordan, a smart, charismatic, overweight police detective with a relentless drive to solve cases.

From there, Jay took writing seriously. What was to become the fourth and longest novella in a Miles Jordan series took on a life of its own. Set in the magical city of Venice, Italy, material for the story came easily. The word count grew, the chapters came together, and the novella became this full-length novel.

Death in the City of Bridges is Jay's debut novel, written over a span of six years on a lot less than part-time basis; it included trips to Venice for research and inspiration.

Visit Jay at jcceron.com or say hello via email at mailbox@jcceron.com.

Other Works

DEATH OF THE SALTWATER BLONDE

Book 1

A tropical getaway. A body in the ocean. Will his single-minded pursuit of the truth reel in a murderer?

Jamaica. NYPD detective Miles Jordan's sharp sense of justice doesn't take time off. So during a glass-bottom boat tour crowded with passengers, it's his eagle-eyes that spot a naked corpse submerged in the clear blue waters. And after the female victim is identified as an American, he shrugs off his vacation and agrees to help the locals solve the brutal homicide.

Wary of the police's motives, Miles is skeptical when a suspect is quickly apprehended and he's ordered to sign off the case. But his instincts push him to continue the investigation on his own… even as his precinct boss threatens to revoke his badge.

Can the relentless cop net the culprit before he loses his career?

Death of the Saltwater Blonde is the breezy first book in the Miles Jordan Mystery Thriller series. If you like intelligent heroes, perplexing puzzles, and lavish destinations, then you'll love J. C. Ceron's killer holiday.

jcceron.com/works

Made in the USA
Middletown, DE
09 September 2024

59993186R00213